I0668002

Venus Rising

Ali Spooner

Venus Rising

Ali Spooner

Affinity
eBook Press
NZ
2016

Venus Rising

© Ali Spooner 2016

Affinity E-Book Press NZ LTD
Canterbury, New Zealand

1st Edition

ISBN: 978-0-908351-50-3

All rights reserved.

No part of this e-Book may be reproduced in any form without the express permission of the author and publisher. Please note that piracy of copyrighted materials violate the author's rights and is Illegal.

This is a work of fiction. Names, character, places, and incidents are the product of the author's imagination or are used fictitiously and any resemblance to actual persons living or dead, businesses, companies, events, or locales is entirely coincidental

Editor: Ruth Stanley
Proof Editor: Alexis Smith
Cover Design: Irish Dragon Designs

Acknowledgments

I would like to thank my fans for following my stories, providing great feedback and encouragement. Writing wouldn't be so much fun without you. Thanks to Affinity, Irish Dragon for the cover art and the team of editors, readers, and publishers who continue to help me grow as a writer.

Dedication

I'd like to dedicate this story to Ruth, an angel of an editor. Thanks for being patient in working with me to make the story better. I appreciate all you've done for me.

Also by Ali Spooner

The Devil's Tree
Shotgun Rider
The Settlement
Ruined
Terminal Event
Love's Playlist
Cowgirl Up
Twisted Lives
The Epitaph
Bailey's Run

Sasha Thibodaux Series
Sugarland
Bayou Justice
Line of Sight

Table of Contents

Chapter One

At age twenty-four, one month away from graduating with her MBA, Levi Johnson sat pondering her future. With numerous job opportunities available upon graduation, Levi was in no hurry to plunge into the serious world of finance. For the last six years, she had studied hard and now she wanted to have some fun before settling down into a career.

Weeks earlier, Levi had been surfing the net searching for a job that sparked her interest when she ran across an advertisement for a bartender at an exclusive lesbian resort in the Virgin Islands. She clicked on the posting and her eyes widened at the sugar-white sand and green water making up the private beach at the resort. *Surely, there would be thousands of applicants for this job.* But she continued to read anyway.

She reviewed the job qualifications and benefits. On a whim, she applied for the position, sending a résumé, cover letter, and picture per the requirements posted in the online advertisement.

"This would be a perfect way to spend the summer," she said to herself as she sealed the envelope.

†

Levi had forgotten about the job on the island until she arrived home three weeks later and found a large package waiting for her when she opened her mailbox. Glancing at the return address, a surge of excitement raced through her. Had the response been a simple thanks but no thanks, she felt it would have come in a much smaller envelope.

Clutching the package in her hand, Levi climbed the stairs to her apartment and once inside sat down at her small kitchen table. Slipping her letter opener under the seal of the envelope, she slid it across the length of the seal. A brochure and airline ticket fell out onto the table. Inside was a letter. Her heart raced as she unfolded the letter, written with beautiful handwriting.

Dear Ms. Johnson,

My partner Liz and I have reviewed your application and cover letter. You've been selected as one of the top candidates from over three hundred applicants. We would like to invite you to our resort to interview for the position of bartender. As described in the advertisement, the position pays minimum wage, but is supplemented by a very generous tipping clientele. The resort provides all meals and the use of a private bungalow.

If you are still interested in the position, we have enclosed an airline ticket for you for Friday, May tenth, so that you may fly down to allow us to assess your potential for joining our staff. That weekend is a very special "Singles" weekend. All resort rooms are booked, so you will be staying with my partner and me if you choose to make a visit.

I look forward to hearing from you soon and would kindly request that you reply by email of your intention to visit.

Sincerely,
Nat Lewis
NLewisVenus1@VIslands.com

Levi couldn't hide the grin on her face as she read the letter again. She powered up her computer and sent a reply accepting the offer of an interview, confirming the tenth as her day of arrival.

✝

Levi had ten days before she flew to the islands for her interview. Until then she had to pack up her apartment. She had already arranged for another graduate student to purchase her furniture and appliances, as well as take over the lease on her apartment at the end of May. If her plans worked out, Levi would be working in the islands before then and her friend would have a free month of rent.

When Levi finished her last exam the following Monday, she spent the next few days closing out bank accounts, paying final bills, and reading through mixology books to sharpen her knowledge of bartending skills.

As an undergrad, Levi had worked as a bartender for several years and had the basic skills needed, but she wanted to make a huge first impression on Nat and Liz during her interview period, so she spent several nights before her departure entertaining friends and using them as human guinea pigs. She experimented with several new cocktail recipes until she developed a concoction she would claim as her signature drink. With the help of her friends, they named the creation, "Tropical Ecstasy" or Tropical E for short. The taste was smooth, sweet, and guaranteed to knock you off your feet. Her friends also brought Levi up to date with the latest dance moves.

As the date for her departure neared, Levi hoped she had formed a plan that would keep the bar rocking while she impressed her future employers.

On Wednesday night, Levi returned home with her MBA in hand. While she was pleased to have finished at the top of her class, she was much more excited about the possibility of a job down in the islands. Even if she only worked for a year or so, it would enable her to sow some of her wild oats before settling down to a career and searching for a mate. *Life is good*, she thought as she packed her diploma away with the last of her boxes.

†

Friday morning Levi woke prior to the alarm going off. She showered, dressed, and carried her bags to the curb to await the taxi she had ordered the day before. As she slipped into the backseat of the cab, she looked at the small complex that she had called home for the last two years. The building held many good memories for her, but Levi knew it was time to move on with her life. As she rode to the airport, she smiled at the memory of her friends ribbing her over taking a minimum-wage job when she could easily be pulling down a six-figure salary, but she knew each of them was envious of the opportunity she had been offered. There was plenty of time in her future for fame and fortune. Right now Levi just wanted to have some fun and frolic in the sun.

At the airport, Levi passed through security with minimal effort and made her way to her departure gate with time to spare. Immersed in a magazine article, Levi was startled when the overhead speaker announced that her flight was ready to board. She passed through the boarding gate and onto the jet way, leaving her old life behind to begin what she hoped would be a welcome respite from her years of academia.

Once on board, she stretched out in a luxurious first-class seat and accepted a glass of wine from the flight attendant while the remaining passengers boarded the jet. Levi had never been terribly comfortable flying, but the wine and luxury of the seat relaxed her and shortly after takeoff, she found her head nodding. She reclined her seat and dozed until the pilot ran into turbulence as he began the descent for landing. She looked out the window, instantly mesmerized by the view. The island was filled with a lush green canopy of trees. Encircled by a pristine white beach that separated the island from sparkling blue-green water so clear you could see the ocean floor beneath it.

The pilot landed the plane smoothly. It appeared they had landed in the middle of a forest as trees surrounded the jet while they taxied to the terminal. Levi emerged from the plane and made her way to baggage claim. She was surprised when a sultry voice said, "Welcome to the islands, Levi."

Levi looked up into the deep, dark eyes of a cinnamon-skinned beauty.

"My name is NeNe. Nat asked me to meet you and bring you to the resort."

Levi shook the offered hand. "Thanks for the warm welcome."

"Is this all you have?" NeNe pointed to the two bags now resting at Levi's feet.

"Yes, I tried to travel light," Levi said, immediately rewarded with a beautiful smile from NeNe.

"Well, let's get you out of here." NeNe bent down to pick up Levi's bags.

Levi took control of the larger bag, and for the first time noticed the uniform shirt NeNe was wearing. "So you work for the resort?"

NeNe smiled again. "Yes, I provide transportation when needed during the day and DJ at the club at night. I have been with Nat and Liz for almost three years and love working at the resort." She held the door open for Levi. "I understand you are auditioning for the role of bartender at the club."

Levi chuckled at her choice of the word audition versus interview, but she was, in fact, correct. Levi would have to perform well to obtain the job opportunity the resort had to offer. "Yes, I hope to make a good enough impression to land the job."

"I'm certain you will do just fine, Levi, and I look forward to working with you."

"Thanks, I hope you are right. I will need some assistance from you tonight though if you are the DJ."

"Just name it and I will see what I can do," NeNe said.

"Do you have the song, "Mambo Number Five" in your mix?"

"As a matter of fact, I do," she answered with a grin.

"At some point tonight, I will ask you to play it for me then."

"Easy enough. Just let me know when."

†

NeNe pointed out a few of the island's highlights as she drove and Levi instantly fell in love with the beauty of the island. Several minutes later, the Jeep slowed and turned down a lush tropical lane that served to seclude the resort from the main road. A few hundred yards off the road, the canopy opened to reveal the majestic Venus Rising resort.

"Wow," was all Levi could think to say as she looked over the grounds of the immense resort. "This place looks magnificent," she finally managed as NeNe drove through a tropical garden to the back of the property.

NeNe parked and helped Levi with her bags. As they walked toward the main section of the resort, a tall red-haired woman appeared from the shadows.

"Welcome to Venus Rising. My name is Liz. After NeNe shows you to the guest room to deposit your bags, I will take you on a tour."

"Very pleased to meet you." Levi followed NeNe inside.

NeNe ushered Levi down a hallway, opened a door to the luxurious owner's suite, and guided her to a huge guest room.

"I'll leave you for a few minutes if you'd like to freshen up a bit," NeNe said, closing the door behind her.

Levi looked around the room and made use of the facilities before unpacking her bag and arranging her clothing in a large walk-in closet. She surveyed the expansive room once more then met NeNe in the hallway.

"All set," she said as she offered NeNe a smile.

"Let's get you started then."

†

Liz was on the phone as Levi and NeNe entered. She motioned for Levi to take a seat across from the desk. NeNe bent down to whisper in Levi's ear.

"Relax, you'll be just fine," she said. "I'll see you in the club later." She gently squeezed Levi's shoulder then walked to the office entrance just as Liz was hanging up the phone.

"Thank you for all your help, NeNe," Liz said.

"You're welcome," she answered, and after shooting a wink to Levi, continued out the door.

Liz fixed her green eyes on Levi and smiled. "Are you ready to start your tour?"

"Yes ma'am," Levi said politely.

"We are very informal here so Liz will do just fine," she said with a grin. "If you will follow me, we'll get started."

Levi stood and followed Liz, listening intently as she described the resort's many amenities and the type of clientele Venus Rising served. The high rate of occupancy the resort maintained was impressive. Liz explained that it was rare that there was a cancellation, but when one did occur there were usually several clients eager to take advantage. Astounded by the size of the resort, Levi was impressed with the many different activities offered, from a full-body massage to scuba diving and deep-sea fishing. She found herself smiling. *This is definitely a place where every woman's dreams can come true.*

Liz told her the resort maintained a staff of seventy-five, and the average length of employment was slightly over four years.

"That's a very impressive retention rate," Levi said. "What event occurred to open this position, if I may ask?"

"Jessica, our previous evening bartender, was swept off her feet by one of our guests and she left to be with her new partner in Boston. As you'll soon find out, our clientele is primarily successful businesswomen, artists, an occasional actress, and our younger crowd hails from Ivy League schools, with large trust funds to enable them to enjoy an exotic lifestyle."

Liz guided them through a lush tropical garden and beyond a huge pool crowded with scantily clad women sunbathing and sipping on cool tropical drinks. Liz noted numerous heads turned to watch as they strolled past and knew Levi would be an instant success with this crowd. She had ample good looks and carried herself quite confidently, as she and Nat had hoped she would.

Designed with multiple levels, the club spread out before them. The top level held tables and booths for the patrons to relax and enjoy their drinks while they looked out onto the pool, the private beach, or down onto the dance floor, which made up the second level of the club. The third and final level held the most beautiful, round, teakwood bar Levi had ever laid eyes on. She grinned as she looked down from the top level onto the bar and she could barely wait to reach her final destination. There were a few afternoon patrons in the club enjoying a cool drink. Levi saw NeNe in the large DJ booth as she prepared her music for the night to come.

Liz led Levi across a catwalk that connected the dance floor to the bar level. Levi looked down to find saltwater aquariums lining the wall between the dance floor and the lounge area above with brightly colored tropical fish swimming freely around the club.

As they approached the bar, a tall, dark-haired woman stood up from behind the bar where she had bent down to retrieve several bottles to restock the mirrored shelves. Levi watched as the two women locked eyes and smiled at each other. She knew then this was Nat.

"I'm Nat." The woman introduced herself as she pointed to heavily cushioned seats surrounding the bar. "Please have a seat, Levi, and let's talk for a bit. Would you care for a drink?"

"Just a bottled water please."

"How about a glass of white wine for you, darling?" Nat asked Liz.

"That sounds wonderful, love," Liz said as she took a seat by Levi.

"So what do you think of our resort?" Nat asked.

"I have never seen anything so amazing in my life. And this bar," Levi shook her head, "is just incredible."

Nat chuckled. "Well, I'm glad you approve. If you are selected to fill the position, this will become your new home from four in the afternoon until two in the morning, five days a week."

"Do I have free rein to run the bar as I wish during my shift?" Levi asked.

"Within reason, yes. We have a fairly standard menu of drinks, but we ask our bartenders to be creative in developing different cocktails to use as their specialties."

"Perfect," Levi said. "What time do I start?"

"Well, it's almost noon, so why don't you and Liz grab some lunch and you can relax a few hours before you come to relieve me for the four o'clock shift," Nat suggested.

Levi picked up a menu and took it with her to study as she and Liz left the club and headed to the dining room. Levi found it hard to contain her excitement as she looked over the drink menu, memorizing the contents of each drink she was unfamiliar with to be prepared for her audition.

Levi was still immersed in the drink menu when Liz said, "May I suggest the grilled fish of the day."

"Yes, that sounds fine."

"I just can't get over how fabulous this place is," Levi remarked as the server left the table.

"Thank you. It has taken us a few years to build up the business, but we have discussed the possibility of starting a second resort in the future."

Levi found it difficult to concentrate on her meal, even though it was as fantastic as everything she had seen at the resort. After the meal, Liz took her back to the guest room and encouraged her to get some rest before her shift would begin.

"Tonight will be full tilt," Liz warned with a grin as she left a totally excited Levi behind.

†

Levi looked at the bed and knew a nap would be very beneficial, but doubted sleep would come. She looked inside the closet to find two freshly starched and pressed uniforms hanging there. On the bedside table was a nametag with her name printed on it. Levi was beginning to feel at home.

As a precaution, Levi set the alarm clock for three to give her plenty of time to shower and dress for her evening in the club.

She stretched out on the bed and was surprised to find she was relaxed enough to drift off to sleep.

✝

Liz joined Nat back in the club after leaving Levi in the guest room.

"So what do you think about Levi?" Liz asked.

"Well, she certainly has the exuberance and looks for the position," Nat answered.

"She definitely turned a few heads while we were touring."

"If she has decent bartending skills, I would feel comfortable making an offer."

"I guess we will find out soon enough," Liz said as the clock above the bar neared the three o'clock hour.

✝

Two hours after she had laid down, the alarm clock jangled to wake Levi from her nap. She quickly showered and dressed in the uniform provided—tan shorts and black muscle shirt that showed off her trim figure and long, tanned legs.

She made her way back through the resort and out to the pool on her way to the club. A small group of women whistled and waved to Levi as she passed. She smiled and waved back.

"I see you have made your first adoring fans," NeNe said as she walked up to Levi.

"Oh hush, NeNe." Levi blushed slightly.

"Hey NeNe and Levi," Nat said from behind the bar.

"Hi Nat," Levi and NeNe said at the same time. NeNe reached over and pinched Levi's arm. "Jinx."

"I can see already that Liz and I are going to have our hands full with the two of you."

"I'm off to the booth, Levi, so good luck tonight."

"Thanks NeNe," Levi replied then turned toward Nat. "Are you ready to show me around?"

Nat showed Levi where all the important items were stored, who and how to call if change was needed and a quick rundown of the register. Levi paid close attention to each of Nat's instructions.

"I will be here for quite a while tonight, observing and evaluating your skills, so if you have any questions just motion for me. After that, if you need me, just have NeNe give me a buzz."

NeNe was completing sound checks on her equipment when the doors opened again and the afternoon sun shone bright.

"This lovely lady is Karen, your assistant tonight. Karen, this is Levi, who is interviewing for the job of bartender."

"Good luck then," Karen said as she began to wipe down the tables and booths even though Nat had left them sparkling clean.

Levi pointed to the black dry erase board that advertised the daily specials. "Mind if I make a change?"

"As of this moment, the bar is all yours," Nat said. She walked from behind the teakwood and sat down at the bar. Levi erased the current drink special then picked up a neon orange pen and began to write...

Today's Special
Tropical Ecstasy or Topical E for short
Smooth, sweet and guaranteed to knock you off your feet

"Sounds interesting," Nat said. "Let's taste one."

Levi went to work blending up the drink and poured one small glass each for Nat, NeNe, and Karen. Each of the women sipped the drink that looked like a banana smoothie. Levi watched their faces.

"Excellent," Nat proclaimed as she finished off the drink.

"I can bet you'll be selling a bunch of these tonight," NeNe said.

"I guess I had better go back to the bungalow and get my rollerblades," Karen teased. "This is very tasty."

"Only one problem I can see," Nat said. The grin of excitement faded from Levi's face. Nat got up and walked into the storeroom. She returned moments later with a new frozen drink dispenser and sat it down beside the daiquiri machine. "I hope you have a recipe for mass production." Nat laughed and started to install the machine for Levi's use.

"That is no problem at all." The grin returned to Levi's face and she began scooping ice into the large blender then portioned out her concoction to create a ten-gallon mix.

"Just as tasty as the first," Nat said when the batch was ready.

The door opened again and Levi looked up to see a group of sunbathers enter the club.

"Come in, ladies, and meet Levi, our bartender for the night," Nat said to the small group. "Have a free shot of Tropical Ecstasy and tell us what you think."

Levi's grin broadened as she poured shots for the six women now seated at the bar. She watched as one by one the women downed the shots. "This is fantastic," one of the women said and the rest of the group agreed wholeheartedly.

"We're on our way to shower and eat dinner, but you can be guaranteed we'll be back for more of these," the woman said. They thanked Levi for the free shots and left the bar. Levi glanced over at a smiling Nat.

"Sell them as shots and help me set up another dispenser," Nat said.

The sun had yet to set and Levi felt her interview was going well. Levi set up the second dispenser then took a break to catch her breath until the after-dinner crowd began to drift in.

†

The ladies who had received the free shots had done an excellent job of advertising the new drink. Tray after tray of shots disappeared into the growing crowd. NeNe was slowly increasing the tempo of the music and dancers began to pack the dance floor. The tips began to pour in as well, and every time a tip of five dollars or more was dropped into her tip jar, Levi would ring the brass bell behind the bar and yell "Hazzah!"

Confident that Levi was doing well behind the bar Nat moved to join Liz, who was watching from a booth above.

"What do you think?" Nat asked as she set down two shots of Tropical E and slid in beside Liz.

Liz grinned and downed the shot. "I think we just found our new bartender."

"She is quick with a smile and the ladies really like her looks," Nat said. "I counted at least a dozen notes with room numbers and invitations passed to her already and this is the mellow early crowd."

"She seems to really be enjoying herself as well. So does this mean my wife will be sleeping all night beside me again?"

"Just as soon as we can get Levi started," Nat promised and kissed Liz softly.

Chapter Two

Levi was indeed enjoying herself. NeNe had the crowd on the dance floor gyrating in a frenzy, and Karen and Levi had to work at a fevered pitch to keep up with the drink orders. Young women kept every barstool occupied, vying for Levi's attention as she served them drinks. On more than one occasion a note with a name and room number was attached to the bar bill payment, inviting Levi to join that particular woman in her room. After the third or fourth such offer Levi no longer blushed and knew she would have to work hard to keep her head swelling from too much attention.

The cash register drawer was rapidly filling and it was still early evening. Liz had showed her how to make a cash drop so Levi counted out a thousand dollars and placed it in an envelope then sealed it before sliding it into a small vault beneath the bar. *If this is anywhere close to a typical evening, Liz and Nat have a virtual gold mine on their hands.* Her business mind whirled as she washed a load of pilsner glasses and calculated the profits they had to be making on the bar alone. This job could be much more than even her wildest dreams could imagine.

When the crowd had settled for a few moments of rest, Levi motioned for Nat to come down to the bar. Levi had been carefully perusing the crowd all evening and had decided on one particular young lady to help her out with her plan to win this job for good. She had spied the woman on the dance floor earlier and watched the woman's seductive moves hold many other women in a trance as she moved from partner to partner.

When Nat arrived Levi asked, "Would you mind taking over for five minutes?"

"Of course not, Levi, take a break."

"Thanks." With a nod to NeNe, she worked her way into the crowd and located the small blonde she had spotted earlier. Just as Levi reached the table where the woman sat, NeNe started "Mambo Number Five."

Levi leaned down to the woman and asked, "May I have this dance?"

Levi led the eager blonde to the nearly empty dance floor. All eyes were on them as the two women danced to the song in perfect rhythm, as if they had practiced for weeks. The crowd went wild with applause, whistles, and shouts. When the song ended Levi slowly dipped the young woman and kissed her softly on the lips. NeNe rolled on to the next song and the reenergized dancers rushed to the dance floor.

Levi escorted the young woman back to her table, thanked her for the dance, and with a killer smile headed back to the bar.

Nat saw the sparkle in Levi's eyes as she again stepped behind the bar, a thin sheen of perspiration covering her face. "Very smooth," Nat said, tossing a clean bar towel to Levi.

Levi caught the towel and patted her face. She looked up to find a new wave of customers crowding the bar with requests for drinks. Nat stayed behind the bar and helped until the wild rush was over. She gave Levi a smile of confidence and left to return to her booth, carrying a glass of wine to Liz.

"Convinced yet?" she asked Liz as she handed her the glass.

"I can feel your naked body lying next to me already. The ladies absolutely adore her and she has each one of them wrapped around her finger." Liz chuckled.

"So why don't we slip away for a little while and enjoy a break until it is time for me to come back to help our new bartender close up shop." Nat stood and offered her hand to her lover.

✝

Levi saw Nat flash her a smile and thumbs-up before she and Liz disappeared out the door. Levi then turned her gaze to the DJ booth and caught NeNe's eyes. She had seen the exchange between Nat and Levi and nodded her head, rewarding Levi with one of her beautiful smiles.

Karen placed her tray on the bar and took a deep breath. "I feel like we have served ten thousand drinks tonight." She grinned at Levi. "I will definitely bring my rollerblades tomorrow night."

"Karen, what do you and NeNe drink?"

"A cold beer for me. NeNe is rather fond of Sex on the Beach."

"Hmm, interesting choice." Levi poured a cold draft for Karen then prepared NeNe's favorite drink. "Would you mind if I make this delivery?"

"Not at all, Levi. I'll try to hold down the fort for a minute or two."

Levi slipped around the bar and made her way through the crowd to the DJ booth.

NeNe opened the door and Levi stepped inside. "You were looking thirsty." Levi handed NeNe the frosty cold drink.

"Thanks. You've made quite the impression tonight." Nene took a sip of the drink. "I wouldn't be surprised if Nat offered you the position later."

"What about the other applicants?"

"Are you kidding me? Nat didn't leave them alone behind the bar, and tonight she has snuck off with Liz for some much needed R&R, so I would say they feel very comfortable with you." NeNe smiled warmly at Levi. "You are a huge hit, my friend."

"Thanks, NeNe. Let me know when you are ready for a refill." Levi slipped back into the crowd and made her way back to the bar.

16

"Oh, thank God you're back," Karen said. "These women are dying for more TEs and the cooler is running low."

"No rest for the wicked." Levi smiled and began mixing up a fresh batch.

Karen headed off with a fresh tray of shots. Levi finished restocking the cooler and turned to fill several orders from the bar. It was nearly midnight when the telephone behind the bar rang.

"The kitchen closes in just a little while. What would you and Karen like for dinner," NeNe asked.

"A juicy burger for me. I'll have to track Karen down to see what she wants and call you back," Levi said.

A moment later Karen walked back to the bar loaded down with glasses. "NeNe is going to place our dinner orders and wants to know what you would like."

"A loaded club sandwich and a set of new feet," Karen said, making Levi laugh.

Levi picked up the telephone and dialed NeNe in the booth. "Karen would like a loaded club and a set of new feet." She turned to watch NeNe burst out in laughter in the booth.

"All right, I will place our orders and join you two at the bar when they arrive."

†

NeNe set up the mixer to play a string of music. When she saw the food delivered from the kitchen, she stepped out of the booth and headed for the bar. The crowd was beginning to thin and the majority of those still in the bar were busy slow dancing or making out in a booth.

Karen made a final pass to check for orders and then joined NeNe and Levi at the bar.

"Damn, that looks good," Karen said as she spied Levi's burger.

"Tastes good too." Levi moaned after she took a large bite.

"Oh you tease." Karen punched Levi in the arm.

"It has taken you all night just to figure that out?" NeNe said with a laugh.

Levi placed her hand over her heart and laughed. "I am so wounded by you two."

"This has been a really good night," Karen said. "If this keeps up we may have to ask Nat for a raise." She took a bite from her sandwich.

"It has been an incredible night," Levi said. "I have already made four cash drops and will probably make another before we close down."

"Your tip jar is about to overflow too," NeNe noted.

"Yes, it should be great after the split." Levi grinned.

"What split?" Karen asked. "That's all yours. I get my tips out on the floor." Karen patted her pouch.

"You have to be kidding me," Levi said. She looked at Karen and then NeNe and both of them returned her smile.

"Damn, I couldn't make that much over a weekend in the States."

"Welcome to Venus Rising." Karen grinned.

†

An hour later, the last of the patrons left for the evening and Karen began wiping down the tables. Levi restocked the bar for the next day. She refilled the coolers with TE mix and filled the ice bins with fresh ice. She was just washing the last load of glasses as Nat walked back in wearing a huge smile on her face. *Someone must have had an enjoyable evening.*

"Well did you enjoy your first night?" Nat asked.

"Immensely. You have a great place here."

"We do have a great place and welcome aboard, Levi," Nat said.

Karen and NeNe applauded Nat's decision and each hugged Levi.

"I can already tell this is going to be a terrific summer," NeNe said.

"You don't know the half of it," Nat said. "When we left the bar tonight, Liz and I had a discussion and we made a very important decision." She sat down on a barstool and made sure she

18

had the full attention of the three ladies before she spoke again. "We have been approached as a new port of call by a lesbian cruise line. Now that we are fully staffed, and have the hottest bartender on the island, we agreed to take them up on their offer."

"That is great news," NeNe said.

"We will need to hire another server to help Karen handle the crowd and a few drivers to handle a trolley service to and from the cruise ship, but I think we are ready for the move." Nat took a deep breath.

"Congratulations," Levi said.

"Thank you, Levi. If this venture works out well, there will be significant bonuses for all of you," Nat promised. "All right, ladies, let's finish closing up so you gals can get some rest."

NeNe washed the windows of the DJ booth while Levi swept the bar floor and Karen vacuumed. Nat cleaned out the cash drawer and emptied the vault into a bank bag.

Nat pointed to Levi's tip jar. "I think you are the proud owner of all the island's small bills," she said. "Would you mind trading some of them out for larger ones?"

"Not at all." Levi took the bills out of her tip jar and started sorting.

"I have two hundred in ones and smaller bills," Karen said. She exchanged the small pile of bills for two hundred-dollar bills and then said her goodbyes for the night and headed for home.

Levi counted out four hundred in small bills, minus the ones with personal messages, and exchanged them with Nat. She continued to count and ended up with over eight hundred dollars in tips for the evening. Shocked by the total amount, Levi knew she had made a good decision to come to the islands.

"Not bad for a first night," Nat said. "Once the cruise line comes in and word of you spreads across the island, don't be surprised if that doubles."

Levi's head was swimming with numbers as she and NeNe walked out with Nat. Nat turned back toward the resort and left Levi and NeNe standing by the edge of the pool.

"You don't look like you are ready to sleep," NeNe said.

"I am way too wired to even think about sleep."

"Would you care to take a walk on the beach with me then?"

Levi smiled at NeNe. "I'd love to."

They took their shoes off and left them by the pool. Levi reached for NeNe's hand and they walked toward the water. The moon glistened across the calm surface as Levi and NeNe walked for a mile or more along the beach, enjoying the tropical night.

"So tell me about NeNe," Levi said as they walked. "Is there someone special in your life?"

"Not at the moment. I've been single for a few months now and I'm just enjoying the summer."

"I am sure you must get plenty of offers from the guests at the resort."

"I do, and I have enjoyed a few nights with a couple of beautiful ladies, but nothing more than a weekend affair has ever developed." NeNe blushed. "You know, what happens in the islands stays in the islands."

Levi laughed at NeNe's spoof of the Las Vegas commercial, but also realized it was true. Most of the women who visited the resort were only looking for a few nights of tropical bliss, leaving the possibility of creating a meaningful relationship in this setting very difficult.

"What about you, Levi?"

It was Levi's turn to blush. "I was hoping to sow my wild oats down here for a while before deciding to settle down and search for that perfect mate."

"Well, from the way you handled the ladies tonight, I would say you will be sowing fields of oats this summer." NeNe chuckled.

Levi's face turned scarlet. NeNe slipped her arm around her shoulder. "Just relax and have fun, Levi, we are only young once."

NeNe raised her hand to stifle a yawn, and Levi looked at her watch to find that it was nearly three in the morning. "You must have gotten up early today to pick me up at the airport and here I am keeping you from sleep."

"It has been a long and exciting day. Do you think you are relaxed enough to sleep now?" she asked as they turned and started walking back to the resort.

"I think so." But Levi still had serious doubts about sleeping.

"Why don't we get some sleep and meet for lunch tomorrow then I'll give you a tour of the island before we have to go on duty," NeNe suggested.

"That sounds like a great plan to me."

They passed some low dunes and heard loud moans of pleasure coming from behind them. A few of the guests were apparently enjoying themselves in one of the secluded dune huts offered by the resort.

"Someone is obviously having fun." Levi said as they reached the stairs leading back up to the pool.

She and NeNe stopped to retrieve their shoes and walked into the resort.

"Thank you for making my first night here a great one." Levi leaned over and softly kissed NeNe.

"My pleasure." NeNe murmured and turned toward her bungalow.

Levi watched her for a moment and then entered the guest suite and stripped out of her uniform. Levi enjoyed a luxurious, long, hot shower and then slipped naked between cool sheets. She'd worried needlessly about being able to sleep. She was gone as soon as her head hit the pillow.

Chapter Three

Levi woke the next morning and decided to have a short run before showering and meeting NeNe for lunch. She pulled on a sports bra, running shorts and her favorite running shoes, and after brushing her teeth and hair, headed down to the beach. The pool was already crowded with sunbathers and when she stepped onto the sand, it was just as crowded with women. Levi stretched for a few minutes then took off at a slow jog down the shore. The sun beating down on her shoulders felt marvelous and the pull of the thick sand made her legs work to maintain her stride. Several other joggers were on the sand and they smiled or waved as Levi jogged by.

Her skin coated with sweat, she jogged past the spot where she and NeNe had turned around several hours ago. Levi continued on her run, seeing the jungle that bordered the beach draw closer. She had moved out of the heavy sand and was running smoothly along the edge of the water, following a lone pair of footprints. She followed the tracks for nearly a quarter of a mile along the shore before they turned toward the jungle. Levi decided to follow.

She followed a clear path for another hundred yards and then picked up the sound of a waterfall. The path veered off to the right and opened to a clearing, which held a small waterfall. Levi came to a halt when she saw a lovely dark-haired woman, totally naked, wading across a small pool. Levi leaned against a coconut palm and watched the woman cross the pool until she stood underneath the waterfall. The water cascaded down her skin and the woman brushed the soaked dark hair back from her face. The woman was breathtaking beautiful and Levi stood transfixed.

Facing away from Levi, the woman's hands stroked down the front of her body as the water caressed her skin. Levi's eyes followed the movement of the woman's hands and she knew the woman was teasing her nipples. When one of the woman's hands disappeared beneath the water, Levi swallowed hard. She knew she should not be watching this woman give herself pleasure, but she could not pull her eyes away from the beautiful woman.

Levi felt her loins ignite as she watched the woman's hips rock against her hand. She was turning to walk away when the woman turned and looked directly at Levi and smiled. Levi stared back into the most beautiful green eyes she had ever seen and stopped dead in her tracks. The woman reached rapture, her lips open as the waterfall muted the cries of her climax. The woman closed her eyes, releasing Levi from their grip and Levi took off back down the path at a full run.

Levi ran and as her limbs worked, her mind kept flashing back to the woman underneath the waterfall, the vision now burned into her brain. When Levi saw the first of the sunbathers come into view on the beach she slowed her pace and then stopped to walk the last three hundred yards. Sweat covered her completely as she reached the catwalk and walked toward the resort. She picked up a pool towel to wipe the sweat from her face and arms as she strolled back to her room for a shower.

Even the coolness of the shower could not erase the vision of the woman under the waterfall from her mind. Levi knew she was in for some serious trouble if she allowed the vision of the woman's to haunt her. She prayed that an afternoon with NeNe would help to erase the memory.

†

NeNe was waiting for her when Levi walked into the dining room. After a hearty lunch, they climbed into NeNe's Jeep and headed out into a brilliant afternoon. NeNe gave Levi a tour of the island, pointing out the various local amenities and hotspots. They drove past her family home, then along a route that would lead them into a small jungle. Banana groves grew along both sides of the narrow road. NeNe took a right turn off the road onto a smaller path.

"This is the most beautiful spot on the island," NeNe said as she pulled into a large clearing.

Stone cliffs ringed the forest. Three huge waterfalls plummeted down their walls. Large flat rocks circled the pool and when Levi stepped onto one, she looked back across the entire island. The beauty of the scenery took her breath away and, for the moment, replaced the woman she had seen under the smaller waterfall that morning.

"This is beyond beautiful, NeNe." Levi turned to face her friend.

"I thought you might enjoy this spot." NeNe sat on the flat rock.

Levi joined her friend and together they sat looking across the island in silence, enjoying the beauty of the day.

"Tonight will be even busier than last night," NeNe said as she looked at her watch. "I hope you are ready to pour your fingers off tonight."

"I will give it my best shot, no pun intended." Levi stood and offered her hand to NeNe and lifted her to her feet. "Thank you for sharing this with me."

The fire of arousal still burned inside her and Levi thought about leaning into NeNe for a kiss. But a moment of clear thought rushed through her and Levi knew if she were to take NeNe in her arms now, it would be with the passion she was feeling for another. Levi wanted any moment with NeNe to be a passion they had inspired together. As difficult as it was, Levi turned away from NeNe and they walked back to the Jeep.

Seeing the glimmer in Levi's eyes, NeNe was sure Levi was going to kiss her so she was surprised and disappointed when Levi turned away from her. Sighing softly, NeNe followed Levi back to the Jeep. She could be patient, but she would not wait forever for Levi to realize there was chemistry between them.

✝

Nat smiled at Levi when she walked through the door. "I hope you rested well," she said as Levi slid onto a barstool across from her.

"I slept like a rock once I hit the bed."

"It's going to be a wild night, so I'm going to take a long nap this afternoon and be ready to come back around eleven. Just in case you need some help."

"I'll do my best."

"I know you will, Levi, but some nights are too busy for just one bartender, and I have a feeling tonight will be one of those," Nat said. "I have also pulled a server from the dining room to help Karen until we can hire a second full-time server for the bar. And, it took some wheeling and dealing with a manufacturer, but I have a surprise waiting for you in the storeroom."

Levi jumped off the barstool and headed straight for the storeroom. Three large boxes were waiting for her. Levi took a box cutter, sliced open the top box, and pulled the flaps open. She let out a roar of laughter when she reached into the box and pulled out a plastic shot glass that had Venus arced over the top, and Rising arcing back up from the bottom and the letters TE in the middle.

"No more need for you to wash hundreds of shot glasses. The patrons can keep them as souvenirs or we can pitch them at the end of the night," Nat said. "And, because that is your signature drink, you will be paid a quarter for each shot served from the bar. I also need you to write down your mixture so I can use it during the daytime and on your off days."

"You mean I actually have to take days off?"

"I'm afraid so, youngin'. Tuesdays and Wednesdays will be your days off for now and if you want to swap them later, we can make the changes. Sharon was the other top candidate for this job, but she is not ready for a full-tilt crowd, so she will work the slower nights and fill in at the pool bar."

"Hey Levi," Karen said as she stepped behind the bar and placed her purse in the storeroom.

"Hiya, Karen, look what the boss bought for us." Levi tossed a plastic shot glass to Karen.

She caught the glass and smiled as she gave it a close look. "Sweet! This should really cut down on the amount of dishwashing for us."

"Jennifer and I will drop in around eleven tonight to help out with the crowd," Nat said. "Since both of you are here, I'm going to head out and get that nap in." She tossed the bar towel to a widely grinning Levi. "See you two later."

Nat held the door for NeNe, who was coming in. She waved at Levi as she disappeared into the DJ booth. Levi wiped down the already immaculate bar and checked the supplies she would need for the evening. She pulled out a stack of trays and laid them next to the TE cooler along with several stacks of the new shot glasses. The door opened and a dozen or more sunbathers walked into the bar and spread out among the lower level booths.

Karen started taking their orders and smiled at Levi as she said, "Two dozen shots of TE, if you please, Madame Barkeep."

Levi chuckled and began placing the filled shot glasses on the tray then handed them across the bar to Karen. "Here you go." She laughed when she realized that Karen had worn her rollerblades as promised.

As the sun set, the first of the after-dinner crowd began to gather. The place was soon hopping with women, drinking, and dancing. The tips poured in as the shots continued to flow. Levi kept a watch over the crowd, searching for the beautiful woman she had seen under the waterfall, only to be disappointed that she hadn't arrived yet.

She was working up a sweat in the heated bar, pouring shots and drawing beers, when the doors opened. She glanced up to see long legs covered in black leather stride through the door. A black silky blouse covered the top half of the gorgeous woman she had seen earlier in the day and the entire bar held its collective breath as she walked in. The beer overflowed the pilsner glass she was filling, snapping her back to reality. Levi handed Karen the beer and returned to pouring shots as the woman walked to the bar and sat down. When she turned to hand Karen a tray of shots, she found the glowing green eyes fixed on her. She smiled, and with her heart racing wildly, walked over to the woman. "What's your pleasure?"

The woman smiled a wicked smile. "You later, but for now, I hear there is a fantastic new shot." She sat back on her stool. "Send me six for starters."

Levi poured six shots and placed them in front of the gorgeous woman. "Thank you, Levi," the woman said, her eyes lowering to Levi's nametag.

"My pleasure." Levi calmly returned to filling drink orders.

She glanced over at the woman as she mixed a drink. The woman had downed the third shot. "Very tasty. Your creation I presume?"

"Yes ma'am, that it is."

"How about starting a tab for me, sweetheart, and charge it to the penthouse."

"Sure thing." Levi handed Karen the drink she had been mixing. "I'll need your room key to validate it on the register."

"Of course you will, sweetheart." The woman stood and fished the key from her back pocket and handed it over.

Levi slid the electronic key across the register's card pad. She handed it back to the woman when it flashed an approval to a Simone Taylor. "Here you go, Ms. Taylor. Just let me know when you need another drink."

"How about pouring a couple dozen of your shots then and place them on a tray for me."

Levi poured two dozen shots, as the lady had requested, and then handed the tray over the bar to her.

"Thanks love." The woman took the tray from Levi and walked over to a booth where four young ladies were sitting.

Levi watched as she introduced herself and joined the ladies at their table. *Now that was smooth,* she thought as she turned to charge the shots to the woman's room.

NeNe had the tempo cranked and Levi watched Simone take the hand of one of her new friends and walk her to the dance floor. More than one head turned to watch the dark-haired beauty as she gyrated to the music, dancing very sensually. Levi felt her arousal stir as she watched her movements. Levi locked eyes with Simone long enough for Levi to feel flushed. She forced herself to turn away from the dance floor and went to the storeroom for a case of beer she really didn't need, but would stock anyway.

She found it difficult to keep her eyes off the dance floor, and was busy trying to concentrate on slicing a bag of limes when Nat walked into the bar and nudged her.

"Looks like a great night," she said, her smile fading as she looked at the bartender. "Are you feeling all right?"

"Yes, I feel fine, Nat, why do you ask?"

"Well you look a little flushed and your shirt is soaked."

"It's just been a very busy night so far," she replied, just as Karen called for another tray of shots.

"I'll get those, why don't you take ten and go out for some fresh air," Nat suggested.

Levi started to protest, but the look Nat gave her made resistance useless.

"All right, I'll be back in just a few."

Levi climbed the steps and stepped out into a cool breeze. She walked onto the catwalk and sat at the top of the stairs leading to the beach, gazing out across the churning surf. The moon glowed brightly over the water and lit up the white-tipped breakers, which crashed and blended with the sugar-white sands on the shore. The water had a very calming effect on Levi and she relaxed under a blanket of stars. She gazed down at the shoreline and watched a pair of lovers holding hands and walking down the beach. For a moment, Levi felt so all alone. The laughter of women walking up behind her brought her gaze back to the stairs and she stood to let them pass on their way to the beach.

Back inside, Levi noticed Simone at the bar talking with Nat. The woman left with another tray of shots. Levi stepped behind the bar just as Karen shouted out an order for six Coronas with lime. Levi went back to work filling the order.

"Welcome back," Nat said as she placed bills in an envelope and dropped them into the cash vault. "How many does this make so far tonight?"

Levi smiled. "That would be number six so far."

"Excellent." Nat resumed pouring a tray of shots that she handed to Jenny to pass around the bar, on the house.

"Have you ordered dinner yet, Levi?" Karen asked.

"No, not yet. I'll give NeNe a call. A burger tonight?" she teased Karen as she picked up the phone.

"Karen says she is starving," Levi said when NeNe picked up.

"I bet she wants a burger tonight."

"Yes, she does and I'll take a grilled chicken sandwich," Levi said. "Do you want anything, Nat?"

"Yes, order me a platter of nachos."

"Add a platter of nachos for the boss too, please," Levi said before hanging up.

Karen skidded to a halt in front of the bar and blew the bangs back from her forehead. "Two dozen more TEs for table six."

"Sit for a minute, Karen, and I'll take these out and give you a breather. You haven't stopped rolling all night." Levi took the tray of shots to the table where the dark-haired woman sat.

Levi had no idea why, but she needed to be close to the woman for just a minute. She set the tray down at the table. Before she could leave, Simone grasped her hand and slid something into her palm. She pulled Levi down so she could whisper in her ear.

Levi's skin burned at the woman's touch and her knees threatened to buckle when the woman whispered in her ear.

"That is only for you, precious." She let go of Levi's hand.

Levi stood and placed the object in her pocket. Returning to the bar, Levi laid the tray down and walked into the storeroom. Pulling the object out of her pocket, she opened her hand to find a hundred-dollar bill smiling up at her and a brief note. *I would love to share your company in the penthouse tonight. S.*

†

Nat caught an odd look in Levi's eye and wondered why she suddenly seemed uncomfortable. "Levi."

"Yes, Nat?"

"I think it's time for 'Mambo Number Five.'"

"You think?" Levi grinned.

"I do." She nodded and flashed a high five to NeNe, who responded with a thumbs-up. Nat watched Levi walk up to the second level and lean down to whisper into an attractive brunette's ear.

The woman nodded her answer to Levi's whispered question as she stumbled away from the table and allowed Levi to take her to the dance floor just as "Mambo Number Five" started to play.

Nat watched Levi guide the giddy woman all over the dance floor and when she dipped her at the end of the song for a kiss, Nat noticed she let her lips linger just a little longer than the previous night, and the crowd went wild. They roared their applause as Levi lifted her partner back to her feet and carefully led the woman back through the crowd as women flocked to the dance floor. Nat's eyes followed Levi as she wound her way through the throng of women. "Nice job," she said as Levi walked behind the counter.

"Thanks boss." Levi's eyes twinkled with excitement.

Nat was relieved to see the look of discomfort gone from Levi's face.

Dinner arrived and NeNe set the mixer to play and joined them. "You sure know how to stir a crowd," she said, sitting down next to Levi.

"Just having some fun, ma'am." Levi smiled before biting into her sandwich.

Karen took a bite of her burger and groaned her pleasure out loud. "Are you glad you went with the burger tonight?" NeNe teased.

"Oh yessss," Karen purred as they all broke out in laughter.

Levi was seated inside the bar. Movement over NeNe's shoulder caught her attention and she looked up to see Simone leading a blonde out of the bar. She winked at Levi as she walked by and graced her with a beautiful smile. Levi returned the smile and turned to refill a glass of soda for NeNe. *Was she foolish enough to think the woman would leave alone?* The hundred-dollar bill burned a hole in her pocket and she suddenly felt cheap. That the woman felt she could buy her affection bothered her. Levi's anger burned inside as she thought of the dark-haired beauty's assumption.

The rest of the evening was a blur and when they finished closing down the bar, NeNe left to meet a date and Nat walked back with Levi to the resort. "Are you sure you are okay? You've been awfully quiet since dinner."

"Yes, Nat, I'm fine."

"You have a least a dozen invitations in your pocket. Why don't you pick one and go have some fun."

"I may just do that." Levi knew she had a much more pressing issue to deal with as she slipped into her room and stripped out of her clothing. She showered quickly and dressed in running shorts and a snug shirt then slipped her running shoes on. She needed to burn off some energy and felt like a run would be the perfect way to do that. She placed her room key inside her pocket and took the hundred-dollar bill in her hand. Her anger flared as she rode the elevator up to the penthouse.

Levi knocked on the door of the penthouse. She shuffled her feet impatiently as she waited for the door to open. When it did, Simone stood before her in a thin robe. Levi could see past her to the young blonde sprawled across the bed. She heard her call out, "Simone, darling. Come back to bed."

31

"I was hoping you would come by," Simone said with a warm smile.

"I just wanted to return this." Levi placed the bill in Simone's pocket. "You don't have to buy my attention." Tears glistening in her eyes, Levi spun on her heel and fled to the elevator.

"That was not what I meant at all," Simone said but Levi was already gone, riding the elevator down to the main floor. Simone watched as Levi ran through the pool area and headed to the beach. Simone closed the door and quickly dressed in running shorts and a T-shirt. She looked at the woman lazing in her bed. "Playtime is over, doll, please see yourself out."

"But baby..." but Simone was already out the door.

✝

Levi ran blindly down the beach as tears blurred her vision. Her muscles started to burn, but she pressed on, her anger fueling her run. After a mile of a dead sprint, Levi's muscles were starving for oxygen. She slowed her pace to a fast jog as her feet splashed in the approaching water. When her legs threatened to buckle, Levi slowed to a walk. She looked around to find that she was at the spot where the path led to the waterfall hidden in the jungle. Her feet carried her to the sounds of falling water and she collapsed onto a flat rock at the base of the fall. Levi stared up at the star-filled sky as the roar of the water filled her ears. The tears continued to fall and Levi closed her eyes tightly in an effort to quell their flow.

✝

Simone rushed to the elevator and pushed the button, then chose the stairs as a faster option. She pushed through the door at the bottom and rushed out into the night. The moon shone brightly on the beach and she could easily follow the tracks that only Levi could have made at this time of night. Running down the beach, she knew instinctively where she would find the beautiful young

32

woman. Their exchange had gone so wrong. Simone knew she had to do something to make it right for Levi. When she reached the waterfall, she stopped and, just as Levi had done earlier that day, she leaned against a palm tree. She caught her breath as she determined what she wanted to say.

"Would you mind lifting the rock and let me crawl out from under it?"

Levi's eyes flew open and she saw Simone standing in front of her. She blinked and when she opened them again, the woman was still there. She sat up on her rock and stared at the woman.

"I know you must think I'm no better than a reptile that would live under a rock, but I assure you that offering to buy your services was not my intent."

Levi blinked again and remained silent.

"May I join you?"

When Levi still did not answer, Simone sat on the rock facing her and looked deep into her eyes. "I meant the money to be a tip for your great service and the fun atmosphere you had created at the bar," Simone said. "I was asking you to join me tonight in the penthouse, but it was not intended in the manner in which you interpreted." Simone rested back on an elbow and continued. "When I saw you this morning, I knew there was something special about you. I wanted to meet you and get to know you better."

"It looked like you had your hands full when I arrived," Levi said roughly.

"I admit I made an error. I was letting off some steam with that woman and had lost all track of time. Watching you today had me so aroused, I needed to work some of that out of my system. I had no plan to make our first, actually, our second encounter a sexual one at all."

Levi frowned as she listened to Simone. Either this woman was incredibly smooth or she was genuine in what she was saying.

Simone waited for Levi to speak. When she remained quiet, she continued. "I am not naïve, Levi. Most of the women at this resort would not have turned away this morning when you came upon me. They would have joined me in the pool for a romp at mindless sex and that would have been all it was, but you turned away and that intrigued me." Levi was making this apology very tough and Simone had to struggle for the words she wanted to say next. "I apologize that my invitation was misinterpreted and I want you to know that I am genuinely interested in you, Levi."

Levi heard the emotion in her voice. She softened a bit and the frown slowly erased from her face. "I think I jumped to the wrong conclusion about you as well. I assumed you could have any woman in that bar tonight and my feelings were hurt when I thought you were offering to buy my services." Levi dropped her head.

Simone leaned closer and took Levi's chin in her hand and lifted it until Levi's eyes met hers. "I can see how you could think that and I should have made my request clear from the beginning." She smiled sweetly. "Do you think we could start fresh?"

Levi's smile broke the tension hanging between them and she reached out her hand. "Hi, I'm Levi."

Simone took her hand. "I'm pleased to meet you, Levi. My name is Simone."

Levi smiled at her. "How ironic is it that we meet here for a second time?"

"Somehow when I reached the beach, I knew you would be here. Maybe we were just destined to be in this spot when we met and we just weren't ready this morning," she suggested. "I just feel awful that I hurt your feelings to get us to this point now."

"It was not all your fault."

"I'll consent to that on one condition."

"Which would be?"

"Well, I'll be at the resort until next Thursday. I assume Nat will give you an off day."

"Yes, I have Tuesday and Wednesday off."

"Well then, I would love to spend Tuesday getting to know you," Simone said.

"I think that could be arranged."

"Very well then. I'll make some arrangements and get back with you later today about the details. If they meet your approval, we'll have a date for Tuesday." She stood and offered her hand to Levi. "Now, I think it would be a good idea for both of us to get some sleep." She pulled Levi to her feet. "We both have a big day ahead of us tomorrow."

Levi stood and walked with Simone back to the beach. "Race you back?" Simone teased.

Levi broke out in laughter. "I used up the rest of my energy getting here. I may not be able to walk tomorrow as it is."

"All right, we'll walk back." They walked together as the sun's rays began to color the horizon. When they returned to the resort, Simone turned to Levi, "I'm glad I finally got to meet you, Levi." With a smile, she was gone.

Chapter Four

When Levi awoke the following morning, the voice mail light was flashing on her telephone. She retrieved the message that let her know a meeting of the bar staff was scheduled for two o'clock. Levi glanced at the clock and found that it was already noon. She called the kitchen to place an order for a salad and went to get ready for work.

NeNe was in the dining room when Levi walked in and she motioned her over to her table.

"Hey, Levi," she said with a bright smile. "How are you today?"

"I'm good, NeNe. How about you?"

"I'm doing great. I thought I would grab lunch before our meeting. Want to join me?"

"Sure."

"Thanks, Cindy," Levi said as the server placed a large salad in front of her.

"Do you have any idea what the meeting is going to be about today?"

"I have no clue," NeNe said. "We don't have meetings often, so it must be something important."

"Well, I guess we'll find out soon enough." Levi dug into her salad. "So how was your date last night?"

"We had a very good time, and made plans to meet up again tonight."

"Good for you, NeNe." Levi punched her friend lightly on the shoulder.

At that moment, Nat and Liz walked by with Simone. Levi's eyes lit up at the sight of the beautiful woman and she felt her cheeks blush.

"You really like that one don't you?" NeNe said, catching Levi gazing after Simone.

"I don't know yet, NeNe, but she's certainly intriguing. We have a date planned for Tuesday, so I guess I'll get to know her better then."

"Levi, you sneaky little devil you!" NeNe returned the punch Levi had given her earlier.

They finished eating and walked to the bar. Karen introduced Lynn, Sharon, and Janie as the other bartenders and servers as NeNe and Levi joined them at a large table. They were busy chatting when the door opened again and Liz, Nat, and Simone entered together. They joined the staff around the table and Levi smiled at Simone, who sat across the table from her.

"Thank you for meeting us today, ladies," Nat said. "We wanted to share some very exciting news with all of you and get your feedback on some issues as well." Nat sat back in her seat and smiled at the group. "We would like to thank you for one of the most successful Singles Weekends we have ever had and when you receive your paychecks this week, we hope you will be pleased with your new raises."

"You have all worked very hard to help us make Venus Rising what it is today and without your efforts, we could not be making the changes we are about to tell you about," Liz said. "But, before we go any further, I would like to introduce Simone Taylor."

"Simone is the owner of Sappho Cruise Lines and is also my sister," Nat said.

Levi felt her heart rush to her throat. Her eyes darted over to find Simone smiling at her. She could feel her cheeks heating up as she thought back to how rudely she had talked to the beautiful woman, who was also her employer's sister. She slumped down in her chair.

NeNe reached under the table to pinch Levi, who had continued to stare at Simone, and brought her attention back to the conversation at the head of the table. Levi struggled to hear Nat over the pounding of her heart in her ears. She tried to return her focus to Nat but could not help but wonder if her actions earlier that morning would have a devastating effect on her continued employment. She again felt like a total heel.

"With the addition of Levi as a full-time bartender," she heard Nat say, "We have decided to enter into a contract with Simone to become a port of call for her cruise line."

Levi relaxed a bit in her seat as she listened to Nat and stole quick glances at Simone.

"In two weeks, the first of Sappho's cruise ships will be in port for several nights, and then weekly after that, so we have a great deal of work to do, ladies."

"Liz will be interviewing to fill a few more server slots and we will add another part-time bartender to handle an additional poolside bar that will hopefully be ready in two weeks," Nat said.

"We will also be adding an outdoor covered patio that will be an extension of the bar. Once it is complete a large door will be added, over there." Liz pointed to an area between the dance floor and restrooms.

"You should expect an additional two hundred and fifty patrons each night the ship is in port," Simone said. "Our clientele is just as exclusive as the resort's, and I think you will find them very generous and appreciative of the great service I have seen from all of you."

"Levi, we will no longer be sanitizing barware here," Nat said. "The kitchen staff will be responsible for the pickup, sanitization, and delivery of clean supplies, which will allow us to concentrate on serving."

"No more dishpan hands?" Levi teased Nat.

"Trust me, you won't have time to be washing dishes," Simone said. "Our crowd is thirsty and loves to have a really good time when they are in port."

"Do you have any questions or suggestions?" Nat asked.

"Will we have at least three servers on duty when the ship is in and can you purchase additional barware?" Karen asked.

"Three for sure and sometimes four when we have special weekends like our Holiday and Singles weekends," Nat promised. "I will also be behind the bar, helping Levi on those nights as well. And yes, the new barware should be arriving in the next few days."

"It all sounds so very exciting," NeNe said.

"Yes, it is, NeNe, and Liz and I want to again relay our appreciation of your efforts in making this venture possible. Thank you for coming in this afternoon and we'll see you back at four for start of business," she said, before dismissing her staff.

✝

Simone stood and looked over at Levi. "Would you mind taking a walk with me before you start your shift?"

"I would love to." Still blushing she followed Simone out of the bar toward the beach.

"So why did you not tell me who you are?" Levi asked as they walked.

"Would it have made any difference?"

"Well, I probably would not have been so rude to you last night if I had known that you were Nat's sister."

"Half-sister," Simone corrected her. "We have the same mother, but different fathers."

"If you weren't her half-sister, and I had treated a potential partner of Nat's that way, I could have damaged their working relationship. I would never have wanted that to occur."

"Will you relax? I have already told Nat that I was a total jerk with you last night."

"Oh dear, and I still have a job today?"

"Yes, Levi, you are her star. I was chastised by Nat for treating you so badly." Simone chuckled. "Fact is, she told me that you were way too good for me and that I would have to court you properly, if I were to have any chance in hell at being with you."

"It is a good thing Nat is your sister and could talk some sense into you," Levi teased. She relaxed as they walked down the beach.

"I plan on spending a week a month down here and I promise to do everything I can to seduce you away from the grasp of my sister," Simone said. "Nat thinks she has the world's best bartender and I plan to prove to her she is wrong."

"Wrong? You don't think I am the world's best bartender?"

"I think you are a great bartender, but you have the potential to be so much more."

"Is that some of your smooth talking or are you being serious?"

"Smooth talking aside, I am very serious. From what Nat has told me about your education, it is evident that you have a very quick business mind. If you let it, your education and experience will take you far."

Levi remained quiet as they walked and she pondered Simone's statement. Neither of them had realized that they had walked past the last line of sunbathers and were rapidly approaching the path to the waterfall.

"I guess this is meant to be our spot," Simone said as she took Levi's hand and they walked the path to the waterfall.

"It does seem that we are destined to be here, doesn't it?" They walked to one of the large boulders and took a seat. "A week a month," Levi said with a grin.

"Do you think you could handle me for a week at a time?"

"It may take some working up to, but I'm willing to give it a shot."

"Please don't think I am trying to prevent you from sowing your oats while you are here. But I would like to spend as much time as possible getting to know you while I'm here."

Levi looked at Simone with a raised brow.

"I realize there are a few years age difference between us, and Nat shared with me that one of your goals in taking this job was to sow your wild oats. So, please don't feel like I expect you to remain celibate when I'm not around." Simone grinned at Levi. "If you see something you want, go after it, and enjoy. Once you have decided to settle down with a mate, then you will be satisfied with that one special someone."

Levi could not believe they were having this conversation. Simone obviously desired her but would give her the freedom to explore her sexuality to the fullest, without demands for fidelity except for their time spent together. Surely, she must be dreaming. Levi looked into Simone's eyes and read the sincerity there.

Simone raised her hand to caress the side of Levi's face. She leaned in for a kiss but the alarm on Levi's watch went off, startling them.

"Time to go to work," Levi said with a soft smile to Simone.

Their first kiss would have to wait for another moment.

Simone stepped off the boulder and extended her hand to Levi. "We can't have you late for work. I think I'm going to get some sun out by the pool and possibly catch a nap, before having dinner with Nat and Liz." They walked back down the path. "Would you mind if I sat at the bar with you tonight, so we can chat when business slows down a bit?"

"I would like that very much."

They walked quickly back to the resort where they parted ways. "I'll see you later," Simone said, and disappeared into the crowd at the pool.

Levi smiled to herself. Feeling like she could suddenly float, she stepped through the door to the bar to begin her shift.

Chapter Five

Though she was busy, the afternoon seemed to drag for Levi. Each time the door to the bar opened Levi looked up only to be disappointed when Simone didn't step through the door. The afternoon crowd was light as guests packed for their return home the following day, but as the sun set, the women began to slowly drift in.

Levi marveled at the variety of women who had come to the resort. Every size, shape, age, and color she could have imagined was under one roof. It was interesting to watch from behind the bar as new couples formed. She couldn't resist smiling when she thought how beautiful it was to watch love bloom. Levi watched carefully as a certain young lady spent a great deal of time sitting in the DJ booth with NeNe and her heart swelled with happiness for her new friend. Levi's face was beaming with a smile when the door opened again and Simone finally walked into the bar and took a seat at the bar.

"Hello, gorgeous."

"Hi, Simone, how are you?"

"I'm much better now, thank you." Simone smiled and raised an eyebrow at Levi. "I hope you've had a great night so far."

"The afternoon was a little slow, but the night has certainly picked up." Levi handed Karen another tray of drinks. "May I get you something?"

Simone chose not to respond with the first answer that crossed her mind, which was filled with sexual innuendo, and instead answered with, "I think I would like a soda for now, until the lobster I had for dinner finishes swimming."

Levi poured a soda and dropped a cherry into the glass. She imagined how sensual Simone would have looked enjoying the succulent, sweet lobster, coated in salty, warm butter. Her insides quivered with the very image of her lips wrapping around a chunk of the sweet meat. Levi had to fight hard to ward off the blush that was threatening to rise to her cheeks.

"Here you are, ma'am." Levi placed the drink in front of Simone.

Between orders, Simone and Levi chatted quietly and learned more about one other. Levi was impressed to discover that Simone had an MBA from Harvard. She had risen quickly in the business world when she started Sappho, growing the fleet from one ship to half a dozen in three short years. Simone told her that she traveled extensively, but hoped to spend more time on the island now that there was someone to grab her interest. Levi chuckled but forced her heart to calm down to prevent it from racing out of her chest.

Over the next hour, Simone watched Levi work and interact with the customers in the club, and Levi watched as women approached Simone with requests to dance. She politely declined their invitations, preferring to remain in Levi's company instead.

"You know, you're breaking so many hearts, including mine, by not being out on that dance floor tonight," Levi said.

"Including yours?"

"Yes, including mine. I admit I really enjoy watching you dance."

"In that case, I will be right back." Simone grinned and stepped off the barstool. She approached one of the women who had previously asked her to dance and, after a quick exchange, walked with her to the dance floor.

Once Simone stepped into her arms, Levi observed how women flocked to be near her. The area quickly became crowded with gyrating bodies. Simone moved very fluidly to the music, and Levi felt charged with energy conceived by Simone's sensual movements. Her eyes followed Simone as she danced a heated dance. When the long set of songs had finished, Simone made her way back to the bar. A light patina of perspiration had broken out across her body, making her exposed skin shine as she approached.

"Good Lord, it is hot on that dance floor." Simone fanned herself.

"Now would you care for something a little more refreshing?" Levi asked.

"How about a half dozen of them."

Levi grinned. Instead of filling shot glasses full of Tropical E, she filled a pilsner and placed it in front of Simone. "Small sips," she cautioned as Simone raised the glass to her lips.

Nat had entered the bar during the dance and now walked up to the bar and sat down next to Simone. "You would not be trying to get my sister inebriated so you can take advantage of her, now would you, Levi?" Nat teased.

"Ouch, boss," Levi exclaimed in mock surprise. "I would never even think of doing that to your sister."

"Oh Nat, now look what you've done. You've gone and spoiled all my fun tonight." Simone laughed.

"Now that, I seriously doubt, sister."

"Levi, why don't you call NeNe with your dinner orders and take a break until the food arrives. I think I can handle the crowd for a little while by myself."

NeNe wrote down the order Levi called in and then asked, "Is it time, Levi?"

"Oh, NeNe, I definitely think it is time. Hit me."

"Dinner is ordered, so there's only one thing left to do," Levi said as the beginning notes to "Mambo Number Five" played and the crowd stirred. Levi looked around the bar, looking for the right partner, and smiled when her eyes met Simone's. "Dance with me?"

"It would be my pleasure." Simone took the hand Levi offered.

They moved gracefully and sensually to the music, their rhythm matching. Levi's heart raced as the song began to fade. Taking Simone in her arms, she locked eyes with her and dipped Simone then lowered her mouth to cover Simone's, their lips brushing softly. Levi pressed her tongue between Simone's lips and their tongues continued the sensual dance their bodies had begun. Neither of them were aware of the roaring crowd or that the music had ended. When Levi lifted Simone to her feet after the kiss, her face appeared flushed. With a soft chuckle, Levi led her from the dance floor.

"We'll be back in a few minutes," Levi said.

Levi and Simone walked out into a beautiful night and down to the end of the pier. Levi hungered for the taste of Simone, but wanted their first time together to be slow and enjoyable. Still, she could not resist pulling Simone into her arms for a deep kiss. Their hands slowly explored one another and their bodies began to sway together to the faint sounds of the slow, pulsing love song playing in the bar.

Simone's hands slid beneath the waistband of Levi's shorts and she attempted to pull her shirt free. Levi stopped her progress, taking her hands and entwining their fingers together as she moved their arms behind Simone's back.

Levi felt Simone's groan of disappointment and frustration vibrating in her mouth and she could feel the arousal quivering in her muscles as she held Simone tightly against her chest. Levi broke the kiss and moved her mouth up to Simone's ear. "I don't want our first time to be rushed, and I promise it will be worth the wait."

"I'm sure it will be," Simone breathlessly whispered, grinding her hips into the thigh Levi had pressed between her legs as they swayed to the music.

Simone rested her forehead on Levi's as they continued their slow dance. When the music ended, she looked up to find the moon shining in Levi's eyes. "You are so beautiful." She leaned in for a tender kiss.

After two more songs and many kisses, Levi escorted Simone back to the bar. Dinner had just arrived and NeNe was on her way to the bar when Levi and Simone reentered.

"I promised Nat we would go to town in the morning and take care of some business, but I would love to meet you for a run and lunch when we return, if that would be possible," Simone said as they pressed through the crowd.

"Can we meet at eleven then?"

"That would be perfect." Simone looked at her watch and decided to call it an evening.

Levi watched her walk from the bar and then sat down beside Karen. "Another burger?" she teased her friend.

"These things are to die for." Karen giggled as Levi opened her box to reveal a burger to match hers.

"Good thing NeNe is eating healthy for us." Levi reached across to snag one of Nat's nachos.

"Someone has to set a good example for you two," NeNe said with a smile and took a bite of her salad.

They ate and chatted while the crowd kept the dance floor packed. Levi knew there would be a rush for drinks once this set had finished, so she made short work of her burger and downed a bottle of water.

"You could have taken the time to chew that burger," Nat teased.

"I have a feeling the natives will be very thirsty when they come off the dance floor," Levi said as she began pouring shots. "We are going to have to convince NeNe to play slow music while we eat." Levi shot a grin to her friend.

"That's right, blame it on the DJ, when in reality it is the bartender that gets them all wound up."

Karen and Nat joined NeNe in laughing at her comment. "I must admit, the hormone levels certainly elevated a few notches after that kiss you gave Simone," Nat said with an elbow to Levi's ribs.

Levi blushed profusely at her boss's comment. "I just couldn't resist kissing those delicious lips."

"Kissing is one thing, it looked more like you were giving her mouth to mouth," Nat continued with her teasing.

"Well, I don't recall the lady complaining."

NeNe and Karen shook their heads as they dumped their trash and went back to work. Nat sat on one of the stools and watched Levi wipe down the counter. Levi looked up and caught Nat grinning at her. "What?"

"I have never known Simone to be patient before when it comes to pursuing a woman she is interested in, but with you something is very different," Nat said. "She has become quite used to her looks filling her bed with ease, but she told me today that she would wait as long as necessary to be with you."

"She certainly is a beautiful woman."

"But…"

"I sense there can be more between us than a casual fling. I want to invest some time getting to know her instead of bouncing into bed with her then finding out we have nothing in common but casual sex."

"I think that's a very wise decision," Nat said. "My dear sister has broken more than one heart and I would hate for you to fall victim to that. Don't get me wrong, Simone is a beautiful, intelligent woman, but no one yet has been able to hold her attention for long."

"Trust me, I don't want to be just another conquest for her. If she is willing to wait until the time is right, then at least she has demonstrated enough interest to convince me to become vulnerable to her charms." Levi shook her head and chuckled. "I know when I interviewed, I told you that I wanted to have some fun and sow some oats, but I never dreamed I would meet someone like Simone so quickly."

"Simone will only be here one week of every month, so there will be plenty of time for you to explore your sexual needs. Simone actually told me that she would not mind you experimenting until you were ready to settle down. Then she could be satisfied that you were with her for all the right reasons."

"She pretty much told me the same thing earlier, but hearing you repeat it makes me more comfortable with the validity of her comment."

"Oh, by no means should you expect Simone to lead you into someone else's arms when she is here, but she will give you the freedom to do as you please in her absence." Nat chuckled. "I do not believe Simone has it in her to share you with anyone else, but she cares enough for you to see you happy. Besides, what hot-blooded woman would not be tempted by all the beauty that comes and goes here?"

Levi raised a brow at Nat's comment. "Even you?"

"Are you kidding me? Liz would kill me in a heartbeat if she caught me in bed with someone else," Nat said with a laugh. "And, I can guarantee it would not be a pretty death. Lucky for me, Liz takes care of all my needs, so I have no desire to step out of our relationship."

Levi nodded her head in agreement and hoped one day she would feel like that for someone.

"Speaking of my needs, if you have everything under control, I am going to leave you and take care of those needs. If you are comfortable in closing, you can drop the money bag and cash register tape by the room when you close down."

"I think I can handle it from here on out. If I run across something, I'll give you a call, but do try to enjoy yourself," Levi said with a devilish grin.

"Consider me gone then."

Chapter Six

Monday morning Levi went in in search of NeNe to ask her friend for a ride into town so she could open a bank account to deposit her tip money and eventually her paychecks. She walked past the dining room and glimpsed inside. She saw NeNe eating a late breakfast with a beautiful young woman and decided instead to drop in on Liz and ask to borrow one of the resort's vans to make her trip.

Levi's knock on the door to the office was immediately answered from inside.

Liz smiled when she saw Levi poke her head in. "Hello Levi, how are you?"

"I'm doing well, thanks. I was wondering if I could ask a favor? I want to go into town to open a bank account this morning and was hoping I could borrow one of the resort vans?"

"Normally, that would not be a problem, but they are all out at the moment shuttling guests," Liz said. "Nat and Simone have our car, but can you ride a motorcycle?"

"I used to have an old Harley."

Liz opened the desk drawer and pulled out a set of keys and tossed them to Levi. "Inside the garage you will find a black Fat Boy that needs to be driven."

"Sweet!" Levi yelped. "Thanks, Liz!"

"Not a problem. Just watch out for Nat. I swear that woman does not know how to drive."

49

"Will do."

Liz chuckled when she looked out the window to see Levi pumping her fist in the air.

The Fat Boy turned out to be a beautiful black monster totally chromed out. Levi sat on it for a few minutes before she turned the key. She let it warm up and then pulled out of the garage and headed downtown. It did not take long to find one of the two banks on the island. Levi pulled into a parking space and turned off the engine. It felt good to ride a bike again and she considered ordering a bike to use for transportation around the island.

Twenty minutes later, she left the bank with a checking, savings, and a certificate of deposit account opened and headed back to the resort. She parked the bike and returned the keys to Liz before returning to her room to change for her run with Simone.

Levi walked out to the pool area to begin her stretching while she waited for Simone. As usual, the pool was packed and she gave the ladies a nice show of skin as she stretched her muscles in preparation for her run.

"Was that you I saw on Liz's bike a few minutes ago?" Simone said as she walked up.

"Yes, she loaned it to me so I could go to town."

"I must admit, you looked mighty fine." Simone leaned down to begin stretching her legs.

"Thanks, I used to have a bike years ago."

"Thinking of getting another one?"

"Maybe. It would make sense for down here."

"Are you ready to run?"

"Was just waiting on you." Levi took off at a slow jog.

Simone laughed and raced after Levi. They increased their pace as they ran down the beach. As they neared the cutoff to the waterfall, Levi looked over at Simone and grinned, but kept running down the beach. At the two-mile point, they turned around and when they got within a hundred yards of the waterfall path, Simone called out, "Race you," and took off at full speed.

It did not take Levi long to catch Simone and they raced to the path at a dead heat. Both were coated with perspiration and breathing hard. "Would you care to cool off with me?" Simone asked as her eyes moved to the waterfall.

Levi bent down and removed her running shoes and then looked inquisitively at Simone. Simone had her hands on the waistband of her shorts but when she caught Levi's gaze, she quickly dropped her hands and reached for Levi instead. Laughing together, they waded across the pool into the cascading fall. The cool water felt refreshing against their heated skin. As they stepped from under the main flow, Levi pulled Simone to her, caressed her face with her hands, and covered her mouth for a slow, deep kiss.

Waiting was torture for Levi but she felt it was the right thing to do. A kiss would be all they shared, and for the moment it would have to be enough.

Levi felt the desire between them, and knew they would be together soon. Simone had been mysterious, so far, about the activities she had planned for their date tomorrow, but Levi felt like there would be an opportunity to make love with Simone in a slow and leisurely manner. She could wait one more day and even though she felt Simone shake with desire in her arms as they kissed, she would make her wait as well.

Simone saw the desire in Levi's eyes as her fingers traced down her face. When Levi took her hands and raised them to her mouth to kiss the tips of her fingers, Simone's knees went weak. From that moment on, Simone knew Levi was the one she had waited for and dreamed of for years. Her only hope was that Levi would feel the same for her.

Their bodies rinsed clean from the cool waters, Levi took Simone's hand and guided her across the pool to sit on the rock. "What do you have planned for us tomorrow?" Levi asked as she looked into Simone's eyes.

"A quiet breakfast in the morning when you wake. After that, I have rented a boat and thought we would do some exploring on a small island just off the coast and have a picnic lunch. And, if you are not tired of me by the end of the day, a delicious lobster dinner at the dining room."

"That sounds like a wonderful day to me. Mondays are usually slow, so we will close the bar at midnight. I can be ready by eight, if that is good for you?"

"Eight would be fabulous." Simone leaned into Levi's shoulder.

"When you leave here, where will you be going?"

"First to Cancun and from there on to Greece. I want to check on how well the ships are doing in each of those ports. Then a week back in the States and finally back here for the first arrival to Venus Rising. Nat and I are putting together plans for a fabulous kickoff for that weekend; I hope we can pull everything together in time."

"I'm sure it will be a huge success with the two of you putting it together," Levi said.

"I hope so. This venture could be very profitable for both of our companies, and will be the driving force to our future success."

Levi looked at her watch. If they were going to get a shower before lunch, they would need to start back to the resort soon. She looked at Simone and caught her smiling at her. Levi leaned down to softly kiss her lips. The tenderness of the kiss made a mockery of the passion burning between them, but Levi did not press the kiss further. Instead, she hopped down from the rock and offered a hand to Simone.

"If we are going to get a shower before lunch we need to head back."

Simone took the offered hand and jumped off the rock into Levi's waiting arms. Levi could feel the quivering of Simone's muscles as their bodies pressed close, and she softly whispered, "Soon."

Levi was tempted to invite Simone into her shower as they walked back to the resort, but they would be rushed and she planned to make their first time together last for hours. She would have to be patient until the time was right and Levi felt that time would arrive tomorrow.

When they reached the resort, Simone kissed Levi and said, "Come up to the penthouse when you are showered and dressed and we will go for lunch."

"I will see you shortly then."

✝

Simone watched Levi walk away, entranced by the way she moved.

"Earth to Simone," Nat said as she walked up to her sister. "She has you hooked doesn't she?" "Who, me? Hooked?" Simone asked.

"Yes, you, dear sister. I have never seen you like this before." Nat jabbed Simone in the ribs with her elbow.

"Levi is such an amazing young woman."

"That she is. Are you meeting her for lunch?"

"Yes, as soon as we shower."

"You had better get a move on then."

"I will see you later, sis." Simone walked to the elevator that would take her up to the penthouse.

✝

Levi enjoyed the soft flow of the warm water over her head and cascading down her shoulders and back. She imagined Simone's hands on her as she bathed and her nipples grew firm under her hand as the soapy cloth bathed her chest. It had been some time since Levi had the pleasure of another woman's attention and she ached to fulfill the need rushing through her veins. *Very soon,* she thought as she dried and dressed for work.

✝

Simone stripped out of her running clothes and glimpsed at her image in the full-length mirror. The running and frequent workouts were paying off and she was pleased with the image that reflected back at her. Maybe this afternoon she would visit the spa

53

for a little pampering while Levi was at work. She had just finished showering when Levi knocked on the door. Wrapped in a thick robe, Simone walked to the door.

"Would you like for me to wait for you downstairs while you finish?"

"That won't be necessary unless you are afraid I will jump your bones." Simone laughed and led Levi over to a comfortable chair.

"I think I'm safe for the moment." Levi took a seat and watched Simone walk across the room to the bathroom.

She stopped before entering the bathroom and turned to look at Levi. "I wouldn't be too sure of that, my dear."

Levi stared at Simone's beautiful body as she let the robe fall from her shoulders then placed it on the hook on the back of the bathroom door. From her vantage point, she had an unobstructed view of the bathroom and the adjacent dressing room. With dampness growing between her legs, she watched as Simone dressed in matching lace panties and bra, her hips swaying in a sensual slow motion as she covered her skin with the sheer fabric. She then slipped on some tight-fitting jeans and a dark blue oxford, leaving the tail of the shirt out for a casual appearance. Simone stepped into a pair of loafers and brushed her hair before joining Levi in the bedroom.

"You look very sexy." Levi stood, her eyes devouring her as she approached.

"Thank you. I hope what you see meets with your approval."

"You are a beautiful woman." Her eyes rose to meet Simone's.

Simone was standing right in front of her, eyes glowing with desire. "This beautiful woman wants to kiss you."

Levi pulled Simone into an embrace, lowering her mouth to meet hers. She felt the electricity between them as their lips met and their tongues danced slowly together. Simone responded by taking Levi's tongue deep into her mouth and sliding her hands down Levi's back, pulling her hips closer and pressing herself deep into Levi, causing her to moan when their bodies made contact.

Levi's hand moved between them, her fingers searching for the nipples she knew would be swollen and straining against the lace of Simone's bra. She was not disappointed when her fingers discovered the firm, sensitive flesh aching for her touch. Simone groaned as Levi's fingers slowly traced her nipple, teasing her to near madness.

Simone broke the kiss. "Unless you are planning to have me for lunch, I suggest we get far away from this bed," she said, her voice thick with desire.

Levi looked over at the large, comfortable bed and then back to Simone. "Are you hungry?"

"I am starving, but not for food."

Chapter Seven

Levi took a step backward and smiled seductively at Simone. Her hands started at the top button of her oxford and slowly began to unfasten each one. Levi's smile grew as the shirt opened further with each button released and the lacy bra came into view.

Simone shivered and her muscles quivered as Levi slid the shirt off her shoulders. The moment she had dreamed of was finally about to happen and she was completely speechless.

The fire burning in Levi's eyes grew brighter as she reached behind Simone to free the clasp of her bra, revealing nipples swollen with excitement. Levi traced the outline of Simone's collarbones, down to her breastbone then slowly down between her breasts. Her fingers grazed the fullness of Simone's breasts, fanning out across the swelling flesh that rose and fell with each breath, igniting flames of desire that quickly spread between her trembling thighs. Levi's hands explored down her stomach, slowly circling Simone's navel before coming to rest on her waist.

With a devilish grin, Levi knelt before Simone and deftly unfastened the button of her jeans then slid the zipper down to expose the deeply tanned skin underneath. Her hands worked the jeans over Simone's hips. Simone toed off her loafers, leaning forward to place her hands on Levi's shoulders for support, and carefully stepped out of the jeans. Levi tossed them to the bed.

Still kneeling before Simone, Levi leaned down to place soft kisses from her knee up to the inside of her thigh. The aroma of Simone's desire danced in Levi's brain as she gently nibbled the soft flesh connecting Simone's thigh to her trunk.

Simone moaned. Levi's hands found the waistband of Simone's panties and she slipped her fingers beneath the silky fabric and began to lower them down Simone's hips. Inch after inch. Simone watched Levi's lips caress the smooth skin uncovered as the panties lowered. When they had moved beyond her thighs, Levi gently pressed Simone backward to sit on the bed.

Simone's eyes glazed over with passion and Levi looked into them as she reached behind her head and pulled her shirt over her head, quickly followed by her sports bra. She released her belt and slid her shorts and panties down as Simone's tongue darted from her mouth to wet her lips. Simone's hands circled Levi's waist and pulled her toward the bed. Levi's breasts were level with her head so Simone took the opportunity to lean forward and flick her tongue across Levi's semierect nipples. Simone continued to tease Levi's nipples as Levi caressed down Simone's back, slowly dragging her nails along her back and leaving trails of goose flesh in their wake. Simone's moans grew louder. She pulled Levi's hips closer and her mouth opened to take a breast into her mouth as her hands kneaded the muscles of Levi's ass.

Levi's head fell back as she leaned into Simone's mouth. She buried her fingers in Simone's hair, pulling her head fully onto the breast she was eagerly suckling. Simone's hand slipped between them; her fingertips stroked lightly over Levi's glistening lips, soaked with the juice of her excitement. Levi's clit was erect and exposed to Simone's touch. Levi knew her body would not tolerate much stimulation before she would be shaking in climax.

Gently pulling Simone away from her breast Levi guided her to lie back on the bed. She spread Simone's thighs wide as she climbed between them and taking Simone's hands in hers, she held them above her head as she lowered herself onto Simone, pressing her into the bed. With her free hand, Levi reached between them and spread Simone's lips and lowered her swollen clit to rest between Simone's soaked lips. Levi groaned as the silky wetness from Simone's body coated her clit. She slowly began to move her hips against Simone. Levi leaned down to softly kiss Simone who locked her heels behind Levi's thighs to hold her close. Simone shuddered as Levi's clit made contact with hers. Their bodies moved in one rhythm, entwined in a dance of sexual bliss. They kissed deeply as Levi increased the force of their bodies grinding together, the heat building furiously between them. Simone attempted to pull her hands free to caress Levi, but Levi held them in place as their hips and tongues danced sensually together.

Levi was rapidly nearing her peak when she reached up and took Simone's hands in each of hers, entwining their fingers together. She could feel Simone's hips bucking against her, the thin sheen of perspiration aiding the fluid movements of their bodies. Levi could feel her nipples drag across the softness of Simone's breast with every movement of her hips and Levi's mind began to reel with pleasure. She broke the kiss to bury her face in Simone's neck as she breathed into her ear, "Come with me, Simone."

Simone needed no further invitation than the sultry words breathed in her ear. Her orgasm ripped through her with violent spasms. "Oh God, yes Levi!" she cried out as their bodies released a flood of excitement, soaking the bed linens as they writhed together passionately.

†

Levi slowed the pace of her thrusts as Simone's breathing began to calm. Her lips caressed the tender skin of her neck. "That was so beautiful, baby," she whispered as her tongue trailed the outer rim of Simone's ear.

"That was utterly fantastic, Levi."

"That is just the beginning." Levi took Simone's earlobe into her mouth, sucking it deep as her hips and hands pressed Simone into the bed.

Simone's body vibrated with excitement with every word from Levi. She hoped she would continue to talk and when Levi released her lobe and began to whisper in her ear, Simone thought

58

she would come again from the sheer sultriness of her voice. The quiver of excitement in Levi's voice left no doubt of the desire she felt for Simone.

"My hands and mouth will explore every inch of your skin," Levi promised as her tongue licked back up to Simone's ear. "My fingers will tease you and delve into the depths of your wetness until you beg me to make you come."

Simone hung on every word. "Oh yes, Levi," Simone said between gasps for air. "Make me come for you, baby."

Levi straddled Simone's thigh as she kissed down her neck. Feeling Levi's wetness on her thigh Simone raised her foot to rest flat against the bed, pressing her thigh into Levi's center. Simone could feel Levi's clit throb against her thigh, coating her skin with wetness. Simone's own excitement increased with every stroke of Levi's tongue against her skin and Simone could feel her arousal flowing from her, trickling between her thighs. Levi cupped Simone's breasts, squeezing them as her tongue licked across her aching nipples. Simone groaned loudly as she watched Levi's mouth move to lick the soft skin beneath her right breast and draw slow circles, moving closer to her nipple with each circuit of her mouth.

†

Levi's hand floated down Simone's stomach and across her hipbones. She could see the pulse in Simone's neck beating wildly. Her eyes searched out Simone's and found passion burning in them. She covered Simone's right breast with her mouth as they locked eyes. Levi's hand disappeared between Simone's thighs where she found a small river of wetness that escaped Simone's body. She followed its trail down her lips to feel the soaked linen beneath her. Her fingers coated in the velvety fluid, Levi raised her hand to Simone's left breast, her fingertips circling her nipple and leaving a trail of wetness that felt like liquid silk against her skin. Simone began to squirm. Her hand caressed its way back down between Simone's thighs, her fingers surveying the soft curls that protected her swollen entrance. Drops of wetness glistened in the

59

dark curls as Levi's fingers teased their way to her sensitive lips. Levi penetrated her slightly and began to stroke upward, brushing across her sensitive clit and Simone growled her pleasure. Her hand found the back of Levi's head and pressed her mouth more firmly onto her breast.

Levi's fingers teased Simone's clit as her mouth ravaged each of her breasts. Leaving Simone's breasts, Levi licked down her sides and across her stomach to her navel. Simone was panting as Levi reached her abdomen and she pressed against the top of Levi's head, urging her downward. Levi resisted, lapping instead at the sparkling drops of salty perspiration resting in the light blond hairs across Simone's stomach. The taste was in sharp contrast to the sweetness of Simone's juices that she had tasted on her breast and it left Levi hungering for more. Levi moaned softly as her tongue licked the soft, smooth skin, hoping to drive Simone crazy with wanton lust.

"Please baby, let me come," Simone pleaded.

"Soon," Levi whispered against her skin as her thumb stroked across the tip of Simone's clit.

Levi kissed her way down Simone's front and she moved to lie between her soaked thighs. Her tongue lapped at the sweet dew that lay nestled in her dark curls. Her thumb continued to stroke Simone's clit as the tip of her tongue started at the bottom of her quivering lips, and licked slowly upward, sliding gently inside her heated core. Levi patiently explored her wetness, diving deeper with her tongue as Simone's wails of pleasure grew with each new stroke. Levi drove her tongue deeply into her, her chin becoming coated with the wetness escaping her eager tongue. Levi rolled Simone's clit between her finger and thumb, tugging at it and pinching it lightly as Simone exploded, filling Levi's mouth with a rush of hot juice. She drank greedily from her as she writhed under her tongue.

"Yes, yes, Levi!" Simone's fingers gripped the bed linens roughly.

She slowly withdrew her tongue and replaced it with two long fingers, burying them deeply on her first thrust as her mouth covered her throbbing clit.

"Oh yes, Levi!" Simone screamed aloud as Levi's fingers drove in and out of her wetness, sliding smoothly into the welcoming cavern within her.

Levi's tongue trapped Simone's clit against the roof of her mouth, rolling it from side to side, causing her to cry out again as another climax rushed through her. Levi rode the wave with Simone, her fingers moving relentlessly inside her, curling as her muscles contracted forcefully around them. The tips of her fingers located Simone's G spot and stroked it smoothly. Violent spasms raced through her.

Several minutes passed before Simone could form a sentence. "Come hold me, please, Levi." Levi withdrew her fingers and softly kissed Simone's clit before she crawled up into Simone's exhausted embrace. Simone wrapped her arms tightly around Levi's waist as she rested her head against Simone's shoulder, trying to catch her breath as well. Levi lay still until the final spasms of pleasure subsided deep within Simone and then looked up to her face, searching her eyes.

Levi was startled to find tears streaming from Simone's eyes. She was confused until she saw the joy in her eyes and the lift of her lips as they formed a smile. Levi smiled back at Simone, comforted knowing that her tears were those of relief and pleasure.

"You are an incredible lover, Levi." Simone played in Levi's damp hair.

"And you, my dear, are absolutely beautiful." Levi's lips nuzzled into Simone's neck.

Content, they rested for several more minutes. When Levi again raised her head, she saw the clock and realized she was due to be on duty within the hour. She kissed Simone softly and said, "Why don't you rest for a while and then come down to the bar after dinner and keep me company?"

"Must you go now?" Simone asked.

Levi chuckled. "I have thirty minutes to prepare for work."

"It can't be that late already." Simone turned her head to look at the clock for validation.

"Time flies when you are having fun," Levi reminded her with a soft laugh.

"That was way beyond fun." Simone searched Levi's eyes. "Will you stay with me tonight?" Levi saw the sparkle in Simone's eyes and knew she could not deny her any request. "I would love to." She kissed Simone before climbing from the bed.

Simone turned onto her side to watch Levi dress, her desire mounting again as her eyes devoured her. Levi finished dressing and bent down to kiss Simone one last time. "I will see you later."

"Thank you, Levi," Simone said as Levi reached for the door.

She turned and smiled at Simone. "The pleasure was mine." She slipped out the door.

Levi rushed to her room, showered and dressed in a clean uniform. She arrived at the bar with barely five minutes remaining until she was to begin her shift. Nat spotted her immediately and recognized the glow that surrounded her young bartender. "I see someone must have had an enjoyable lunch," Nat said as Levi approached the bar.

Levi blushed at Nat's comment. "Is it that obvious?"

"My dear, you are simply glowing." Levi blushed furiously. "I can only imagine my sister at this moment."

"I would think she is sleeping soundly about now."

"My, my, I am impressed."

"Why is that?"

"I have never known anyone to wear Simone out." Nat laughed.

"Well, there's always a first." Levi beat her fists against her chest, causing Nat to roar with laughter.

"I guess there is, my young friend." Nat tossed a towel at Levi. "I will see you at midnight," she said as she walked around the bar. "Call if you need anything."

Chapter Eight

The afternoon passed quickly for Levi and she watched the door closely as the dinnertime crowd began to filter in. The new guests were very excited about the week and eager to hit the dance floor. Levi stayed busy behind the bar. Karen rushed to keep up with the orders as the thirsty dancers pulsed and gyrated. NeNe kept the pace of the music fast and the dance floor stayed packed.

It was almost nine before Simone entered the bar. She looked refreshed and her smile grew wide as she met Levi's eyes. Levi watched the sensual sway of her hips as she maneuvered her way through the crowd and walked up to sit at the bar.

"You look gorgeous." Levi leaned on the bar toward Simone.

"You, my love, look good enough to eat. For now I will have to settle for a kiss though." She leaned forward and kissed Levi softly.

"Did you have a good afternoon?"

"Yes, I did. Thank you," she answered. "I slept very hard for several hours then showered and met Nat and Liz for a fantastic dinner. Then I went for a long stroll down the beach and had some very pleasant thoughts of a lovely young bartender." She grinned.

Levi smiled at Simone's last comment. "Can I get you anything to drink?"

"No, I am good for now, thank you. Have you had a busy evening so far?"

"The afternoon was a little on the slow side as the new guests were getting settled in, but they certainly become energized after dinner."

Simone looked at the tip jar swelling with bills and the stack of handwritten invitations, piled up by the cash register. She remembered her own feeble attempt at luring Levi to her room and winced at the look of pain in her eyes when Levi arrived and misunderstood her invitation. That was history though, and she had shared one of the best days of her life with Levi, which she hoped would be the first of many yet to come.

Levi smiled at her. "Are we all set for tomorrow?"

"Yes, the kitchen will have our picnic basket ready by the time we finish breakfast and Nat promised to give us a ride down to the marina."

"Fantastic. I can hardly wait to go exploring with you," she said with a wink.

Simone spent several hours chatting with Levi when business would slow down for a few minutes, and she accepted several offers to dance, much to Levi's delight. Around eleven, she decided to head back to the penthouse and prepare for Levi's arrival.

"I am going to head out for the night, Levi," Simone said as she returned from the dance floor. She handed Levi a key to the penthouse with a mischievous grin. "I'll be waiting."

"As soon as I get done here, I will drop by my room for a quick shower and then I'll be there." "Not soon enough for me." Simone faked a pout. "I guess I'll just have to be patient." She spun around on the barstool and leaned over the bar to kiss Levi before she walked across the bar and into a beautiful night.

Levi had not noticed the young woman who had walked up to the bar as she watched Simone's departure. When she turned her attention back to the bar, she found the young woman smiling at her. "Your girlfriend?"

"Just friends for now," Levi said as she smiled back to the dark-haired beauty who had taken a seat at the bar. "What may I get you?"

"I hear this drink called Tropical E is really good."

"Would you care for a shot or a tall one?"

"Better make it a tall one." The woman watched Levi closely while she moved to the frozen cooler to pour her drink.

"Welcome to Venus Rising," Levi said as she placed the drink in front of the woman. She took the ten the woman handed her, and returned a moment later with her change.

The woman placed the bills on the bar and took a sip from the drink. "My, this is good," she said. "Would you mind if I keep you company for a while? I am not ready for all this mingling."

"Not at all." Levi reached out her hand. "My name is Levi, and I hope your stay here will be very pleasant."

"I have heard incredible stories about this place from friends back in Boston, so I finally decided to come down and judge for myself." She again sipped from her drink and then smiled warmly at Levi. "My name is Lynn."

"From Boston, I take it." Levi chuckled.

"For another month or so, yes," Lynn said. "Then I will be moving to New York to start work at a law firm."

"Ah, an attorney." Levi smirked.

"Yes, but we all aren't bad people, so don't hold that against me," Lynn said, obviously used to the numerous lawyer jokes.

"What is your specialty?"

"Corporate law. I was none too keen to deal with hit men and mobsters so I shied away from criminal law." She was becoming more relaxed as she talked with Levi.

"So are you down for a little bit of fun before you put your nose to the corporate grindstone?"

"Yes, something similar to that," Lynn said. "After all those years at law school and studying for the bar exam, I felt I was due for a little reward."

"Agreed." Levi raised her bottle of water. "I took this job in hopes of having a summer of fun and frolic before settling down as well."

"What is your profession?"

"Finance," Levi said. "I have several offers pending on Wall Street that I'm considering."

"So we could end up as neighbors." Lynn laughed softly.

"Indeed we could." Levi returned her smile.

Levi looked up to see NeNe flashing her a five sign. "Do you dance, Lynn?"

"Yes, some, why?"

Levi nodded to NeNe. "We have a tradition here that you are now a part of." Levi walked from behind the bar and took Lynn by the hand as "Mambo Number Five" began to play.

Levi led Lynn onto the dance floor, which was clear, and when they began dancing, the few dancers on the floor stopped to watch as Levi and Lynn glided across the floor. Lynn was grinning wildly at Levi as she took her in her arms and dipped her low before leaning down to kiss her lips. When the song ended, and Levi raised Lynn back to her feet, she was blushing profusely and more than slightly out of breath.

"Thank you for the dance, Lynn," Levi said as they walked back to the bar.

"My pleasure," Lynn stammered. "Do you do that often?"

"Do I do what often?"

"Sweep totally unsuspecting women off their feet and seduce them on the dance floor?"

"Every night that I work," Levi replied with a wink and a grin.

"My, my, I can see why my friends enjoyed this place so much then." She finished her drink and stifled a yawn. "I think I will get a good night's rest tonight and then hit the pool tomorrow. Will you be here tomorrow night?"

"Not as a bartender," Levi said. "I have the next two nights off, but I'm sure I'll see you around the resort. Do you see that adorable DJ over there?" Levi pointed toward NeNe.

"Yes, and she is cute."

"Her name is NeNe and if you need anything while I'm off, be sure to ask her for assistance."

"Thanks, I will definitely keep that in mind, Levi." Lynn stood and placed a fresh ten in the tip jar. "Enjoy your time off."

"Thanks, I shall." She watched Lynn make her way through the thinning crowd and out the door. NeNe announced last call for drinks, and Karen approached the bar with a request for five pitchers of Tropical E to go. Levi chuckled at a large group of young college women who were obviously planning to continue their party after the bar closed.

As the last patrons of the night left the bar, Levi stepped out to vacuum the small area between the bar and dance floor as Karen wiped down the last few tables. NeNe closed up the DJ booth and joined them at the bar just as Levi and Karen finished. Levi picked up the bank bag and they all headed for the door. NeNe and Karen both wished Levi fun on her days off. "Don't do anything we wouldn't do," Karen teased.

"No worries, Karen," Levi quipped. "I probably wouldn't do half the stuff you do."

"Oh, Levi, I am so hurt." Karen laughed and with a wave she was gone.

"I really do hope you have a great couple of days off," NeNe said as they walked toward the pool. "Are you spending them with Simone?"

"At least tomorrow. After that, who knows?" She knew full well she wanted to spend every available moment getting to know Simone better.

As they approached the pool, they heard a splash as a couple of the late night partiers had jumped into the pool. The crowd was loud and they were having such a great time on their first night on the island. One of the women saw NeNe and Levi approach and called to them. "Won't you join us, ladies?"

Levi grinned at NeNe. "You go right ahead. I have a previous commitment, so I will drop the bag off while you stay and have some fun."

"Thanks for the offer, ladies, but I have other plans," Levi said to a chorus of disappointed sighs. "May I have a rain check?"

"You may have anything you want," one of the young ladies said with a giggle, already well past her sobriety limit.

"You better watch this crowd, NeNe." With a quick kiss to NeNe's cheek, Levi left the pool area.

✝

Levi chuckled as she entered the resort and headed straight for Nat and Liz's suite. She knocked on the door and heard Liz invite her inside. She was eager to make her drop and meet Simone. Liz could see her excitement.

"Okay, no shop talk tonight. Get out of here and have some fun." Liz walked Levi to the door.

Back in her room, Levi slipped into her shower and dressed comfortably in loose shorts and a baggy T-shirt before heading to Simone's room. She slipped the key in the lock and her jaw nearly hit the floor when she opened the door and walked into the bedroom. Dozens of candles lit the room, and two large vases of yellow roses were positioned on each side of the bed. On the bed itself, Simone was propped against the headboard, a sheer white teddy revealing plenty of her silky skin. She held a glass of champagne in her right hand and reached out with her left to offer a glass to Levi.

"Welcome back, Levi," Simone said, her eyes already undressing Levi as she walked toward the bed. "Why don't you lose those clothes and join me in a toast."

Levi easily slipped from her clothes and crawled onto the bed beside Simone, taking the offered glass.

"To us."

"To us," Levi echoed. She returned Simone's smile as she raised the glass to her lips.

They talked while they drank the champagne, making idle conversation. Simone was eager to have Levi in her arms again. She reached for her glass and set it on the bedside table then turned and reached for Levi, who willingly melted into her embrace as their lips met and they kissed deeply. Simone pulled Levi on top of her and Levi could feel the heat of Simone's body as it welcomed her. Their hands and mouths explored one another, Levi's hands eagerly removing the sheer garment that prevented them from lying skin to skin.

Entwined in passion they made heated love for several hours until both lovers were sated and their bodies exhausted. The last conscious memory Levi had before drifting off to sleep was Simone resting her head on her shoulder with an arm draped across Levi's stomach and a loud contented sigh.

A few short hours later, the telephone rang for their wake-up call. Simone lifted the receiver to listen to the message and then returned the handset to the cradle. Levi snuggled back into Simone's warmth and looked into her bright eyes.

"Good morning, lover," Simone whispered.

"Good morning, Simone." Levi laid her chin on Simone's shoulder. "Did you sleep well?"

"Very well, thank you and yourself?"

"A terrific night's sleep."

"How long will it take you to get ready for the day?"

"Not long at all. I packed a bag yesterday and it will only take me a few minutes to shower and dress this morning."

"Great, why don't you go shower and meet me in the dining room for a quick breakfast and we'll get started," Simone suggested.

Levi kissed Simone and climbed out of the bed. Simone watched her leave the room and smiled. Levi had given her an intense workout the previous night and she could feel stiff muscles cry out as she sat up in bed. Praying the shower would loosen her up, Simone crept from the bed and into the bathroom.

Chapter Nine

Simone reached into the shower to turn the water on and looked back into the mirror to find she was still smiling. It felt good to be with Levi and she hoped the feeling would last for some time to come. Levi was more than just another fuck buddy for her and she hoped their physical attraction would blossom into a permanent relationship. She stepped under the water and moaned as the steamy water massaged her aching muscles. Her hands gently bathed her breasts, still sensitive from the passionate suckling Levi had given them barely hours ago. Just the thought of Levi made her core grow damp with excitement and Simone finished bathing and dressed as quickly as she could.

She picked up her beach bag and headed downstairs. She was pleased to see Levi waiting and walked quickly over to her table. Levi stood and smiled at Simone's approach.

"You certainly look refreshed," Simone said as she kissed Levi and sat down in the chair next to her.

"It is amazing what a shower can do," Levi said with a sly grin.

"Yes it is. Have you ordered yet?"

"No, I was waiting for you."

"What can I get for you ladies this morning?" the server asked.

"I think I feel like eggs Benedict," Simone said. "The workout you gave me this morning has given me a good appetite."

"Sounds good, but I think I'm going for the tall stack of pancakes for the instant carbohydrate boost."

The server smiled as she wrote their orders down and returned to the kitchen. Nat walked across the room toward them and stopped the server to add some breakfast of her own to the order. "Mind if I join you two?" she asked as she reached the table.

"Not at all," Levi said.

"Good morning, sister," Nat said to Simone. "You look a little tired this morning. Did some handsome young bartender keep you up too late last night?" She winked at Levi.

"Nothing a good breakfast and a relaxing day out on the water won't cure," Simone answered.

"Oh, that does sound good," Nat said. "Doing some island hopping?"

"I promised Levi that we would explore the islands just off the south coast."

"The larger of the two is called Tipu, and has some beautiful small falls near the middle of the island," Nat said. "The scenery is amazing if you don't mind a short hike."

"Sounds like the perfect spot for us," Levi said as she placed her hand on Simone's thigh.

When they had finished eating, Nat went into the kitchen to pick up the picnic basket Simone had ordered. She returned to the table and placed the basket in front of them. "You are just going for the day, right?"

"Yes, why do you ask?" Simone asked.

"This basket is heavy enough to hold a few days' worth of food."

Without missing a beat, Simone said, "Well, Levi has a healthy appetite." Levi nearly sprayed the table with the mouthful of apple juice she had just taken.

"Me?" Levi said in mock astonishment.

71

"No worries, Levi, I know how ravenous Simone can get. I am going to get the van while you two finish eating." Nat picked up the basket and left the dining room.

Simone ate the last bite of her eggs and laid her fork on the plate. Smiling at Levi, she asked, "Ready?"

"Waiting on you." Levi stood and took Simone's hand and led them from the dining room into a brilliant morning.

Nat sat behind the wheel of the van and waited as they climbed in. She drove them into town and delivered them to the marina. "Pick you up here at six?"

"Sounds great, sis, and thanks for your help."

†

Levi carried the picnic basket as they walked toward the marina office and after a few minutes of conversation with the owner, they headed down the pier toward a small charter boat. Simone took the basket and stored it while Levi started to untie the mooring lines.

Simone started the motor and they slowly idled out of the marina into open water. Levi sat beside her and watched as Simone expertly guided the small boat through the harbor as they headed south. As they picked up speed, Levi propped her feet up on the console and laid her head back to enjoy the warmth of the sun on her face as the wind blew through her hair.

Levi was almost dozing to the soft purr of the motor when Simone touched her arm and pointed to the pair of dolphins swimming alongside them, keeping pace with the boat until they passed the southern edge of the island. Then the pair drifted back and returned toward the harbor. Several miles to the south, they could see the two islands Nat had described and Simone guided them toward Tipu.

Simone slowed the boat and circled the island until they located a small beach clearing. Thirty feet from shore, Simone dropped the anchor and the boat drifted to a stop. Levi took off her shorts and shirt and jumped over the side of the boat into the waist-deep water. She took the basket Simone handed her and watched as Simone slipped out of her clothes and slung her beach bag over her shoulder. She took Levi's hand and joined her in the warm water. They waded to the shore and found a small sandy trail that appeared to lead into the interior of the island.

They disappeared into the dense green foliage. Several yards down the trail they could hear falling water ahead. They stepped into a clearing and found the trio of small falls Nat had told them would be there. Simone took a blanket from her bag and spread it in front of a small cave located between the falls before taking the basket from Levi. The sun shone down on the small pools of water, which Levi found surprisingly warm as she waded into the waist-deep water. Simone dove into the water and swam for the fall, surfacing underneath the pelting water. Entranced by the glow of Simone's skin under the shimmering water, Levi watched Simone's hands brush her hair back from her face. Her hands then moved down her back to unfasten her bikini top. With a wicked grin, she tossed it over to the blanket, soon followed by her bottoms. She stood naked under the flow of the water. Levi had waded closer and her dark eyes burned with desire as they caressed Simone's skin, lingering on her erect nipples as the water cascaded across them. Now within arm's reach, Levi lifted Simone's breasts into the full flow of the water. Simone's nipples grew firmer under Levi's touch and from the pounding of the water. Levi stepped under the flow and leaned forward to cover Simone's mouth with hers as her fingers rolled Simone's swollen nipples. Levi's tongue snaked into her mouth, stifling the low groan from Simone as her nipples responded to Levi's touch.

Simone encircled Levi's waist with her arms and pulled her hips closer, intensifying the kiss, as their tongues wove together in a sensual dance. Simone's hands moved down Levi's back to slip the fastener on her top and slide it off her. Her hands caressed up to Levi's shoulders and she put soft pressure on them until Levi broke off the kiss and moved down to cover Simone's breast with her mouth as they stepped from under the fall.

Levi nipped at the sensitive flesh of Simone's nipple and Simone's groans of pleasure echoed loudly in Levi's ears. Her hand slipped beneath the water and her fingers sought the silky wetness hidden between Simone's thighs. Levi suckled her breast as her fingers parted Simone's full lips and her fingers plunged deep, causing her to cry out in pleasure.

Simone struggled for breath as she rocked in rhythm with Levi's thrusting fingers, reaching climax quickly. Her legs gave way as she crumpled into Levi.

Levi took Simone in her arms and lowered her into the water. She knelt and placed Simone's legs over her shoulders. Simone's muscles continued to tremble with the intensity of her orgasm as Levi began kissing up the inside of her left thigh. She held her hips just above the surface of the pool as Levi's fingers parted her swollen lips and her tongue swirled in a sensual kiss around Simone's pulsing clit.

Levi struggled to keep Simone afloat as her tongue licked and probed into her sweetness, savoring each drop Simone's body offered. Her tongue drove Simone into a frenzy of passion, the orgasm so intense Simone fainted.

Levi took Simone in her arms and carefully carried her from the pool, placing her spent lover on the blanket to rest. Smiling, Levi stretched out beside her and watched as her eyes fluttered and then opened. Slightly confused, she asked, "What happened?"

"I do believe you passed out, lover."

"Oh my word, Levi, that was so intense." She lifted a weary hand to Levi's face.

"Rest now." Levi snuggled into Simone's naked body, placing her head on her shoulder. Levi listened as Simone's breathing deepened and slowed, signaling she was asleep. She closed her eyes for a short nap too, exhausted from the previous night's lovemaking and the lack of sleep.

.

Chapter Ten

Levi woke with a start as the wind whistled through the trees. Simone was curled in a tight ball and Levi hated to wake her, but the weather was rapidly changing and she feared they needed to find protection from the coming storm.

"Simone, sweets, you need to wake up," Levi whispered as she gently shook Simone's shoulder.

Simone stretched out to Levi's touch and rolled onto her back. "Hey baby. What's wrong?" she asked when she saw the frown on Levi's face.

"I'm afraid we have a storm coming up and we need to find some shelter."

"What do you mean a storm? The harbormaster said we would have a perfect day out on the water."

"Well, like most weather forecasters, he blew this one." Levi tugged on her bikini top. "We don't have time to make it back to the boat, and I'm not sure it would be safe anyhow, so we better find some shelter."

They both looked at the mouth of the cave and decided that would probably offer the most protection for them. "Why don't you take our blanket and food inside and I'll collect some wood," Levi said as she helped Simone to her feet.

The winds were picking up quickly and the sunshine was replaced by heavy, dark clouds looming over the canopy of trees covering their secluded spot. Levi quickly found an armful of small branches and carried them inside the cave to the spot Simone had chosen to set up their blanket. *This should be a safe distance for us.* She dropped the wood on the floor of the cave and went in search of more. Storms could blow up quickly in the islands and Levi silently prayed this one would move through quickly and leave them safe and sound.

Large raindrops pelted her skin as she ran back toward the cave with a second armful of wood. The skies opened up, releasing flashes of lightning and loud claps of thunder. Simone looked at her with fear in her eyes as she placed the wood in a large pile. "Relax, sweets, we'll be just fine. We'll have our picnic by campfire and wait out the storm," Levi said in her most confident voice. A large crash of thunder close by made Simone jump, and Levi took her in her arms and held her close. "It's fine, baby, we are safe from the storm here. Why don't you lay out some food while I see if I can get a fire started?"

The calmness in Levi's voice helped get Simone moving. She busied herself with the picnic basket, taking out bowls of fruit, cheese, and finger sandwiches the kitchen had prepared for them and opening a bottle of wine. Thankfully, Levi had placed a book of matches in her beach bag and after several attempts had a small fire started and burning slowly. The temperature had dropped quickly and the fire would add some heat to the small cave while also giving them the comfort of light, should it grow darker outside. Levi placed several larger pieces of wood across the growing flames and joined Simone on the blanket.

"This looks delicious," Levi said as she sat beside Simone.

Simone smiled weakly and poured each of them a glass of wine.

"To us." Levi touched her glass to Simone's, her eyes sparkling with excitement.

"I am starving," Levi said with a soft chuckle, taking the sandwich Simone offered. The flames from the fire reflected in Simone's eyes and Levi felt drawn to them. She leaned in to Simone and kissed her softly on the lips, the sweetness of the wine lingering between them, then picked up a slice of melon to offer Simone.

Simone smiled and opened her mouth, allowing Levi to feed her the sweet melon and take her mind off the storm, now in full rage outside the cave. A trickle of juice flowed from the corner of Simone's mouth and Levi's tongue slowly licked at the escaping liquid, tracing its path back to Simone's lips. Simone moaned softly as Levi's tongue traced her lips sensually, barely brushing them.

Levi had a unique talent of stirring desire in Simone and she parted her lips to invite Levi's tongue into her mouth. Instead, Levi picked up a small wedge of the juicy melon and placed it in Simone's mouth, her fingers tracing her lips. Simone's face flushed with the heat of excitement stoked by Levi's touch and the look of desire in her eyes as she slowly fed Simone, satisfying one hunger while evoking another.

They finished the food, taking turns feeding one another as they attempted to ignore the storm and the wailing winds that whipped around their shelter. Levi pulled a thick towel from the bag and wrapped it around Simone's shoulders as she shivered from a chill, then stood to add more wood to the fire. She put away the remnants of their picnic and wrapped the blanket around them.

Simone pressed Levi onto her back then rolled on top of her and kissed her deeply as the shadows of the flames danced on the walls of the cave. It had become dark as midnight outside and the light from the fire flickered in Levi's eyes as Simone rolled her hips into Levi. Levi spread her thighs, settling her lover between them and joined Simone's rhythm as their tongues and hips moved together. Levi cupped Simone's ass, pulling her deeper into her as her desire took control and her climax began to grow. Simone's hand disappeared underneath the fabric of Levi's swimsuit and she buried two fingers inside her aching core. Levi's hips moved in a frenzy of passion, driving Simone further into her with each thrust of her quivering body. Simone buried her face in Levi's neck, her fingers plunging in and out of her lover's wetness. "Come for me, baby," she breathed into Levi's ear and Levi exploded, her cries of pleasure echoing in the small cave, driving Simone over the edge, and she convulsed with bliss as she joined Levi in ecstasy. Their

Ali Spooner

movements slowed and they lay panting in one another's arms, heartbeats still racing as their bodies glowed with pleasure.

✝

Nat looked out across the resort from her office window and frowned at the storm approaching from the south. "I hope Levi and Simone are safe in this weather," she said to Liz.

"I think they are clever enough to take shelter from the storm." Liz walked to Nat and wrapped her arms around her waist. "They are probably snuggled up somewhere safe together at this very moment."

"You're probably right. But, I won't feel assured until I see them back on solid ground tonight." Liz turned her lover around to face her. "Quit worrying, my love, I'm sure they are just fine." Still not convinced, Nat kissed Liz and tried to appear that she was less concerned, but the dark clouds looming over the coast did little to ease her mind. She moved away from the window and busied herself reviewing paperwork until the first of the rain started pelting the glass and she found herself drawn again to the large picture window.

✝

Levi felt the trickle of sweat as it rolled down her side. Tucked into the blanket, the two women were safe from the outside chill and the heat from their lovemaking added to the warmth of the fire. Simone's eyes began to close. Levi watched her lover slip into dreams and then turned her attention to the storm raging outside. She saw the palms blowing furiously in the wind as lightning lit up the sky. Their day on the island had turned out to be much more exciting than expected, but any time spent with Simone was turning into a treasure for Levi. Her fingers played in the softness of Simone's hair as she slept peacefully on Levi's chest. She smiled at the sleeping form of the woman she was quickly growing to love.

78

As the flames of the fire began to dwindle, Levi carefully rolled Simone onto her side. She crept from underneath the blanket to add more wood. The skies were still dark outside and though it was late afternoon, Levi was certain darkness would fall before the storm passed. She added wood to the fire and then picked up a burning branch and walked beyond Simone deeper into the cave. She crawled over a large boulder and slid into a smaller opening, her curiosity getting the better of her. Levi walked bent over for approximately ten feet and then felt the coolness of open space greet her. When she again stood straight and lifted her torch, Levi stood in the middle of a much larger cavern.

Chapter Eleven

Nat picked up the telephone and called the harbormaster to see if Levi and Simone had made it back in. The man assured her that even though they had not returned, he felt certain the two women were sheltered safely. There had been no emergency calls made from the boat, so he assumed they were safely sheltered on one of the islands.

"The electrical storm we are having prohibits any search vehicle from leaving the harbor, but I assure you, Nat, just as soon as the weather subsides, I'll send out a rescue boat, to find them," the harbormaster said.

Unsatisfied, but destined to wait out Mother Nature, Nat returned the telephone to the cradle and cursed as lightning strikes landed close to the resort. Liz walked into the office and saw the worried frown on her lover's face.

"Don't worry, Nat, those two are probably snuggled up and having a great time," Liz said, trying to put her lover at ease.

"I know you're right, Liz, but I still can't help but worry." Nat paced across the room. "Simone is my only sister and I don't know what I would do without her."

✝

Levi walked deeper into the cavern and up to the edge of the small pool. She bent down and dipped her hand in the water, smiling when she discovered the pool was a hot spring. The weather looked like it would remain nasty for some time yet, and Levi thought a dip in the hot spring would be a nice way to pass the time. She searched and found enough wood to start a small fire in a pit, left by a previous visitor, and managed to light the cavern with a low glow. Excited, she made her way back to the cave's mouth to find Simone awake and staring out into the rain.

When she heard footsteps behind her, Simone turned and smiled at Levi. "There you are. I was worried about you when I woke to find you gone."

"I thought I would do some exploring while you slept and found something really interesting." Levi dropped her torch back into the fire. "Grab our blanket and basket and follow me." She picked up an armful of wood and her torch.

Simone draped the blanket over her arm and picked up the beach bag and basket with the remaining food then followed Levi through the tight channel in the rock. Levi dropped the wood next to the small fire and turned to watch Simone spread the blanket out and place the basket in the center.

"We have plenty of food and some wine left, if you are hungry," Simone said.

"Later." Levi lowered the bottom of Simone's suit and dropped it onto the blanket, soon followed by her top. "We have something else to enjoy first." Levi quickly shed her suit and reached for Simone's hand.

They walked to the small pool and Simone moaned when she stepped into the warm water. "This is a terrific find, Levi." She stepped deeper into the pool.

Levi floated on her back across the pool. Simone reached out and grabbed Levi's ankles and pulled her across the water toward her. Levi stood and walked into the outstretched arms of Simone. "This has turned into such a lovely day," Simone said as she pulled Levi close.

"Yes, it has," she agreed. "I just hope Nat and Liz aren't too worried about us."

Simone chuckled. "If I know Nat, she will be pacing by now."

"Well, there is nothing to be done except wait this storm out and then hopefully make it back to the harbor."

Simone's fingers traced the length of Levi's cheek. "I feel very safe with you, Levi."

"I think we are very safe, and hopefully in a few hours we can head back to the resort."

"I'm in no hurry." Simone bent forward to softly kiss Levi. "I'm really enjoying having you all to myself, with no one around to interrupt."

Levi moved closer to Simone, her leg pressing between Simone's thighs as they shared long, deep kisses, hands caressing one another's bodies. The storm was beginning to fade outside, the pounding of the rain subsiding, but the two lovers deep inside the cave were oblivious to anything other than the sensations they were sharing. Levi's fingers descended between them, opening Simone's lips and sliding inside her as they rocked together in the warm water. Thrusting against Levi's thigh Simone reached down to enter Levi, her fingers slipping smoothly into the silky wetness. She moaned as the quivering muscles inside Levi pulsed around her fingers. Their tongues and fingers thrust and swirled as their climaxes approached. They came together with loud groans, reaching their peak in unison, embracing one another tightly in the warm pool as they shook with pleasure.

Once their bodies returned to normal, Simone took Levi's hand and walked from the pool. They dried themselves before sitting back on the blanket. Levi opened the basket, pulled out the bottle of wine, and poured them a glass while Simone made them both a sandwich with the last of the meat and cheese.

They finished their snack and Levi decided she would walk back through the cave to check the weather.

"Hurry back, lover," Simone purred.

Levi picked up a torch from the fire pit and walked back through the channel to the front of the cave. Darkness had fallen, but the rains had passed and there was a light breeze blowing. She felt it would be safe to return to the boat and head back to the harbor. As Levi turned to walk back into the cave, a shiny object caught her eye in the glow of the fire. She knelt down to pluck the object from the soft soil and found it to be a small gold coin of some sort. Levi turned the coin for closer inspection. Obviously buried for some time, the winds that had whipped through the front of the cave had unearthed the small treasure from its hiding place. Curious, Levi brushed through the surrounding soil, but there were no other coins present. She tucked her find safely inside her bikini bottom and, picking up her torch, walked to the back of the cave.

Simone had dressed and collected their belongings while waiting for Levi's return. Levi filled the empty wine bottle with water from the spring and soaked the embers in the small pit, the hissing of the fire echoing in the great cavern. Satisfied the fire was extinguished they walked from the cavern, back through the cave and into a cool evening.

The torch carried by Levi gave off enough light for them to find their way back to the beach by the path they had traveled earlier that day. When they walked from beneath the cover of the trees, they were in awe of the clearness of the skies, and the millions of stars glittering across the dark backdrop. The sight was beautiful and brought smiles to their faces, however the smiles quickly faded when their eyes lowered to the horizon and their boat was nowhere in sight.

"I know I anchored the boat right over there," Simone said.

"Well, our adventure is destined to continue. We might as well get comfortable and wait until someone comes to our rescue," Levi said. "Find us a nice comfy spot. I'll go back to the cave for the last of our dry wood."

Not keen about being alone in the dark, Simone bravely nodded and watched Levi disappear back into the trees. She found a large fallen tree, and placed the blanket in front of it and waited for Levi's return. Leaning against the tree, she again looked up into the night sky and was lost in the beauty, until she heard Levi's approach.

Levi dropped the wood on the sand and dug out a small fire pit. She arranged a stack of wood and held her torch underneath it until the dry wood caught fire. She then gathered more wood and placed it around the pit to dry, hoping that it would burn long enough to allow rescuers to find them. Levi sat beside Simone and snuggled into her warmth as they wrapped the blanket around them and gazed up into the night sky.

Chapter Twelve

Lulled to sleep by the enchanting night sky, they slept until the drone of a motor awakened Levi. She looked up to see the lights of a Coast Guard rescue boat. A searchlight scanned the shore and when the crew caught sight of Levi's fire, they raced toward shore. Levi nudged Simone awake and then covered the embers of the fire with wet sand to extinguish the flames. Simone folded up their blanket and tucked it away in their now empty picnic basket.

Tethered behind the Coast Guard cutter was the boat they rented, bobbing along behind the larger boat like a small toy. Simone and Levi waded into the water to meet the approaching boat. A deep, masculine voice announced over a bullhorn, "Ms. Taylor and Ms. Johnson, I presume."

"That would be us," Levi replied as the man directed the light at a small ladder.

Levi handed the picnic basket to one of the men on the deck and then followed Simone up the ladder.

"Sorry it took us so long, but the weather was wicked for a while. I'm Captain Jones." He extended a hand. "Are you both in good health?"

"Yes, we are, thank you," Simone said. "A little tired, but we were able to weather the storm in safety." She grinned at Levi.

"I'm glad you are both safe," Jones said. "We found your boat adrift a few miles back and there was no sign of either of you aboard, so we hoped you were safely on one of the islands."

"I thought the anchor would hold, but I guess not in that kind of storm," Simone said.

"You were very lucky to be on solid land during that storm," Jones said. "I wouldn't have wanted to be in that boat on open water when that monster hit. That was one of the most powerful pop-up storms I have ever experienced."

One of the mates handed them thick blankets to wrap up in. "Ready to go home, ladies?" Captain Jones asked,

"Most definitely," Levi said.

"Why don't you join me in the cabin and we will head for home." He held the door open for them.

"Thank you, Captain," Levi said as she ushered Simone through the open door.

"Was there much damage on the island from the storm?" Simone asked.

"Surprisingly enough it was very minimal, downed power lines and trees, but no major structural damage."

"That is great news," Levi said, worried for the resort and its visitors.

"All is fine, ladies, just sit back and we will have you on home ground in just a few minutes." He increased the throttle and the cutter lunged to full speed.

Levi was thankful for the warm blanket. Even inside the cabin, the coolness of the night air seeped through and brought a chill to her. She snuggled closer to Simone and watched as the lights of the island came into view. "That is a welcome sight," she said to Simone.

"I am ready for some hot food, a warm shower, and a comfortable bed."

"Amen to that. My place or yours?"

"Hmm, mine I think," Simone said with a smile. "I will call room service for the two biggest steaks they have and we can shower while we wait."

"My stomach is growling already," Levi said.

As they slowed and approached the harbor, Levi could see the resort's van. She also noticed Nat pacing up and down the sidewalk. "Someone doesn't look very happy."

"She has been harassing me for the last four hours to go out and find you," Captain Jones said. "I think she is just worried about you both."

"She can be a wee bit aggressive," Simone said. "Her heart is in the right place though."

"I would be the same way, if it were my sister lost at sea," Captain Jones said.

"Regardless, I will grab our gear out of the boat while you deal with Nat."

"Now Levi, you know Nat's bark is worse than her bite," Simone teased.

"Maybe so, but I've had enough excitement for one day."

"Really," Simone said with a mischievous look.

"Really." Levi was bone-tired and just wanted a warm meal and a good night's sleep, even if it did disappoint her lover.

The crew cast the mooring lines to the men waiting at the dock, and Levi took the opportunity to jump onto the pier from the back of the boat. One of the Coast Guard crew had already boarded the small boat and handed Levi their clothes and personal belongings. Levi put on her shorts and top and picked up the rest before walking to meet up with Nat and Simone.

"I am just happy the two of you are safe," she heard Nat say as she hugged Simone. "You had me worried when the storm came up."

"Levi took very good care of me, sis."

Nat turned around and hugged Levi tightly. "I'm glad you were with Simone today and even happier that you made it back safely. NeNe and the crew down at the bar have been calling all evening to check on you."

"We were safely tucked away," Levi assured Nat. "Is everything okay at the resort?"

"The wind shredded one of the canopies and we were running on generator power for a short while, but no major damage."

"Great," Levi said as they walked toward the van.

It was almost eleven when they reached the resort. Levi could feel her head nodding on the ride. "You two go get cleaned up and I will have your food sent up," she heard Nat say as she dropped them off at the front of the resort.

"Thanks, Nat." Simone took Levi's hand and they started toward the elevator. They were both eager to wash the salt from their bodies and headed straight for the shower when they arrived at the penthouse. They stripped down and stepped under the warm flow, enjoying the comfort of the soft water.

Levi had completely forgotten about the gold coin she'd tucked into the bottom of her bathing suit. The coin had pressed into the skin just below her hipbone, where it remained stuck until the water washed it away. The coin fell to the floor of the shower, unobserved by either woman. The coin lay shining near the shower drain as the women slipped from the shower and dried off. They wrapped thick robes around their bodies and walked into the bedroom just as the food arrived.

They took the food out onto the balcony and devoured the steaks, eating as if it were their first meal in days. Levi's eyes grew heavier with each bite and when she was full, she pushed back from the table. "Simone, I just have to lie down." Levi kissed her forehead and headed back to the bedroom.

Simone chuckled and finished her meal. She pushed the food cart in the hallway and turned to walk back to the bed. She smiled at Levi who was sound asleep and crept into bed, snuggling into Levi's warmth and closed her eyes.

The next morning Simone woke before Levi and sat drinking coffee when a gentle knock came to the door. Simone opened the door, held a finger to her lips, and pointed to Levi, still sleeping on the bed.

The housekeeper nodded and walked quietly into the bathroom to deliver fresh towels and robes. She reached inside the shower to retrieve the used washcloths and noticed the coin lying on the floor. Curious, she reached down and picked up the coin, staring at it closely. Her eyes grew wide and she dropped the coin immediately upon recognition. She fled the bathroom, screaming out a prayer in Spanish.

Simone had settled back with her coffee and was about to reach for the paper when the housekeeper's shrieks rang out from the bathroom. The woman ran from the room as if her hair was on fire. Levi shot up from the bed at the sound of the woman's screams, totally confused by what was happening. Simone jumped up and ran out the door after the woman, but saw nothing but the back of her head as she ran down the hallway, still screaming loudly.

Simone stepped back into the penthouse and found Levi staring at her. "What the hell just happened?"

"I have no idea. The woman came in to bring fresh linens, and when she was in the bathroom she started screaming and ran from the room," Simone said.

"That must have been one hellacious spider she saw." She climbed out of bed, pulling the robe around her nakedness. She looked at Simone who was already walking toward the bathroom. "Call if you need my assistance." Levi went to the table to pour herself a cup of coffee.

Simone expected to find a huge spider or some sort of insect in the bathroom, but was unable to find any creepy crawler. As she stepped closer to the shower, her foot came to rest on something cold. She moved her foot back and saw the gold coin the housekeeper had dropped prior to her hasty exit from the room. Simone picked it up and examined it closely, wondering how the coin had made it to the floor of her penthouse bathroom. After another glance around the room to search for something that could have frightened the housekeeper so badly, and finding nothing, she left the bathroom with the curious coin in her hand.

"So what was it?" Levi asked.

"I couldn't find any spider or anything that could have scared the woman, but I did find this." Simone opened her palm to show her the gold coin. "I wonder where this came from?"

"I forgot all about that." Levi reached for the coin. "I found it in the cave yesterday and had tucked it away in my suit for safekeeping." Levi turned the shiny coin in her hand.

Simone opened her mouth and was about to ask Levi another question when the telephone next to the bed rang interrupting her.

Chapter Thirteen

"What on earth did you do to Maria?" Nat asked

"What do you mean what did I do to her?" Simone growled into the phone. "I didn't do anything to her. She walked into the bathroom to replace the linens then ran out of the room screaming at the top of her lungs. Trust me, I'm as baffled about what happened as you are."

"All I could get out of her was something about a curse."

"Well, I certainly don't have any idea what she is talking about. Where is she now?"

"Liz has her in the office and is trying to get her calmed down enough to find out what she is so upset about. If I can find out what it is I will call you back."

Simone returned the telephone to the cradle and walked back to Levi. "That was really odd. Nat says the housekeeper was screaming something about a curse."

"A curse? That sounds totally ridiculous." Levi absentmindedly toyed with the coin. "What on earth could she have seen that would have terrified her so badly?"

"I have no idea and neither does Nat. Liz is talking with Maria now to try to figure this out. Why don't we shower, dress and go down for a late breakfast and check in with Nat to see if she has gotten to the bottom of this?" Simone suggested.

"I need to go to my room to get clean clothes, so I'll meet you in the dining room in thirty minutes," Levi said.

"That will be fine." Simone watched Levi drop the coin in her robe pocket and pick up her dirty clothes.

Levi kissed her lips. "I'll see you soon."

After Levi left, Simone sensed a strange electric quality in the air but dropped her robe on the foot of the bed and walked to the shower. She turned on the shower and within minutes had forgotten the odd sensation. There had to be a simple explanation for what had happened here earlier and she was certain Nat would solve the riddle.

†

Levi dumped her dirty clothing in the growing pile and headed off to the shower. She took the coin from the pocket of her robe and placed it on the vanity as she stepped into the shower. With her head full of shampoo lather, Levi reached for the soap. It slid through her fingers, falling to the floor of the shower. With her eyes clenched shut, she stepped forward cautiously to find the soap. As she bent to retrieve it, her foot slid on soap-slippery floor and she fell forward, striking her left arm on the tiled shower wall. "Damn!" Levi cried out at the pain searing up her arm. One look at the awkward angle of her wrist was all she needed to know she had broken bones. She struggled through the pain, but managed to rinse her hair and body before turning off the water. Her left wrist was swelling rapidly and she cursed her luck. She knew she had no other choice but to seek medical attention. *There goes my relaxing day off.*

Levi managed to dry herself and dress as best she could with one hand. She brushed her teeth and hair and after slipping the coin in her pocket, went down to the dining room to find Simone.

†

Nat was the first person Levi saw as she stepped off the elevator, and Nat knew immediately that something was broken when she looked at the swelling and growing bruises on Levi's arm. "It looks like you need to take a trip to the emergency room to get that arm taken care of, my friend."

"Yes, I think you're right." Levi winced from trying to manipulate the broken bones.

"Let's get some ice from the kitchen and get you wrapped up before we head into town," Nat suggested and hurried off to the kitchen.

Levi sat down on a couch in the lobby to wait for Nat. "What's wrong, baby?" Simone asked, walked up to Levi.

"I slipped in the shower and hit my arm on the wall. I think my wrist is broken. Nat has gone to the kitchen to make an icepack and then will take me to the emergency room for evaluation."

Liz came rushing down the hall as Nat returned from the kitchen. She handed Nat the Ace bandage she had called for and assisted Nat in wrapping the bandage around Levi's damaged wrist and the large icepack Nat had made.

"Did you get anything out of Maria?" Nat asked.

"Yes, but it will wait until Levi has this arm taken care of. I sent her home for the rest of the day, but I think she'll be fine. Do you want me to go with you to the hospital?" she asked Nat.

"I think the two of us can handle one broken wrist," Nat said as she shot a grin at Simone.

"Well, then just call if you need anything." Liz handed her lover the keys to their Tahoe. "And be careful."

"I will, my love." Nat helped Levi to her feet. She kissed Liz and walked from the resort with Levi and Simone, who seemed to be shocked speechless.

Nat helped Levi and Simone into the backseat and then drove them to the hospital. Levi was in obvious pain as each bump in the road jarred her and sent another jolt of pain up her arm. She looked at Simone and saw that the color had drained from her face. Levi hoped Simone wasn't about to faint. "Are you feeling okay, Simone?"

93

"Yes, Levi, I am just worried about you." Simone smiled weakly.

"Don't be, everything will be just fine."

Nat dropped them off in front of the emergency room and parked the car while Simone got Levi checked in. The nurse working the triage station called Levi back, carefully removed the wrapping and ice pack, and looked at Levi's swollen lower arm. "That looks pretty painful. How did this happen?"

"I was taking a shower and dropped the soap," Levi said. "My head was full of shampoo lather and when I tried to find the soap, my foot hit it. I lost my balance and struck my arm against the wall."

The nurse worked hard to stifle a chuckle, busying herself taking Levi's vital signs.

Levi noticed her attempt to hide her laughter. "I know, it sounds like something from a Three Stooges movie."

"Yes, it does. I'm almost certain your wrist is broken, but we'll get an X-ray to determine how bad the damage is." She wrote out an X-ray order and made a call while Levi put the icepack back in place.

Levi winced from the pain of the weight of the ice touching her wrist but welcomed the dulling cold.

"Would you like something to ease the pain?" the nurse asked.

"That would be great."

"You didn't hit your head during the fall did you?"

"No, just my arm."

"You are going to be here for a while yet, and I won't tell you that it's not going to hurt when they set those bones for casting, so I think you'll need something to take the edge off."

Levi smiled to the nurse. "Thanks."

The nurse returned with a small white cup and a glass of water and handed them both to Levi. "This should help. I have put in the order for your X-ray and the technician should be here soon to take you back. Do you want to stay here or join your friends in the waiting room?"

"I'll wait out there." Levi nodded her head in the direction of the lobby.

"Very well. Let's get you up and into a wheelchair and I'll wheel you out there."

With the nurse's assistance, Levi stood and walked across the small room to a wheelchair. She was amazed at how quickly the narcotic was taking effect and was thankful for the strong hand at her elbow guiding her to the chair. The nurse wheeled her out to where Nat and Simone were sitting.

"Ms. Johnson will be going back for X-rays in just a few minutes but wanted to sit with you while she waits. I've given her a medication to ease some of the pain, so she will need to stay in this wheelchair. We can't have her taking another spill on us now can we, Levi?" the nurse teased.

"No ma'am," Levi said with a goofy grin. She felt like she had lost control of her facial muscles and was grinning like the Cheshire Cat. Whatever the pill was, it was some good stuff, and she couldn't help but giggle.

"Well, I think it's safe to say the pill is taking effect," the nurse winked at Nat, "so watch her closely."

"Will do," Nat said as the nurse walked back into the small room.

With words that were beginning to slur, Levi turned to Nat. "The nurse said it's going to be a while before I'm done, Nat, so you can go back to the resort if you need to."

"No need, my friend, Liz and the crew can hold down the fort for a little while until we get you fixed up."

"You want to go?" Levi asked Simone a little drunkenly.

"Of course not, baby. I will stay right here with you,"

"Great, we can have a party then," Levi said with a goofy grin.

"Wait just a minute," a sexy voice spoke from behind them. "There is no partying allowed in the waiting room."

"Oh, here comes the party wrecker." Levi chuckled.

"Hi ladies, my name is Lisa, and I have been tasked with taking our patient here upstairs to get some pictures of that arm of hers."

"She's a little loopy," Nat warned as the woman leaned down next to Levi.

"I promise to take good care of her and will have her back here as quickly as I can."

"I can't go back with her?" Simone asked.

"I'm afraid not. From here on out Ms. Johnson will be in our hands, but I promise we'll take good care of her," she said to a clearly disappointed Simone. "Are you ready, Ms. Johnson?"

"No worries, baby, I'll remember to smile when they take my picture," Levi said. "Let's go."

Lisa wheeled Levi through the electronic doors as they headed to the elevator. "How did you hurt your wrist?"

"I slipped on the soap in the shower." Levi's head bobbed with the movement of the chair.

"That killer soap will get you every time," Lisa said. Levi howled with laughter.

†

Two hours later, Levi returned to the emergency room, her left wrist wrapped in a soft brace. Lisa wheeled her out into the waiting room.

"We have good news and bad news, ladies," Lisa said as she approached them. "First the good news, Ms. Johnson has a clean break to her ulna."

"That's the good news?" Nat asked.

"Yes," Lisa said. "The bad news is that we cannot cast her wrist until the swelling goes down, so we have to release her for today, but she has to come back tomorrow afternoon to get casted."

Levi, still loopy from the effects of the pill, giggled. "I love you, Lisa."

Simone stiffened in her seat and frowned at Levi's words.

Lisa handed Nat a bottle of pills. "She is going to have a painful day, so one of those every six hours is recommended if she needs some pain relief. Hopefully, she will sleep the day away and we'll see her back here tomorrow afternoon." She looked at Nat and Simone. "Who is driving?"

"I am," Nat said.

"If you will pull your vehicle up to the curb, I'll roll Ms. Johnson out for you."

"I can do that." Simone glared at Lisa.

"Sorry, but it's hospital rules," Lisa said, adding fuel to the rage burning inside Simone.

Simone grabbed the keys from Nat and stormed out of the emergency room to retrieve the van. The warm air outside did little to soothe her rage as she stomped through the parking lot. She unlocked the door and snatched it open crawling in behind the wheel. She pulled the van up to the curb and parked it, fuming while she waited for Nat, Lisa, and Levi to arrive.

Nat helped Levi into the backseat and secured her in the seat belt before closing the door behind her. "Thanks Lisa," she said as the young woman headed back into the hospital. Nat then walked around to the driver's door and opened it. "Outside now," she said roughly to her sister.

Simone stepped out of the van and Nat closed the door behind her. "What the fuck was that all about?" she demanded.

"It seems that Levi enjoyed the time she spent with Lisa."

"You're a damned fool, Simone. Can't you see that Levi is high as a kite?"

"High or not, that was uncalled for."

"Grow the fuck up and get your ass in the van," Nat said, totally disgusted with her sister's attitude.

Nat waited for Simone to climb into the backseat and then drove as carefully as she could back to the resort. She helped a sullen Simone get Levi into her bed and left Simone to watch over her.

Simone sat next to Levi's bed until she fell asleep, her anger still flaring. Once Levi appeared settled and resting quietly, Simone left the room. She stopped by the office, tossed Nat the bottle of pills for Levi. "Here, you go babysit. I'm going to have some fun."

Shocked, Nat and Liz looked at each other as Simone stormed through the door and headed out to the bar. "What the hell has gotten into her?" Liz asked.

"I have no clue, but I don't think Levi needs to be left alone right now," Nat said.

"Let me go sit with her then while you find out what is happening with that sister of yours."

Chapter Fourteen

Liz let herself into Levi's room and sat on the love seat close to the bed. She watched Levi and saw the grimace on her face when her arm moved during her sleep. Levi looked adorable, her handsome features fully relaxed and her lips curling into a soft smile as she dreamed of something pleasant. Simone would be lucky to have someone as genuine as Levi in her life. Liz hoped Simone would come to her senses soon and realize how good Levi was for her.

Levi stirred and softly whispered Simone's name and then settled back to sleep. Liz's heart ached at the thought of Simone's callousness and the selfishness she had demonstrated earlier in the day.

Liz curled up on the love seat and tucked a pillow under her head as she watched over Levi. The calm darkness of the room eventually began to tug at her consciousness and Liz found herself drifting off to sleep.

✝

NeNe watched Simone walk up to the bar and order a large drink before finding a table close to the dance floor. The afternoon crowd was light, but the ladies were having a great time drinking and dancing as they got to know each other. Concerned for Levi, NeNe set up the automatic play and left the DJ booth to talk to Simone.

"Hi, Simone. I'm surprised to see you here. How's Levi?"

Simone looked up at NeNe, her eyes flashing with anger. "She'll survive," she snarled. "She has a broken wrist and is medicated to sleep through the night. Hopefully, the swelling goes down and she can be casted tomorrow."

"You left her alone?" NeNe asked in surprise.

"Yes, I did. It's not my job to babysit her."

"No, I guess it isn't, Simone, but I thought you cared enough about Levi to want to be with her even in difficult times. But I guess I am wrong on that account."

"I guess you are," Simone answered as she took a deep drink from her cocktail.

Refusing to be a victim of Simone's black mood, NeNe had started back across the bar when she saw Nat walk through the door. NeNe had worked for Nat and Liz long enough to read their body language and the sight of Nat told NeNe that a bad storm was brewing and to steer clear for the moment. She walked past Nat silently and could hear her mumbling to herself as she focused on Simone.

NeNe picked up the telephone in the booth and called down to the bartender on duty. "Will you send me up a large TE? Yes, I know it's early for me, but I think I need a drink." She replaced the receiver into the cradle just as Nat reached Simone's table.

NeNe could see the tension in Nat's shoulders as she loomed over the seated Simone. Nat was usually the most calm and laid-back person NeNe had ever met so the anger she sensed between the two women shook her to her core. She had no idea what was happening, but from the stern looks and the harsh words she felt sure were exchanged between them she knew it was unsettling.

†

"Do you mind telling me just what the fuck you are doing here when the best woman you have ever met is hurt and in pain?" Nat demanded.

Simone took a sip from her drink and set it on the table. "Well, it is obvious that Levi manages just fine without me."

"Just where do you get that, Simone? You know Levi is head over heels in love with you."

"Yeah right, that is what I thought too, before today. I guess she proved us both wrong at the hospital."

"You fool! You know Levi was heavily medicated and was just being nice to Lisa."

"Even so, that comment was totally uncalled for. I will not be treated like that by anyone."

"Simone, you need to come down off your high horse and go be with Levi."

"I have no intention of watching her sleep when I could be having some fun instead." Simone looked at the group of women on the dance floor.

"For once in your life, Simone, you should forget about your needs and care about someone else," Nat challenged her. "Levi is the best person that has ever come into your life and I can't believe you are going to turn your back on her now."

"Well, that's life, big sister."

"No, Simone, that's your miserable life."

"Fair enough, but it is my life." Simone stood and walked past Nat to the dance floor.

Nat was incensed, but knew she was not getting through to her sister. She shook her head and stormed back out of the bar.

†

NeNe watched the interaction as she sipped her drink and knew the night was going to be a long one. She watched in disbelief as Simone joined the dancers on the floor, and within minutes had culled an attractive blonde from the group and was entertaining her at her table. Disgusted by the way Simone fawned over the blonde she was not surprised when an hour later the two of them left together. There was no doubt in NeNe's mind that the two would end up in the penthouse wrapped in a heated embrace before the next hour ended. All she could do was shake her head as she watched Simone leave the bar with the young blonde draped all over her.

†

Nat left the bar in a rage and took a long walk down the beach to cool her heated mind. The soft breeze wrapped around her and the sound of the gentle waves calmed her anger. She decided to go check on Levi and Liz. As Nat walked back into the resort, Simone and a blonde guest stepped into the elevator, and her anger flared again. Nat walked to Levi's room and slipped her master key into the door and stepped quietly into the room. She smiled as she found Liz sleeping soundly on the love seat and Levi dozing peacefully on the bed. She sat in an oversized chair and relaxed as she watched the pair sleeping. For the life of her, Nat could not understand Simone's behavior. She pondered over the day as she listened to the soft snoring of Liz and Levi.

Night was falling swiftly and Nat realized she was hungry. She crept from the room and walked down to the kitchen to order dinner for the three of them. It would soon be time for more medication for Levi and Nat hoped some food in her system would help her rest well for the evening. She called down to the bar and asked the relief bartender to pull a double shift. Nat had decided to stay with Levi through the night to make sure she did not have a reaction to the medication. She was walking back to Levi's room when she crossed paths with NeNe, who was also going to Levi's room.

"Hello, NeNe."

"Hi, Nat, I was just going to drop by and check on Levi during my break."

"Liz is with her and they were both sound asleep when I left them a few minutes ago."

"I saw Simone, and all she said was that Levi's wrist was broken and she was sleeping it off," NeNe said with a frown.

NeNe saw Nat tense up at the mention of her sister's behavior. "I don't know what is going on in that head of hers. I will stay with Levi tonight, though, and make sure she has a comfortable night."

"Why don't you let me stay with her tonight after I get off work and you can at least share a bed with Liz."

"Are you sure you wouldn't mind?"

"No, not at all Nat." They stopped outside Levi's door.

"Well, why don't you come inside and let's see if we can wake the two sleepyheads for some dinner."

NeNe chuckled softly and followed Nat into the room. Nat kissed Liz softly to wake her and then moved to the bed to sit beside Levi. A light knock on the door signaled dinner had arrived and Nat asked NeNe to let the kitchen staff in. She gently shook Levi to awaken her. Levi's eyes cracked open as she tried to focus her vision.

"Simone," she said.

"No, Levi, this is Nat."

"Where is Simone?"

Nat was startled into silence. She was not prepared to answer that question and was thankful when Liz came to her rescue.

"Simone needed some rest, so we sent her to her room to get some sleep."

"That's right." Nat followed Liz's lead. "We are going to stay with you until you get some food in you and go back to sleep. Then NeNe is going to stay with you the rest of the night."

Levi looked even more confused and faltered when she tried to sit up in the bed. Nat quickly supported her as she sat up and leaned against the headboard. Nat had ordered her favorite, a cheeseburger fully loaded, and Levi's mouth watered as NeNe carried the tray of food over to her.

"Cut it in half and split it with me please, NeNe," Levi said.

NeNe smiled and set the tray beside the table. She cut the burger in half and handed a portion of it to Levi, who smiled in appreciation. NeNe sat beside her and took up the other half as Liz and Nat settled into the love seat to eat their meals.

Levi grew more alert as she ate. Her wrist was still very painful and she was thankful when Nat brought her a pain pill. She finished as much of the burger as she could and then took the pill. NeNe looked at her watch and saw that it was time to go back to work.

"I'll see you later, my friend." NeNe placed the plate back on the tray.

"Thanks, NeNe," Levi said, her energy starting to fade as the pill started to take effect.

Levi could barely hold her eyes open after NeNe left. Nat helped her move back down in the bed and covered her with the bed linens. "Tell Simone I love her and miss her," she said. Then her eyes closed and she slept.

Nat gritted her teeth against her anger and she stalked back to the love seat. "That bitch," she mumbled as she sat down next to Liz.

"It will all work out for the best," Liz said as she snuggled into Nat.

"One way or another." Nat wrapped an arm around Liz and they watched Levi sleep.

Chapter Fifteen

NeNe knocked on the door around one and handed Nat the bank bag as she walked into Levi's room. "How is she doing?"

"She has rested well so far tonight, but is due for another pain pill soon. So if she starts showing signs of pain I would recommend waking her for another dose."

"Good, I am really worried about her."

"Levi is going to be fine. I'll take her back to the hospital in the morning and once she has a solid cast, she should start feeling much better. Are you sure you're fine to stay the night?"

"Yes, I'm good. You and Liz go get some rest."

"Very well, just give us a call if anything changes or you need anything." Nat gently woke Liz.

"I will," NeNe promised as she walked them to the door. NeNe sat on the love seat and watched Levi sleep, the faint light from the bathroom shining on her. She was less concerned about the broken wrist than she was about her potential broken heart. She was worried how Simone's behavior was going to affect Levi. Levi had fallen hard for Simone and NeNe feared that Simone's reluctance to be with Levi would be devastating when Levi realized Simone's affections were so superficial. She sighed and walked to the window to look out at the brilliant stars that were twinkling against the dark sky.

NeNe was lost in her thoughts when Levi stirred in the bed. "Simone," she called out as NeNe turned toward the bed.

"No, Levi, it's NeNe." She walked to the edge of the bed.

"Hello, NeNe. I thought you were Simone standing there."

"I haven't seen Simone tonight," NeNe said, which really was the truth. She had not seen her since earlier in the day when she left the bar with the blonde draped all over her.

"Oh."

"How are you feeling?"

"My arm is on fire."

"It has been enough time for another pain pill."

"In a few minutes. Why are you here? Not that I'm not thankful for your company, but where is Simone?"

"I don't have the answer to that," NeNe said. "Liz and Nat stayed with you until I got off work and then I sent them off to bed."

A frown grew on Levi's face as she started to piece the puzzle together. She realized Simone had played her for a fool. If Simone had truly cared for her the way she had claimed, then she would be here to watch over her instead of NeNe. Her eyes grew moist with tears, yet she was determined and fought them back. "I will take that pill now." She lifted herself up in the bed long enough to take the pill from NeNe and wash it down with a sip of water.

NeNe turned to walk back to the love seat but was stopped by Levi's voice. "If you insist on staying will you at least share a bed with me, NeNe? That love seat is not the most comfortable place to sleep, you know."

NeNe walked around the bed, kicked her shoes off and climbed under the covers. She rolled onto her right side and watched as Levi's eyes grew heavy from the medication. "Sleep well, my friend," she whispered and moments later, Levi began to softly purr.

†

When Liz walked up to the front desk the next morning, the clerk informed her that Simone had checked out earlier in the morning and had left the island. Liz spun on her heels and walked back to their suite to wake Nat up with the news.

Liz handed Nat a cup of coffee and sat on the edge of the bed. "I just don't understand what has gotten into Simone," Nat said. "I have never seen her as happy with anyone as I thought she was with Levi. I had hopes she would finally settle down."

"I have no clue either, my love. Like you, I thought things were marvelous between them. It just seems like since they returned from the island, she hasn't been the same person."

"How do we break the news to Levi?" Nat asked.

"I see no other way than to tell her the truth, as painful as it will be for Levi. I'm sure when she wakes up and Simone is nowhere in sight, she will start to comprehend what is going on."

"I hate that Levi ever met Simone now," Nat said. "She's too good of a woman to be treated so terribly and my heart goes out to her. I guess when I take her back to the hospital this morning I will tell her Simone has left the island."

"Do you want me to do it?"

"No, Simone caused this pain, so I think I should be the one to talk to Levi, but thank you for offering, my sweet woman." Nat kissed Liz's soft lips.

"Finish your coffee. I'll go help Levi get ready while you shower and dress."

✝

NeNe woke and watched Levi sleep until well after the sun rose. In such a short time, NeNe had grown to love her new friend and she prayed that she would be strong enough to help Levi through the hurt that was yet to come. The physical pain would be so much easier to bear than the broken heart that was looming on her horizon. NeNe was furious with Simone for hurting Levi and planned to seek her out today just to tell her what a bitch she was being. She was lost in thought when Levi woke.

"What are you thinking about that has you frowning so?"

Levi's question startled NeNe from her thoughts. "I was just thinking how lucky I am to be lying here next to such a beautiful young lady."

"Yeah right. If I look half as bad as I feel, you should be running from the room screaming in fright," Levi said with a grin.

"Aside from a bad case of bed head, I think you look pretty darn nice."

"Go put your contacts in, my friend. I can feel the dried drool on my cheeks and I feel like my eyes are almost swollen shut."

"Hmm, let me see." NeNe moved closer to Levi. "Mmm, nope, still the same beautiful eyes you have always had," she said, with a soft laugh.

Levi tried to raise her arm and instantly decided to leave it lying on the bed. NeNe saw the painful grimace. "Do you need another pain pill?"

"No, I need to be able to get up out of this bed today. I do need your help though, NeNe."

"What can I do for you?"

"Two things actually. Will you go down to housekeeping and get a small plastic bag to tape around my arm, and second, will you wash my hair?"

"Of course I will." NeNe crawled from the bed and headed to the door.

"NeNe," Levi called out, stopping her in her tracks.

"Yes, Levi?"

"Thanks for staying with me last night and being my friend."

"My pleasure." NeNe bounded out the door. As she walked past the elevator, the doors opened and Liz stepped out.

"Good morning, NeNe, how is our patient this morning?"

"She is awake and ready to attempt a shower," NeNe said. "I am off to housekeeping to get a small plastic bag to wrap around her arm and will be back in just a minute."

"I'll stop by the office then for some tape and will meet you there. Oh and by the way, NeNe..." "Yes, Liz?"

"Simone checked out this morning and is gone."

"Just like that." NeNe shook her head. "What a bitch." NeNe realized she had spoken her thoughts out loud. "I'm sorry, Liz."

"Apparently so," Liz said with a sigh.

"I know she is Nat's sister, but she is being a real bitch."

"Agreed, and no one is taking it harder than Nat right now," Liz said. "She plans on telling Levi when she takes her back to the hospital this morning."

"I don't envy Nat that task," NeNe said.

"Me either."

Liz knocked lightly then pushed the door to Levi's room open. Levi was sitting upright in the bed and smiled at Liz as she walked in. "This room hasn't seen this much female company since I got here," Levi said with a sly grin.

"Now don't complain, Levi," Liz mock scolded her. "If you weren't so picky, this bed could be filled every night with beautiful women."

"I guess I can be a little picky."

"There's nothing wrong with having scruples. Now, Nat has sent me to get you moving about and some food in your stomach before she takes you back to the hospital."

"NeNe..." Levi started to say but was interrupted by NeNe coming through the door.

"NeNe went to get you a plastic bag," NeNe said, finishing her comment.

Liz and NeNe carefully placed the bag over her hand and lower arm before gently taping it to hold it in place. NeNe went into the bathroom and started the shower, placing a towel nearby for Levi's use. "Can you get undressed or do you need help?"

"I think I can do it," Levi said with a bashful grin.

"Okay, then call out when you are ready and I'll come in to wash your hair." NeNe closed the door and walked back to sit by Liz.

"Are you okay with washing her hair?" Liz asked.

"Believe it or not, I have seen a naked woman before, Liz," NeNe said with a feigned look of disgust on her face.

"I know, but none of them have ever been Levi." Liz was fully aware of the attraction NeNe secretly held for Levi.

Knowing Liz had just busted her out, NeNe's face grew scarlet. "Is it that obvious?"

Liz chuckled. "Only to the well-trained eye. I don't think even Levi knows how you truly feel about her, but I can sense that you would love more than a friendship with her."

Still a brilliant shade of red, NeNe said, "All right, you can stop there, Liz, or I won't be able to make it into that bathroom when she calls."

"Fair enough, I will drop it for now."

Silence fell between them as they both thought about what Liz had just revealed. NeNe jumped when Levi called from the bathroom.

"Call if you need any help," Liz teased as she stretched out on the love seat.

NeNe stepped into the steamy bathroom and slowly opened the shower curtain. She didn't have time to prepare for the sight her eyes beheld as they took in Levi's nakedness. She quickly reached for the shampoo and busied herself washing Levi's hair as she tried to keep her eyes averted from Levi's body. "Are you good from here?" she asked when she finished washing her hair.

"I think I've got it." Levi turned away from NeNe to step under the water to rinse.

NeNe took in the view from behind which was just as adorable as she knew it would be. "Call if you need help." She stepped from the bathroom.

"Thanks," she heard Levi call out as she closed the door.

"Mission accomplished." She sighed as she sat back down on the bed.

"Do you want to go shower and meet us in the dining room for a late breakfast?" Liz asked.

"That sounds like a good idea."

"I'll help her get ready and meet you downstairs in a short while then."

Venus Rising

†

Simone rested her head against the back of the first-class seat and stared out of the window on her flight to Miami. She didn't understand why she was so compelled to leave the resort, but it felt like she would suffocate if she stayed any longer. When she woke up in the middle of the night with the blonde tangled up in the sheets, she knew she had made the biggest mistake of her life. She could not remember why she had been so angry with Levi or recall how she had ended up in bed with the blonde that she didn't even have a name for, but Simone was sure she had ruined what chance she had to be with Levi.

All she could think to do was to get as far away from the island as she could. She had slipped from the bed, showered, and called for a cab while she dressed and packed her bags. The telephone rang as she closed the final bag, the front desk notifying her that her cab had arrived. Without a final look at the naked woman in her bed, Simone had fled the penthouse that held so many memories of Levi and rushed downstairs. She called to the front desk staff to bill her credit card as she passed by and walked straight to the cab. The driver put her bags in the trunk and Simone climbed into the backseat. With her heart racing, she had left the resort before the sun peeked over the horizon.

Chapter Sixteen

Simone barely made her connection in Miami, and when she settled into her first-class seat, she ordered a single malt scotch even though it was barely nine in the morning. The tightness in her chest began to fade as the smooth liquid burned down to her stomach and she began to relax. She downed the rest of the drink and ordered another shortly after takeoff, reclining her seat to enjoy the second drink. In a few hours, she would land in Cancun and spend two days there before taking a flight to Greece to check on the cruise ships that would be in port. Then she would return to the States for a week and consider how she was going to handle the debut of her cruise line arriving at Venus Rising. Nat would surely be highly upset with her sudden disappearance and her treatment of Levi, but she would come up with a plan to smooth things over. She always found the right thing to say and this would be no different.

Simone had no clue what had gone so wrong between them. She had thought things were progressing well with Levi and then this morning she woke up with the weight of an elephant sitting on her chest. Her only choice was to run and hope the distance would help to clear her head.

She sipped the scotch and rested her head against the seat as her thoughts returned to Levi. Her lips curled into a smile as she replayed the last few days spent with Levi and her heart felt heavy with loneliness. Simone knew Levi was the woman she was destined to be with, but her actions over the past twenty-four hours had ruined any chance of a future with Levi. Simone downed the rest of the drink and, still thinking of Levi, closed her eyes for a nap.

†

Levi and Liz joined NeNe and Nat in the dining room for a late breakfast. "You're looking better, Levi," Nat said. "How are you feeling?"

"Still a little drugged from the medications, but I do think I'll live," Levi said with a grin.

Nat was thankful that many of the staff and guests of the resort stopped by their table to inquire about Levi as this kept the topic off Simone and her behavior. She dreaded telling Levi that her sister had left the island without as much as a good-bye.

When Levi finished her meal, Nat pushed back from the table. "Are you ready to go get that arm taken care of?"

"Now is as good as ever." She stood and, after saying her thanks and good-byes to NeNe and Liz, she and Nat left for the hospital.

Nat closed the door behind Levi and walked around to the driver's side of the van.

As Nat reached for the key, Levi asked, "What's the story with Simone? No one has mentioned her this morning and I find that odd."

Nat's hand froze and she looked over at Levi. The pain written on her face told her that Levi knew what was coming next, which did not make the task any easier.

"Levi, there is no simple way to say this, but Simone left the island early this morning."

"Why?"

"I have no idea, my friend, but she was gone before the sun rose."

"She left without even saying good-bye to you?"

113

"She slipped out without a word," Nat said. "To be honest, I have no idea what has gotten into Simone. For the life of me, I cannot understand why she would walk away from the best thing that has ever happened in her life."

Levi grinned at Nat's comment. "Thanks Nat, I thought things were going well between us, and I don't understand this at all."

"That certainly makes two of us, Levi." Nat turned the key to start the motor. "I have tried calling her several times, but just get her voice mail, I will keep trying though until I can get to the bottom of this. I promise."

"Thanks, Nat." Levi smiled weakly. "I thought I was more than just another of Simone's conquests."

"I know that you are, Levi, and that's what's so baffling with her behavior. Simone is totally smitten with you, which makes it even more bizarre."

They had reached the hospital and Nat got Levi checked in as Lisa took her back to the X-ray lab for more films. She sat in the waiting room while Levi was x-rayed, her fracture set, and her lower arm covered in quick-drying plaster. As she waited, she contemplated what on earth could be going on with her sister and could come up with no clue to what Simone was doing. Nat had left numerous voice mails on Simone's cell phone, however, she had not had any of her calls returned, causing Nat to be even more baffled.

✝

Simone was jolted awake by the landing of the jet in Cancun. She reached into her bag and turned on her cell phone as she waited for the jet to reach the terminal. There were five voice mails from Nat, each growing more hostile as she demanded to know where Simone was and what she thought she was doing, running out on Levi the way she did. Simone had no answer for that either and went on to the next voice mail. Simone's heart sank to her feet as she heard the report that her cruise ship entering Cancun had misjudged a turn and had received damage from an outcropping of underground reefs. The damage was not enough to sink the vessel, but it would take at least a full day in port to have the repairs made. "That is just fucking great," Simone grumbled. "What next?"

Simone gathered her luggage in baggage claim and headed outside to rent a car service to take her down to the port. She maintained an owner's suite on each of her cruise ships and would drop her luggage off and then track down the captain, Vanessa Jones, to find out what happened to cause the accident. Simone was fuming when she stepped onto the loading plank and saw the large gaping hole on the bow of the vessel. A valet jumped to attention when she saw Simone stalking toward her and then dropping her bags at the woman's feet. "Take these to my suite," she barked rather roughly. "Do you know where Vanessa is?"

The young woman grabbed up Simone's bags. "The captain is up in the control room." She darted off with her bags, glad to escape the wrath of Simone that was soon to hit like a typhoon.

Simone walked into the control room and spotted Vanessa going over some charts with one of the other officers. "What the fuck happened, Vanessa?" Simone said loudly as she approached.

The captain looked up from the chart she was reviewing and returned Simone's glare with a smile. "We had some bad weather and miscalculated a turn and clipped a reef."

"I thought we had equipment installed that would prevent that."

"It was an accident, Simone, pure and simple," Vanessa explained. "No one was hurt and the damage looks worse than it actually is. Some new metal plates and some fresh paint and we'll be ready to go by tomorrow night."

"Another day in port is going to cost thousands, not to mention the cost of repairs," Simone said with a shudder.

"The repair will be less than two grand. If it will make you feel any better, take it out of my salary," Vanessa said, losing patience with the angry Simone.

"Any more mistakes like that and you won't have a salary."

115

Vanessa straightened and loomed over Simone by a good three inches. "If you are not happy with my service, say the word and I will be gone."

Vanessa's aggressive response rocked Simone back onto her heels. She was temporarily shocked into silence with Vanessa's challenge. She was being a bitch and everyone in the room would gladly agree with her if given the chance. "I'm sorry, Vanessa," Simone said to break the silence. "I was already having a bad day and then I got this news on top of everything else going on."

"Just relax, Simone, and let us do our jobs. The repairs are underway, the guests certainly did not mind spending another day in Cancun, and we will be on our way again before the end of tomorrow. I will come find you if I need your assistance with the repairs." Vanessa calmly walked Simone to the door.

"I'll check back with you later," Simone replied as Vanessa ushered her out of the control room.

Vanessa turned back into the room and gazed at the crew of officers grinning broadly at her. She knew she had handled the situation with Simone in a way that did not allow Simone to escalate the issue and cause more drama than necessary and her crew appreciated that quality in their captain. "Back to work, you slackers," Vanessa said with a grin as she resumed reviewing the charts.

✝

Simone walked into her suite and turned on the spigot to draw a nice hot bath. This day had started horribly and was not showing signs of improvement. She needed to take a step back and trust in her staff and their ability to operate the ship. Simone had hired the best crew she could and she would damned sure get her money's worth out of them. Weary from the flight and the stress, she slipped into the hot water and willed her mind and muscles to relax.

†

Levi walked back through the swinging double doors, a fluorescent green cast encasing her lower left arm. She saw Nat in the waiting room and managed a small smile for her. The last thing Levi felt like doing right now was smiling, but she knew Nat was doing everything she could to make her feel better.

"That is so your color," Nat said as she stood and hugged Levi. "I'm glad to see you survived that ordeal. Did it hurt much?"

"I won't lie, it felt like someone drove a truck over my arm."

"That good, hmmm? Do you still have some pain medication or do we need to stop for a refill?"

"I still have several left. I can make it without the drugs. I need to get back to work."

"Not today, sunshine. I am working tonight's shift and you, my dear, are going to rest."

"Nat, I can't stand to lie in bed all day."

"Who said anything about bed? I think an afternoon out by the pool would do you a world of good, then a nice relaxing dinner and off to bed early with you."

"Nat, why did she leave?" Nat looked at Levi and saw the tears that were about to spill and her heart ached for her young friend. She placed a protective arm around Levi's shoulders as they continued to walk. "Levi, if there is one thing I have learned in life, it is that I will never understand women," she said with a grin. "To be completely honest, I have no clue what Simone is doing or why, but if I could get my hands around her neck, I would shake her until she rattled."

Levi smiled at Nat. "You would have to beat me to her. I just don't know where I went wrong."

"If anything, you are too good for Simone," Nat said. "Simone has bounced from woman to woman for years, always thinking only of her own needs with no regard for her lover. When she met you, I thought I saw a change in Simone, the way she doted over you, but I guess I was wrong. If there was any way I

117

could undo the hurt she has caused you, Levi, I would do it in a heartbeat."

Levi stopped and turned toward Nat. "There's nothing I would change, Nat. Yes, it hurts that Simone is gone, but I would not trade a minute of the time we spent together."

Nat closed the door behind Levi and took a deep breath. She knew Levi was hurting, but was also confident that she was strong enough to survive and move forward with her life. Still, she wished there were something else she could do to help Levi deal with the pain her sister had caused.

"Simone, I am going to kill you," Nat mumbled as she walked around to the driver's door and climbed inside.

Chapter Seventeen

Nat parked the van in the resort garage and they walked in the front door. Maria, who was walking past the front door, crossed herself and hurriedly walked away from them when she saw Levi. Levi looked at Nat, who shrugged her shoulders. "I have no idea. Let's go see Liz and find out if she has come to the bottom of this mystery with Maria."

Liz looked up from the file she was examining when she heard them walk in the office. Her smile to Nat lit up the room. "Welcome back, you two. Nice color." She grinned and nodded toward Levi's cast.

Nat and Levi took a seat across from Liz. "Have you found out what has disturbed Maria so badly?" Nat asked. "We just passed her in the hall and she crossed herself and scurried away from us like we have a plague."

"I think I have come to understand Maria enough to figure out this mystery," Liz said. "When she went into Simone's bathroom to replace the towels, she saw a gold coin that had dropped in the shower." She looked at Levi. "Where is that coin by the way?"

"I have it in my pocket."

"According to Maria, that coin and the hundreds like it are cursed."

119

"Cursed?" Nat asked. "I know there are some strange superstitions in the islands, but a cursed coin? That is almost unbelievable in this day and age."

"Well, that coin is very old and not a part of this day and age, my love, and therein lies the issue," Liz explained. "I did some research on it after Maria left. The history of the coin Levi has in her pocket is steeped with evil, beginning hundreds of years ago." Levi reached to take the coin from her pocket, but Liz stopped her. "Leave it alone for now, Levi."

"I think you have our attention, my love, so please continue with this tale," Nat said.

"The story of the coin begins with the slave trade in America. Ships were packed tight with victims of kidnapping from the coastal areas of the continent of Africa." She ignored the ringing telephone on her desk to continue her story. "The atmosphere of these slave ships and the treatment of these people was deplorable, as history has taught us, and many of the weaker passengers died during the voyage to America."

"What does this have to do with Levi's coin?" Nat asked.

"The coin was used as payment to the slave traders for their delivery of slaves into the port of Charleston, South Carolina, minted from Spanish gold, and prized by the greedy slave traders." Liz paused for a moment. "After one such delivery, the slavers headed south on their return to the African coast and their ship fell under siege by a pirate ship. Unprepared for battle on the ocean, the slave ship fell easily to the better armed and manned pirate ship. The pirates took the chest of gold from the captain of the slave ship and set the crew to sea in a small boat."

Liz smiled at Nat and Levi, who were both leaning forward, listening intently to her story. "After looting the ship, the pirates set it on fire and watched as the carrier of such tortured souls was burned and sank to the bottom of the ocean while the crew drifted in the small boat cursing at the pirates."

"So the evil began as payment for the captured Africans who were taken from their homes and transported across the wide ocean to be sold into slavery to serve the plantation owners and wealthy northerners?" Levi asked.

"Yes, Levi, the slave captain was punished for his treatment of the slaves by having his payment stolen and his ship destroyed, barely escaping with the lives of his crew," Liz said.

"So now the gold coins are in the possession of the pirates, but how did Levi's coin get to the island just south of here?" Nat asked.

"As the pirates sailed south toward the Caribbean, their ship was assaulted by a horrendous storm and the ship sank off the coast of the Virgin Islands. So the chest of cursed coins rested on the bottom of the ocean with the bones of the crew of the pirate ship, until treasure hunters found the wreckage a hundred or so years later." Liz leaned forward to rest her arms on the desk as she looked at Levi. "The tides played havoc on the sunken treasure and the chest that once held hundreds of these gold coins was scattered across the ocean floor. When the treasure hunters located the pirate ship they were able to discover about two hundred of these coins while the others were carried away by the ocean tides."

"Did the treasure hunters bring the coins to the islands?" Levi asked.

"No, ironically the curse of the coins continued. The treasure hunters planned to take their bounty back to America, but as they passed the southern tip of Florida their ship disappeared into what is now known as the Devil's Triangle, or Bermuda Triangle, and was never seen again."

"So everyone that has come into contact with these coins has been destroyed by their evil?" Nat asked.

"As the legend tells it, yes. Anyone who has taken possession of one of these coins has experienced bad fortune and many have lost their lives trying to possess the gold," Liz explained.

"When Maria saw your coin, Levi, she recognized it immediately as one of the cursed coins and fled in terror before she was tempted to hold it any longer."

The coin felt suddenly warm in Levi's pocket and she placed her hand over it. "Did Maria tell you how to break the curse?"

"Several islanders have found the coins over the years and the legend says that the person or persons who came into possession of a coin, must return it to the sea."

"I still don't know how it came to rest in the soil of that cave," Levi said as her hand rubbed across the coin in her pocket.

"I would guess that it either washed ashore or was buried there by someone who was trying to break the curse," Nat said.

Liz sighed. "The problem we face now is that Simone needs to be present when Levi returns the coin as she was with Levi and has touched the coin."

Both Liz and Levi looked at Nat. "I've tried to call her, but she is not returning my calls."

"You have got to get it through to her that she must come back to help Levi break the curse," Liz said. "If not, both of them will continue to be plagued by misfortune."

Levi sat back in her chair, exhausted by the events of the morning and the news that Liz had just dumped in her lap. "So what should I do with the coin?"

"I would hide it away from view for now until we can get Simone back down here. Don't touch it or look at it any more than you have to," Liz warned.

"I'll do that," Levi said as she stood. "If you will excuse me, I think I will take a nap."

"Are you in pain?" Nat asked.

"Not too bad, Nat, but I am suddenly very tired."

"I'll do my best to reach Simone and then I'll come by to check on you in a couple of hours."

"Thanks for everything you two have done for me," Levi said.

"You are very welcome, Levi," Liz said as they walked with her to the door.

†

Levi walked to her room and located a small velvet jewelry bag with a drawstring top. She fished the coin from her pocket and dropped it inside the bag. She struggled to lift the

122

mattress off the bed and placed the bag under the center of the mattress, away from easy reach when the housekeepers changed the linens. Levi replaced the mattress and removed her shoes before lying across the bed. As she rested, her arm began throbbing from the exertion. Levi sat up, and took one of the pain pills before lying back down. The gentle whooshing of the ceiling fan lulled her to sleep and she dreamed of Simone.

†

Liz left the office to make her rounds. Nat sat down behind her desk and dialed Simone's number. She was shocked when Simone answered after three rings.

"Hello, Simone, it's Nat."

"Before you jump all over me, Nat, let me tell you this has not been a good day," Simone said, the stress evident in her voice.

"Well, it is about to get worse." Nat told Simone the story of the cursed coin.

Simone listened to the story and waited until Nat had finished. "Nat, I know that leaving Levi the way I did was a terrible thing, and I understand how much you like her, but do you really think I'm going to fall for a story like that just so you can get us back together?"

"This is not a ploy, Simone," Nat said, angry at her sister's response. "Besides, Levi is way too good for you."

"Well, I have my hands full here at the moment and I can't drop what I am doing to deal with some fairy tale. I have a cruise ship that nearly sank and every day it's in port I'm losing money."

"What happened to the ship?"

"It hit a reef coming into port at Cancun."

"Don't you think that is a little odd, Simone? A ship with that kind of technology running into a reef sounds ridiculous to me."

"Nat, you can't seriously believe in the mumbo jumbo of a curse, and you can't blame the ship's damages on one stupid coin," Simone raved across the phone.

"Just think for a moment, Simone. Until Levi found that coin, relations between the two of you was fantastic, and since then, Levi has a broken wrist, you ran off in a jealous huff and now your cruise ship was damaged. Doesn't that sound at least a bit coincidental?"

"Things just happen, and I don't see how a damned coin can have anything to do with any of the events that have happened."

"If you won't do it for your own good, at least do it for Levi."

"I'll think about it. I have to go now, Nat."

Simone disconnected the call, dropped the phone on the bed, and burst into tears. She did not understand why she was crying, but she could not stop the flow of tears as they rushed down her cheeks.

Chapter Eighteen

Simone cried herself to sleep and awoke two hours later to the sound of the ship's horn blaring in the early evening, signaling the passenger dinner was about to begin and to head back to the ship if they wanted the meal onboard. Simone dressed in jeans and a snug-fitting black blouse. She had long been attracted to the good looks and confidence of the handsome captain; maybe a night spent with her would help her clear her mind of her misfortunes. Smiling confidently to her image in the mirror, she brushed back her hair before heading to the bridge in search of Vanessa.

Vanessa was leaning over the railing, supervising the last strokes of the paint gun as workers painted the newly welded plate to match the rest of the ship. They would allow the paint to dry and head out to sea the following afternoon. Simone was impressed with the crew's ability to get the repairs made in such a timely manner and to provide additional activities for their guests during the extra day spent in port. She looked across the brilliant blue water as the sun began to sink into the horizon.

Simone walked up beside Vanessa and placed a hand on her shoulder. Vanessa turned to look at her and smiled warmly. "Let me apologize for being such a bitch today," Simone said, offering Vanessa one of her sweetest smiles.

"There is no need for that, Simone. I fully understand your concern for the safety of the passengers and the ship."

"I still feel awful for snapping at you like that; I know you are an excellent captain. I hope you will let me make it up to you by allowing me to take you ashore for dinner tonight."

"That really isn't necessary, Simone, and I already have plans for the evening. The repairs are complete and we'll be ready to depart by lunchtime tomorrow. I promised the repair crew a night out on the town for their expedient work. If you'll excuse me, I need to go prepare for the evening." Vanessa walked past Simone.

Had she remained a moment longer, Vanessa would have seen Simone's jaw drop in shock. Simone had never experienced hearing "no" from a woman she was interested in, and Vanessa's refusal rocked her back on her heels. She was left standing against the rail, alone and lonely as Vanessa walked toward the setting sun and disappeared beneath the deck. Her confidence shattered, Simone walked to the elevator and descended to one of the many lounges. She sat on a barstool and ordered a double scotch on the rocks and sat brooding over her crushed feelings. Several women tried to approach her as she drowned her sorrows with the alcohol, but one angry look from Simone quickly sent them on her way. Two hours later, completely inebriated, Simone stumbled back to her suite and fell across her bed.

†

A quiet knock on Levi's door woke her after a long nap. She opened the door to find NeNe standing in her doorway. "Hey there, Levi, I have the afternoon off and have been given permission to kidnap you for an afternoon by the pool."

Levi chuckled. "By which one, Liz or Nat?"

"Both actually. It is scary to think of what Liz will do in my DJ booth today, but hopefully she won't do major damage. Are you hungry?"

"Yes, I think I am."

"You get your suit on and I'll order us a burger and drinks by the pool, if that's fine with you?"

"A burger sounds great. Give me a few minutes to change and I'll meet you down by the main pool."

Levi stripped out of her clothes and walked to the dresser to pull out a green suit, bright enough to match the cast on her arm. She slipped into it before pulling a large cover-up over the suit. She stepped into a pair of leather sandals.

She easily found NeNe and joined her friend near the pool where guests quickly surrounded them. They were all concerned about Levi and glad to see she was doing well. Levi blushed from all the attention and was relieved when NeNe sent the well-wishers away so they could enjoy a pleasant lunch.

"You have quite a following, my friend," NeNe said with a chuckle. "If you had not surfaced today to prove to them you were still alive, I think your room would have been stormed."

"Yeah right, NeNe."

"I'm not kidding, everyone in the resort has been asking about you. They all wanted to know when that gorgeous bartender was coming back."

Levi chuckled. "I will be back to work tomorrow."

"Good, the ladies have really missed you."

"It will be good to get back to work."

"How are you coping?"

"I'm dealing. I still don't understand what happened or why, but life will go on." Levi forced a smile.

"Yes, it will." They fell silent as they finished their lunch.

Afterward, Levi lay back on a lounge chair and enjoyed the warmth of the sun on her skin. The music pulsed out of the speakers as the crowd around the pool grew until every seat was filled. When she rolled onto her stomach, Levi placed more weight on her left arm than she should and the sharp pain in her wrist reminded her that she was not one hundred percent yet. She grimaced in pain as she flopped down on the lounger.

✝

Simone awoke late the next morning, her head pounding from the scotch she had consumed the night before. Sunlight seeped through the seams of the heavy drapes and when she could muster the courage to stand, she stumbled to the window to seal out the light. Even the slightest ray made the pain in her eyes burn deeply into her head. She located her hygiene bag, doled out three aspirin, and downed them with a glass of purified water. Simone squinted to focus on the clock, finding it was nearly ten. She would have to shower, dress, and pack her bag to depart the boat by noon, when Vanessa said they would be leaving port. Simone struggled against the temptation to crawl back into bed, but instead turned on the water in the bathroom for a cool shower, hoping it would help to invigorate her suffering body.

With the assistance of a nervous cabin steward, Simone managed to pack her bag and meet the car the service had sent to transport her to the airport for her flight to Greece. As Simone settled back into the dark limo, she looked up to see Vanessa standing on the bridge, barking out commands as her crew prepared to leave port. What a wasted trip she thought as the car slowly pulled away from the curb. The pounding in her head had subsided to a dull throb and her dark shades helped block the painfully bright rays of the sun. Within a half hour, Simone had arrived at the airport and awaited the call to board the jet that would take her to Greece.

As she waited, Simone briefly considered calling Levi, but lack of words prevented her from dialing the number she had memorized. There was just no sense in calling her now, the damage she had done was not repairable by mere words. Simone dropped her phone back into her bag and slumped in her chair until it was time to board.

Chapter Nineteen

With Nat's blessing and assistance, Levi returned to work the following day and the remainder of the week passed without incident. In the early morning hours as she lay in the bed waiting for sleep, Levi could feel the coin pulling at her consciousness. Even though she was tempted to remove the coin from underneath her mattress, she left it concealed, heeding Maria's warning.

The resort buzzed with activity as last-minute preparations were completed for the arrival of Simone's cruise ship. Construction of the bar addition had been completed and staff had been added to assist with the increase in business. Levi was in charge of training the new bartenders and was pleased with the performance of the four young women she and Nat had selected. Levi embraced the extra work as it helped to keep her mind off Simone. A week had passed since she left the island so abruptly and Levi had not received any word from Simone. She didn't understand why she still cared, but she hoped Simone was not experiencing any ill effects from the curse and was safe and sound.

✝

Simone had survived the trip to Greece without incident, but on her return to the States, her jet was struck by lightning, forcing it to make a very rough emergency landing. Strange events in her life began to make Simone wonder if indeed there was some truth to the curse of the coin. She did not want to believe the warning that Nat gave her, but she was experiencing the worst string of luck in her entire life. Maybe it really wasn't coincidence, as she struggled to make herself believe.

She would be returning to the cruise ship in two days to sail on the maiden voyage to Venus Rising and she would work with Levi to put this nonsense to bed once and for all. She had spent much of the last few days thinking about Levi and was determined to win her back when she returned to the island.

She started her efforts the following morning, sending a dozen roses to Levi, hoping her gesture would open the door to Levi's heart and she would welcome her back with open arms. She followed up the roses with a phone call, but only reached Levi's voice mail. Still unsure of the right words to say, Simone ended the call without leaving a message and finished packing for her trip.

✝

Levi and the new bartenders were trying out recipes for cocktails when her cell phone vibrated on her waist. She picked up the phone and saw Simone's cell number flashing across her screen. Levi replaced the phone in its case and continued her experimentation. Several new concoctions showed great promise and she glowed with pride at her staff for their hard work during the week. Nat and Liz joined them for samples of the new house drinks and agreed with Levi that the drinks would be a smashing success during the busy week to come. Levi sat with Nat and Liz while the new bartenders stored the last cases of liquor.

"How is your arm feeling, Levi?" Liz asked.

"The pain is all but gone, but it is itching like crazy."

"That's a good sign it's healing then." Nat chuckled.

"I suppose so. I still can't wait to get this cast off so I can scratch the itch."

"Another week or so, Levi," Liz said.

"Not a moment too soon," Levi answered. "So are you two ready for the big weekend?"

"As ready as we can be," Nat answered. "I'm certain there will be something that comes up we aren't prepared for, but I'm confident our group can tackle anything that arises."

Levi nodded her head in silent agreement.

"I received a telephone call from Simone and everything is on schedule from her end," Nat said. Both she and Liz watched Levi's face closely as Nat brought up Simone. Levi's expression did not waver as she listened to Nat.

"Sounds like we are good to go then," Levi said.

"Are you ready?" Liz asked.

"The bars are well stocked, we have competent staff, and it looks like the weather is going to be beautiful."

"That's not exactly what I meant, Levi," Liz said. "Are you ready to be face-to-face with Simone?"

"I promise I will be professional during any interactions with Simone."

"Professionalism aside, Levi, are you emotionally prepared?" Liz asked a bit more direct this time.

"I'll deal with it just fine. I'm sure it won't be easy, but NeNe has been terrific at keeping me occupied and not allowing me to dwell on Simone."

"You know NeNe cares very deeply for you," Liz said.

"Yes, and I appreciate NeNe's friendship very much, but there is no romantic chemistry between us."

"Well, you can't have too many close friends," Nat chimed in.

"Very true, my love," Liz said with a slow sigh. She had hoped that NeNe and Levi would fall in love, but Levi had just made it clear that her feelings for NeNe were strictly platonic, dashing Liz's hopes. Liz was worried about Levi, who was sinking herself in her job and not taking much time to deal with the situation between her and Simone. She was a strong-willed woman, and Liz knew Levi would deal with her feelings for Simone in her own time and in her own way.

NeNe entered the bar carrying a box full of new CDs. "Hey ladies," she said.

"It looks like NeNe has been busy too," Nat said.

"I have spent the entire day burning some new mixes for the club." NeNe grinned proudly.

Everyone buzzed with excitement as they prepared for the weekend. NeNe carried her new music to the DJ booth and started cataloging it. Nat and Liz watched the Friday night crowd begin to filter in. They would have one last night of solely resort guests before the cruise ship arrived midafternoon on Saturday. Then there would be nonstop partying until Thursday when the ship would sail from port.

"You have been working very hard the last few days, Levi," Nat said. "Why don't you stick around to monitor the new staff and once you feel comfortable, take off and have some fun, maybe mingle with the guests a little," she added with a wink.

"I might just do that," Levi said as she left the table and walked over to the bar.

Nat and Liz left the bar and went to the dining room for an early dinner. They would also need to relax and rest up for the busy weekend ahead. They sat in the dining room overlooking the pool and watched as Levi went back and forth between the two bars checking on staff and mingling with the resort guests. Liz shot a smile at Nat when they saw Levi tap a guest of the shoulder and ask her to dance out by the pool.

"Levi will be fine. How about a slow dance of our own back at the room," Nat said, grinning mischievously.

"I'm waiting on you, lover." Liz stood and walked briskly from the dining room, Nat closely behind her.

†

Levi finished her dance and walked out onto the pier. The water was as smooth as glass and the full moon hung low in the sky sending bright rays of shimmering light across the water. Giggles from under the pier broke the solitude of the moment, painfully reminding Levi of how lonely she was. Even surrounded by a resort full of beautiful women she had never felt so alone. She had never felt as deeply for anyone as she had for Simone and her absence left her feeling empty inside. Disgusted with feeling sorry for herself, she turned away from the railing and walked down the pier. Most of the pool crowd had drifted into the main bar and Levi slipped past unnoticed and disappeared into the resort. Her nose was assaulted by the sweet fragrance of roses when she opened her door. The light beside her bed was on and a beautiful arrangement of roses sat next to her bed.

She plucked the card from the center of the flowers, breathing in a lungful of the sweet aroma. She opened the card and saw the words *Please Forgive Me* scrolled across the card with no signature. Levi sat on the edge of the bed, still holding the card as she stared at the three words. Could she forget the hurt Simone had caused her so easily she wondered? Levi still harbored a love for Simone; that had not changed, but she would always question Simone's commitment and motivation. It had been painfully apparent how easily Simone could walk out on someone and Levi feared it could just as easily happen again. With her eyes full of tears, Levi stretched across the bed, listening to the soft whir of the fan and felt the gentle breeze as it kissed her heated skin.

Chapter Twenty

The next morning Levi awoke, still dressed from the night before. She looked over at the clock to discover it was nearly seven. In two hours, she was due to help Nat supervise the last-minute touches before the ship's arrival, so she showered, dressed, and went to the dining room for breakfast.

Levi could feel the excitement as staff buzzed around the resort. The arrival of the cruise ship today was a huge landmark for the *Venus Rising* and it appeared every staff member was aware of the significance, not only for the resort but also the entire island community. The increased revenue from the cruise line guests would fund the improvement of the island's tourism rating and would generate revenue to boost the economy.

Levi was lost in thought, sipping the last of her juice when Liz walked up to her table and placed a large box in front of her.

"Good morning, Levi."

"Morning, boss, how are you?"

"I'm doing great, Levi, and you?"

"Rested and ready for one heck of a weekend." Levi grinned.

"Excellent."

Levi was eying the box with curious glances. "What's in the box?"

"Nat and I bought a surprise for you. Go ahead and open it."

Levi easily broke through the tape holding the box shut and opened the flaps. Her eyes lit up when she spotted the tall green plastic shot glasses. She reached inside and pulled one out to inspect it more closely. *Welcome to the ladies of Sappho One,* printed in white lettering on the side of each glass.

"Nat had a wonderful idea." Liz nodded toward the box of glasses. "Since this is such a special event, she thought it would be grand to have the bartenders serve each arriving guest a shot of Tropical E in a souvenir glass as they arrive at the resort."

"That's brilliant! Not only does it officially welcome them to the resort, but it also whets their appetite for more Tropical E," Levi said with a chuckle.

"Exactly! You didn't think I married Nat just for her good looks, did you, Levi?"

"Heavens no. The two of you make a terrific pair of businesswomen and I have already learned so much from both of you," Levi said with genuine appreciation.

"Her ears must have been burning," Liz teased as she watched Nat enter the dining room. She and Levi broke out in laughter.

"Now that is a heavenly sound," Nat said. "It is so good to hear you laughing again, Levi, so I won't even ask what the joke was."

"Good morning, boss."

"The maintenance staff is ready to hang the banner across the drive if you two are ready. They are just awaiting the go-ahead from us to put the last piece into place," Nat added.

"I am ready if you are, Levi," Liz said.

"Let's do it then." Levi stood up from the table.

Liz flagged down one of the waitstaff and asked her to take the box of shot glasses to the bar and then joined Levi and Nat for the walk to the front of the resort. The guests from the cruise ship would take a trolley from the port to Venus Rising and the staff would welcome them with the shots and take them on a tour of the resort. Two of the ship's photographers would arrive ahead of the guests to take pictures as part of the cruise package in front of tropical backdrops, already built and put in place. The staff raised the banner welcoming the Ladies of Sappho Cruise Lines and the final preparations were complete. All that was left was to wait until the first of the trolleys arrived from the port.

✝

Levi had requested the maintenance staff set up a frozen drink cooler in the gazebo in the center of the drive. She and one of the new bartenders went to work creating a large cooler of Tropical E and stocked the gazebo with the new shot glasses and serving trays that they would use during the arrival process.

With the temporary gazebo bar set up and ready to serve, Levi completed a final walk-through of the bars with Nat and found everything in order for the weekend. Nat had ordered an ice machine for the main bar; every cooler and shelf was well stocked with every imaginable liquor and mix.

They joined Liz in the dining room for a quick lunch as they waited for the first trolley to arrive. Every staff member looked sharp, and the grounds were in immaculate condition. Liz and Nat were proud of their resort. The three chatted excitedly as they ate salads and awaited the call from the harbor that the first trolley was on its way. There would be two trolleys working the port, each carrying twenty-five passengers. The trolleys would continue to run every hour once the ship's occupants had arrived to *Venus Rising* or other destinations. When the call came at five minutes past one, Levi, Nat, and Liz walked to the front of the resort. Levi would pour the shots as Karen served them to the guests. Nat and Liz would welcome the guests and after the pictures, they would assign them to a tour group.

NeNe was ready to serve as a tour guide for the first few groups that arrived, then she would head off to the main bar to get the music thumping when the party began. She winked at Levi as she passed the gazebo. "Are you ready, gorgeous?"

"All set," Levi said then she set up the tray of shots for Karen when the trolley came into view.

Simone was the first woman to step off the trolley. She hugged and kissed Liz and Nat then turned to watch her guests depart the trolley. She accepted the shot from Karen and turned toward the gazebo. She locked eyes with Levi and raised her glass in a silent salute. Levi returned Simone's smile and began setting up the next round of shots while Nat finished her welcoming speech and the tour began.

The first trolley full of cruise guests had barely finished their shots when the second trolley arrived and the weekend was underway. It would take ten rounds of the trolleys to transport all the cruise guests and then another five rounds to transport the ship's staff. For another two hours, guests arrived by trolley and Levi watched while women of every age, size, shape, color, and nationality arrived at the resort. Simone was lost in the throng of women and Levi stayed busy serving the new guests.

When the final trolley pulled up with the bright white-clad cruise ship officers, Levi had poured the last of the drinks. She was cleaning up the workstation as she watched the crew arrive. Simone had returned to join Nat and Liz as they welcomed her staff. Levi had turned her back for a moment, and when she turned back around, she saw Simone introducing Captain Vanessa Jones to Nat and Liz. *Handsome*, Levi thought while she took in the stark white uniform and the tanned arms of the captain, slowly working her way up past the black curls to the most amazing set of gray eyes that she'd ever seen. Even more surprising, they were locked on and smiling broadly at Levi. When she realized she was caught gawking, Levi blushed and turned away to finish preparing the cooler for transport back to the main bar.

Liz witnessed the look between Vanessa and Levi and turned to find that Simone had also observed the exchange between the two women. She saw the muscles in Simone's jaw working as she tensed and her body language seethed with jealousy. Liz could not help but grin at the thought of Simone being jealous. Serves her right for treating Levi so badly, she thought as she took Vanessa's arm and started a personal tour for the captain and her crew. Levi deserved someone who appreciated her for the beautiful person she is and she would do everything in her power to feed the sparks of chemistry that ignited between the captain and her young bartender at first sight.

Nat and Simone joined the tour group as Levi made her way down to the main bar. The resort guests had immediately begun to mingle with the women of the cruise ship and the party was in full steam. The pool area was packed with women dancing and drinking and when she arrived at the main bar, she found that the women had spilled out into the new addition. The sight was a bit overwhelming at first, until Karen rolled by on her rollerblades, already flushed. "You going to give us a hand here, Romeo, or you going to stand there all night gawking?"

Levi chuckled until she reached the bar then jumped in to begin taking orders from the crowd of customers waiting for attention. Levi could barely catch a glimpse of NeNe through the packed bar. She was busy spinning the music and chatting with a small group of women who had her surrounded in the DJ booth.

The rush of orders continued for another two hours before groups started relaxing in the booths and tables and Levi could actually find a space on the dance floor to make her way out to the patio bar. Tina, the outside bartender, was soaked with perspiration as she served drinks to the crowd. "You need a break?" Levi asked.

"That would be fantastic, Levi, thanks." Tina walked from behind the bar and headed toward the pier for some fresh air.

Levi replaced Tina behind the bar and turned toward the ladies seated at the barstools. "So ladies, what do you think of our little resort?"

"This place is incredible," one woman answered and the others agreed. "I can't ever remember seeing so many women in one place all having such a great time."

"Venus Rising is a very special place. Women come here to find new love or to revitalize a stagnant relationship or just to make a ton of new friends," Levi said with a chuckle.

"I bet it's a blast to work at this place," one of the women said.

"I have really enjoyed myself the short time I have been here. It has been a lot of hard work, but the ladies you meet make it all worthwhile."

"I bet you have to beat the women off with a stick," one woman said, making Levi blush. "Anyone special in your life?"

"Not at the moment." The roar of applause and cheers made Levi blush even more.

"So, gorgeous, what plans do you have for tomorrow?" another woman asked.

"If I survive tonight, hopefully a little beach time before it's time to start all over again," Levi said.

"I'll be sure to save you a spot at the beach right beside me then," the woman said with a wink.

Levi was relieved to see Tina making her way back to the bar. "Welcome back, you have a live crew out here." Levi chuckled. "I'll be back later to check on you, but call if you need anything."

When Levi returned inside, she noticed they were running low on some items and went to the storeroom. She carried several bottles and placed them on the shelf under the bar and when she stood, she was looking into the smiling gray eyes of the sexy captain.

Vanessa smiled at Levi. "Hi, I am Vanessa Jones." She offered Levi her hand.

"Levi Johnson." She shook Vanessa's hand. "What may I get you, Captain?"

"Vanessa, will do just fine, and I think I will have another of your wonderful concoctions."

"Feel up to a tall one?"

"I think I can handle it."

Levi placed a frosty pilsner full of Tropical E in front of the captain. "Go easy, they are exceptionally potent tonight," Levi warned with a grin.

Vanessa lifted the glass to her lips and took a sip from the frozen drink. "You definitely have a winner on your hands here. This place is amazing." She looked around at the bar full of women.

"Yes, it is." Levi caught Liz waving from an upper deck booth. She held up three fingers and Levi poured three drinks and passed them over to Karen. "Karen, take these up to Liz, Nat, and Simone, please."

"Sure thing, Levi." Karen whisked off on her rollerblades.

"Smart lady to wear those in this crowd," Vanessa said.

"Survival of the fittest in this business," Levi said. "You adapt to the crowd or the crowd passes you by for another club."

"I can honestly say this is the best arrangement I have seen. You already had a crowd from the resort and now the cruise travelers double your business."

"Nat, Liz, and Simone are all brilliant businesswomen."

"Ah, speaking of which, I can feel the daggers in my back from Simone as I sit here innocently talking with you. Is there something between you two that I should know to protect myself from further harm?" Vanessa asked with a grin.

"I doubt that you would have any difficulty dealing with Simone. We had a brief encounter, but that's over."

"Well then, my boss is not as intelligent as I gave her credit to be."

"I guess I can be added to the list of Simone's conquests," Levi said with bitterness in her tone. "But that's a long story I would rather not get into tonight."

"How about tomorrow then," Vanessa asked.

"What?"

"How about you meet me tomorrow and I will give you a tour of the ship and you can tell me your long story," Vanessa said with a dashing smile.

"Why, Captain, are you asking me out on a date?"

"Well, I think it is only fair, Levi." Vanessa grinned.

"How is that?"

"My crew and I toured your resort so I think it is only fair that you offer me the same courtesy and come to tour the *Sappho One.*"

"Excuse me, Romeo," Karen said. "Do you think I could get a tray of TE shots while you chat up this lovely lady?"

"Are your staff always this pert?" Vanessa asked with a chuckle.

"Always, especially this one." Levi shot a wink to Karen.

"By the way, Romeo, I agree with the captain. I think you should go on her guided tour tomorrow." Karen picked up the tray of drinks and headed into the crowd.

Vanessa laughed heartily as Karen disappeared. "So we have a date then?"

"I have to work tomorrow afternoon, so it would have to be tomorrow morning."

"Tomorrow morning would be perfect, I am usually up by five," Vanessa said.

Levi laughed. "I am just getting to sleep by five, so how about nine instead?"

"Nine works."

Levi noticed NeNe was frantically waving at her from the DJ booth. NeNe flashed a high five signal to her and Levi nodded her head. "Do you dance, Captain?" she asked.

"Not well, but yes."

"Great, may I have the pleasure?" Levi stepped around the bar and reached for Vanessa's hand.

NeNe cranked the music up loud as "Mambo Number Five" brought the crowd alive and Levi led Vanessa to the dance floor. Levi gracefully guided Vanessa across the floor and, as had become the tradition, when she dipped Vanessa at the end of the song, she gently leaned down to brush Vanessa's lips with a soft kiss.

It was Vanessa's turn to be flustered as Levi stood her back on her feet as the crowd roared with applause. When they returned to the bar, Vanessa took up the stool and said, "I can see why Simone would pursue you."

"And you, have you been one of her conquests?" Levi asked.

Vanessa chuckled and shook her head. "I have been fortunate to have been blessed with the willpower to withstand Simone's womanly charms." Vanessa saw Levi flinch from her answer and immediately regretted the answer she gave. "I'm sorry if my comment upset you in any way."

"Not at all. I was just delusional in thinking we had something more."

"Simone was a fool to hurt you, Levi," Vanessa said. "I hope her actions have not jaded you to the possibility of someone falling for you. I think you are a very special woman and I hope you will allow me to get to know you this week. I am not a player and I will not try to seduce you as a conquest."

"Do you come with instructions?" Levi joked.

Vanessa smiled another of her totally disarming smiles. "You won't need instructions with me, I promise, Levi." Vanessa glanced into the mirror and saw Simone headed toward the bar. "You are about to have company. I will say goodnight now and I look forward to seeing you tomorrow."

"I look forward to the tour, Captain," Levi said as Simone sat beside Vanessa.

"Hello, Levi," Simone said.

"Hello, Simone."

"I see that you have met the dashing Captain Jones."

"Yes, I have, Simone, and she has promised me a personal tour of her ship tomorrow."

"Speaking of which, I had better return to make sure everything is in order for your visit tomorrow," Vanessa said with a wink. "It was a pleasure to meet you, Levi."

"The pleasure was mine." Levi smiled at Vanessa, who turned and walked away.

"I was hoping that maybe you and I could get together and talk tomorrow, Levi," Simone said as Levi watched Vanessa walk away.

"I'm sorry, Simone, I already have plans for tomorrow."

"Maybe Monday then. Nat says we need to take care of that coin and I want to do my best to make up for hurting you."

"Monday will be fine. I'll book a boat for the morning. We can replace the coin and be done with this curse forever. There is no need to make up with me, Simone. It was a hard lesson to learn, but surviving your actions has made me a stronger person."

"I never meant to hurt you, Levi, I love you so."

"That love walked out with you when you left the island without as much as a good-bye. But this is not the time or place to be discussing this."

"You're right, Levi, I will see you on Monday then." Simone spun on her heel and walked back to the booth to join Nat and Liz.

Chapter Twenty-one

The evening remained so busy that Levi did not have time to think about Simone or the enchanting Captain Jones. She knew she was vulnerable to a charming woman at this point and did not want to make the same mistakes she had with Simone. Vanessa was certainly a charmer, quite handsome and confident, not unlike Simone and yet very different. Still, Levi would have to remain on guard to protect her heart from another hurt so closely after Simone.

†

Vanessa stepped off the trolley and walked aboard her ship.

"Back so soon, Captain?" one of the young stewards asked.

"That place is packed with a wild crowd, Heather," Vanessa said. "I was ready for a little peace and quiet. What time do you get off duty?"

"In another thirty minutes," the young woman said with a smile.

"Don't worry. That crowd will be cranked for at least another three hours. I wouldn't be surprised if they have to toss them out at closing time. Will you do a favor for me and stop by my cabin before you go ashore?"

"Sure thing, Captain."

"Thanks, see you in a little while." Vanessa returned to her cabin and walked to her desk. She rummaged through charts and papers until she found an envelope and a notepad.

Dear Levi,

It was a great pleasure meeting you tonight and I look forward to your visit tomorrow. Congratulations on a successful first night. I hope the remainder of the week goes as smoothly. I have no idea of your work schedule, but it would be my honor if you'd be my guest at the beach feast Nat and Liz are hosting for my crew Wednesday evening. See you tomorrow.

With warm regards,

Vanessa

Vanessa folded the small sheet of paper and placed it inside an envelope before she reached for the cabin telephone. She called one of the onboard gift shops and asked to have a single sterling silver rose delivered. When the rose arrived, she placed it with the note to Levi. Was she being too corny? She wondered as she thought of the words she had written. What the hell, she would take a chance. A soft knock came to the door. She picked the rose and envelope and carried it to the door. Heather stood there, dressed in tan shorts and a green midriff top.

Vanessa handed the rose and note to the grinning steward. "Would you mind making a delivery for me?"

"Of course not, Captain. Who's the lucky lady?"

"A young bartender by the name of Levi. She's working in the main bar; I'm sure you'll know exactly which one she is. Just look for the crowd of women surrounding the bar." Vanessa chuckled.

"That's one lucky bartender."

"Thanks, Heather, I appreciate the favor. Now off with you. Go have some fun," Vanessa said as she walked from the cabin with the steward. Vanessa stood at the rail and watched Heather board the trolley and disappear into the darkness.

The night breeze was cool on the water and Vanessa allowed her fingers to trail down the smooth wooden railing as she walked the length of the deck. She had fallen in love with the ship the first time she had laid eyes on her and she took pride in the way her crew maintained the richly grained woods, plate glass, and metal. Vanessa stopped at the bow railing and gazed across the water, the image of the full moon glimmering on its surface.

†

Levi had walked out on the pier to catch a few minutes of fresh air. She, too, found herself drawn by the reflection of the full moon on the water, and for a moment, she lost herself in the peacefulness of the image. The door to the bar opened and Levi could hear the thumping bass of the music and it shattered the serene calm. Levi looked to her right and she could see the faint lights of the *Sappho One* twinkling against the dark night. Her mind drifted to Vanessa and her deep gray eyes that held her spellbound in her gaze. "Careful, Levi," she whispered to herself. Shaking her head she walked back to the club.

"Thanks for the break, Nat," Levi said as she returned to the bar. She noticed Simone was no longer sitting at the booth and Levi wondered where she had gone.

"No problem, Levi. Julie should be here soon to work out the remainder of the shift. Liz and I were thinking of stopping off for a midnight snack, if you would care to join us."

"Thanks, but I think I will hit the shower and get some rest tonight. It has been a long day."

"Yes, it has, and from the looks of your tip jar, I would say quite a profitable one too. If it stays like this, you will need to find an investment project. Looks like you have quite a few invitations in there as well. I hope you won't forget to have some fun," Nat said in her best motherly tone.

†

Heather pressed her way through the crowd to the head of the bar. "You must be Levi."

"Yes, I am, how may I help you?"

"I have something to deliver." Heather handed the single rose and envelope to Levi.

"Thank you." Levi accepted the young woman's offerings.

"What, another secret admirer?" Nat asked as Levi lifted the rose to her nose and then opened the card.

"From the captain," Levi said. "She has invited me for a tour of her ship in the morning and wants to know if I will join her Wednesday for your beach feast."

"Well, I just happen to know you are scheduled off that night, so I hope you tell the lovely captain yes."

"I just might at that." Levi smelled the fragrant rose again.

Julie walked up to the bar to relieve Levi. "Looks like a great night," she said.

"It has been insane tonight, Julie. You may have your hands full clearing this place out at closing time." Levi smiled as she emptied out her tip jar.

Levi exchanged several bills with Nat and, tucking her tips into her pocket, picked up her note and the rose and left the bar. Stopping just outside the pool Levi looked up at the sky. The stars blazed brightly in the night sky, brilliantly lit by the moon, the island seemed at peace.

When she reached her bungalow, Levi sat on the edge of the bed. She opened Vanessa's note and read it again before laying in on her nightstand and slipping from her clothes and walking to the shower. Levi knew that Simone would be up in the penthouse and probably not alone. She silently cursed the woman who had brought her senses alive, and then disappeared. She ached for the touch of Simone as the water caressed her skin. Levi was conflicted with emotion. She could go to Simone, forgive her for being such an ass, pick up where they left off, and risk being crushed again, or she could allow Vanessa a chance at getting to know her and start fresh. She turned the water off and dried her skin, pushing thoughts of both women as far from her mind as possible. The last thing Levi needed tonight was erotic dreams twisted between Simone and Vanessa. Levi slipped between her cool sheets and allowed the rhythmic thump of the fan to lull her to sleep.

✝

Vanessa entered the captain's cabin after walking the entire ship. She had begun her nightly walks early in her career as a lesson taught by her seafaring father. "You always want to make sure your ship in is tidy shape before you retire for the evening," she could still hear him saying. "Your ship is like a beautiful lady, Vanessa, and you must be sure to treat her right." Sadly, her father had died two years before Vanessa had taken charge of her first ship, but she knew he was watching over her and was proud of what she had accomplished. With pleasant memories of her father still present in her mind, Vanessa climbed between the sheets of her large bed and allowed the ever-gentle rocking of the ship to lead her into dreamland.

✝

Simone buried her hand in the hair of a dark-haired guest as the woman's tongue drove in and out of Simone's wetness. Simone was still seething over Vanessa making an approach on Levi and Levi's rebuke of her attempted apology. Her frustration followed her into bed and she was unable to appreciate the efforts of the young woman to bring her to climax. Completely frustrated, angry, and full of rage, Simone finally sent the disappointed woman on her way, then tossed and turned until her exhausted body collapsed for several hours of broken sleep. Her dreams were plagued by visions of Levi, the smile she wore while talking with Vanessa, and the various faces of women Simone had used to rid her mind of Levi. When she awoke the next morning with a start, her lips whispered Levi's name to a cold and empty room.

Chapter Twenty-two

Levi woke earlier than expected the next morning and decided to take a run along the beach. She slipped on running shorts and a short top before sliding into her most comfortable pair of running shoes. The staff was out cleaning the pool area and preparing for the morning crowd that would be surrounding the pool in an hour or so. Levi stretched her taut muscles and started down the walkway to the stairway leading to the beach.

As she stepped onto the crystal white sand, she was amazed to find the beach completely empty. Granted it was barely seven, but usually even by then someone was on the beach. Odd, but she set the thought aside as she took off at a slow jog across the sand washed clean by the morning's high tide. Hers were the first footprints of the day to penetrate the cool, wet sand. As she lengthened her stride and picked up her pace, Levi thought of nothing but the pounding of her heart and focused on the lighthouse miles ahead.

†

Fifteen minutes later, Simone stepped out on the beach. Levi's footprints were already disappearing in the surf. Her head throbbed, but she hoped a nice run would clear her muscles of the toxins she had so eagerly consumed. Her skin had already broken out in a sweat as she slowly began to jog.

†

Vanessa had been up for an hour and had walked the ship after dressing in another of her sharply pressed white uniforms. She walked into the main dining room and joined some of her staff for breakfast. "Good morning, ladies." She greeted them with a smile.

"Morning, Captain," came a chorus of less than well-rested voices.

"The usual, Captain?" a young server asked.

"Yes, please, Susan. Did you ladies have a good time last night?"

"I think it's safe to say a good time was had by all, Captain," reported Killian her first mate and most trusted staff. "I think more than half your officers closed the bar down this morning before returning home."

"Present company included?"

"Why yes, Captain. Someone had to make sure they all made it safely home."

"Good job, Killian, it looks like they all made it home, albeit some look like they could use a few more hours of sleep."

"Aye, Captain, I do believe as soon as the shift ends, more than a few will be napping," Killian answered with a grin.

"It should be an easy day, so try to get them off duty as soon as possible."

Susan returned with a fluffy omelet, juice, and coffee. "Here you go, Captain." She placed the plate in front of Vanessa.

"Thanks, Susan," Vanessa said before slicing off a bite of the omelet.

"I hear you have a special guest coming aboard for a tour this morning," Killian said.

"News travels quickly, I see, but yes, Levi Johnson is coming aboard."

"We will ensure everything is perfect then, Captain." Killian stood to leave the table.

"I would expect nothing less from you, Killian."

"I'll see you on the deck later then, my Captain." Killian left for morning inspections.

✝

Simone began noticing footprints in the sand in front of her as she ran. In the distance she could barely see the outline of a figure running toward her. The alcohol she had consumed last night was gushing out her pores as she plodded along the hard-packed shore. The figure appeared familiar as it drew closer and when she recognized Levi running toward her, she picked up the pace.

Levi saw Simone jogging in her direction, her skin already covered in sweat. She could not deny the physical attraction she still had for Simone, and the way her body reacted as they ran toward one another was an unwelcome reminder for Levi. She felt butterflies stirring in her stomach as she watched Simone's fluid movement through the humid morning.

Simone slowed and called to Levi as she approached. "Can we talk now, Levi?"

"Not now, Simone, I have an appointment to prepare for." Levi continued running, never slowing as she passed Simone.

Frustrated, Simone reversed her direction and ran after Levi. She used up a good portion of her remaining energy to catch Levi. "If not now, when?"

"I have a boat reserved for us at nine tomorrow morning," Levi said as she left Simone in her wake.

"Fine, see you at nine then." She groaned as she stopped and bent over, trying to catch her breath. Simone looked up in time to see Levi wave to her and then she disappeared from the beach.

✝

Vanessa waited for Levi at the small gangplank that served as a walkway between her ship and the concrete pier. She smiled as Levi approached and walked out to meet her. "Good morning, Levi."

"Good Morning, Captain."

"I am so happy you came this morning. I look forward to showing you the *Sappho One* when you are ready. Have you had breakfast?"

"Yes, I have."

"Shall we begin the tour then?"

"I'm all yours," Levi said to a widely grinning captain.

For the next hour and a half, Vanessa showed Levi every inch of the large ship from the huge galleys where the food was prepared to the engine rooms that provided all the power to the ship.

"This is simply amazing," Levi said as they walked the well-polished deck floor. "I have never seen a cruise ship so meticulously maintained. There is not even a lounge chair out of place."

"The crew is very well trained and takes great pride in their positions."

It was obvious the way Vanessa spoke of her crew and to them as they passed on the decks of the great ship that she was very proud of them. She called each and every one of them by name as they toiled in their work and each was wearing a broad smile and welcomed Levi aboard.

"They seem to be very proud of their captain too," Levi said.

Vanessa blushed slightly. "We all work very closely together as a team to ensure our guests have the best time possible."

Their tour had reached the bridge where they met Killian. "Good morning, Ms. Johnson, welcome to the *Sappho One*," she said as she shook Levi's hand.

"This lovely lady is Killian, my first mate, second in command here on the ship."

"Very nice to meet you, Killian," Levi said, returning the woman's smile.

With Vanessa's consent, Killian gave Levi the tour of the bridge, explaining the navigation charts and the equipment they used to sail the ship.

"All of this is so amazing." Levi began to realize how complicated it was to operate a ship of this size.

"Every crew member here has a specific duty to fulfill and when we all work together, the ship runs smoothly and efficiently," Killian explained. "Even when we are in port, the team has to work together to ensure guests are prepared for their excursions and the ship is maintained at ready status," she explained as they walked back toward the door. "Hopefully you will have a chance to sail with us in the future, Ms. Johnson, to experience the full amenities the ship has to offer."

"I would like that very much. Maybe in the fall when the island slows down a bit."

"Would you like to see some of the cabins?" Vanessa asked.

"That would be great."

Vanessa ushered Levi into a waiting elevator and went down two floors. Vanessa used her master key to open a sample of each type of stateroom for Levi to observe. Levi was amazed at the size of the rooms. Even the least luxurious rooms were amply furnished with plenty room for two guests. The penthouse suite was incredible with its wet bar and the private view it showed from the balcony that ran the length of the room. "This must cost a small fortune," Levi said.

"About six thousand for two guests. The typical guests who book this type of accommodations are successful businesswomen or a couple celebrating a honeymoon or other special occasion. They have their own private waitstaff and can have their meals privately served out on the balcony. They have champagne brunches and other special amenities that allow them the privacy and romantic encounter they desire."

Levi smiled. "Sounds heavenly."

"We rarely have complaints from a guest. If there is a problem on board, we deal with it quickly to resolve the issue." Vanessa closed the door behind them. "Sappho's philosophy is to have long-term guests who return frequently to cruise with us, and we have been successful with that goal so far."

"Very impressive," Levi said as she followed Vanessa down a hallway.

"I hope you don't mind, but I have arranged for lunch in my cabin."

"Not at all, your tour has worked up my appetite."

"That's good," Vanessa said. "One of our chefs has prepared a signature lunch for you."

Vanessa led Levi into a luxurious cabin, not quite as lush as the penthouse suite, but more than comfortable to meet the captain's needs. A large king-sized bed was the centerpiece of the room. Complemented with a workstation, Vanessa used the area to review the charts and files she'd arranged in organized stacks. It had a small dining room where lunch was waiting for them. They feasted on tender filet mignon and a lobster tail that was so flaky, the meat melted in Levi's mouth. The meal was complete with bananas Foster, served still flaming to the table by one of the kitchen staff. The meal was as incredible as the ship and when Levi finished off the dessert, she was pleasantly full. Vanessa took her over to a small sitting space where they enjoyed a rich blend of coffee.

Levi noticed a picture of a younger Vanessa and an older man, standing on the deck of a small fishing boat. "Your father?"

"Yes. I was raised in the Northeast. My father was a lobsterman and fisherman all his life." She smiled remembering the man she loved. "Every chance he could get, he took me out on the ocean with him. He instilled his love for the water so deeply in me there was no other choice of a career for me. After a short stint in the Coast Guard, I went to school and obtained my captain's license and I began sailing private yachts for customers. It was on such a vessel that I met Simone, and she offered me a position sailing *Sappho One*. That was nearly two years ago, and I could never ask for a better job

"May I be bold and ask again about the relationship between you and Simone?" Vanessa asked. "I felt her eyes stabbing in my back last night as we talked, but I have a sense from you the attraction is one sided."

"Simone came to the island and swept me off my feet. We shared a very special relationship for several days and I was feeling that we had a solid future, until she disappeared in the middle of the night after my accident." Levi raised her plaster-encased arm.

"What happened to your arm?"

"Simone and I had chartered a small boat to do some island hopping. While on one of the islands, we got caught by a freak storm and we took shelter in a cave." Levi thought back to that day and she could see herself reach down to pick up the cursed coin. "I was searching for firewood when I found a small gold coin that I slipped inside my suit for safekeeping. After the storm had passed we were rescued and returned to the resort." Levi paused in her story to sip the rich-smelling coffee. "The next morning I went down to my room for clean clothes and a shower and when I was showering I slipped on the bar of soap I had dropped and hit my arm on the shower wall."

"That must have really hurt," Vanessa said.

"It did. After struggling to get dressed I went downstairs and Nat and Simone took me to the hospital, and it was there that Simone started acting strangely. She was rude to the hospital staff and to Nat. When we returned to the resort, Nat and Liz cared for me while Simone carried on with her partying." Levi sighed. "It was all very strange, but Simone ended up leaving the island very early one morning without a word of good-bye." Levi paused again in her story. "After Simone left, we found out from one of the housekeeping staff that the coin I had found is supposedly cursed, and the curse could only be broken by returning the coin to where I found it. I had to wait until Simone came back to the island, because she has to be with me when the coin is returned."

"That is an incredible story, but based on what Simone has told me it sounds true," Vanessa said.

"What do you mean?"

"Simone flew into Cancun to meet us in port there. We'd had a small accident. During bad weather we hit some hidden reefs as we approached and had to spend an extra day and a half in port for repairs."

Levi had known about that from Nat but was startled by what Vanessa said next. "Then, as she was flying from Greece, her jet was struck by lightning and they had to make an emergency landing. It sounds like your curse has affected Simone more than she cares to admit."

"I have a charter boat reserved for tomorrow, so hopefully we can put the coin back to rest and break this curse before someone gets seriously hurt."

"I hope so too," Vanessa said with a warm smile.

Levi looked at her watch and was amazed at how quickly the time had slipped away. "Thank you for a beautiful morning, but I need to go back to the resort to get ready for work."

"It's been my pleasure. Have you considered my invitation to the beach feast?"

"I would love to be your guest," Levi said as she stood. "Thank you also for the flower and such a lovely meal."

"You are most welcome, I will send your compliments to the chef."

"Will I see you tonight?" Levi asked as they walked to the elevator that would take them to the gangplank.

"You can be assured you will see me tonight."

As Levi reached solid ground again, she turned and softly kissed Vanessa's cheek. "Thanks again for a wonderful morning."

"See you later," Vanessa said and watched Levi walk to the waiting trolley. When she turned she looked up to find the crew watching her from the bridge, grinning and appearing to be cheering. Vanessa shook her head and returned to her station.

Chapter Twenty-three

On her way to work, Levi walked past the pool packed with resort and cruise ship guests, smiling and waving at several women who called to her. The sun was still shining brightly and she had to stand at the door of the bar for a minute while her eyes adjusted to the lighting inside. She looked around and was amazed at the size of the crowd that had gathered so early in the afternoon.

She and Karen kept the crowd hydrated as NeNe cranked up the music and the dance floor swarmed with dancers. Levi hardly had time to think of her morning as the crowd kept her busy at the bar, but she could not resist looking toward the door each time it opened, searching for Vanessa.

"Waiting on someone special, Romeo?" Karen teased as she caught Levi looking at the door.

"Maybe, maybe not." Levi grinned.

"Personally, I hope it is that ship's handsome captain," Karen said, causing Levi to blush. "Ah, so it is her, great choice." Karen laughed as she picked up a tray of drinks and skated off.

Another hour expired before a group of the ship's officers entered the bar with Vanessa in the center of the group. She and Killian walked to the bar as the rest went in search of a table.

"Good evening, Captain," Levi said. "Good to see you again, Killian."

"Good evening, Levi," Vanessa and Killian said in unison.

Levi took the opportunity to give Vanessa the once-over as they exchanged greetings. Vanessa looked completely delicious in jeans and a dark blue oxford shirt. She had her sleeves rolled partially up her arms and looked very casual and relaxed. "What can I get you ladies?"

"For starters, how about a dozen tall Tropical Es," Vanessa said.

"Coming up." Levi began to pour the drink and set them on a tray. Before she could place the last of the drinks on the tray, Vanessa took it from her hand. With a nod to Levi, Killian took the tray and headed for the table of her crewmates.

"Would you mind if I sit at the bar with you for a while?" Vanessa asked as she handed Levi a credit card.

"Not at all, I would enjoy your company. This round is on me."

"Thank you, Levi, but will you start a tab for me? Trust me, the natives are thirsty and restless, so I'm sure they will keep you busy tonight."

"Very well." Levi scanned Vanessa's card and returned it to the handsome captain.

Vanessa took a sip from her drink. "I sure hope Nat and Liz are giving you a percentage of this incredible drink's sale."

"A quarter each sale. I feel slightly guilty taking a salary from them with the great tips and a cut of the TE sales."

"Don't feel guilty, you are the hot commodity here, Levi, and business would not be nearly as good if not for you. I'm certain Nat and Liz will do anything they can to keep you happy."

"I am happy here."

"With all this money you are raking in here, you should consider some investments. What are your dreams of the future, Ms. Johnson?"

"If you had asked me three weeks ago that would have been an easy question to answer. I came to the island with the intention of having a summer of fun. Then I was going to be off to New York or Boston to seek my career in finance, and a good woman to share my life with."

"What has changed that dream?"

"I think seeing the success Nat and Liz have had with the resort has really made me think," Levi said. "Why should I spend my career making money for others when I could be making it for myself? With the right idea and the start-up capital, I'm sure I could be successful as well."

"Do you have that idea yet?" Vanessa asked.

"I have been toying with a few ideas, but haven't settled on one plan yet. What about you, Captain, what are your plans to spend all the money Simone is paying you?"

"Well, I have my dad's insurance money, and the profit from the sale of his fishing business tucked away in investments, but like you, the right opportunity hasn't surfaced yet. So for now, I am content to continue working for Simone, who, after all is said and done, has treated me fairly."

"Like her sister, Simone knows a good thing when she sees it." Levi intended her comment to be a compliment.

"Obviously not, or she wouldn't have treated you the way she did." Vanessa immediately regretted her rash comment. "I'm sorry, Levi, that was foolish of me to say."

"No, Vanessa, it was an honest opinion and you are right. If she were as smart as I give her credit for, she would have done things very differently."

"I hope her behavior does not jade you against love."

"Not a chance." Levi laughed.

"Great," Vanessa said. "I would hate to see that happen to such an incredible woman."

Levi blushed and turned away from Vanessa. An idea popped into Levi's mind. "Excuse me for a minute, please," Levi said before she walked over to the telephone. "Liz, this is Levi. May I borrow your bike Tuesday?"

"Of course, Levi, you can take the bike anytime. Just stop by and pick up the keys when you want."

"Thanks, Liz." Levi hung up the telephone. Returning to where Vanessa was sitting at the bar, she asked, "Do ship's captains get a day off?"

"I think I could spare a day, what did you have in mind?"

"Tomorrow Simone and I have to take care of the coin business, but I'm off on Tuesday. Liz has a Harley and has promised to loan it to me if you would like to spend the day doing some exploring on the island."

"I can't think of a better way to spend a day off."

"It's a date then, I'll pick you up at the ship at nine, if that's a good time for you."

"That would be perfect but are you sending me on my way now?"

"Actually," Levi shot a wink to Karen, "I was about to ask you to dance."

"Will you take over for me for a short break, Karen?"

"Take all the time you need, Levi," Karen said with a grin.

"Would you care to dance then, Vanessa?"

"I would love to, Levi."

NeNe saw them walking across the floor and switched tempos to a slow song as they stepped onto the dance floor. Levi took Vanessa in her arms as the music pulsed slowly through the bar. Vanessa's body felt incredible to Levi and she allowed herself to rest her head on Vanessa's shoulder as they moved to the music. Vanessa's warmth and the movement of her hips so close to hers made Levi's pulse race. As much as she tried to fight her attraction to Vanessa, Levi could not deny the woman made the blood rush through her veins with the heat of molten lava.

Vanessa's hands moved down Levi's back, pulling her close as Levi's lips brushed softly against her neck. It took great restraint to stifle the moan trapped deep inside her as Levi kissed up her neck. "You are on dangerous ground, Levi," Vanessa whispered a warning in her ear.

Levi chuckled softly and was about to speak when Vanessa lifted her head and kissed her. Surprised by Vanessa's action, Levi relaxed and allowed Vanessa's tongue to part her lips and swirl around her tongue. Vanessa was fueling a fire that had lain dormant until Simone had brought it to life. The desire Levi was feeling made her tremble in Vanessa's arms. The kiss remained soft and sensual throughout their slow dance and when the music ended, they stood together for a moment, searching one another's eyes.

†

Simone had joined Nat and Liz in their booth before Levi and Vanessa left the bar to dance. She seethed with rage now as she watched the exchange between Levi and Vanessa on the dance floor, barely able to contain her anger.

Sitting across from Simone, Nat watched Simone's eyes follow Levi on the dance floor. "You had your chance, Simone, and blew it. Now let her be," she said in a stern tone to her sister.

Simone's angry eyes flashed at Nat. "I have no intention of letting her go that easy."

"You had better prepare yourself for a fight then. Vanessa appears to have Levi's favor at the moment and I doubt she will be foolish enough to turn her back on her," Liz said, further driving her words home.

"We'll see about that." Simone left the table and headed to the dance floor.

Chapter Twenty-four

Simone reached the bar just before Levi and Vanessa returned, taking over the barstool Vanessa had vacated. "I'm going to go check on the crew, Levi," Vanessa said.

"I'll see you in a bit then." Levi slipped behind the bar.

"You two seem to be hitting it off well," Simone said as calmly as she could. She was still seething with jealousy, but knew that showing it would accomplish nothing other than turn Levi off.

"Vanessa is an amazing woman." Levi watched her interact with her staff. She could not help but smile when Vanessa looked up and caught her eye.

"Yes, that she is. Vanessa has been a big hit with the ladies too."

"I can only imagine," Levi said, artfully dodging the spite in Simone's voice. "I would think that she would be fantastic to any woman who was lucky enough to catch her fancy. May I get you something to drink?"

"A scotch on the rocks please."

"Yes ma'am, coming up." Levi busied herself preparing the drink.

"So what is it that we must do tomorrow to break this silly curse?" Simone asked as Levi set the drink down in front of her.

"We have to return it to the island and I have to bury it where I originally found it."

"Then will all this bloody curse nonsense be over?"

"I sure hope so, Simone."

"Will everything go back to the way it was before, Levi?"

"I think we will both be released to move forward with our lives, Simone."

"I was hoping that we could go back to the way we were, that you would be in love with me again."

"Simone, I will always love you, but I realized when you left, we weren't in love with each other. To try to force that would be a huge mistake."

Angered by Levi's rejection, Simone reached across the bar and grabbed Levi's arm. "You know you still want me, Levi, so quit playing games, and tell me what I have to buy you to win you back."

Levi pulled her arm from Simone's grasp. "That's just the point, Simone, you can't and never could buy my love. I don't function like that."

✝

Vanessa saw Simone grab Levi's arm and stood to bolt across the room. Killian placed her hand on Vanessa's shoulder. "Wait a minute. Give Levi a chance to handle this alone."

Vanessa sat back down, but continued to watch the exchange closely. The rest of the table also watched the interaction between Levi and Simone and threatened to break out in applause when Levi pulled away from Simone. "See, Levi is doing just fine, Captain," Killian said.

"Yeah, I guess so. But she is only getting five more minutes with Levi then I'm going back down there," Vanessa said rather stubbornly.

Killian chuckled. "Levi has really gotten to you, hasn't she, boss?"

Vanessa looked at Killian and smiled. "I guess I'm acting a little overprotective."

"Just a little. May I buy you a drink, Captain?"

"That would be lovely." Killian picked up the tray and filled it with empty glasses.

"I'll be right back then," she said with a grin.

She walked down to the bar. "How about another round please, Levi?" Killian said. "Those drinks of yours go down so easy, I'm afraid we'll keep you very busy tonight."

"That's fine with me, Killian."

"Good evening, Ms. Taylor," Killian said. "How are you tonight?"

"I'm doing well, thank you, Killian, and yourself?" Simone managed to say.

"I'm fantastic and enjoying the island immensely. The guests really seem to be enjoying themselves as well." She nodded toward a group on the dance floor.

"So it seems." Simone took another sip of her drink.

"It may be hard to get some of them back on the ship when it is time to leave the island." Killian chuckled.

"You could be right, Killian," Levi said. "I would certainly do a close head count before you depart."

"I hear you may be cruising with us later this fall." Killian grinned as she noticed Simone's posture stiffen.

"I may indeed." Levi placed the last of the drinks on the tray and handed it back to her.

"Thanks, Levi." Killian took the tray and walked back to the table.

"Just let me know when you are ready to take a cruise and I will make sure you have the best of everything," Simone offered.

"Thanks, Simone, but I think I can do that on my own."

"Suit yourself." Simone spun around on the barstool and walked back to where Nat and Liz were sitting in the booth.

"Welcome back, sis," Nat said as Simone took a seat. "What's wrong?"

"Levi is just being a total bitch."

"Did you really expect Levi to bow down to you with forgiveness just because you came back?" Liz asked.

Simone shot Liz a look of pure hatred. "Well, considering we have both been cursed, I was hoping for a little more compassion for my actions from Levi."

"Oh, so now you admit you believe in the curse?" Nat teased.

"What else could it be?" Simone said rather blandly.

"Maybe it could be you are finally getting a dose of your own medicine, Simone," Nat said. "For years you have been treating women badly and maybe your karma has caught up with you."

"Very funny." Simone stood and walked to the dance floor, joining a small group dancing.

Seeing the barstool vacant once again, Vanessa left the table where her crew sat and returned to the bar.

"Welcome back."

"Did you miss me?"

"As a matter of fact, I did." Levi smiled.

"You are off duty at midnight correct?"

"Yes, I am. Why?"

"I was hoping that maybe if I hung around until then that you and I could take a walk on the beach."

"I would really like that, Vanessa. Listen, it's almost time for our dinner break, would you care for anything?"

"No, we had a big meal on the ship before we came to the resort, but thanks."

"If you will excuse me, then, I'll order dinner and be right back then." She called NeNe in the booth, and then called the kitchen to order dinner for Karen, NeNe, and herself.

"Order something good?" Vanessa asked when Levi returned to the bar.

"The kitchen makes the most sinful bacon cheeseburger," Levi said with a grin.

"Sounds delicious."

Killian and the crew walked up to the bar and she grabbed Vanessa by the hand. "Come on, Captain, you have been elected to dance with us," Killian said with a wild laugh.

165

"Save my seat," Vanessa hollered as her crew dragged her onto the dance floor.

Levi watched them surround Vanessa. It was obvious how well loved Vanessa was by her staff. Twirled, and dipped by several of them, they danced in a tight group around her. When Vanessa escaped ten minutes later, she returned to the bar breathless and still laughing at her crew.

"Sweet Jesus," she wiped sweat from her brow with a napkin, "that bunch will wear you out if you let them."

"It's obvious how much they adore you, Vanessa."

"I admit I'm a little attached to them too. Besides being a great crew they are also some wonderful women," she added with an affectionate smile as she looked back at them still dancing wildly.

The tray from the kitchen arrived with dinner. "I'll head back to the table and let you enjoy your meal. See you at midnight." Vanessa walked back to the table where the crew was slowly returning from the dance floor.

Karen and NeNe noted the arrival of the food and made their way to the bar.

"I'm starved," Karen said as she rolled up and took a seat next to NeNe.

"That makes two of us," NeNe said.

"Let's make it unanimous," Levi added with a chuckle.

†

After they finished their meals, Levi began cleaning up the bar, wiping down equipment and stocking the coolers in preparation for Julie to come in and finish out the shift. Julie arrived early, allowing Levi to check out and walk over to the table where the cruise ship staff was sitting.

"Pardon me, ladies. Your captain has promised me a walk on the beach, and I have come to collect," Levi said with a grin.

"Don't forget your way home, Captain," Killian teased as Vanessa stood.

"Don't worry about me. You just make sure this lot makes it back safely."

"Goodnight then, ladies," Levi said and they left the bar.

Chapter Twenty-five

Levi and Vanessa walked to the steps leading down to the beach. They sat down to remove their shoes, and Vanessa rolled her jeans to mid-calf, then slipped their shoes under a stair step and began their walk down the beach. Vanessa reached over and took Levi's hand as they walked in silence, enjoying the quiet serenity of the empty beach. The moon shone over the water, reflecting across the small waves that brought whitecaps rushing to shore.

They shuffled their feet in the white sand and laughed at the sparks of phosphorescence that ignited during their steps. They walked down the beach until they reached an area where someone had taken great pains in creating a sand sculpture of the *Sappho One*. Levi and Vanessa sat down on the soft sand to admire the artist's work.

"That is a beautiful rendition," Vanessa said. "It makes me regret that I didn't bring a camera."

"It is quite realistic isn't it?"

"All the way down to the small portholes on the lower decks," Vanessa said. "I wonder if the artist is one of my crew. There is so much detail it had to be created by someone with intimate knowledge of a cruise ship."

"You're probably right. So much love was put into this piece and it's a shame that when the tide comes in it will be washed away to remain only a memory." She cocked her head at Vanessa. "That does give me an idea though."

"I'm listening," Vanessa said.

"Why don't we have a sand sculpture contest as one of the beach activities?"

"That is an excellent idea."

"I bet we could convince Nat to donate a hundred dollar bar tab to the victor."

"I'll check with Simone to see what she is willing to donate as well. We have a penthouse vacant, so maybe if the guest is a passenger with us, they could receive an upgrade for the voyage home. If it is a resort guest, then they could be given a free upgrade to join us on a future cruise," Vanessa said, the wheels of her imagination turning.

The moon shone down on the sculpture and the small portholes were alight with moonlight, bringing the ship to life. It was an amazing visual and Levi was happy to be sharing this moment with Vanessa.

"Are you ready for tomorrow?" Vanessa asked.

"I'm ready for this whole ordeal to be over. I hope the trip goes smoothly and we can be back at the resort by noon."

"I can be available for moral support if nothing else."

"That is very sweet of you to say, Vanessa, but this is something I must do with Simone. I would love to have you with me, but we have very specific instructions to follow."

"Would you mind if I was waiting for you upon your return then?"

"Not at all. I'll treat you to lunch in town if you would."

"I would like that very much," Vanessa said with a warm smile.

Silence fell around them like a curtain as they smiled at one another. Levi's squeal broke the quiet when the incoming tide reached her feet, surprising her. Vanessa began laughing and Levi pushed her back onto the sand.

"Think that was funny, do you?" Levi asked as she leaned over Vanessa.

"Why, yes ma'am, I do," Vanessa said as she started to get up off the sand.

Levi pushed her back down. She grinned as she lowered her head until she was inches from Vanessa's lips. "I don't hear you laughing now," Levi whispered before she placed her lips on Vanessa's.

Vanessa parted her lips, enticing Levi's tongue to enter her mouth. Her arms encircled Levi and pulled her down until their bodies were touching as their tongues danced sensually. The oncoming tidewater and the sand sculpture forgotten as their bodies melted together in the soft beach sand.

Levi's body soared with desire for Vanessa and she was certain from the soft moans vibrating in her mouth that Vanessa was feeling the same. Her skin burned with a need to be naked next to Vanessa. She broke their kiss. "Have you ever been skinny-dipping, Vanessa?"

"Yes, but not since I was a teen."

"Come with me then." They brushed the sand from their clothing, and Levi took Vanessa's hand, leading her to the path that would take her to the waterfall.

When they reached the source of the sound of water, Levi guided Vanessa to the large flat rock. Her fingers manipulated the buttons on Vanessa's shirt until one by one, they came undone and the shirt fell open. Her fingertips brushed across Vanessa's heated skin as she removed first her shirt, then her bra. Vanessa took her jeans off while Levi removed her uniform. Reaching for Vanessa's hand, she led them through the pool toward the cool flow of water falling from the cliff above and pulled Vanessa into her arms.

Their mouths melded together as their hands explored one another. Hard nipples brushed together as fingers teased and nails scratched slowly over hypersensitive skin. Levi shuddered with desire and Vanessa pulled her close.

"Are you all right?"

"I am more than all right. I want you so badly, Vanessa," Levi spoke softly between groans as Vanessa's hands fondled her ass.

They made their way back to the flat rock. Vanessa draped a leg between Levi's thighs and pressed her hips into Levi. Their mouths joined in a heated kiss as they lay back on the rock. Vanessa caressed Levi's skin, working slowly down between her trembling thighs, her fingertips gently probing between her hot soaked lips. Levi whimpered as Vanessa's fingers stroked lightly across her throbbing clit while their tongues continued their seductive dance.

Levi reached down between Vanessa's legs to find she was equally wet. It was Vanessa's turn to moan as Levi's fingers teased her hard clit. Vanessa's fingers parted Levi's lips and two fingers penetrated her. Levi mimicked her movement and entered Vanessa. Fingers stroked and bodies rocked together as Vanessa and Levi approached the apex of pleasure and, with perfect timing, the two lovers came together in a rush of passion, leaving them breathless and trembling in one another's arms.

✝

The moonlight illuminated the lovers' bodies as they lay quietly together. Simone, who had been watching them from a distance, silently slipped into the dark night. The vision of Vanessa and Levi danced before her eyes, making her quiver with excitement. She needed to find a lover of her own for the night.

Simone's timing was excellent. As she walked back into the bar, a redhead she had been dancing with earlier was standing to leave for the night. Simone gave the woman her best smile. "Would you like to spend the night with me?"

The woman, enthralled by Simone's charms and her beauty, gratefully accepted Simone's invitation.

They walked into the resort just as Levi and Vanessa climbed up the stairs from the beach.

"Would you stay with me tonight?" Levi asked.

"I would love to, Levi, but my commitment to the ship demands that I be onboard. Why don't you pack a bag and spend the night with me? I promise I will wake you and see that you have an excellent breakfast before you have to meet Simone."

Levi thought about the suggestion and then remembered the cursed coin resting beneath her mattress. "I would have to bring the coin onboard and I will not chance that."

"Tomorrow night then," Vanessa said.

"Most definitely, tomorrow night."

Levi walked with Vanessa to the trolley stop and they shared a slow kiss as they waited for the trolley to arrive.

"I will see you tomorrow at the harbor then," Vanessa said as she stepped onto the trolley.

"Goodnight, Captain." Levi winked and turned to walk back into the resort as the trolley pulled away.

Chapter Twenty-six

The next morning Levi awoke to a brilliant red sunrise. She remembered the old saying "Red skies at night sailor's delight, red sky at morning sailors take warning." She hoped the weather would hold off long enough for her and Simone to make it back from the island. She was looking forward to ending the curse and even more excited about having lunch with Vanessa.

Levi carefully lifted her mattress and reached for the bag that held the cursed gold coin. She could feel the warmth of the coin through the fabric as she stuffed it into her pocket. Levi did not want to look at the coin any more than necessary, but felt drawn to touch and hold the coin. Pushing the temptation aside, Levi picked up a light jacket and headed down to meet the trolley.

†

Simone was already waiting for Levi when she arrived.

"Good morning, Levi."

"Good morning." Simone looked like she had barely slept and Levi knew what would have kept her up all night. She pushed the thought away. The last thing she wanted to think about this morning was Simone tangled in sweaty sheets with someone else.

The trolley pulled up to the station and Levi followed Simone on board. Levi looked out across the water, a concerned

173

look on her face. "I hope we can beat this weather." She nodded toward the growing cloudbanks.

Simone turned to look at the clouds. Maybe they would get to the island and get caught up in another storm, she hoped, just like the last time. It would be all too ironic, she thought, and Levi would not be able to resist her attempts to seduce her.

✝

At the harbor, Levi went into the harbormaster's office to get the keys to the boat she had rented. "How long will we have before this weather hits?" she asked.

"I would guess about three hours." He handed Levi the key.

"Plenty of time to get there and back," Levi said.

"Should be, if you don't get distracted." He glanced to Simone.

Levi chuckled. "Not this time." She turned and walked out to where Simone was waiting.

They boarded the boat and after a few minutes were on their way to the island. As soon as Levi cleared the no wake zone, she opened up the throttle and steered for the island. "The wind feels great blowing through my hair," she said, then added, "I can understand why Vanessa loves her life on the sea."

Simone watched Levi. Good God you are gorgeous, even though you have snubbed my return to the island, I still want you so badly.

Levi turned to her and smiled, her eyes sparkling with joy as they sped across the water and Simone wondered what Levi was thinking.

✝

Levi couldn't help but think back on the first time she and Simone had traveled to the island. It was a completely blissful day,

174

even when they were trapped by the weather. A smile played on her lips as she thought about the way they had made love under the warm sun and then later in the hot spring inside the cave. When she turned to look at Simone, she knew there was still a spark of that desire glimmering through all the hurt Simone had caused her.

Simone returned her smile and Levi felt butterflies in her stomach. She turned her attention back to the water ahead and tried to force the image of a naked Simone from her mind.

As the island grew near, Levi searched for the exact spot they had landed before. She remembered Liz's warning that everything needed to be the same as it was before, the same people involved and the same locations visited in order to remove the curse. Levi concentrated on remembering the exact spot where she found the coin.

Levi steered the boat into the small harbor area and this time made certain the anchor was firmly in place before she jumped overboard and helped Simone into the water. They waded to shore and found the path that led them into the island. They walked the same footpath past the small pool and headed directly into the cave.

Simone reached for Levi's hand and was surprised when Levi did not immediately pull away from her touch. They walked in silence through the entrance to the cave, each lost in their own memories.

"You need to walk through the tunnel to where the hot spring is," Levi said. "I have to locate the spot where I found the coin and when I'm finished I will come get you and this curse business will be done."

"I'll be waiting." Simone dropped Levi's hand and walked into the tunnel.

Levi sat on a small boulder and concentrated on remembering the location. She remembered her search for firewood and seeing the glint of the coin as it caught her eye. When she was sure she had the spot, Levi opened her eyes and walked across the cave. Digging a small hole with a piece of driftwood she reached into her pocket to retrieve the coin. She opened the small pouch and poured the coin into her palm. The warmth of the coin on her skin felt comforting. Unable to resist the draw of the coin she picked it up and rolled it between her fingers. It would be so easy just to slip it back into her pocket. No one would be the wiser, she thought as the coin glowed in her eyes. Levi was about to put the coin in her pocket when a sharp pain ran through her injured wrist. Levi was startled by the sudden sharp pain—her wrist hadn't hurt for days—but it reminded her of the reason she was on the island, to end the curse. With her fingers noticeably shaking, Levi knelt and dropped the shiny coin in the hole she had dug and covered it with the soil from the cave. For a moment, she contemplated placing a rock over the hole, but did not veer from the plan. With the coin gone from sight, Levi stood and walked toward the tunnel.

†

Simone reached the hot spring and couldn't resist taking a dip in the warm water. She stripped off her clothing and waded into the water. She was floating on her back when Levi walked from the mouth of the tunnel into the small clearing.

Levi saw Simone's naked body floating on the water and stopped in her tracks. Her memory had not played a trick on her. Simone was just as beautiful as she remembered and the stirring in her body increased.

Simone spotted Levi standing at the edge of the pool. "Won't you join me one last time?" she purred.

Levi started to undress then realized that if she entered the pool, she would again fall into the trap of Simone's seduction. "I don't think so, Simone. You enjoy yourself, but I'll wait outside for you." Levi heard Simone's soft laughter echoing in the tunnel as she walked quickly away from the hot spring.

Minutes later, Levi turned at the sound of footsteps and saw Simone walking toward her. Her hardened nipples outlined by her damp shirt and the soft sway of her hips lured Levi, but her willpower again resisted the enchantment of the seductress walking toward her.

They walked back to the boat in silence, Levi pleased the deed was done and Simone quieted by Levi's rejection of her advances.

✝

Vanessa stood on the deck of *Sappho One* and watched as a small boat appeared on the horizon. She hoped it was Levi and Simone returning without incident. As the boat drew closer, Vanessa left the ship and headed for the pier to meet Levi. Levi was securing the mooring lines as Vanessa stepped onto the pier. She watched Levi offer a hand to help Simone from the boat. Simone took Levi's hand and as she stepped onto the pier, she took Levi in her arms in a passionate kiss. Shocked into inaction, a few moments passed before Levi gently took Simone's arms and stepped back from her kiss.

Vanessa stopped a few yards away and decided to let Levi deal with Simone. The breeze carried Levi's words to her.

"It is all over now, Simone. What we had was nothing more than the brief fling it turned out to be, and now I am moving on." Levi walked away, leaving Simone standing in shock on the pier.

Vanessa waited at the end of the pier and Levi's pace quickened as she walked toward the handsome captain. Vanessa smiled and when their eyes met, Levi's heart melted. She gave Vanessa a soft kiss. "It is so good to see you." She took Vanessa's hand and they walked off the pier and dropped the keys at the harbormaster's office.

"Did everything go well for you?"

"Very smoothly, thank you." As they turned onto a sidewalk, Levi glanced back to see Simone still standing at the end of the pier glaring at them before they disappeared behind a building.

"I was beginning to worry about the weather," Vanessa said as they walked.

"I was too. I'm glad we made it back before this storm comes on land. Are you hungry?"

177

"I'm starving," Vanessa said.

They went to a small diner and feasted on seafood platters as they watched the storm approach the island. As they stepped outside the diner the first raindrops began to fall. Vanessa looked at Levi and grinned. "My place?"

Levi reached for her hand and they laughed as they ran toward the cruise ship and stepped on board just as the skies opened up and the rain began in earnest. "Welcome aboard, Ms. Johnson." Levi looked up to see Killian smiling at them.

"Thanks Killian, how are you?"

"I'm great thanks and yourself?"

"I'm wonderful."

"Are we prepared for the storm?" Vanessa asked.

"All secure, Captain. The weather reports say this will pass in an hour or so."

"Very well then, we will be in my cabin if anything comes up."

"Yes, Captain."

Vanessa walked Levi into her cabin and removed the jacket from her shoulders. Levi stepped toward Vanessa and wrapped her arms around her as their mouths melded together in a kiss. The rain pelted the ship's portholes as Vanessa undressed them. She and Levi made love to the sounds of the storm raging outside her window. The cries of their lovemaking were lost in the wailing of the winds, and the rumble of thunder as the ship rocked them through wave after wave of pleasure. Sated, they collapsed in one another's arms and slept.

Chapter Twenty-seven

Levi awoke, startled to find that she had less than an hour to return to the resort, shower, and dress for work. She crept from the bed and dressed before she bent down and kissed Vanessa awake.

"I'll see you later I hope."

"You can bet I'll be at the resort later. Have a great afternoon, Levi." Vanessa attempted to sit up on the bed.

Levi put a hand on her shoulder and stopped her. "Relax for a while and let Killian run things for a bit."

With a final soft kiss, Levi left the cabin and the ship, managing to catch a trolley just as it was about to pull off. She looked down at her wrist again and smiled at how quickly the afternoon had flown by.

Levi walked into the bar to find Nat relaxing beside Liz on a barstool.

"Has it been a quiet afternoon?" she asked.

"It has been slow for the last hour or so. How did your morning go?"

"The coin is back where it should be."

"How did things go with Simone?" Liz asked.

"She tried to entice me into the hot spring with her, and she kissed me when we returned, but I told her that we were done once and for all."

Nat sensed Levi was on the verge of saying something else, but thought better of speaking her mind. "What else, Levi?"

Levi hesitated for a moment. "I know it may seem odd, but I almost feel sorry for Simone."

"Why's that, Levi?" Nat asked.

"She looked so dejected when I left her standing on the end of the pier. It made me sad for her."

"Simone was overdue for a reality check," Nat said. "I know she is my sister and I love her dearly, but she must learn she can't treat people the way she treated you."

"I know you're right, Nat, but still, I hate knowing that my actions hurt her."

"That is the biggest difference between the two of you," Liz said. "You care about hurting others and she only thinks of her own feelings."

"Until Simone learns that lesson I'm afraid she would have continued to hurt you time and again," Nat said.

"You're probably right, Nat." Levi wiped a towel across the bar counter. "I can't help but wonder what would have happened if I hadn't found the coin."

"In many ways I think finding it was a blessing," Liz said. "The curse allowed you to see who Simone really was and not the fantasy image of the woman she wanted you to see. You are a smart and caring woman, Levi, and you would have eventually seen through Simone to what she is really like. The coin kept it from dragging on for months."

"What I have seen from the two of you interacting together, I would say that you and Vanessa are growing close," Nat said. "You know, if I weren't so in love with Liz, I just might be tempted to chase after that handsome captain myself." Nat giggled.

Liz reached over and punched Nat in the shoulder playfully. "What makes you think the captain would have the likes of you?"

Levi roared with laughter at the shocked look on Nat's face.

"Dear Lord, Levi, please don't encourage Liz with your laughter or I won't hear the end of this all night," Nat said with a wink.

"Yes, boss." She tried but struggled to quell her laughter.

"Are you still planning to take her island hopping on the bike tomorrow?" Liz asked.

"Yes, I am, if that is still good with you."

"Just drop by for the keys when you are ready."

"Thanks." Levi turned to fill an order for Karen.

"We are going to have some dinner, but will probably be back later," Nat said as she and Liz stood.

"Have a great dinner you two." Levi handed Karen a tray of drinks.

†

Levi kept busy making an inventory of supplies at the bar while business was slow. She made a note of what supplies she needed and was loading the cooler with bottles of beer when she looked up to see Simone sitting at the bar.

"I'm sorry, Simone, I didn't hear you come up."

"No problem, Levi, I was enjoying watching you work," Simone said with a warm smile.

"What may I get you to drink?"

"I think it's time for a tall Tropical E. That's still my favorite drink."

"Coming up then."

Levi set the drink in front of Simone and, for a moment, looked into Simone's eyes, wondering what could have been if she had not found the coin.

A crowd of young women burst through the door and their laughter ran throughout the bar. Several of the women waved to Levi as they took a table close to the bar.

"Hi, Levi," one beautiful young woman said as she approached the bar.

"Good evening, how are you ladies doing?"

"Fantastic! We had a great day at the beach and have worked up a thirst for some Tropical E. Would you please set us up with a tray full and start a tab for me?" the woman asked, handing her a credit card.

"Certainly." Levi ran the woman's credit card through the cash register and filled a tray with her fruity drinks. "Karen is on duty tonight and, if you like, I can send her to check on you ladies regularly."

"Are you kidding?" the woman asked. "Then I wouldn't get a chance to flirt with you."

Levi broke out in laughter. "Fair enough," she said her cheeks suddenly warm with a blush. She handed the woman the tray. "Just let me know when you are ready for more."

Simone watched the exchange closely. "You certainly have a way with the women, Levi."

Levi smiled at Simone. "Thanks."

"It's true. I bet there isn't a woman in this bar that you couldn't charm."

"I don't know about that, Simone. I just try to be kind and treat people the way I want to be treated."

"I guess there is a lot I could learn from you." Simone offered Levi a warm smile.

"Maybe so," Levi returned her smile.

✝

Vanessa had quietly entered the bar and stopped on the upper deck to watch the interaction between Levi and Simone. For a moment, she considered returning to the ship, but she had made a promise to Levi. After hiking her overnight bag up on her shoulder, she continued down to the bar.

"Good evening, ladies," Vanessa said as she walked up to the bar.

"Hey Vanessa," Levi said. "Here let me put that behind the bar for you." She reached for her bag.

"Good evening, Captain," Simone said. "How are you this fine evening?"

"I couldn't be better, thanks, boss." Vanessa sat on a barstool next to Simone.

"May I buy you a drink?" Simone asked.

"Sure, how about one of those Tropical Es, please."

"Coming up." Levi turned to pour the drink.

"Cheers." Vanessa offered her glass to Simone.

Simone raised her glass and tipped it into Vanessa's. "Cheers."

"How has your day been, Levi?" Vanessa asked.

"It started off kind of slow, but has been picking up over the last hour. How was your afternoon?"

"It was great, thanks," she said with a wide grin. "I thought I would stop by before going to the dining room for dinner. Would you care to join me, Simone?"

Simone carefully hid her surprise at the offer. "That would be nice, Vanessa."

It was Levi's turn to watch the interaction between Vanessa and Simone. It made her wonder what they were plotting. The competition for her attention was obvious and she was somewhat surprised by Vanessa's dinner invitation. Levi suppressed a chuckle. *I will never understand women.* Her smile broadened when she realized she had echoed Nat's earlier sentiment.

They took their drinks, and after saying good-bye to Levi, left the bar. NeNe watched them leave the bar together and then looked at Levi, who just smiled and shrugged her shoulders. NeNe shook her head, and laughed, then cranked the music louder.

†

"Holy shit," Nat said, her fork stopping midway between her plate and her mouth. "Don't look now but Vanessa and Simone just came in together."

Liz couldn't help but turn and wave at Vanessa and Simone. "Would you two care to join us?" she asked as they walked toward the table. She ignored the sharp blow to her shin from Nat's foot.

Vanessa looked at Simone, who nodded her head. "That would be great, thanks." Vanessa pulled out a chair for Simone and then sat next to Nat.

"What are you two lovelies up to tonight?" Liz asked.

"Just stopping in for a bite to eat," Simone said as a server walked to the table.

"What would you recommend tonight, sister?" Simone asked Nat.

"The steaks are always good, if you want red meat, and there are several fantastic fresh fish choices tonight."

"Steak sounds good to me," Vanessa said. "Is that a filet you're eating, Liz?"

"Mmmm-hmm, tender as a mother's love," she said between bites.

"Good enough for me then." Vanessa winked at Liz.

"I think I will have the fresh grouper," Simone said.

"Good choices, ladies. May I offer you some wine?" Nat asked as she lifted the bottle.

Vanessa offered Nat her glass.

"I think I will pass, but thank you, Nat," Simone said.

"I hear you have a big day planned with Levi tomorrow, Vanessa." Liz gracefully dodged Nat's foot under the table.

"Yes, she has promised me a day on the island on the back of your bike."

"That sounds like a fun way to spend the day," Simone said. "Just don't do any treasure hunting."

"Spending the day with Levi is treasure enough for me," Vanessa said.

The next few moments passed in tense silence, broken by the delivery of salads for Vanessa and Simone.

Nat finished her meal and winked at Liz. "If you ladies will excuse me, I think I will go check on Levi."

Chapter Twenty-eight

Nat found Levi busy, but well under control behind the bar. She sat on one of the empty barstools and watched Levi pour up a tray of drinks and hand them over to Karen.

"Now that it is just you and I, Levi, tell me how you are really doing," Nat said during a lull.

"I'm doing just fine, Nat." Her voice quivered slightly and even she wasn't convinced.

"You have quite a lot going on in your life right now, Levi, so if you need to talk I hope you know you can talk to me anytime."

"Thanks, boss."

"You look like you've had things on your mind these last few days."

Levi exhaled loudly. "I have never been so confused in my entire life."

"Are there too many women on your mind?"

"I really thought I was over Simone, but I just can't seem to let her go. I know she treated me badly, but I wonder how much of her behavior was caused by that damned coin."

"I can't answer that for you, Levi," Nat said. "Simone has always been a selfish person, but I admit I did see a change in her when you two first met."

Nat picked up a napkin and dabbed at a water ring left by a beer bottle. "What are your feelings for Vanessa?"

"I wish I knew for sure. There is definitely a physical attraction between us, but Simone still enters my mind often, and many times when she shouldn't." Levi flushed.

"Well, I know you have plans with Vanessa tomorrow and again Wednesday night for the Beach Feast. Vanessa will be gone the next day and Simone will still be here for the remainder of the week. Then you should have a week without the influence of either woman before Vanessa returns with the next cruise ship arrival."

"So, you think I should try to spend time with each of them and then afterward try to sort out my feelings?"

"That is exactly what I am thinking. I know you are in a difficult situation and one or the other will have to deal with heartache." Nat watched as Levi blanched at the word heartache, but that was the bitter truth. Whomever Levi didn't choose, would have to deal with losing a great woman.

"Both Simone and Vanessa are attracted to you and they are both aggressive and competitive women, so you will have to be the one to make the decision." Nat chuckled. "Neither of them is going to give up easily, you know. I think they are both making a valiant effort to get along and not cause any more drama for you than necessary. In fact, I left Liz eating dinner with them to come check on you."

"Thanks, Nat. I appreciate your advice and support. I know it's up to me to decide what is best for me at this point in my life."

Karen rolled up to the bar and took the seat next to Nat. "I need two more dozen shots please."

"Why don't you let me take over for a few minutes and you grab some air," Nat suggested.

"Thanks, Nat." Levi walked from behind the bar and went outside.

†

Vanessa and Liz walked into the club and sat down at the bar. "Where's Levi?" Liz asked.

"I sent her out for some fresh air," Nat said.

"Is everything okay?"

"It will be." Nat smiled at her lover. "Where's Simone."

"She said she was going back to her room but would be down in a while."

Nat pulled out two bottles of water and placed them in front of Vanessa. "If I had to bet, I would say that Levi is sitting down at the end of the pier."

"Thanks, Nat." Vanessa picked up the bottles and headed for the door.

"So, what's up, baby?" Liz asked.

"Levi is really confused with her emotions right now. She has some thinking to do and a very difficult decision to make. She still has feelings for Simone and is very attracted to Vanessa as well."

"Levi has a good head on her shoulders. I know she will choose well, but it won't be a pleasant situation for her," Liz said, taking the glass of wine Nat offered.

†

Just as Nat had predicted, Vanessa found Levi sitting at the end of the pier, staring across the water.

"Would you mind some company?" she asked as Levi turned to look up at her.

"Not at all." She took the bottle of water Vanessa offered. "Thanks."

Vanessa sat down beside her.

Levi twisted the cap off the water and took a long drink.

"Are you all right, Levi?"

"Yes, why do you ask?"

"You seem a little preoccupied tonight."

"I just have a lot on my mind."

"Simone?"

"Yes, Simone, and you. I have feelings for both of you."

"I can understand that. I have very strong feelings for you, Levi, and I think we could make a great life together, but if you want I will walk away. By no means am I giving up on us, but if you would be happier with Simone, I would not interfere."

"Thanks, Vanessa, that means a lot to me. I have some serious thinking to do over the next week or so." Levi sighed.

"Would you prefer I go back to the ship tonight then?"

"No, Vanessa, I need you to stay with me. I hope that doesn't sound selfish of me, but I need you to hold me tonight."

"That is not selfish at all," Vanessa said. She took a drink of the water and looked out over the ocean.

A few minutes of quiet companionship passed then Vanessa turned to look at Levi and found tears rolling down her face. She laid a protective arm around Levi's shoulder.

"Relax, sweetheart, I am sure everything will turn out for the best." Vanessa hugged her close then wiped the tears from Levi's face and kissed her forehead. Levi trembled as she held her and Vanessa sensed the torment her young lover was experiencing. She took Levi's chin in her hand and lifted her face until she could read her eyes.

"I believe I'm in love with you, Levi, but I'll honor whatever decision you make and try my best not to add to the pressure that you are feeling right now."

She stood and offered a hand to help Levi up. "Would you mind if I grabbed my bag and went on up to your room to relax?"

"No, I wouldn't mind at all. I have an extra key at the bar, so you can take this one."

Vanessa started back toward the club.

"Vanessa," Levi called to her.

Vanessa turned back to face Levi. "Yes, Levi?"

"Thank you for caring so much for me."

"My pleasure, ma'am." Vanessa smiled and walked away.

Vanessa retrieved her bag from behind the bar under close scrutiny from Liz and Simone, who had joined Liz at the bar.

"I'm going to call it a night, ladies. I'll see you tomorrow."

A few minutes later, Levi returned and stepped behind the bar. Liz, Simone, and Nat looked at her, waiting for her to speak. "What?" she asked when she realized they were all looking at her.

"Is everything all right?" Liz asked.

"Everything is fine. Vanessa decided to make it an early night is all."

"Is she going back to the ship?" Liz asked.

Levi chuckled. "No, if you really must know, she's going to my bungalow."

"Oh, all right then," Liz said with a grin.

Levi went back to work filling orders for Karen while Nat restocked. Liz and Simone sat at the bar talking until a slow song started to play.

"Would you mind if I stole your bar mate, Nat?" Simone asked.

"No, go ahead. I think I can handle business for a few minutes."

"May I have this dance then, Levi?" Simone asked.

"Sure." Levi stepped from behind the bar and allowed Simone to lead her to the dance floor.

Simone held her close as she rested her head on her shoulder and breathed in the delicious smell of her perfume. She could see Simone's pulse beating in her neck as they swayed slowly together on the dance floor.

Simone raised her hand to softly stroke across Levi's cheek and when she lifted her head, she could see the passion glowing in Levi's eyes. She was tempted to lean down and kiss Levi, but she clearly remembered Levi's words to her earlier in the day. The look Levi was giving her told her that Levi still wanted her, but Simone would not make the first move.

"I still love you and will wait however long it takes," Simone whispered in Levi's ear as she pulled her close.

Levi did not respond, but remained pressed close to Simone during the remainder of the song. When the song ended, Simone smiled at Levi.

"Thank you for the dance."

189

"You're welcome," Levi said as they walked back to the bar.

Simone left shortly before midnight and Levi's relief came in a few minutes later.

"I hope you have a great day off tomorrow with Vanessa," Liz said. "By the way, catch." She tossed the keys to the Harley to Levi.

Levi caught the keys and grinned widely at Liz. "Thanks. See you two sometime tomorrow."

"I hope not," Nat said. "Enjoy your time off."

Chapter Twenty-nine

Levi slid her key into the door and quietly slipped inside her bungalow. The faint glow of the bathroom light bathed Levi's bed and played softly across Vanessa's face as she slept. Levi tiptoed into the bathroom, slipped out of her uniform and pulled an oversized sleep shirt over her head. Returning to the bedroom she sat in the chair next to the bed. Vanessa had rolled onto her side and the sheet slipped off, exposing her bare shoulder.

Levi smiled at the sight of Vanessa's tan skin and listened to the soft purr of Vanessa's breathing as she watched her lover sleep. She lost track of the time and when the chiming of her clock struck one, she realized she had been watching Vanessa for nearly an hour. She sat pondering her thoughts, asking herself, Is this the woman I want to spend my life with?

She was so lost in the intensity of her thoughts that when she looked at Vanessa a short time later, she found that her eyes were open and watching Levi curiously.

Vanessa lifted the sheet and smiled at Levi.

Levi returned her smile then climbed into bed and snuggled into Vanessa. Vanessa draped the sheet over them, wrapping her arm around Levi's waist and burying her face in Levi's neck. Levi felt Vanessa's warm breath on her skin and she closed her eyes and allowed sleep to take her.

†

When Levi woke the next morning, she was alone in bed. Vanessa's bag was still sitting on the edge of the couch, but the room was silent except for the soft hum of her ceiling fan. She glanced at the clock to see that it was almost nine. She couldn't believe she had slept so late. She wiped the sleep from her eyes and sat up in the bed just as she heard the click of a key in her door.

Vanessa carefully pushed her way through the door carrying a room service tray and smiled when she saw Levi sitting up in the bed.

"Good morning, sweetheart."

"Good morning. I can't believe I slept so late. Have you been up long?"

"Just long enough to shower and go down to get us some breakfast."

"Smells great."

Vanessa placed the tray on the end of the bed and lifted the plate cover. Underneath was a large ham and cheese omelet and a portion of hash browns. She added two slices of wheat toast to the plate and handed it to Levi.

"Breakfast in bed for you, my dear." She set a glass of juice on the bedside table. "Would you like some coffee?"

"Yes, please." Vanessa poured them each a cup of the rich-smelling coffee.

Levi took a bite of the omelet and moaned her approval. "This is almost sinful this morning."

Vanessa pulled the chair up next to the bed and began eating her own breakfast. "This is really tasty."

Levi took advantage of the opportunity to give Vanessa a once-over. She was wearing a pair of jeans, black Harley boots with a sea-foam green T-shirt that showed off her nicely tanned and muscular arms. Levi's eyes worked their way up Vanessa until they reached her eyes, sparkling brightly with excitement.

When they had finished breakfast, Vanessa offered to return the dishes to the kitchen while Levi took a shower and got dressed.

"You know, the kitchen staff will pick those up if you set them outside the door."

"I know, but I don't mind taking them back while you're getting ready."

Twenty minutes later, Levi wrapped a thick towel around her waist after her shower and walked into the bedroom to find Vanessa sitting on the love seat reading a newspaper.

Stepping in front of Vanessa Levi lowered the paper from in front of her face and leaned down to kiss her softly on the lips.

"Mmm, what was that for?" Vanessa asked as she put the paper on the table.

"Do I need to have a reason?" Levi teased as she sat down in Vanessa's lap.

"No ma'am, as a matter of fact you don't." Vanessa wrapped Levi in her arms.

Levi reached behind Vanessa's neck and pulled her head down for a soft, leisurely kiss. Vanessa's hand trailed up Levi's leg until it reached the bottom of the towel where it stopped. Levi covered Vanessa's hand, guiding it beneath the towel where Vanessa's hand continued its journey up Levi's thighs. Levi spread her legs, causing the towel to fall open across Vanessa's lap.

Vanessa caressed the inside of Levi's thighs, her fingers lightly brushing across the soft, damp hairs causing Levi to shiver with anticipation. Vanessa's tongue swirled seductively inside Levi's mouth and her soft moans filled the room. The tips of Vanessa's fingers gently parted Levi's full lips, slowly drawing the moisture up to circle her growing bud, strumming across it with her thumb. She teased Levi with soft touches until she felt her back arching, begging for a firmer touch. Her moans vibrated in Vanessa's mouth as her long fingers pressed between her soaked lips and entered her deeply. Her fingers curled upward, reaching for Levi's most sensitive spot as her thumb continued to stroke across her throbbing bud.

Levi broke the kiss long enough to whisper to Vanessa. "Oh yes, fuck me slowly," she breathed and then pulled Vanessa's mouth to her own.

Vanessa's fingers slid slowly in and out of Levi as she gently rocked with their rhythm. She kissed her way down Levi's neck and chest until her lips hovered over an erect nipple. She flicked her tongue across the nipple with the same rhythm she used to stroke Levi's g-spot. Levi growled her pleasure and arched her chest toward Vanessa, wanting more. Vanessa grazed the tip of the nipple with her teeth and then took it between her teeth, nibbling on the sensitive skin.

"Oh yes, baby," Levi purred.

Vanessa opened her mouth and covered the swollen flesh of Levi's aroused breast, sucking it deeply into her mouth. Levi's hand covered Vanessa's hand that was buried deep inside her and thrust her hips roughly against it, driving Vanessa's fingers deep inside her. Her muscles clutched around the strong fingers penetrating her and Levi exploded in orgasm.

Levi shook with pleasure and Vanessa covered her face with soft kisses until Levi sagged against her. "That was beautiful," she whispered into Levi's ear.

"That felt so good." Levi turned to look in Vanessa's eyes. "I'm definitely in need of another shower though. Would you care to join me?"

"If I do, we may not make it out of this room today."

"Well, I could think of much worse ways of spending my day off, but I did promise you a day of discovering the island."

"Yes, you did."

"I guess I had better hurry then." Levi retrieved her towel from Vanessa's lap and disappeared into the bathroom.

†

A few minutes later Levi emerged from the bathroom and stepped into the closet to slide into jeans and a tight-fitting T-shirt. She sat down on the bed, slipped on socks before lacing up her boots and with a wicked grin to Vanessa announced, "I'm ready."

She slipped the bike key into her pocket along with some cash and reached for Vanessa's hand. They walked to the garage together. Levi started the bike and backed it from its parking spot. Vanessa climbed on behind her. Snuggling in close to Levi's back she could smell the fragrant shampoo in Levi's still damp hair as they pulled away. She slid her hands around Levi's waist and could feel the vibration of the powerful Harley engine run through Levi's body as she twisted the throttle and the bike picked up speed.

Chapter Thirty

The bike handled like a dream as they wound their way around the island, their hair blowing in the wind. Vanessa hugged Levi close and the feeling of Vanessa pressed into her back was comforting to Levi.

They cruised along the highway until Levi spotted a small side road, more of a lane, really, barely wide enough for one vehicle at a time. She turned the powerful bike onto the path and they disappeared beneath a canopy of trees, heading into the island's interior.

Levi found an even smaller trail that ended in front of a small mountain of rock. She killed the engine and looked back at Vanessa.

"Are you up for a climb?"

"This looks like a great spot." Vanessa stepped off the bike.

Levi locked the front fork of the bike and slipped the key into her pocket then reached for Vanessa's hand. Finding a path to the top, Levi led Vanessa over the rocks, slowly picking her way upward until she reached a plateau that looked out over the island. They sat on the edge of a large flat rock and looked at the area before them.

"Beautiful," Vanessa said.

"Breathtaking isn't it?"

"It almost seems like you could step out on the clouds as they drift by." Vanessa's smile broadened.

They sat on the perch for over an hour watching the movements of the island. Vanessa pointed out her beloved ship, a wisp of smoke puffing from one of the large stacks. "She looks so small from up here."

"But still so much larger than anything else in port," Levi replied.

"Will you stay there with me tonight?" Vanessa turned to look at Levi.

"I'd love too."

"I really hate to admit it, but being away from her for more than a day is almost unbearable."

"I can understand that. I'm beginning to feel the same way about the resort."

Vanessa smiled. "I think we have both found our passions."

"I do believe you're right. I planned to spend the summer here and then head back to the States, but now I'm not so sure."

"So you think you will stay at the resort permanently?" Vanessa asked.

"At least for a while longer than originally planned."

"Great, I'll be able to see you a couple times a month then." Vanessa grinned sheepishly.

"Yes ma'am, I do believe you will. At least until I can figure out what I want to do with the rest of my life."

Levi noticed the shadows changing and realized the day was rapidly slipping away from them.

"If we are going to see more of the island, we had better climb down from this spot soon."

Vanessa stood and offered Levi a hand. "I'm right behind you."

They picked their way down the mountain of rocks carefully and had nearly reached the bottom when Levi's boot skidded on a rock and she lost her footing. Vanessa grabbed for her, catching her right arm and preventing a fall, but Levi had instinctively reached out with her left hand to brace herself. She cried out when a pain shot up her casted wrist.

Vanessa steadied Levi in her arms. "Are you all right?"

"Yes, I just put too much weight on my wrist, but I'm fine."

Vanessa took the lead down the remainder of the path until they were safely at the bike.

Levi turned on the ignition but when she reached for the brake with her left hand she found she did not have the strength in her fingers to pull back the brake. Levi turned off the bike.

"What's wrong?"

"I hope you can drive a bike," Levi said, turning back to Vanessa. "I can't pull back on the brake calipers with my left hand. So you're going to have to drive."

"No problem, I have a bike almost identical to this one at home." She dismounted and Levi slid back on the seat.

Vanessa straddled the bike in front of Levi. "Do you need to go to the hospital to get checked out?"

"No, I'll be fine. I just can't brake well enough to drive safely. Why don't we ride down and take a walk on the beach," Levi suggested.

"Sounds good to me." Vanessa reached down and turned on the ignition.

Several minutes later, they were back on the main road that circled the island, Levi's arms wrapped around Vanessa and her head rested on her shoulder. The farther they rode, the fewer people they saw on the beach. After a mile of seeing no one else on the beach, they decided to pull over in a small lot. They pulled off their boots and socks and rolled their jeans up their shins.

Hand in hand they walked down the beach toward the sun. They walked in the shallow surf, playfully splashing one another as the afternoon slid toward evening. As the glowing orb approached the horizon, they sat on a dune to watch it sink then disappear completely. There was a faint glow in the sky as Vanessa turned toward Levi and kissed her softly.

"I don't know about you, but I'm getting hungry," Vanessa said when she broke the kiss.

"I could go for a seafood platter myself." Levi stood and began to walk back toward the bike. "My treat though," Levi insisted.

They put their socks and boots back on and Levi climbed on the back of the bike. Vanessa started to mount the bike in front of her and Levi stopped her.

"Turn around."

"What?" Vanessa asked.

"Turn around and face me."

Vanessa mounted the bike facing the back and settled in mere inches from Levi's lips.

"Is this what you wanted?"

Levi reached up and pulled Vanessa toward her. "This is what I wanted." She covered Vanessa's mouth with a passionate kiss.

Feeling suddenly amorous and excited by the thrill of discovery, Levi pulled Vanessa closer by draping Vanessa's thighs over hers, pressing their bodies together.

She caressed Vanessa's back, their kiss growing in intensity. She leaned forward, pressing Vanessa backward until her shoulders were resting between the handlebars. Levi's hands tugged at Vanessa's T-shirt, pulling it free from her jeans and raising it above her breasts, her fingers grazing Vanessa's hard nipples. Levi was ecstatic to find Vanessa was wearing a front closure bra. Her fingers deftly worked the fastener. Levi's hands covered Vanessa's breasts, rolling her nipples between her thumb and forefingers. Oblivious to any potential traffic on the road, Levi kissed down Vanessa's neck, her tongue leaving a trail of moisture on Vanessa's skin. Levi licked across her aching nipples causing Vanessa to moan loudly.

She unlaced Vanessa's boots and slipped them off her feet then unfastened her jeans and slowly pulled them down Vanessa's legs. Vanessa raised her hips to assist Levi and her undulations gave Levi an idea. Once the jeans were gone, Levi planted light kisses down Vanessa's stomach and draped Vanessa's knees over her shoulders.

Using her shoulders to support Vanessa's hips she lowered her head between Vanessa's legs and gently parted her lips with her fingers. She planted feather-light kisses on Vanessa's clit as her fingers teased her opening.

Vanessa began to slowly grind her hips into Levi's face. Levi drove her tongue deep into Vanessa's wetness, her thumb stroking across her throbbing clit. She probed and licked Vanessa into a frenzy of passion, and when she cried out she was coming, Levi replaced her tongue with two fingers and sucked Vanessa's clit deep into her mouth.

Vanessa convulsed violently as she climaxed, her hips still thrusting against Levi's fingers extending her orgasm beyond anything she had ever experienced. She gasped for breath, begging Levi not to stop, until her body collapsed in exhaustion.

Levi lowered Vanessa's legs back down across her thighs and took her in her arms, holding her close as tears streamed down her cheeks. They shared a few moments of complete bliss before they realized headlights were coming their way. Vanessa struggled to fasten her bra and pull her T-shirt down as Levi reached for her jeans.

Vanessa had barely slipped her jeans over her hips when the beam of the headlights reached them. Levi burst out in laughter and pulled her close.

"A few minutes sooner and they would have seen quite a sight," she said between chuckles.

"Oh my word, Levi, that was incredible." Excitement still glowed in Vanessa's eyes.

"You think you can still drive?"

"I may be a little shaky but I can get us back to town."

Chapter Thirty-one

They dined on fresh seafood before riding back to the resort.

"Did you ladies have a great ride?" Liz asked when they returned the keys. She smiled inwardly as she noted the glow on their faces.

"It was a great day all around," Vanessa said. "We had a fantastic tour of the island and a fabulous meal."

"Will you be joining us at the club later?" Liz asked.

"No," Levi said, "I think we're going to have a quiet evening on the ship and rest up for tomorrow's feast."

"Oh, that reminds me. Simone asked me to tell you she has a couple of Jet Skis reserved for tomorrow afternoon if you and Vanessa would like to join her for a day on the beach before the feast," she said.

Levi looked at Vanessa who was grinning and nodding her head. "I guess you can tell Simone that we will see her on the beach tomorrow then." Levi chuckled.

"I'm sure she'll be thrilled," Liz said as Levi and Vanessa turned to leave. "See you two tomorrow."

"Thanks again for the use of the bike," Levi said.

"It's yours to use anytime you wish," Liz said, dropping the keys back into the desk drawer.

✝

"I need to go to my room and pack some fresh clothes," Levi said. "Why don't you go have a drink and I will meet you at the bar soon."

"That's a good idea." Vanessa leaned over to kiss Levi. "I'll see you in a few then, love."

Levi watched Vanessa walk toward the bar, smiling as she thought about how Vanessa moved with cat-like grace. Lost in her thoughts, Levi turned and nearly ran into Simone, who was standing right behind her.

"Hey Simone," she said, startled by her closeness.

"Hello Levi," she softly purred. "Liz just told me that you and Vanessa accepted my invitation for an afternoon at the beach."

Levi raised her left arm. "No jet-skiing for me, but I am sure you and Vanessa can enjoy them without me."

"Damn, I didn't think about your cast." Simone frowned.

"It's no problem. I can sunbathe while I watch you two playing."

"Great, I look forward to it," Simone said. "Are you coming down to the club later?"

"Only to retrieve Vanessa. I'm going to pack a bag and we're going to have a quiet night on the ship."

"Very well, I'll see you tomorrow." Simone turned and walked toward the elevator.

Levi reached her room and packed a small bag of clothes for the next day. She instinctively reached for the bag with her left hand and felt the painful twinge in her wrist. Since her slip earlier in the day she had felt a dull ache in her wrist and now it was beginning to slowly throb with pain. Levi tossed the bottle of pain medication in her bag, hopeful that she would not need them, but prepared if the pain grew worse. She closed the bag and lifted it over her shoulder and walked down to the club.

✝

Levi found Vanessa sitting at the bar chatting with Nat while she drank a beer. She looked over at the DJ booth and shot a smile and a wave at NeNe, who eagerly waved back at her friend.

"Good evening, boss," Levi said as she walked up to the bar.

"Hello, Levi."

Levi slid onto the barstool next to Vanessa. "Hiya cutie, may I buy you a drink?" She winked at Vanessa.

"That would be very nice."

"Two of whatever the lady is having please," Levi said.

"Coming right up." Nat walked to the cooler for the cold beers.

"I hear the two of you will be joining Simone for some beach time tomorrow," Nat said as she placed the beers on the bar.

"Word travels quickly I see," Levi joked.

"I think someone is excited to be on a Jet Ski."

Vanessa grinned. "What can I say, I love being on the water."

"Oh really, Captain, as if we couldn't tell." Levi elbowed Vanessa lightly in the ribs.

"How are you going to wrap that wrist?" Nat asked.

"I'm not. I'm going to let Vanessa and Simone do all the water play while I bake slowly on the beach and enjoy a nice cold drink."

"Damn, I forgot about your wrist, Levi," Vanessa said. "I'm sure we can talk Simone into changing plans."

"Don't you dare, I plan to have a totally lazy day on the beach while I watch you two wear yourselves out."

"Are you sure, baby?" Vanessa asked. "I am sure we can find something we can all do together."

"I am positive, sweetie."

They finished their drinks and said goodnight to Nat. Levi reached for her bag and cringed at the pain that shot up her arm. "Damn," she said.

"Are you sure we don't need to get you checked out," Vanessa asked as she took the bag from Levi.

"I'm fine. I think I just irritated my wrist today."

"Well, promise me you will have it checked if it is not better tomorrow."

"I promise." Levi slipped her hand inside Vanessa's as they walked to meet the trolley that would take them back to the ship.

✝

Vanessa placed Levi's overnight bag on the bed. They removed their riding clothes and walked into the bathroom for a shower. Levi had grown accustomed to bathing one-handed, but tonight she allowed Vanessa to bathe her with soft caresses and tender kisses. She felt totally pampered by Vanessa's attention and enjoyed every moment. After rinsing off, they dried their bodies and slipped between the fresh, clean sheets.

Levi rolled on top of Vanessa and again cringed with pain.

"Did you bring any painkillers with you?"

"Yes, but I don't want to take them," Levi said with a wicked grin.

"There is no need for you to be in pain." Vanessa rolled her onto her back, and walked to the bathroom for a glass of water then fished the bottle of pills from Levi's bag.

Vanessa handed the bottle to Levi and waited until she retrieved a pill to hand her the glass of water.

"It has been a long and beautiful day, Levi, so why don't we just cuddle and call it an early night."

The frown of her disappointment was evident on Levi's face, but she was hurting and gratefully accepted the water from Vanessa.

"Are you sure you don't mind?"

"I am perfectly content to hold you in my arms until you fall asleep, baby," Vanessa said with a warm smile.

Levi swallowed the pill and handed the glass back to Vanessa. "Come snuggle me then." She rolled over to face Vanessa.

Vanessa set the glass on the table and crawled between the sheets. She took Levi in her arms, kissing her softly as her hand

204

slowly caressed Levi's back. She watched Levi's eyes grow heavy and finally close. "Sleep now." Vanessa listened to the deepening of Levi's breathing, a sweet smile playing across her lips.

"I love you, Levi," Vanessa softly whispered as Levi slipped from this world into sleep.

Chapter Thirty-two

Levi awoke the next morning to find Vanessa propped up on an elbow smiling at her. It was nearly nine and Levi tried to shake off the aftereffects of the pain medication and keep her eyes focused.

"Good morning," she said with a warm smile. "I hope you slept well."

"Good morning, Levi, and yes I slept just fine."

She didn't need to mention the several times she was awakened by Levi's moans of pain resulting from her fall yesterday. Vanessa had simply cradled Levi in her arms until she fell back into a restful sleep and then snuggled into her warmth.

"How are you feeling this morning?" Vanessa asked.

"A little groggy, but the pain seems to be gone."

"Great news. Are you hungry?"

"Starved."

"Let's shower and I'll order some breakfast for us."

"Sounds great to me."

"Would you mind if I slipped off for an hour or so before we head to the beach to make sure the ship is ready for departure tomorrow?" Vanessa asked.

"Not at all. I think I will try my luck in your casino while you're gone," she said with a grin.

"Just don't break the bank." Vanessa lifted the covers and walked into the bathroom to start the shower.

Once more, Vanessa bathed Levi with loving care, her hands caressing her skin, stirring her arousal. Vanessa pressed her body into Levi's while she stroked down her sides and stomach.

"That feels so good," Levi whispered over the sound of running water.

Vanessa dropped the sponge in the rear of the shower and maneuvered their bodies under the stream of water to rinse. Her hands parted Levi's thighs and her fingertips teased Levi's clit as her lips brushed Levi's neck.

"May I make it feel much better for you?" she whispered in Levi's ear.

"Oh yes, " Levi moaned as Vanessa's fingers rubbed across her swollen bud.

Levi spread her legs wider, giving Vanessa better access as her fingers parted the silky wet lips and entered Levi. Levi turned her face toward Vanessa, their tongues dancing sensually as Vanessa's fingers plunged in and out of Levi while they rocked together in the shower. Vanessa turned Levi and pressed her against the back of the shower, fingers still driving deep inside her, and she knelt in front of Levi and sucked her throbbing clit deep inside her mouth.

The sounds of their pleasure echoed in the shower stall as Levi released and flooded Vanessa's hands and face with sweet nectar as she convulsed in orgasm. Vanessa slowed the movement of her fingers and drank freely from Levi's center. Levi sighed and her inner muscles relaxed, releasing Vanessa's fingers. Vanessa slowly removed her fingers, causing ripples of pleasure to vibrate deep inside Levi, and stood to kiss her.

They stepped under the shower's flow again and washed away the remains of the pleasure they had just shared. Helping Levi from the shower, Vanessa patted her dry before sending her off to dress.

Levi put on her swimsuit, and slipped a pair of shorts on before returning to the bathroom.

Vanessa had wrapped a towel around her waist and was bent over the sink brushing her teeth when Levi reentered the bathroom. The soft sway of Vanessa's breasts caught Levi's attention. She pressed her hips into Vanessa's backside and her hands reached around to cup her breasts, her thumbs rubbing across the rapidly growing nipples.

Vanessa wiped her face and caught Levi's stare in the mirror. "Did you find something you like?" she asked rather coyly.

"Uh-huh, I did." Levi felt a shiver run through Vanessa. "I plan to spend more time with these tonight." Levi softly pinched Vanessa's nipples.

"That definitely gives me something to look forward to." Vanessa turned and took Levi in her arms for a long, deep kiss.

"Okay, we have to stop or we'll never leave the ship," Vanessa said, reluctantly pulling away from Levi.

Levi smiled as Vanessa dropped the towel and went into the bedroom. She gathered up towels and sunscreen for the beach trip and walked to the bedroom to find Vanessa sitting on the bed holding a small box. Vanessa handed her the box.

Levi took the box with trepidation. "What's this," she asked before sitting on the bed next to Vanessa.

"Just open it."

Levi lifted off the lid and found a gold bracelet shining up at her. She took the bracelet out and placed the box on the bed beside her.

"This is beautiful, Vanessa," Levi said with tears in her eyes and a voice filled with emotion.

"I wanted to give you this as thanks for the great time we've had this week," Vanessa explained. She took the chain from Levi's hand and carefully placed it on her wrist.

"It's beautiful, but…" Levi started.

"No buts, just accept it as a gift from me, Levi. No expectations." Vanessa planted a soft kiss on Levi's lips.

"Thank you." Levi held Vanessa close for a moment.

"My thanks to you," Vanessa said.

The embrace was too soon interrupted by a knock on the door that signaled the delivery of their breakfast. Thirty minutes later, Levi walked into the casino and Vanessa climbed to the bridge with an agreement to find Levi as soon as she was finished.

Levi located a vacant slot machine and inserted a twenty-dollar bill. The bright gold of the bracelet glittered on her tanned wrist and brought a smile to her face.

✝

Killian was looking over a clipboard of reports when Vanessa walked onto the bridge.

"Captain, I do believe you are glowing."

"I believe you may be right, Killian."

"The look is definitely a good one for you."

"Thank you, my friend." Vanessa placed a hand on Killian's shoulder.

"So things are going well with Levi?"

"As well as can be expected right now."

"Good. You two make such a cute couple."

"Thanks. Are we all set to sail tomorrow?"

"Just a few more supplies to take on and we'll be ready."

"Great, have you checked the weather reports yet?"

"Not yet, that is next on my list."

"I'll take care of those." Vanessa sat down at a computer terminal and began to key in information and print out forecasts. "It looks like we will have a smooth ride back home," she said, reading over the last report.

"That's great, but, you know, I could get a little spoiled here on the island."

Vanessa laughed. "I know exactly what you mean, Killian, but we will be back here again in a week."

"That's true. What plans do you have for today?"

"Levi, Simone, and I have an afternoon at the beach planned."

Killian raised a brow at the mention of Simone. "Playing with the competition?"

Vanessa smiled up at her over the report she was reading. "We were invited by Simone, so I didn't have much of a choice. I'm sure we will have a great time though." She tried to sound confident for Killian as much as for herself.

"Where is Levi, by the way?"

"She decided to try out the casino while I came up here."

"You better go get her then and get out of here."

"Why is that?"

"Well, first off, we don't need her cleaning out the slots. Second, I'm about to leave here for the afternoon and if I find her alone in the casino I might be tempted to steal her away from both you and Simone," Killian teased. "You know how charming I can be."

"Very well, I'm out of here. I can't be held accountable for Levi falling for the likes of you." Vanessa winked at her good friend.

"See, Captain, I knew you would come to your senses and see things my way."

Vanessa stood and walked toward the door. "I'll see you later at the feast, but I'll be on the beach if you need me for anything."

"For goodness sakes, Captain, will you go already and let me finish my work."

"All right already, I'm out of here."

†

Levi had won a small jackpot and was raking coins into a bucket when Vanessa walked into the casino. Their eyes met and Vanessa smiled at her.

"Looks like I had better get you out of here quick," Vanessa said, nodding toward the stash of coins Levi had accumulated.

"Not too much damage." Levi lifted her bucket. "Let me cash out and I'll be ready."

Levi collected her winnings and joined Vanessa who was observing a poker game. "All set."

"Are we still planning to come back here before the feast to shower and change?" Vanessa asked.

"I think that's the plan." Levi reached for Vanessa's hand as they stepped out into the warm afternoon's bright sunlight and walked to the trolley stop.

Simone was already at the beach and waiting for them. She had reserved three beach lounges and was sipping a cool drink when Levi and Vanessa arrived.

"Hi ladies," Simone said. "I thought I would come down and get us set up."

"Hello, Simone," Levi and Vanessa said in unison.

Vanessa set the beach bag down and spread out towels along their loungers as Levi and Simone chatted.

Simone was sipping on a tall Tropical E. She flagged down a server to order one for Levi. Vanessa had declined the offer, thinking it unwise to mix alcohol and Jet Skis, but knew better than to suggest otherwise to Simone.

"In twenty minutes we can go get the skis," Simone reported as she handed Levi her drink.

Levi took the drink and placed it on the small table and resumed rubbing tanning oil onto her skin.

"Do you want me to put some of that on your back before we hit the water?" Vanessa asked.

"Yes, please." Levi handed Vanessa the bottle of tropical-smelling oil.

Vanessa smoothed the oil over Levi's back as Simone watched closely, a hint of jealousy in her eyes as she sat back on her chair.

"Mmm, that feels good," Levi moaned as Vanessa rubbed the oils across her shoulders.

"Just don't forget to turn," she reminded her as she handed the bottle back to Levi.

"I'll set the timer on my watch, just in case. I know once you two get out on the water I won't see you for a while." She stretched out on her stomach.

Levi really didn't know which one was more excited about the Jet Skis. She knew Vanessa was chomping at the bit, while Simone also fidgeted on her chair.

"Why don't you two start walking," Levi suggested. "I'm sure they won't mind if you arrive a few minutes early."

Simone grinned at Vanessa and they took off down the beach, walking quickly as Levi chuckled and watched them go. When they disappeared inside a small building she closed her eyes. The effects of the medication were still hanging with her and adding a Tropical E just made her that much more sleepy.

Levi had barely drifted off when she heard what sounded like a swarm of angry bees. She opened her eyes and raised her head to see Vanessa and Simone flying past on the calm waters. She lifted her hand to wave to them. Both women smiled and waved back to her and then turned out to sea. Content, Levi lay back down and drifted off again.

Levi's alarm went off to remind her to change positions. She rolled over to lie on her back and elevated the lounge chair so she could look out across the water. She could see a dozen or more Jet Skis in the distance and strained to pick out Vanessa and Simone from the small crowd. They were riding off to the east of the small pack and appeared to be heading back toward shore. The water was no longer smooth as glass and had become choppy since she had first laid down, but she could still hear the squeals of laughter rolling across the water.

She reached for her drink and took a sip. As Levi turned back toward the water, her heart sank to her toes and she jumped to her feet, mindless of spilling her drink and ran toward the water.

Chapter Thirty-three

Levi ran as hard as she could across the thirty yards of sand until she reached the water, waving her arms frantically, trying to gain Vanessa's and Simone's attention. She covered the distance in seconds, but to Levi it felt like the world had stopped and she was moving in slow motion. Her heart was thundering against her ribs as she ran parallel to the water, waving her arms. Shouting to them proved to be a waste of time, her voice drowned out by the pounding of the waves that were increasing in size every passing moment.

Her attempts were futile and Levi could only watch in horror as the scene rapidly unfolding before her eyes. The two skis were racing parallel to the shore and neither of the women could see the large rogue wave that was building behind them, growing to a height of twelve feet.

Both riders were completely oblivious that the wave was about to crash down upon them, possibly changing their lives forever. Levi could not identify either rider as they raced along at high speeds but not fast enough to outrun the wave. Levi collapsed to her knees when she witnessed the first rider disappear under the crushing water, the wave still chasing the other rider. The wave crashed into the second rider, although at a slightly smaller size than the original impact, and Levi watched the ski roll underneath the wave, tossed about like a toy.

Screaming for someone to call 911, Levi watched the water's surface for any sign of her two lovers. She saw one head break the surface and her hopes began to rise. There was no sign of the other craft or its rider on the water.

†

Simone was riding the first ski overcome by the wave. The force of the water drove the ski into the bottom of the ocean, ramming the nose of the craft two feet into the sand. Thrown forward at impact, her right shoulder struck the handlebars splintering her collarbone. The unnatural angle of her broken shoulder allowed the life jacket to become snagged on the handlebar, preventing her from rising to the surface. Forward momentum carried Simone over the handlebars and she struck her head on the hood of the ski, knocking her unconscious, her body trapped under the surface.

†

Vanessa felt the impact of the wave and instinctively tucked her head low as she felt the ski start to roll with the cresting of the wave. For several eternal seconds the ski rolled continuously, underneath the surface of the water, as Vanessa struggled to hold on. Unable to maintain her grip any longer, Vanessa dove from the ski. The floor of the ocean looked dark and she forced herself upward to the light of the sky. She broke the surface of the water, her lungs screaming for oxygen and looked around her to find the ski swamped, a large breach in the hull quickly taking on water and the craft beginning to sink.

Vanessa looked around. Simone could not have trailed too far behind her at the speed they were traveling, but she was nowhere to be seen. Vanessa began swimming toward the spot where she thought Simone should be but there was no sign of her or the craft. She looked toward the shore and saw Levi entering the water; she dove, searching for signs of Simone. The sand on the bottom of the ocean was stirred by the churning wave and Vanessa could only see a few feet ahead of her. When the water cleared to give her a better view, she could make out the shape of the crashed craft, nose impaled in the ocean's bed. Simone was unmoving, floating slightly above the ski.

Vanessa swam hard to reach Simone. Realizing that her life preserver had snagged on the handlebars and she was trapped, Vanessa began ripping at the fasteners to free her from the ocean's grasp. She could clearly see that Simone was unconscious and her shoulder hung at an awkward angle. She choked back her panic, focusing on untangling Simone from the Jet Ski. Once Simone was freed, Vanessa encircled her shoulders and lunged for the surface.

☦

Levi scanned the ocean's surface and gasped when she saw Vanessa's head pop up in the water, holding Simone's limp form above the surface as she swam for shore. Levi dove through a wave and swam as fast as she could, reaching them twenty yards later. She and Vanessa worked together to pull Simone toward shore, fighting the waves and a rip current that was growing in strength. An hour seemed to pass before they reached an area where they could touch bottom and once on their feet they were able to move much faster.

Levi heard the scream of sirens racing toward them as they neared the shore. Moments later, other swimmers reached them. They took Simone from them rushing her to shore on fresh legs as the paramedics arrived on the beach. Levi and Vanessa were both breathless when they finally reached the beach and collapsed close to where the paramedics were working on Simone. They had begun CPR, but there were no vital signs registering on their equipment. They continued their attempts at resuscitation as a second crew arrived to assist them and Simone's lifeless body was prepared for transport.

☦

Simone's world was totally black and she was growing unbearably cold. She could feel herself carried across the waves, and then the cool air hit her skin as she left the salty water. She could hear Levi's cries in the background and desperately needed to tell her she was going to be fine, but she could not open her eyes or speak. The cold crept deeper into her body. She felt hands all over her and lifted up again, this time moving very fast. The wailing of the sirens was the last thing she heard before time stopped and she felt or heard nothing more.

✝

Levi convulsed with sobs as the paramedics placed Simone on a backboard and then lifted her onto a stretcher. Within minutes, they rushed her away in a screaming ambulance. Levi turned to look at Vanessa and saw the blood streaming down her face.

"Vanessa, you're bleeding!"

Vanessa, completely exhausted, was suddenly aware of hot liquid running down her face. She was barely maintaining a grasp on Levi for support, but Levi's panic-stricken look and the feel of blood rushing down her face drained the last of her strength and she collapsed on the beach.

The remaining two paramedics rushed over to them and began working on Vanessa. She was breathing regularly as they hooked up monitors and quickly stabilized. Wiping the blood from her face revealed a deep two-inch gash above her eyebrow. One paramedic placed a pressure patch over the cut as they quickly readied her for transport to the hospital. Levi had the sense to grab the beach bag as she chased the paramedics and climbed in behind them as they loaded Vanessa into the ambulance.

Levi sat against the wall of the EMS unit trying to stay out of the way as paramedics continued to check Vanessa for other signs of injury. Levi dug the cell phone out of the bag and struggled to dial the resort's number. The operator transferred her to Liz right away.

"Liz, there's been an accident! Get Nat and come to the hospital now," Levi cried.

"What happened?" Liz asked.

"I can't explain it now, Liz, just bring Nat and hurry please," Levi pleaded.

"We will be there as fast as we can."

Soon after she hung up Levi heard the ambulance's radio crackle and a voice over the airwaves.

"Bus one ETA, one minute, with a drowning victim, ambu bag initiated and a weak and thready pulse evident after electrical stimulation times four, request immediate assistance upon arrival."

"Ten-four, bus one, emergency crew on standby at the ER awaiting your arrival."

Simone was alive, just barely from the sound of it, but alive, and at least she had a chance of survival, Levi thought.

"Have faith. Your friend is going to make it through," said the paramedic who was working on Vanessa. "This one is going to be fine as well. A bad cut to her eyebrow, loss of blood, shock, exhaustion, and a probable concussion, but with a night or so in the hospital and some stitches, she will be as good as new.

"What happened out there?" the paramedic asked, trying to piece the puzzle of the accident together.

"My friends were riding Jet Skis and were overtaken by a rogue wave neither of them saw coming," Levi said. "Vanessa was able to make it through the rolling of the ski, but from what I could get out of Vanessa, Simone's ski was impaled into the floor of the ocean, and her life preserver was snagged on the handlebars holding her underwater."

"Do you have any idea how long she was under?"

"It seemed like forever," Levi said. "Everything seems so blurry now, but I would guess three or four minutes before Vanessa found her and brought her to the surface and then several more before she reached shore."

The paramedic tried to hide the frown on her face as she added up the minutes without oxygen.

"How are you?" the paramedic asked, inquiring about her wrist.

217

"A broken wrist almost two weeks ago."

"Well, once we get your friends settled in we need to check you out and replace that cast."

"Okay," Levi said. Exhausted, emotionally and physically, she slumped back against the ambulance's wall.

"Try to relax and we will be at the hospital in just a few minutes."

"Killian," Levi said out loud.

"Excuse me," the paramedic said.

"I have to get in touch with Killian." Levi grabbed up the cell phone and hit Redial.

"May I speak to NeNe?" she asked the resort's operator and moments later NeNe picked up.

"NeNe, it's Levi, there's been an accident. I need you to go to the ship and find Killian and bring her to the hospital please."

"I'm on my way," NeNe said, and then her voice was gone.

The ambulance reached the hospital and backed into an emergency room stall. The doors opened and the stretcher holding Vanessa was pulled out and rushed to the emergency room. Levi stepped out and allowed the driver to lead her inside.

The paramedic was talking with a doctor about Simone, filling him in on how long she'd been deprived of oxygen. Levi didn't like the look on the doctor's face as he listened. He turned to walk back into the room where Levi presumed they were treating Simone.

"Is she going to be all right?" Levi asked the paramedic.

"We are doing the best we can for her now," she said. The paramedic took her into a small examination room. "Wait here and I will bring you an update as soon as I can." She pulled the curtain to allow Levi some privacy.

Levi suddenly felt all alone. She could hear the hospital staff rushing in and out of rooms as they attended to Simone and Vanessa, but had no clue as to what was going on. She began to cry, and was holding her face in her hands when she heard a familiar voice call her name.

Chapter Thirty-four

Liz slammed on the brakes in front of the emergency room entrance and Nat flew out of the van. Liz screeched away to find a parking spot.

Nat rushed to the reception desk. "I am Simone Taylor's sister. What in hell is going on?" she demanded.

"Calm down please, miss. Your sister and her friends are being cared for now. If you'll take a seat, I will let the doctors know you are here."

"Take a seat my ass," Liz heard as she walked up beside Nat, "I want to know what is going on!" Nat's voice was louder than Liz had ever heard her speak.

The paramedic who had brought Vanessa and Levi in came out of the ER at the sound of shouting. "I'll handle this, Mary," she said. "Come with me please, ladies."

Liz and Nat followed the young woman into a small room and they all sat down. "There was an accident at the beach," she started.

"What kind of accident," Nat demanded.

"Calm down, baby." Liz placed her hand on Nat's arm.

"According to Ms. Johnson, a rogue wave of approximately twelve feet slammed down upon the two women riding Jet Skis," the paramedic said.

"How are they?" Liz asked.

"Vanessa will be fine. She has a nasty head gash and a probable concussion but will recover well. Your sister, I'm afraid, wasn't as fortunate. Her life preserver caught on the handlebars of the ski and she lost consciousness, probably from hitting her head. It was several minutes before she could be located and rescued."

"Simone drowned?" Nat asked, then crumpled into Liz's arms.

"Yes, but thanks to Levi and Vanessa's quick response and the work of the medical teams she has been revived. She is not out of the woods yet, and her condition remains very critical, but she is breathing again on her own and her vital signs are improving."

"When can we see her?" Liz asked.

"It will be a long wait still," the woman answered. "I would recommend you follow me back to where Ms. Johnson is awaiting treatment. She is terrified and exhausted and I know she could use your support right now."

"Is Levi hurt?" Liz asked.

"Physically no, I don't think so, but she is an emotional wreck and is fighting with shock. As soon as the others are stabilized the staff will examine her and replace the cast on her arm." She stood up. "She needs you both to be strong right now. Are you ready?"

Nat dried the tears from her eyes, took a deep breath, and nodded.

"Follow me then." They left the waiting room and walked through the corridor to the examination rooms.

A curtain flung open as a nurse hurried out to rush down the hallway. Liz caught a glimpse of Simone's body lying prostrate on the examination table. Her skin was incredibly pale, tubes and machines connected to her. She was relieved that Nat could not see in as they passed.

"I will let the doctors know you are here waiting," the paramedic said when they reached Levi.

"Thank you for all your assistance," Liz said as the woman walked away.

"Levi," Liz said in a tender voice. "Are you okay?"

Levi looked up to find Liz and Nat standing just inside the room with her. "Oh Liz, it was so horrible." She broke out in tears.

Liz and Nat sat on either side of Levi and took her in their arms in a group hug.

"Everything is going to be all right, Levi," Liz said, silently praying her words would come true.

Levi lifted her face and looked at Nat with bloodshot eyes. "I tried to warn them, Nat, but I couldn't."

"I know you did everything you could, Levi, and because of that Simone has a fighting chance," Nat said. "For that I am truly grateful to you."

"How is she, do you know?" Levi asked.

"Her vital signs are improving and she is breathing again on her own," Nat said, trying to reassure Levi. "You know Simone is a strong-willed woman, Levi, and there is no way she will give up the fight."

"Have you seen Vanessa?"

"No, not yet. Why don't you stay with her, Nat, and I will go check on Vanessa," Liz suggested.

Liz walked two rooms down and peeked inside the curtain. A doctor, bent over Vanessa, was stitching the cut above her eye. He looked up and saw her. "Come in, I'm almost finished."

Liz stepped inside the room and looked at Vanessa. Her right eye, covered with an angry-looking purple bruise, was swollen shut. She looked down and saw an IV line in Vanessa's right hand.

"Friend or family?" the young doctor asked.

"Friend. She is the captain of the cruise ship docked down at the harbor," Liz said. "How is she doing?"

"I just put twenty-four stitches in her to close up the wound above her brow and I believe she will be taken upstairs in a short while to have a CAT scan to determine if she has a concussion from the blow to her head. We'll probably be keeping her for a few days of observation if no other treatment is needed."

"Why isn't she awake?"

"We gave her a mild sedative while we get some fluids into her. She is also suffering from exhaustion, so a brief rest will do wonders for her. By the time she gets back from the CAT scan she will more than likely be awake and alert."

"Thank you, Doctor." Liz took Vanessa's hand and held it in hers.

"Do you have any information on the patient next door?"

"Friend?" he inquired again.

"No, this time family," she said with a smile.

"She is fighting very hard to pull through," he said. "She was deprived of oxygen for a long time, so we'll have to wait a while to determine if there is neurological damage. She was lucky. Another few minutes and there would have been no hope of survival."

"When will we be able to see her?" Liz asked.

"Her oxygen saturation levels are steadily rising, so once she reaches 100 percent I think you can visit briefly, but she won't be conscious for a while yet."

"Thank you, Doctor."

"I will be on duty all night, so when she is ready I'll send for you." He disappeared behind the curtain.

Liz felt a shiver pass through Vanessa and reached down to pull the blanket up over her, carefully avoiding the IV line. She wiped a stray lock of hair that had fallen into Vanessa's face. She smiled as Vanessa moaned softly in her sleep.

"I'll be back soon to check on you." Liz bent over to kiss Vanessa's forehead.

She stepped from the room and walked back to where Nat and Levi sat speaking quietly.

"Vanessa is all sewn up and they have her sedated to help her recuperate," Liz said as she sat down next to Levi. "The doctor said they would be taking her for a CAT scan to rule out a concussion and then she should start to awaken."

"Did he share any news on Simone?" Levi asked.

"Just that she was getting stronger and he would send for us later tonight if she progressed well enough for a quick visit."

Levi shivered from the cold in the room. Liz stood up to search for a blanket. "Nat, will you go see if you can find some coffee, I think we are in for a long night."

†

Simone woke with a start. The blackness still surrounded her, but it was lighter, almost a shade of gray. She struggled to open her eyelids, but they were too heavy. The cold had begun to subside and she could feel warmth returning to her body. She could also feel gentle hands bathing her skin and examining her closely. When the hands reached her right shoulder she felt a dull ache and when her right arm was lifted a jarring pain seared right into her brain and the blackness returned.

†

When Nat walked out of the emergency room, she ran into NeNe and Killian in the hallway.

"I'm on my way to the snack bar for coffee, so take a walk with me," she said. She brought the two up to date on the accident and everyone's status as they waited for fresh coffee.

"This is horrible," NeNe said. "How is Levi holding up?"

"She is holding her own, but is very distraught, as you may well imagine. She was shivering with cold so Liz sent me for coffee."

"After I see her I'll go back to the resort to get her some warmer clothes," NeNe volunteered.

"That would be great, NeNe, it's cold in the room, but shock has also added to her discomfort." Nat handed them each a coffee and picked up a tray holding three more cups to take back to the emergency room.

"Hey NeNe," Levi said as she took a cup of steaming coffee. Tears welled up in her eyes when she saw Killian. "I'm so sorry, Killian."

"You have nothing to be sorry for. From what I heard you did everything possible to warn them. The captain will be up and about in no time. I have a feeling she is going to make a horrible patient and I pity the poor nurse who has to keep her in bed," she added with a chuckle.

"She isn't awake, but do you want to see her?" Liz asked Killian.

"That would be great, Liz."

They left the room as a nurse entered to check on Levi.

"No one told me we were having a party," she teased with a smile. "I need to cut that cast off and take a look at that arm, Ms. Johnson."

"I'm going to run back out to the resort and get you some warmer clothes, Levi. Is there anything else I can bring you?" NeNe asked.

"Thanks, NeNe, but I can't think of anything else."

"I'll be back in a bit then."

"Do I need to leave?" Nat asked the nurse.

"No, you're fine. I think Ms. Johnson enjoys the company, besides I need someone here in case I slip," she teased as she raised the saw she would use to cut off the cast.

"You miss with that thing and I'm certain you will have another patient," Nat teased, causing the nurse to laugh.

"Hey, hey, I need her to have steady hands here, boss, so cut the laughter," Levi teased.

Liz and Killian returned to Levi's room. They reported that Vanessa had been taken up for her CAT scan, according to a nurse who walked by, and would not return for at least an hour.

The nurse activated the power on the saw and Liz, Nat, and Killian watched with interest as she carefully sliced through the cast on Levi's arm. When she reached the end, she turned the saw off and carefully split the water-soaked cast open with gentle hands. She then cleaned the dead skin and debris from the water from her arm. Levi's arm itched and she was thankful the nurse applied a moisturizing lotion to the pale skin.

"Now we need to get you x-rayed and apply a new cast. I'll call the X-ray department and get you on the schedule. Have you eaten today?"

"Not since breakfast."

The nurse looked at Nat. "Try to get something in her system if you can, even if it is just toast."

"Do you think you can handle some toast?" Nat asked Levi.

Levi looked at the four women staring at her, waiting for her response. "Doesn't look like I have much of a choice, since I'm outnumbered here. Wheat toast with some grape jelly, please."

"I think I can handle that assignment," Killian said and walked from the room.

"Just don't let her attempt any handstands or any other form of acrobatics," the nurse instructed them, and with a chuckle, left the room.

Killian soon returned with toast and jelly. They watched as she ate the two slices of bread and finished her coffee.

"May I get you something else, Levi?" Killian asked.

"Thank you, Killian, but I am fine for now."

NeNe returned with some clothing for Levi and, with great care, Liz and NeNe dressed Levi in jeans, a sweatshirt, thick socks, and her running shoes.

"That feels so much better already. Thank you, NeNe," Levi said with a weak smile.

"You are very welcome."

"Knock, knock," sounded a familiar voice from outside the curtain. Lisa, the x-ray technician who had assisted Levi before, pulled back the curtain.

"Oh no, you again? I thought I was rid of you weeks ago," she teased with a wink.

"I had to take an unexpected dip in the ocean and ruined your handiwork," Levi said.

"Not a problem, I'll fix you up as good as new in no time," Lisa said. "Hop in and we will be off. If you ladies will follow me, I'll show you to a private waiting room where you can await our return."

The small group walked behind the wheelchair like a flock of baby ducks following their mother.

"Help yourselves to coffee and if there is anything you need, just let one of the staff know," she said, then rolled Levi toward an elevator.

Chapter Thirty-five

"Are those your friends who were in the Jet Ski accident?" Lisa asked as they rode up the elevator.

"Yes. What have you heard?"

"One most definitely has a concussion and will have one heck of a headache when she wakes up, but will be released in a day or so if no other complications arise," she said referring to Vanessa.

"Your other friend has a broken collarbone. I took a portable x-ray machine down to the ER and it is most definitely broken."

"Was she awake when you saw her?" Levi asked.

"I'm afraid not. It's going to take a while, Levi," Lisa said, to Levi's obvious disappointment. "She has suffered terrible trauma, but is getting the best care possible at the moment. You'll just have to wait and pray things will turn out well for her."

"Thanks Lisa," Levi said, knowing she could be in trouble for divulging information.

✝

Killian poured them each a cup of coffee, and they sat quietly listening to the tick-tock of the clock. A light tapping on the door caused them to jump and a young female doctor stepped into the room.

"Good afternoon, ladies, I'm Dr. Green," she announced. "I have been assigned to Vanessa's care and wanted to stop in and give you an update. Vanessa did receive a concussion from the blow to her head, but there does not appear to be any further damage. She is on her way back from the CAT scan lab and is semi-alert, so if you want to visit one at a time for a few minutes each that would be fine."

She paused for a moment to allow the information to sink in. "As soon as the room is ready, she will be taken upstairs, and you will be able to remain with her as long as she can tolerate it."

"Thanks, Dr. Green," Liz said. "Any news on Simone?"

"No, I'm sorry. Dr. Hall is assigned to her case, so I don't have any details to share other than she is fighting hard."

"So who is going first?" she asked and everyone turned to Killian.

"Looks like you're it," Dr. Green said to Killian. "Follow me."

Killian followed Dr. Green back to the examination room where Vanessa had just returned.

Vanessa was awake and smiled weakly as Killian stepped into the room. The pain from her swollen face made her grimace, and regret attempting the smile.

"Hey there, Captain," Killian said with a winning smile. "How are you feeling?"

"Like I've been stomped on and run over by a herd of elephants." Her throat was dry and her voice sounded raspy.

"Can she have some water?" she asked Dr. Green.

"Yes, but take small sips," she instructed. "I'll leave you two to visit now."

Killian found a cup, poured some cool water into it, and raised it to Vanessa's lips.

She took a small sip and then another. "How are Simone and Levi?" she whispered.

"Levi is fine. She is upstairs getting x-rayed and a new cast." Killian was relieved when Vanessa smiled regardless of the pain.

"Simone?" she asked again.

"Simone is still in critical condition, but from the limited reports we have received she is fighting very hard."

"Good thing she is a stubborn woman," Vanessa said.

Killian sat down on the bed beside her. "Is there anything I can get you?"

"A new head would be nice, this one is killing me."

"Dr. Green says you have a concussion and will have a whopper of a headache for a few days," Killian told her. "She also said you are going to be moved upstairs as soon as a room is ready."

"Looks like you are going to have to take the *Sappho One* home," Vanessa said.

Killian hadn't thought of the ship's departure and Vanessa's words suddenly struck home. A panicked look crossed her face.

"You're ready," Vanessa assured her. "Just do me a favor."

"Anything, Captain."

"Don't get too used to being captain because I will be back."

"I could never replace you, Captain, but I'll do my best to make you proud," Killian promised.

"I know you will, Killian, and you'll do just fine. You know and love that ship as much as I do and you will take her home safe and sound."

A nurse came into the room. "Would you like something for that headache?"

"Dear woman, you are an angel of mercy," Vanessa said as she watched the nurse inject the medication into the IV line.

"This shouldn't take long to hit your system," the nurse promised and left.

"I will go so Liz and Nat can visit with you before you fall asleep, Captain. I'll stay until I know you are settled and then return to the ship to prepare for departure tomorrow. I'll call daily to check on you, so if there is anything I can do please let me know."

"Killian."

"Yes, Captain?"

"You are the best first mate and friend I could ask for and I thank you for that."

"Thank you, Captain. I will see you upstairs."

Killian returned to the waiting room. "The nurse just gave her some medication so if you want to visit you had better hurry."

"I will go for a quick visit," Nat said and left the room.

"How is she?" NeNe asked.

"She is hurting and looks like the loser of a twelve-round boxing match, but she will be fine."

"Great." NeNe patted the seat beside her and smiled at Killian.

†

Vanessa had turned her face away from the curtain and Nat at first thought she had fallen asleep. Then she turned to look at Nat.

"I am so sorry, Nat," Vanessa said.

"There is nothing to be sorry for, Vanessa. It was an accident and if it hadn't been for you, Simone would not be alive right now. You know Simone well enough to know that she is as stubborn as the day is long and we just have to have confidence that she will fight her way back."

"She is hardheaded," Vanessa agreed.

"That she is. Can I do anything for you?"

"Thanks Nat, but the nurse just gave me a heavenly shot which has helped to ease the throbbing in my head, so I guess I am good."

A moment of silence followed and Nat watched as Vanessa drifted off into a drug-induced sleep. She turned and walked back to the waiting room.

229

†

"I have to sail *Sappho One* home tomorrow, but can I call you and get updates?" Killian was asking NeNe as Nat entered the room.

"Of course you can, Killian," NeNe answered and placed a comforting hand on Killian's shoulder.

"I hadn't thought about that," Liz said.

"The captain had to remind me too," Killian said.

"Vanessa has raved about her confidence in you, Killian, and knows the ship is safe in your hands," Nat said as she sat down next to Liz.

The door to the waiting room opened again and Lisa rolled Levi into the room, a brand-new blue cast on her arm.

"Here you go, ladies, safe and sound and all in one piece," Lisa said.

"Welcome back, Levi," Nat said.

"Thanks, Nat, and thanks for everything, Lisa," Levi said, taking a seat next to Nat.

"No problem, I will check on you ladies before I get off tonight," Lisa said and rolled the chair from the room.

"Is there any news?" Levi asked.

"Vanessa definitely has a concussion and is going to be moved to a room, but nothing yet on Simone," Nat said.

There was a knock on the door and a tall, gray-haired man stepped into the room.

"Good evening, ladies, I'm Dr. Hall, Ms. Taylor's primary physician, and I'm sure you are anxious for an update."

Nat took the lead and introduced everyone to Dr. Hall. "How is my sister?"

"She is stable for now, her oxygen saturations rates are back up and we have started IV antibiotics to prevent pneumonia from setting in since she aspirated so much saltwater."

"Is she conscious yet?" Liz asked.

"No, I'm afraid not. She has a broken right collarbone, which we have immobilized, but she has not regained consciousness yet. I have done all I can for her in the ER so I am transferring her to the Intensive Care Unit for close monitoring."

"Is she going to be all right?" Nat asked.

"Other than the broken collarbone, she did not suffer any other external injuries," he replied, but his face still wore a frown.

"What is it that has you so concerned?" Liz asked.

"Her lack of consciousness worries me, and I cannot tell if there will be any long-term brain damage due to the deprivation of oxygen until she awakens. So for now, all we can do is wait and pray that she awakens soon. I'm sorry I can't tell you more promising news, but for now that's as much as I know." He stood to leave the room. "I will have the nurses notify you when she is moved."

"May I see her?" Nat asked.

"Yes, it may help to have someone talking to her right now. I can't tell you if she hears you, but I can't tell you she won't either. I would suggest you all get a good meal and prepare for a long night. I know it won't do any good to encourage you to go home, but please try to get some rest," he added.

"Thank you, Dr. Hall," Liz said and watched as Nat followed him from the room.

†

Nat stepped into the examination room where Simone was and stifled a gasp as she looked upon her sister. Her skin was so pale and there were IV needles in both arms; monitors were hooked to her chest and head. The only sounds in the room were the beeping monitors and the rasping sounds made by the ventilator. Dr. Hall had told her that Simone was still on a ventilator, but only as a backup in case her respiratory system failed. Simone was breathing regularly on her own, a fact that gave Nat some measure of comfort.

Nat wasn't prepared for the sight of her sister lying so silently on the examination table. Tears flowed down her cheeks as she took Simone's left hand. "I am here for you, Simone, and we are all praying that you will wake up soon. Vanessa and Levi will be fine and send their love. We know you are a strong woman and know you are fighting hard, but you must continue, sister, and not give up the fight." She squeezed Simone's hand.

Simone heard Nat's soothing voice from far away and struggled to open her eyes. She felt Nat take her hand. Her eyes remained tightly shut, despite her attempts, frustrating Simone, so she focused on moving her fingers and very lightly squeezed Nat's hand.

Nat felt the movement of Simone's fingers and jumped in shock. "Yes, that's it, Simone, you have to fight. I know you can hear me. We are all here waiting for you to awaken." Nat's heart soared with renewed hope.

Simone squeezed again, stronger this time. She could not speak but, by God, she was going to let Nat know she was not about to give up.

Nat continued to talk to Simone until she heard the curtain open and the nurses came into the room.

"They are ready for Ms. Taylor in ICU," one of the nurses said. "If you will take the elevator to the third floor, you will see signs to the ICU waiting room and you can wait there. I'll let the nurses know to come get you once she's settled and you can stay with her. It is very important someone she knows is with her now and talking to her. It will serve to give her comfort throughout this critical night."

"There are several of us, friends and family, that will take shifts sitting with her." Nat leaned down to kiss Simone's forehead. "I will see you in just a little while, sister," she said as the nurses prepared Simone for travel.

Chapter Thirty-aix

When Nat returned to the waiting room, Levi's head was propped on NeNe's shoulder. She had drifted off to sleep as they waited.

"They are ready to move Simone to ICU and have asked us to wait in the ICU waiting room," Nat said quietly.

"That's good news," Liz said. "Was she awake at all?"

"No, but I did feel her squeeze my hand a couple of times, so I feel she hears what is said. The doctor is allowing us to take turns sitting with her," Nat said.

"That is good news," Liz said.

"Why don't we go upstairs and let Levi sleep a little longer, if NeNe doesn't mind being a pillow." Liz giggled.

"That sounds fine to me," NeNe said. "Killian, Levi, and I will stay here until Vanessa is moved to her room and then we'll join you upstairs."

"We'll see you later then." Nat reached for Liz's hand as they left the room.

"So, you will be taking over as captain tomorrow," NeNe said.

"Merely standing in while the captain is away," Killian said.

"That has to be exciting for you, even under these circumstances."

"Exciting yes, but also a little terrifying. I know Vanessa will kill me if I put a scratch on her ship," Killian admitted.

"I don't think she has to worry about that at all. By the way, what's a girl have to do to get a tour of that beautiful ship?"

"Just ask someone with connections." Killian winked. "I'll gladly give you a tour when we return."

"I would really appreciate that. Levi raves at how beautiful it is."

"She is a wondrous ship."

NeNe saw the sparkle in Killian's eyes as she spoke of the *Sappho One* and wondered if her own eyes sparkled when she spoke with pride of Venus Rising. She was about to ask Killian another question when the door opened and a nurse came into the room.

"Vanessa has been moved to room 305," she said. "That is as close to the ICU unit as we could get. You can go in and visit with her anytime you are ready."

"Thank you," Killian answered with a smile.

"Levi," NeNe whispered softly. "Levi, it's time to wake up."

Startled, Levi jumped in her seat. "What, what's happened?"

"Everything is fine, Levi. They have moved both Vanessa and Simone up to the third floor," NeNe said. "Nat and Liz are with Simone and we can go see Vanessa now if you would like."

"I would like that very much," Levi said as she stood up.

They rode the elevator to the third floor, stepping out into a madhouse of activity. Hospital staff moved about like ants rushing to and fro as they attended to their duties. They wove their way through the maze of activity until they located room 305.

Inside, they found Vanessa sleeping soundly in the dimly lit room. An IV pole stood by the bed, a bag of sucrose dripping slowly into her veins to hydrate her and aid in relieving the exhaustion Vanessa was suffering. Levi moved a chair close to the bed and took Vanessa's hand in hers.

NeNe and Killian also located chairs and moved them quietly into a circle around Vanessa's bed.

A nurse walked in and smiled at them. "I just have to check her IV," she said as she made her way past Levi. "She will be asleep for a while yet." She noted the level of fluids remaining in the bag. "My name is Mary and you can ask for me at the nurse's station if there is anything you need."

"Thanks, Mary, but I think we're fine for now," Levi said, returning her smile.

Killian watched the tears well up in Levi's eyes as she sat beside Vanessa's bed and her heart went out to her. She knew the dilemma Levi was in, loving both her captain and Simone, and she knew this crisis only added to her stress.

"NeNe, I think I'm getting hungry," Killian said. "Why don't we go get some burgers from downstairs for everyone? Would you mind if we leave you for a few, Levi?"

"No, not at all, Killian."

After NeNe and Killian left the room, Levi placed her forehead on the edge of the bed and allowed her tears to spill. She relived the few horrific minutes that threatened to rip both Vanessa and Simone from her life, and it was still unclear if Simone would pull through. She could not control her tears as they soaked the edge of the bed. She tried to gather her courage and raised her head to wipe her tears away to find Vanessa watching her.

"Hey baby. I guess you caught me," she said with a bit of embarrassment.

"It's all right to cry, Levi," Vanessa said as she took her hand and lifted Levi's chin. "You've had a very stressful day and if it helps, cry your heart out, sweetie."

Levi smiled up at Vanessa who painfully grimaced when she returned the smile.

"Damn that hurt, so please don't make me laugh," Vanessa teased.

"I thought I was going to lose you both today, Vanessa. I saw that wave coming for you and my heart stopped. Then when I saw you both go under I thought my world was coming to an end."

"You can't get rid of us that easy." Vanessa smiled, and then cringed.

"I don't ever want to lose either of you."

"How is Simone doing?" Vanessa asked, trying to shift the conversation.

"She is just down the hallway in ICU for close monitoring, but all reports so far have been good."

"Great news, and you, my love, how are you?"

Levi held up her new blue cast. "All fixed up as good as new."

"Nice color," Vanessa said. "Have you seen Simone yet? Is she awake?"

"No, I haven't. Nat and Liz are with her now, but the doctor says we can take turns sitting with her tonight."

"That's wonderful," Vanessa said. "If she wakes while you are there, please tell her I send my regards."

"I'll do that just for you, Vanessa." Levi leaned forward to softly kiss her lips.

"Ah, sleeping beauty awakens," Killian teased as she entered the room. "A kiss was all it took."

"Not just any kiss, Killian my friend, but a very special kiss from a very special lady," Vanessa said.

"Now I know you hit your head," Killian teased, "you've gone all mushy on us."

"She hasn't always been mushy?" Levi asked.

"Oh, no ma'am. Levi, I think you've gone and ruined her," Killian teased, with a deep chuckle.

Vanessa laughed at Killian and then winced as the tight skin around her eye reminded her of her injury. "Damn, that hurts."

Killian set a bag on the bedside table. "Has your appetite returned with your sense of humor?"

"As a matter of fact, it has, and I can smell a bacon cheeseburger in that bag of yours," she said.

"Well, that blow to your head didn't damage your sense of smell," Killian said as she pulled a burger from the bag.

"Levi, will you raise the head of the bed so I can sit up?"

Levi found the electronic control box and slowly raised the bed until Vanessa nodded her head. "Thanks."

"NeNe is taking burgers to Liz and Nat and will be here in just a minute, but you go ahead and get started," Killian said to Vanessa. "I even remembered to get sweet tea for you."

"You are way too good to me, Killian," Vanessa said as she took the cup and took a short drink.

"Tell me something I don't know." Killian handed two burgers to Levi.

"I love pickles," Vanessa said.

"Ha, I knew that and I have you covered then, Captain," Killian said with a hearty laugh.

Levi took the burger from the wrapper and handed it to Vanessa after spreading a napkin in front of her.

"If these taste half as good as they smell we are in good shape," Levi said.

"Mmm," Vanessa moaned as she took a bite. She chewed slowly and swallowed. "Pure heaven, Killian," she told her and took another bite.

✝

NeNe found Nat in the waiting room. "I've brought burgers for you and Liz." She handed the bag to Nat.

"Thanks, NeNe, they smell great."

"How are you holding up, Nat? Is there anything I can get for you?"

"I'm doing fine, NeNe. I think these burgers should hold us for a while, but thanks for asking."

"Vanessa's room is only three doors down, so if you need anything just give a shout."

"There is one thing, NeNe."

"What is it?"

"I don't know how long you plan on staying, but I was hoping you would go back to the resort to make sure the beach feast goes on as planned," Nat said.

"If that is what you wish, then I'll go in just a little while."

"The staffs of the resort and cruise ship have worked so hard I would hate to cancel it."

"I'll make sure everyone has a great time then."

"Thank you for all that you do, NeNe."

"My pleasure, Nat. You, and Liz have always treated me like family and I appreciate that."

"Well, you are family," Nat said with a smile.

NeNe smiled at Nat. "Eat before it gets cold and I'll see you later tonight."

Chapter Thirty-seven

NeNe walked back into Vanessa's room, and sat beside Killian to eat her burger. "Nat asked me to go back to the resort to make sure the beach feast goes off as planned."

"That's a good idea. I think Killian should join you, to ensure our guests and staffs have everything they need."

"No problem, Captain," she answered and smiled at NeNe.

Levi was pleased to see Vanessa with a hearty appetite. She ate nearly all of her burger and drank all of her tea. She rested against the bed afterward and they could tell her strength was fading.

"If you don't need anything else, I'll head back to the ship, my Captain," Killian said.

"Take good care of her as I know you will," Vanessa said as Killian stood to leave. "I will see you as soon as possible."

"Take all the time you need, Captain. I'll have everything in order when you return."

"Thank you, Killian."

"My pleasure, Captain."

"Have some fun for us at the feast tonight, ladies," Vanessa said as they walked toward the door.

"We will, Vanessa," NeNe said as she reached for Killian's hand.

Vanessa turned to grin at Levi. "Another romance in the making?"

"You never know." She returned her grin, thinking NeNe and Killian would make a cute couple.

"After you fall asleep, I'm going to check on Simone," Levi said.

"Why don't you lower my bed and go now. I have had all your attention this afternoon. Go, I will take a nap and see you later."

Levi lowered her bed and leaned down to kiss Vanessa. "I will be back soon. Rest well, my love."

"I will have the sweetest dreams of you." Vanessa grinned as she watched Levi walk away.

Liz was in the ICU waiting room, flipping through a magazine when Levi entered.

"Levi! How are you?" Liz jumped up to give her a hug. "Are you coming to visit Simone?"

"I'm fine, Liz. Yes, I thought I would give you and Nat a break."

"Why don't you go on in then. Nat and I will keep an eye on Vanessa for a while."

"She will probably be asleep by the time you get there. She was fading fast when I left."

"We will watch her sleep then," Liz said with a chuckle. "Simone is through that door and the first bed on the right." Liz looked at Levi. "Prepare yourself, Levi, right now she doesn't look like the Simone you know."

"I will." Levi took a deep breath and walked from the room.

Nat was sitting next to the bed talking quietly to Simone as Levi entered. She did not hear Levi approach and jumped when Levi placed her hand on her shoulder.

"Time for you to take a break," Levi said. "Anything new?"

"Not really. She moans from time to time in her sleep, but no signs of waking up yet," Nat said with disappointment in her voice.

"You know Simone won't be rushed."

"Very true, but I won't rest easy until I hear her voice again."

"I understand," Levi said. "I think Liz was going to stop in to check on Vanessa. Her room is three doors down and to the right."

"Thanks, Levi. I'll see you in a bit."

Levi took the seat Nat vacated and reached to take Simone's hand in hers. "I know you can hear me, Simone, and I want you to know we all love you and are praying for you to recover quickly."

Levi looked at all the monitors and lines leading into Simone's body and shivered. She could see the mass of her arm, immobilized against her chest to protect her broken collarbone and she wondered if Simone felt pain.

"You two had me so worried today. I was sleeping so soundly and when I woke, I found the two of you had drifted into such peril. I swear, I just can't take my eyes off you without you getting into some sort of trouble."

Levi watched Simone's face for any sign of acknowledgment, but there was none.

Simone sensed there was a change in the room and knew Nat had left. The one that had replaced her spoke with a sweet voice, but she could not determine whose voice it was. She strained harder to listen and to put a face to the name, but could not do so, so she relaxed and listened to the soft tones of the pleasing voice.

Levi found a bottle of lotion and poured some of the rich liquid into the palm of her hand. She knew Simone had received a bed bath in the emergency room, but the salt from the ocean had a drying effect on skin. She softly caressed the lotion into Simone's exposed arm. She lifted the covers off one leg, massaging the lotion into her skin and then moved to the other side of the bed to the other leg, repeating her motions. She talked to Simone as she

241

covered her skin with lotion, soothing the moisturizer into her thirsty skin.

"Vanessa is just a few doors down from you and is recovering well," Levi said. "She has actually eaten one of those greasy cheeseburgers from the snack bar and other than a humongous headache and nasty cut she seems to be doing fine."

Levi placed the lotion back on the nightstand and leaned down to brush the hair back from Simone's brow. She could see Simone's eyes darting from side to side, as her mind was lost in dreams.

"I hope you are having sweet dreams," Levi whispered as she softly stroked Simone's hair.

Levi sat in the chair and held Simone's hand as she watched her sleep. She felt her eyelids grow heavy, but struggle as she might, she could not keep her eyes open and she nodded off to sleep.

†

Levi startled to attention when she heard an alarm sounding in the room. Her eyes flew open and she saw that Simone had pulled the vent tube from her throat, causing the alarm to sound. Seconds later, a nurse rushed into the room to assess the situation.

"I'm sorry, I must have drifted off to sleep," Levi apologized.

"Relax, Ms. Taylor is just fine," the nurse said to comfort Levi.

She reached up and turned off the monitor attached to the ventilator and checked the other monitors. After an initial spike in heart rate, Simone's vital signs returned to normal.

"Ms. Taylor felt the irritation of the tube in her throat and relieved herself of the invading tube," the nurse told Levi. "That is an excellent sign that she is struggling back. If she is aware of painful stimuli she is slowly waking."

"That sounds like good progress," Levi agreed.

"Most definitely. I'll call the doctor to inform him of the latest status, but I doubt he will feel a need to replace the ventilator."

Nat walked back into the cubicle as the nurse was leaving. "What happened?"

"Simone pulled the vent tube out while she was sleeping, but the nurse says that's a good sign that she is improving," she reported.

"Excellent," Nat said. "You look exhausted, Levi. Why don't you go crash on the spare bed in Vanessa's room. Liz and I can watch over Simone while you get a nap in."

"Thanks, Nat," Levi said as she left the cubicle.

Chapter Thirty-eight

Levi walked into Vanessa's room and found Liz staring out the window. She looked up when Levi entered.

"Has she been awake much?" she asked, nodding toward Vanessa.

"Nope, she has been sleeping sound since I arrived. How is Simone?"

"The nurse says she is beginning to come around. She caught me dozing and pulled out the vent tube. The nurse assured me that it was a good sign that Simone is starting to awaken."

"That is excellent news."

"Nat sent me down here to catch a nap."

"You do look exhausted. If you want to sleep for a couple of hours, I will be sure to wake you if anything changes."

"Thanks Liz." Levi started toward the empty bed.

"Why don't you come snuggle with me?" Vanessa said.

Both Levi and Liz turned to find Vanessa awake and smiling at them.

"Why, Captain, what do you think the hospital staff will say if they find me snuggled up to you?" Levi teased.

"I honestly could care less what they would think," Vanessa said with a grin. "So hush and come here." She raised the covers from the bed.

Levi looked at Liz. "Go ahead. I'll stay until you fall asleep and then I'll go check on Nat."

Levi slipped out of her shoes and carefully climbed onto the bed, laying her head on Vanessa's shoulder and resting her aching wrist on Vanessa's hip. Vanessa lowered the covers over them and the warmth beckoned Levi to surrender to sleep. She closed her eyes and listened to the beating of Vanessa's heart as she relaxed, slipping into dreamland.

Liz watched over them as promised. Her heart warmed by the smiles that played across their faces.

Just after midnight, a light knock on the door jarred Liz from her nap. She too had drifted off to sleep, and was surprised to see Killian and NeNe come into the room.

"Welcome back, ladies," she said to them.

"Thanks Liz," Killian said. "I see these two are resting well."

"How is Simone?" NeNe asked.

"I haven't had a report in the last few hours, but if you will stay here I'll go check in with Nat."

"Not a problem," NeNe said. She and Killian found chairs to sit in. "Take your time, we are in no hurry. Oh, you can tell Nat the beach feast went off without a hitch," NeNe excitedly added.

"Great news. I'll be sure to tell her." Liz slipped from the room.

"They look comfortable don't they?" Killian chuckled.

"Yes, they do."

Sensing a change in the room, Levi awoke to find NeNe and Killian smiling at her.

"Hey you two, what's up?"

"We thought we would stop by and check on everyone before calling it a night," NeNe said.

Levi slowly sat up on the side of the bed, her movement waking Vanessa.

"Hey ladies, how was the party?" Vanessa asked.

"It was great," NeNe said. "We just finished seeing everyone off the beach."

"What time is it?" Vanessa asked.

245

"Just past midnight," Killian said. "I know, I should be off to bed soon to be prepared for tomorrow, but I just had to see you again to make sure you were doing okay."

"It is good to see you too, Killian," Vanessa said. "You probably won't sleep much tonight as it is. I trust your judgment."

"I am a bit nervous," Killian admitted.

"I would be worried if you weren't. Just relax and you'll be fine," Vanessa assured her first mate.

Nat entered the room. "Hey ladies."

"How is Simone?" Levi asked.

"She's resting well. I think we shall see great improvement tomorrow," she predicted. She looked at Levi, who still appeared exhausted. "Why don't you go back with NeNe and Killian and get a good night's sleep."

"I can't leave Vanessa and Simone right now."

"Yes, you can," Vanessa said. "We're just going to sleep tonight, so please follow Nat's advice, and get some rest, my love."

"I promise to bring you back bright and early in the morning," NeNe said.

"It's settled then," Killian said. "I will see you soon, Captain."

"We'll wait for you in the hall," NeNe said as she and Killian left the room.

Levi looked to Nat for support.

"If anything changes, I will call," Nat said.

"Goodnight then, my sweet." Vanessa reached for Levi and pulled her down for a kiss.

"I will see you for breakfast," Levi said. "Is there anything I can bring you and Liz?"

"No, I don't think so, Levi. We'll return to the resort when you get here in the morning and catch a few hours of sleep."

"See you tomorrow then." Levi joined Killian and NeNe in the hall.

"Are you ready to go?" NeNe asked.

"Not really, but it seems I'm outnumbered."

"Yes, I do believe you are," Killian said as they walked to the elevator.

Levi rode to the ship with them and after a short good-bye to Killian, she and NeNe were on their way back to the resort.

"You and Killian seem to be getting very close," Levi said with a grin.

"She is such a wonderful woman. I can't wait for her to come back so we can spend some time together."

"Look out, ladies, there is a sparkle in those eyes."

"I can believe that. She makes me laugh and feel so special."

"Not to mention, you two make an adorable couple."

"Thanks, Levi. How are you holding up through all of this drama?"

"I'm extremely tired, my friend. I feel like I could sleep for a week."

"I'll drop you off up front and go park the Jeep."

"You will do no such thing. Park and I will walk with you."

They walked to the staff bungalows. "Call me when you are ready to go to the hospital in the morning," NeNe said.

"Thanks for everything, NeNe."

"You're welcome, my friend, now go and sleep well."

†

"I'm fine here, Nat, so why don't you go sit with Liz," Vanessa suggested. "I'm just going back to sleep."

"You won't be chasing the nurses down the hallways then?" Nat teased.

"Definitely not tonight. Go, and I will see you tomorrow."

"Very well, but if you need anything I am just down the hall."

Nat stepped quietly into the ICU cubicle and placed her hand on Liz's shoulder. "Would you like some coffee?"

"That does sounds good, but why don't you let me get it?" Liz said. "My legs could use a stretch."

Liz kissed Nat and went in search of fresh coffee. Nat took Simone's left hand in hers and was relieved to find it warm to her touch.

"I'm back, sister."

Nat watched in disbelief as Simone's eyelids fluttered and her eyes opened.

"Welcome back," Nat said as she leaned across Simone's bed. "You had us worried for a while there, sis."

Liz stepped back into the room and was shocked to see Simone's eyes opened.

"Hello, Simone," she said.

Simone struggled to focus. She realized it was Nat sitting next to her. She could not make out the figure of the woman at the end of the bed, but recognized the voice as Liz. Her tongue snaked out of her mouth and wet her lips. She tried to speak. After several attempts, she managed a weak, "Hi sis."

"Hush, don't try to talk right now," Nat said. "Just relax. There will be plenty time to catch up later."

Simone was able to nod her head and Nat could see tears pooling in her eyes.

"You are going to be just fine, Simone," Nat said. "It will take time, but you are going to be just fine."

"You gave us quite a worry," Liz said. "It's so good to see you awake. Are you hurting anywhere?"

Simone shook her head and squeezed Nat's hand. "What happened?" she asked in a faint whisper.

"You, Vanessa, and Levi were having a day on the beach," Nat said. "You and Vanessa were out riding Jet Skis when a rogue wave overwhelmed your skis."

Simone frowned as she tried to remember what had happened to cause her to be in the hospital.

"Levi and Vanessa were able to bring you ashore and you were rushed here for treatment," Liz said.

Simone's eyes closed and she slipped back to sleep.

"That was very encouraging," Liz said.

"Yes it was." She was concerned that Simone could not remember the accident, but she supposed that was normal for such a traumatic event. Regardless, Simone had regained consciousness, and spoke. She appeared to recognize her and Liz, so Nat was hopeful that tomorrow would hold even greater promise.

She took the cup of coffee from Liz and smiled at her beautiful lover. "Simone is going to be just fine," she said.

Ali Spooner

Chapter Thirty-nine

Levi woke and showered before going to the dining room for some breakfast. Most of the guests were still sleeping, so Levi dined in peace and quiet. Several of the staff stopped by to speak to her, and to inquire of Vanessa and Simone. All were relieved to find Vanessa doing well and shared their hopes that Simone would continue to show signs of improvement. Levi stared out the window and watched the sun rise across the deep blue-green water and she found herself smiling.

"A penny for your thoughts," NeNe said from behind her.

Levi turned to look at NeNe. "The sunrise here is more beautiful than any I have ever seen."

"I always thought it was due to the sun's light reflecting off the brilliant water, but whatever the reason it does seem special here," NeNe agreed.

NeNe ordered breakfast and ate while she and Levi chatted.

"Will you go see Killian off this morning?"

"I thought I might just drive down that way after I drop you at the hospital."

"I think that is an excellent idea," Levi said with a devilish grin.

They finished breakfast and drove to the hospital.

"I will stop back by after I say good-bye to Killian."

"Thanks, tell her to hurry back." Levi stepped out of the Jeep.

"Oh I will." NeNe winked and drove away.

†

Levi made her way up to the third floor and found Nat sitting with Simone.

"Good morning, boss," she said. "How is Simone?"

"She actually woke up during the night and spoke a little," Nat said with a huge smile.

"That's awesome news. I'm going to check on Vanessa real quick, then I'll be back to sit with Simone so you and Liz can go get some rest."

Levi left and walked to Vanessa's room, finding her lover sitting up in the bed and finishing breakfast. Vanessa looked up and smiled when she saw Levi.

"Good morning, sunshine," Vanessa said, her smile lighting up the room.

"Good morning, sweetie, how are you feeling?"

"Still a bit of a headache, but the doctor says I'll be discharged later today. I still can't fly for a few more days, so it looks like you are stuck with me a little longer."

"That is great news." Levi turned to smile at Liz. "How are you this morning?"

"I'm good, thanks Levi."

Levi bent down and kissed Vanessa. "I told Nat I'd sit with Simone so she and Liz can go get some sleep," she told Vanessa. "I'll be back soon to check on you."

"No problem, I'll just kick back and be a lady of leisure until the doctor sets me free."

"Come on, Liz, let's get you two going. I know you've got to be exhausted."

"I'm most definitely ready to snuggle up with my baby and snooze for a while," Liz said. "I'll see you later today, Vanessa."

"Sleep well and thanks for keeping me company," Vanessa said.

"My pleasure." She leaned down to kiss Vanessa's cheek.

"Later babes." Levi winked.

"Nat told me Simone woke up for a little while last night," Levi said as they walked back to ICU.

"Yes, it was amazing to see her awake. I hope she continues to improve today."

"Me too," Levi said as they entered the cubicle.

"We'll see you after lunch," Nat said as she stood to leave.

"I'll be back at the club tonight so you and Liz can focus on Simone."

"I'm sure I could get someone to cover for you," Nat said.

"That's all right, Nat, I feel like I've been neglecting my duties."

"Hardly, my friend, so just let me know if you change your mind."

"Will do." Levi walked them to the door of ICU. "Get some sleep."

"See you later, Levi," Liz said.

Levi poured a fresh cup of coffee and returned to sit beside Simone who was resting quietly. She talked with Simone and covered her skin with lotion, massaging the muscles of her arm and legs as she talked. She was sitting back, sipping her coffee when the ICU door opened and the curtain was pulled open.

Vanessa was sitting in a wheelchair smiling at her.

"What have we here?" Levi asked the nurse standing behind Vanessa's wheelchair.

"Someone who said she must get out of bed. The head nurse said she could join you for a while but if she gets too rowdy, it's back to bed for her."

"I promise to be good," Vanessa said with a sheepish grin.

"No worries, I'll keep her out of trouble," Levi promised.

"I'll see you in a couple of hours then."

"You must be a real smooth talker to be allowed in here," Levi said.

Vanessa grinned at her. "So how is Simone?"

"Still resting well, but she hasn't been awake since I've been here."

Vanessa looked at Simone. "Sleep is probably the best thing for her right now."

Levi sighed. "I know you're right, but I won't rest easy until I hear her talk."

Vanessa reached over and took Levi's hand. "She'll be just fine, Levi."

The morning was rapidly slipping away when one of the ICU nurses stepped inside the cubicle.

"Aren't you the captain of the cruise ship in port?"

Levi grinned at her. "My, my news does travel quickly here."

"Yes, ma'am, I am," Vanessa answered.

"You might want to see this then. Follow me please."

The nurse led Vanessa and Levi into a small atrium just outside the ICU, which provided an excellent view of the harbor.

Vanessa's eyes lit up as the harbormaster guided *Sappho One* out of the harbor. "Isn't that a beautiful sight?" Levi said as she and Vanessa watched her ship leaving port.

"Yes, it is. It's the first time I've ever seen her leave without me though," Vanessa said with tears pooling in her eyes.

"You'll be back on her soon," the nurse replied. She walked away, giving them a private moment.

"You do love that ship, don't you?"

"Almost as much as I love you," Vanessa answered, shocking Levi.

Neither of them had spoken those words before and Levi was surprised. She bent down and kissed Vanessa softly. "I love you too," she whispered.

They watched until the *Sappho One* left the harbor then turned back to Simone's room. When they entered, Dr. Hall was finishing his examination.

"Good morning, ladies," he said. "Ms. Taylor is progressing well. I hope the two of you're doing well also."

"Just fine, thanks," Vanessa said.

"I'll stop back later today then."

"I don't think I want another round of hospital food," Vanessa said. "Would you please go downstairs and get us another of those incredibly sinful cheeseburgers?"

Levi chuckled. "I think that could be arranged. Do you want bacon or a plain cheeseburger?"

"Oh yes, bacon and extra pickles please, and more sweet tea too."

"I'll be back in a few minutes. Don't run off while I'm gone."

Wearing a huge smile, she answered, "I'll be waiting right here." She watched Levi leave and turned to Simone. "We have quite a lady, I hope you know that, boss."

Simone did not give any sign that she had heard Vanessa.

Levi's trip to the snack bar was a quick one and soon she and Vanessa were eating bacon cheeseburgers. Levi was cleaning up the trash from the meal when they heard a weak voice say, "Do I smell cheeseburgers?"

Vanessa and Levi whipped their heads around to see Simone awake and looking at them.

"Why yes you do, boss. Bacon cheeseburgers to be exact."

"That is so cruel, Vanessa," Simone croaked.

Vanessa grinned at her. "Hey, a woman's got to eat you know."

"Who's your gorgeous friend, Captain?"

Vanessa looked at Levi and Levi stared back at her. "Who are you trying to kid, Simone?" Vanessa asked.

Simone's face looked like a blank page. "Come on, Vanessa, the least you could do is introduce us."

Vanessa looked back at Levi who was in complete shock. "It's Levi, Simone."

"Levi who?" Simone asked sincerely.

"Levi Johnson. The hottest bartender on the island," Vanessa reminded her.

There was still no sign of recognition on Simone's face.

"Well, it's very nice to meet you, Levi Johnson, hottest bartender on the island. Pardon me if I don't shake your hand, but I seem to be a little restrained at the moment."

254

"Nice to meet you too," Levi stammered, completely overwhelmed by Simone's failure to recognize her.

"That must have been one hell of a Jet Ski ride we took," Simone said. "You look like you lost a twelve-round boxing match."

"I've seen better days for sure, boss," Vanessa told her.

"Were you there at the beach, Levi?"

"Yes, I was. Excuse me please." Levi rushed from the room.

Hurrying to the atrium where she and Vanessa had watched the cruise ship earlier Levi found a seat. She covered her face, but could not hold back the flood of tears that burned down her cheeks. How was it possible that Simone remembered the accident and Vanessa but not remember her, she wondered. Completely bewildered, Levi sat alone in the atrium, drowning in self-pity. After all that had happened with Simone over the last few weeks, this memory loss was the proverbial straw, and left Levi completely distraught.

✝

Vanessa looked out from behind the curtain but didn't see any sign of Levi. She worried Levi's heart must be shattered by Simone's behavior. She didn't know what she would say to Levi, but felt that how she did react would be crucial in their future relationship.

Vanessa was turning her wheelchair around to leave the room when Nat and Liz stepped in. Liz was the first to notice the absence of Levi and the frantic look on Vanessa's face.

"Where's Levi?"

"I'm afraid we have a problem, ladies. Push me down the hall please, Liz."

Liz looked at Nat who stared back at her.

"Hello, sis," Simone said from the bed.

Nat turned and smiled at Simone.

"Welcome back, Simone," Nat said.

"We'll be back soon." Liz quietly rolled Vanessa's wheelchair down the hallway.

"What's going on?" Liz asked.

"Simone doesn't remember Levi."

"What do you mean, Simone doesn't remember Levi?"

"I mean just that. Simone has no clue who Levi is or what she feels for her. At first we thought Simone was just teasing, playing a cruel joke, but she really has no idea who Levi is. She thinks she just met her for the first time today."

"Holy shit," Liz sank back against the wall. "Where's Levi now?"

"I have no clue," Vanessa said. "She fled from the room a few minutes ago and I haven't seen her since."

"Can you wheel this contraption around?"

"I think I can manage," Vanessa said.

"Go find Levi. I'll go back and explain to Nat what's going on then I'll find you.

"There's an atrium just down the hall, I think that's where she might have gone."

"I will join you in a few minutes then." Liz took off in the direction of the ICU.

This shit just keeps getting weirder and weirder. How much more trauma could Levi endure when it came to Simone. Levi deserved so much better than she was getting and Liz's heart ached for her.

✝

Vanessa rolled down the hallway and turned into the atrium. As she had expected, Levi was there, sitting with her face in her hands. The sight of the woman she loved in tears broke Vanessa's heart. She quickly rolled over to where Levi was sitting.

Levi looked up to see Vanessa in front of her and collapsed into the arms waiting to hold her.

"I'm so sorry, baby," Vanessa said and took Levi in her arms.

Chapter Forty

When Levi could stop her tears, she raised her head from Vanessa's tear-soaked shoulder. "After all we have been through, how can Simone not remember who I am?"

"I have absolutely no answer for you there, Levi. The only explanation I can think of is that the brain is a very intricate organ and the lack of oxygen slightly damaged Simone's short-term memory."

"I just can't believe she can recall the accident, but is clueless in recognizing me and what I thought I meant to her."

"Stop right there." Vanessa lifted Levi's face. "Never doubt that Simone loves you, because she does. She might not be able to draw upon those feelings at this moment, but Simone is very much in love with you."

"How can you say that?"

"I have known Simone long enough to recognize when she is in love."

Vanessa watched as Levi digested that information. She had to smile when she thought back over her words. She sounded like a commercial promoting Simone and had to stifle a chuckle. Her thoughts were ridiculous, but the atmosphere was thick with tension and if she broke out in laughter even at herself, Levi might not understand.

"What should I do, Vanessa?"

"Right now, all you can do is be patient with Simone and see if her memory returns."

"And if her memory of me doesn't return, then what?"

"Well, you'll have to make that decision when the time comes, Levi, but for now you just have to wait and see what the future holds."

"After all the pain that woman has caused me since we met, why do I even care?"

"Because, my dear, it's obvious that you love Simone."

Levi stared into Vanessa's beautiful eyes for several seconds, trying to read the emotion lying there. She knew Vanessa loved her and it must be difficult for her to encourage Levi to have faith in Simone. Most of the women Levi knew in the past would have jumped on the opportunity to take advantage of the situation for their own personal gain, but Vanessa was not that type of woman. She fully understood that if Levi chose to love her, it would be of her own volition. There was no one who could coerce Levi into showing feelings that were not genuine.

Levi knew she loved both Simone and Vanessa. She briefly considered that maybe the accident and Simone's memory loss was Fate's way of helping her choose between the two women.

"I love you both so much." Levi hugged Vanessa close.

"I love you too."

Levi and Vanessa were in a lover's embrace when Liz walked into the atrium. Levi pulled away at the sound of her approach and looked at Liz with bloodshot eyes.

"I'm sorry about Simone's memory loss," Liz said. "I know it must have shattered your heart, but I hope you know that Simone does really care for you."

"Vanessa has been telling me the same thing, Liz. That I must be patient and see if her memory returns."

"I always knew you were a smart one, Captain."

"I think I may have an idea of what part of the problem is," Liz said as she sat next to Levi.

"What would that be?"

"A staff from the Jet Ski rental dropped off Simone's bag this morning and as I was going through it, I found this." Liz reached into her breast pocket and pulled out a small velvet bag.

"Please tell me that isn't what I think it is?" Levi groaned.

Liz nodded, with a frown. "Simone must have returned to the island and recovered the coin sometime after your visit."

"She did not witness me burying the coin, but I guess it wouldn't be that difficult to discover. But why would she do that?"

"I can't say for certain, but knowing Simone's ego I'm sure she wanted to prove to you that the curse business was nothing more than island superstition," Liz said.

"That sounds about right," Vanessa said. "Simone would not want to admit that something as small and insignificant as a cursed gold coin could alter her life plan."

"It almost ruined her life plan," Levi said as she held tightly onto the small bag. "I will take care of this once and for all, curse be dammed. I will be back before I have to go to work to check if you are ready for discharge." She leaned in to kiss Vanessa.

"Do you want me to go with you?" Liz asked.

"Thanks Liz, but I think it's better that no one sees where I put this damned coin this time."

"Do you think it will work without Simone?"

"Well, it didn't seem to work well with her in the picture, so we'll see."

"Take the van." Liz handed Levi the keys. "I'll try to keep this one out of trouble while you are gone." Liz reached over and ruffled Vanessa's hair.

"Good luck with that," Levi teased. "I'll be back soon."

Liz observed the way Vanessa stared after Levi as she walked down the hall. When Vanessa returned her attention to Liz, she found Liz smiling broadly at her.

"You do love that woman, don't you?"

"With all my heart," she answered with a smile.

"It must be a very difficult situation for you to be in at the moment, stuck in the middle of this crazy triangle," Liz said.

"There have been tough moments, but then I see Levi's smile or hear the sweetness in her voice. That makes it all worthwhile."

Liz placed her hand on Vanessa's shoulder. "Levi is a very lucky woman to have met you."

"Thanks Liz, but I feel like I am the lucky one. Levi makes me feel so complete."

"That's such a sweet and romantic thing to say, Vanessa."

"I can't help it, I want to take her in my arms and hold her forever."

"If circumstances change and Levi chooses Simone, then what?"

"If that happens, then I'll hold on to some very precious memories and still love Levi for the wonderful woman she is."

"Levi would be very fortunate to have you in her life," Liz said. "I know your love for her is sincere and Levi deserves only the best."

"Thanks, Liz." Vanessa didn't want to imagine her life without Levi. "Should we go back and check on Simone and Nat now?"

"That's probably a very good idea. I know this is a hospital, but I swear those two could get into trouble anywhere." Liz chuckled.

Liz pushed her friend down the hall to the ICU. When they moved behind the curtain, Nat looked up. "Where's Levi?"

"Levi is on a mission, and will return later this afternoon," Liz told her lover.

"Welcome back, Captain," Simone said to Vanessa.

"Thanks, how are you feeling Simone?"

"Better now that you are here," Simone flirted.

Vanessa looked at Liz who shrugged her shoulders and smiled back at her.

"So who is this Levi?" Simone asked.

"She is our newest bartender at the resort," Liz replied, unsure how she should answer her question.

Liz looked at Nat, who knew nothing of what was happening, and winked at her. Nat trusted Liz and though completely baffled by this conversation, would follow Liz's lead.

"She looks to be very fond of you, dear Captain," Simone said. "Do I need to be jealous?"

"I'm very fond of Levi as well," Vanessa said. "There's no need to be jealous though, boss."

"I would hate for my best captain to be stolen away by a mere island bartender."

Liz saw the hackles go up on Vanessa's neck.

"Levi's much more than a mere island bartender, Simone," Vanessa growled.

"Oh, so she is someone very special to you then," Simone said with a mischievous grin.

"Yes, she is and I hope you'll mind how you treat her and talk about her." Vanessa's voice rose just a notch to show her irritation.

"Please accept my apologies, Vanessa, I didn't mean to make light of your girlfriend."

Liz wanted to reach across the bed and knock some sense into Simone, but Vanessa expediently put Simone in her place.

"Simone, I think you would do well to take some lessons from Levi," Vanessa said. "For a mere bartender, she knows much more about treating people with kindness and love than you have ever shown."

"Point taken, my friend," she answered.

"Liz would you like to step out and get some coffee?" Nat asked.

"I would love to, baby. Vanessa, would you like some?"

"Yes. Cream and sugar please, Liz."

Nat and Liz walked down the hall toward the break room.

Nat turned to look at Liz once they moved away from the ICU room. "Would you care to fill me in on exactly what the hell is going on here?"

"Well, my love, it seems your dear sister has a bit of a memory lapse when it comes to Levi," Liz said, shaking her head as she tried to explain what was happening.

"Good Lord."

"She remembers the accident and everyone, but Levi."

"How is Levi taking this?"

"As well as can be expected," Liz said. "She's shattered and confused by Simone's latest behavior, but is holding up well. I told her about the coin and she has gone to deal with it once and for all, we hope."

It was Nat's turn to shake her head in disbelief. "Poor Levi. It has been one thing after another with Simone, hasn't it?"

"Yes, it has. I don't know how much more we can expect her to take. I think we should encourage her to stay away from the hospital for a few days until we see how Simone progresses."

"If Vanessa gets discharged today, she should be able to keep her fairly busy." Nat chuckled.

"I think Vanessa would willingly take on that challenge. I think Levi intends to return to work too."

"That may not be a bad idea to keep her mind occupied and off this crazy mess. Let's go see what Vanessa thinks then, my love." Nat picked up several cups of coffee and they returned to Simone's room.

Simone had drifted off to sleep. Nat handed Vanessa a cup of coffee. "Liz and I have talked and we think maybe it would be best if Levi refrained from coming to the hospital once you're discharged. Do you think you can keep her busy for the next few days, at least until we know more about what's happening with Simone?"

"I think I can handle that, being the invalid that I am," Vanessa said with a grin. "I'll sit with her at the bar during her shifts and keep her busy on the beach or at the pool during her off time."

"That way, at least, Levi won't have to be hurt any further by Simone's lack of memory. Lord knows Simone has already hurt her enough."

Vanessa nodded her agreement with Liz's statement.

"I'll do my best to keep her mind off Simone," Vanessa promised.

The curtain opened up and Vanessa's nurse walked in.

"I hate to break up this party, but if you are to be discharged I'm going to have to steal you away to perform your final exam and prepare your discharge orders. I hope someone brought you some clothes, unless you want to be released in a hospital gown or scrubs," she teased.

"Killian brought a small bag for you and I placed it in the closet," Liz told Vanessa.

"Thanks Liz, I hear these hospital gowns can get breezy. I guess I'll see you a little later."

The room fell silent as Liz and Nat watched Simone sleep. "How are we going to fix this?" Nat asked.

"I have no clue, love, but we'll think up something." Liz took Nat's hand in hers. "We always do."

Chapter Forty-one

Vanessa went through her final exam, and then dressed in white Bermuda shorts, a dark blue pullover and slipped her feet into her leather loafers. She never dreamed it could feel so good to be wearing clothes again as she dropped the hospital gown on the bed.

She tucked the prescription for the painkiller into her bag and zipped it shut. She walked down the hallway to the ICU and stepped inside.

Liz looked up and smiled as she entered the room. "Well, look what we have here. You're looking much better now."

"Thanks, it actually feels wonderful to have real clothes on again."

"What, did you get tired of that cool breeze on your bum when you walked to the bathroom?" Nat teased.

Vanessa laughed. "I was hoping no one noticed."

"Not a chance we would miss that view," Liz said with a wink and a wicked grin.

Vanessa returned her grin. "How's Simone doing?"

"Still sleeping on and off, but she seems to be waking more often," Nat reported.

The curtain opened and NeNe stepped inside. "Am I missing the party?"

"Nope, you're just in time," Vanessa said.

"I just wanted to stop by and see how everyone is doing," NeNe said. "Have you been discharged already?"

"Yes, I am just waiting for Levi to return and then I'm out of here."

"Where's Levi?" NeNe asked.

"She had a little business to attend to, but she'll be back later," Liz said.

"Very good. Well, I'm going to head back to the resort unless there is anything I can get for anyone," NeNe said.

"I think we are good, but thanks, NeNe."

"Would you drop me down at the harbor?" Vanessa asked.

"Of course I will, but why the harbor?"

"I'll tell you on the way." Vanessa stood and picked up her bag. "Please give me a call if there is anything you need," she said to Nat and Liz.

✝

Levi rented a small boat at the harbor and easily navigated the waters. Once she was clear of the no wake zone, she poured on the fuel and sped across the open water. She was still fuming at Simone for going back for the coin. Her arrogance nearly got the best of her. Levi would make certain there was no way the coin could come into their lives again.

On the ride across the water, Levi contemplated burying the coin in the cave where she had originally discovered it but decided she would locate a spot on the island where it was less likely for anyone to find. She pulled the boat into a small harbor and dropped anchor. Slipping over the side of the boat, she waded to shore and headed down the now familiar path. Instead of following it to the caves, however, Levi turned left when the trail split and walked deeper into the island.

She located a clearing ringed by coconut palms and found a spot where the ground was sandy enough she could dig a small hole with her hand. Levi dug the hole about a foot deep and dropped the coin inside. She covered it quickly before the allure of the coin could trick her into returning it to her pocket. She tamped the soil down with her foot and found a flat rock to place over the area. Levi leaned back against the tree and gazed up into the sky. Hopefully the coin would remain safely buried and no one else would have to experience the curse of the pirate's gold. Her life had been so different before she discovered the cursed coin, filled with happiness and self-adventure. Since discovering the coin, she found herself adrift in a maelstrom of drama and disappointment. Sighing deeply, Levi stood and made her way back to the beach.

With her mission accomplished, Levi waded out to the boat and headed back to the harbor. The ride on the water had taken her mind off all the drama occurring in her life, but as the harbor came into view, everything rushed back, leaving Levi overwhelmed by the sadness of Simone's memory loss. She struggled to hold back the tears that threatened to flow and concentrated on steering the boat back into the harbor.

†

"What's going on now?" NeNe asked Vanessa on the way to the parking lot.

"When Simone awoke earlier today, Levi and I were sitting with her and she had absolutely no clue who Levi was."

"You're kidding, right? How could she not know who Levi is?"

"I wish I was teasing, NeNe, but it's the truth. Simone does not remember Levi."

"That's just too bizarre," she said, shaking her head. "Levi has to be devastated."

"She's taking it very hard as you would expect. I'm beginning to really worry about her."

"So where has Levi gone, and what is this business she is taking care of?"

Vanessa shook her head as they climbed inside NeNe's Jeep. "This is where it gets even more bizarre."

"Is that even possible?"

"Unfortunately yes, it is. When Liz and Nat returned to the hospital, Liz said Simone's bag had been returned to the resort. She opened it and found the gold coin that Levi had discovered."

"The cursed one you mean?"

"Yes, that one," Vanessa said. "When Levi found out, she was furious and left the hospital to return the coin to the island, hopefully for the last time."

"Why on earth would Simone do that?"

"Nat thinks Simone wanted to prove to Levi that the coin wasn't cursed and she was placing too much faith in a silly island superstition."

"That is a plausible story, knowing Simone's ego," NeNe said.

NeNe started the Jeep and drove the short distance to the harbor. "Would you like me to stay and give you a ride back to the resort?"

"No thanks. Levi has one of the resort vans. We'll drop it back at the hospital and then walk back here to catch the trolley."

"Don't worry about that. I'll get one of the staff to take another van to the hospital and will follow behind to give them a ride back. You and Levi just head back to the resort."

"Thanks NeNe." Vanessa stepped from the Jeep. "I'm planning on going to work with Levi tonight, so I guess I'll see you later."

"That you will, my friend. See you soon."

Vanessa took her small bag and walked down the sidewalk to the harbor. She gazed across the water searching for a sign of Levi's return. There was nothing to see but open water. She looked at the spot where the *Sappho One* had been in port and her heart felt heavy. She missed the ship and her crew. Even though they had been gone mere hours, it felt like days to her.

She walked down the pier, found a small bench, and took a seat as she waited for Levi's return.

†

Dr. Hall walked into Simone's room just minutes after she awoke again. Pleased to see her awake and alert, he did a quick examination and told her that she would transfer to a private room, and if she continued to make such good progress, discharge would follow in a few days.

Relieved by the good news, Nat followed him out into the hall.

"Dr. Hall, Simone is having difficulty remembering things," she said. "More importantly she has no memory of someone very significant in her life. What are the chances of her recovering her memory?"

"At this point in time it would be very hard to make an accurate prognosis, but if I had to guess, I would say she has an even chance of recovering the memory. I wish I could tell you it was a sure thing, but there's still so much we don't comprehend about the brain's function."

Nat nodded her head. "I understand. Thank you, Dr. Hall."

"I'll see you again before Simone's discharge, so if you have any questions, just let me know."

†

Vanessa heard the angry buzz of an engine approaching from the open water and strained her eyes to see a small boat entering the harbor. She picked up her bag and waited to see which slip Levi would enter.

Levi saw Vanessa standing at the end of the pier and her heart raced with excitement. She was surprised to see her out of the hospital so soon, but happy she was here to welcome her back from the island. She pulled the boat into a small slip and tossed a mooring line to Vanessa.

"Welcome back, darling."

"Thanks. I'm surprised to see you here. How did you manage?" Levi asked.

"NeNe rescued me from that dreadful place and brought me here to wait on you."

"You're a sight for sore eyes," Levi said as she stepped from the boat and took Vanessa in her arms. She hugged Vanessa tightly to her and, as she stepped back, brushed Vanessa's lips with a soft kiss.

Vanessa picked up her bag and reached for Levi's hand as they walked down the pier to the resort van.

"NeNe also took care of getting a van to the hospital for Nat and Liz, so we can go directly to the resort."

"Thank God for NeNe," Levi said. "I really didn't want to go back there today except to bring you home, of course," she added, with a wink. "I'll have just enough time to shower and get ready for work as it is."

"Would it be okay if I sat at the bar with you tonight?"

"I would like that very much." Levi reached over and took Vanessa's hand. "If the noise gets to be too much for you, you can crash in my bungalow until I get off duty."

"That sounds like an excellent plan to me. I'm also ready for some decent food." She chuckled.

Chapter Forty-two

Vanessa lathered Levi's hair while they showered and her eyes caressed Levi. It was such a shame they only had minutes before Levi was due to start her shift; she looked so lithe and inviting under the soft flow of water. With a soft sigh, she rinsed Levi's hair and reached down to turn off the water. Her eyes met Levi's when she looked up and Vanessa could see the sparkle of excitement lying there.

"Too bad you have to go to work." Vanessa grinned as she stepped from the shower and wrapped in a towel.

"It will wait until later tonight," Levi whispered into her ear.

Vanessa reached for another towel and gently patted Levi dry. Levi took the towel from her and ruffled her hair.

"Have I told you lately you have the cutest ass?" Levi asked.

"Not in at least a few days," Vanessa said.

"I'm terribly remiss in my duties then." Levi turned and cupped Vanessa's cheeks in her hands. She leaned closer and tenderly kissed each of Vanessa's closed eyelids. "I will definitely have to remedy that."

Levi's hands stroked up Vanessa's back as she leaned into her for a slow, leisurely kiss. She could feel the dampness growing between her thighs as their tongues swirled in a sensual dance.

"Why don't you take a nap and then come down to the club later?" Levi suggested, pulling away from the kiss and the temptation of Vanessa.

"That sounds like a good idea," Vanessa said. "What time will you take a dinner break?"

"We normally order from the kitchen around nine."

"Double whatever you eat and I'll see you at nine," Vanessa slipped on an oversized shirt and sat on the bed to watch Levi dress.

"You, my dear, have a deal." Levi tucked in her shirt and kissed Vanessa goodbye. "See you soon."

Vanessa crawled under the covers and listened to the dull thrumming sound of the ceiling fan as she drifted off to sleep, still savoring the taste of Levi's kiss on her lips.

†

Levi met NeNe out by the pool and they walked to the club together.

"Killian sends her regards to you and Vanessa," she said with a warm smile.

"Thanks NeNe, I hope everything is going well with her."

"They are halfway home. She misses Vanessa terribly from the sound of it."

"I bet Vanessa isn't the only one she's missing right now." Levi smirked.

"I believe you could be right. I miss her too," NeNe said with a blush. "I hope this week passes quickly."

"The time will fly by and before you know it, the *Sappho One* will be back in port."

"Does Vanessa plan on staying here until the ship returns?"

"I'm not really sure, NeNe. I think she may plan on flying back Tuesday or Wednesday to return to the ship, but she has to be cleared by her doctor before she can fly."

"Lucky for you then," NeNe said with a grin.

"I'll definitely enjoy her company," Levi said as she opened the door for NeNe. "She'll be here later to have dinner with us."

"Great, I'll look forward to dinner then." With a wink NeNe walked toward the DJ booth.

Karen was wiping down the bar when Levi walked up to it.

"Welcome back, Levi, I'm glad to see you."

"Thanks Karen, it's good to be back."

Levi walked behind the bar and began taking inventory of the items she needed to stock and walked to the back room. Gathering her supplies, she had just finished making a fresh batch of Tropical E when the club doors opened, and a small group of guests walked in.

A spiky-haired blonde walked over to the bar and sat in front of Levi.

"You must be Levi, the hot bartender everyone raves about," she said. "My name's Del."

"Pleased to meet you, Del." Levi extended her hand. "What can I get you?"

"Well, since you're not on the menu, I guess a tray of your Tropical E shots will have to do."

Levi blushed and looked over Del's shoulder to count the number in her party. "Four of you, so will a dozen do for starters?"

"For starters, yes. I hope you'll save me a dance later tonight. Something slow and seductive," Del added with a wicked smile.

"I think maybe that could be arranged." She turned to begin pouring the shots.

"I'll bring them out to your table if you don't want to wait," Karen said.

"I don't mind the wait," Del said. "The view is so nice." Her eyes traveled down Levi's backside.

Karen laughed and rolled over to talk to NeNe. "I just don't understand it, NeNe, how does she do it?"

"Who and what?" NeNe asked, playing coy.

"How does Levi have every woman that comes in here eating out of her hand?"

NeNe broke into hearty laughter. "Levi has great looks, but it is her charisma that attracts women."

Karen just shook her head as she watched Levi at the bar with Del.

"See, right there." They watched Levi smile warmly at Del as she handed her the tray of drinks. "That smile makes women feel really special, and keeps them coming back for more."

"Still, it is so unfair," she groaned. "She turns down more women in one night than I have slept with in my entire life."

NeNe chuckled. "That's Levi for you." She looked Karen in the eye. "Most women our age would jump at the chance to be seduced by so many women, but Levi is different."

"True, but I would love to have her looks for just one night." Karen sighed.

"You and a hundred others."

"Do you want anything to drink?" Karen asked.

"How about a Coke?"

"One Coke coming up, my dear." She smiled at NeNe and spun away on her rollerblades.

"Later," Del said, taking the tray from Levi as Karen rolled up to the bar.

"How about pouring a Coke for NeNe, Romeo?"

†

Over the next hour, the club slowly filled with women, and Levi, Karen, and NeNe were kept busy. Even with the cruise ship gone, the club was packed with beautiful women. Orders and tips rolled in as well as offerings of dates for Levi, who just smiled and tucked each strip of paper into her pocket.

Around eight, Liz came in and sat at the bar. "Business looks good," she said.

"It's been steady since we opened. How is Simone?" Levi asked.

"Simone is better. She was downgraded to a private room earlier this evening, so Nat, and I decided to come home. We'll go visit again tomorrow."

"That sounds like good news."

"I think it is," Liz smiled and asked, "Where's Vanessa?"

Levi looked at her watch. "She should be here soon. She promised to be here for dinner and then sit with me the rest of the night."

"Dinner sounds good. Nat should be down soon, so when you order how about adding a burger for me and a steak salad for Nat."

"Consider it done."

Liz stood and walked through the crowd, mingling with guests. She left each table of women smiling with laughter as she moved through the club. Liz was a great businesswoman and could teach her much, Levi thought.

"Hey sexy." Levi turned to see Vanessa sitting in front of her. The angry bruise above her eye was changing colors and the swelling was almost completely gone.

"Hey baby." Levi reached across the bar to softly stroke Vanessa's face. "Did you have a good nap?"

"I was a little lonesome, but I rested well, thanks. I'm starved," she said with a grin.

"I have already ordered dinner, so it should be here soon."

Liz slipped onto the stool next to her. "Hi, Vanessa, how are you feeling?"

"Much better now that I am out of the hospital."

"It's good to have you back at the resort."

"It's great to be here too, Liz."

"How long will you be staying?"

"I'll probably hang around until the doctor releases me to fly—I'm hoping that will be by Wednesday—and maybe fly back to meet the ship before we set out to return here," Vanessa said. "That is, if Levi can put up with me for a few more days."

"I think I can handle that." Levi handed Karen a tray of drinks. "What can I get you two to drink?"

"Soda for me please," Vanessa said.

"A cold beer for me please, Levi," Liz said as she turned around to see Nat walking into the club.

Levi grinned. "You always seem to know when she walks in."

"It's a connection we have. I get vibes when I know she's close."

Levi smiled at Vanessa. "I hope we have that one day."

†

The food arrived from the kitchen and they sat at the bar to eat. Nat smiled at the looks passing between Vanessa and Levi. It was obvious to all how close they had grown. The tenderness in the looks and the soft touches were much more frequent and Nat knew Levi was falling helplessly in love.

They had finished eating and were talking around the bar when a slow song began to play. Levi looked up, intending to ask Vanessa if she wanted to dance, but saw Del standing at the bar smiling at her.

"Would you ladies mind if I steal your bartender away for a dance?" she asked.

"Not at all." Vanessa smiled at Levi.

"Well then, a promise is a promise." Del reached for Levi's hand.

"I'll be back in a few minutes." Levi tossed a bar towel to Nat.

When they reached the dance floor, Levi took Del in her arms and held her close as they swayed to the music, their bodies pressed together as they listened to the beat of the music. Del laid her head on Levi's shoulder and whispered softly into her ear. "I would love to lay with you tonight, skin on skin." She reached up to Levi's face and trailed her fingers down Levi's jaw.

"That's quite an offer," Levi said. "I'm afraid I'll have to pass though. I already have a date with that sexy brunette at the bar, tonight and for many nights yet to come," Levi whispered back.

"She is an incredibly lucky woman. If you change your mind, or want some company, give me a call."

"I'll keep that in mind," Levi said and hugged Del close as they finished the dance.

"Thanks for the dance, Levi," Del said when they returned to the bar. "You're a lucky woman," she added as she passed Vanessa on her way back to her table.

"Yes, I know."

"Hold on tight to her," Del said with a wink.

"Oh, I have every intention of doing just that."

"You sure know how to stir up the women." Nat said, watching women gyrate on the dance floor.

"It's good for business."

"That it is, my friend," Nat said.

"Are you about ready to get some sleep?" Liz asked.

"Sleep, no, not quite yet, but I am ready to head upstairs with you." She grinned.

"Now that sounds promising. We'll see you in a couple of hours when you make the midnight drop, Levi." Liz took Nat by the hand to lead her from the bar. "Goodnight Vanessa."

"So you plan to hold on to me tightly," Levi said.

"As tightly as you'll allow me," Vanessa answered.

"That's very good to hear." Levi turned and began to fill an order for Karen. "May I get you something to drink?"

"No thanks, Levi. If you don't mind I think I'll head back up to the room."

"Not a problem, are you feeling okay?"

"Just a bit of a headache, that I want to get rid of before you get off work."

Levi walked around the bar and embraced Vanessa. "I'll see you in a few hours."

"Yes, you will." She kissed her softly.

†

The remainder of the evening passed quickly for Levi, and when Susan came in to relieve her, she quickly closed out the cash register and prepared for the night's drop. She stuffed her tip money into her pocket without sorting through it and waved at NeNe as she left the club.

Del was lying in wait for her in the shadows of the pool, and stepped out in front of Levi as she approached.

Startled by her sudden appearance, Levi stopped abruptly in her tracks. "Damn, Del, you scared me."

"I'm sorry, Levi. I just had to see you one more time tonight." Del stepped forward and took Levi in her arms, leaning in to kiss her.

Levi gently pushed Del away. "I already told you, I'm not interested."

Del stepped back and smiled at Levi. "I know, but you can't blame a girl for trying though."

"For the last time, Del, I'm not interested." Levi pushed past Del and stormed toward the resort.

"See you around, Levi," Del said as she reached the doors.

Agitated by Del's actions, Levi punched the elevator buttons rather harshly as she waited for the doors to close. Her heart was racing with anger at the thought of Del trying to force a kiss on her and she jumped when the doors open and she found Vanessa waiting.

"I was just coming down to meet you," she said as Levi stepped out of the elevator. "Are you okay?"

"Yes, I'm fine. I just wasn't expecting to see you here. It's a pleasant surprise though. How are you feeling?"

"Much better thank you."

They walked to Liz and Nat's suite to drop off the moneybag and then went to Levi's bungalow. Levi could hear soft music playing and when she opened the door, she smelled the scent of roses. Candles provided a soft glow around the room, and a dozen or more red roses sat beside the bed.

"I just wanted to remind you that I love you," Vanessa said as Levi turned toward her.

Levi took Vanessa into her arms. Their lips touched and their bodies began to sway softly with the music. Their hands caressed one another as they danced, mouths locked in a passionate kiss. When the song ended, Vanessa took Levi over to the bed and undressed her, kissing her neck tenderly as her clothing dropped to the floor. Levi was trembling with excitement as she gently pressed her backward onto the bed. Vanessa pulled the shirt over her head and dropped her shorts onto the small pile of clothing lying beside the bed.

With a seductive smile, Vanessa climbed onto the bed. She spread Levi's thighs with her knee and lowered herself onto her. Their bodies fit together so perfectly. Vanessa kissed her way up Levi's neck and ran her tongue lightly over Levi's lips as her hips began to slowly undulate. Levi locked her heels around Vanessa's thighs and their bodies moved in a single rhythm. Vanessa parted Levi's lips with her tongue, flicking the tip of her tongue across Levi's.

Levi moaned when Vanessa rolled her hard nipple between her fingers. She ground her wetness into Vanessa, oblivious to anything but the strong fingers on her nipple and the warm mouth covering hers. She had no idea what Vanessa had planned when she took Levi's hands and raised them over her head, pinning them together. Vanessa broke the kiss only long enough to slip each of Levi's wrists into a soft cuff and then covered her mouth, stifling the moan of surprise when Levi found her hands securely restrained above her head.

"Trust me," Vanessa whispered as her mouth puffed warm air into Levi's ear.

"I do." Levi barely breathed as Vanessa's fingertips caressed down her face. Levi closed her eyes.

Chapter Forty-three

Vanessa covered Levi with tender kisses, starting with her eyelids and moving down to the tips of her toes, all the while her hands gently massaging her. Levi's moans grew louder as Vanessa's hands and mouth tortured her with silky caresses until Levi thought she would explode from the intense arousal.

Vanessa caressed the insides of Levi's thighs, and when she looked into Levi's eyes, they begged for release. Vanessa smiled at Levi and lowered her head between Levi's thighs, her tongue flicking across the sweet dampened lips. Levi writhed with pleasure, trying to lift her hips to meet the movement of Vanessa's tongue and end the agonizing torment she was suffering. However, Vanessa's strong forearm across Levi's pelvis pinned her in place.

"Please, make me come, Vanessa," Levi begged, shivering with intense pleasure. "Take me anyway you wish, but take me now."

Vanessa's thumbs gently opened Levi's lower lips and she took her quivering clit deep into her mouth. Levi groaned loudly. Two fingers penetrated Levi, slipping deeply into the silky wetness flowing deep within. Her tongue circled Levi's clit, licking and nibbling before lightly touching her tongue to her quivering clit. Vanessa could feel the pounding of Levi's heart as it raced to fill the sensitive flesh with blood. She sucked Levi's clit slowly in and out of her mouth while her fingers curled deep inside her.

Levi's juices spilled onto the sheets as Vanessa chased them with her eager tongue. Her fingers stroked deeper inside Levi until Vanessa felt her muscles shiver with the onset of orgasm. With a final deep thrust, Levi was overtaken by violent spasms, flooding Vanessa's mouth and hand with her sweetness.

Still lapping at the juices coating her lips, Vanessa slowly removed her fingers from Levi.

Levi looked into Vanessa's desire-filled eyes. "I want to taste you."

Vanessa moved up the bed to release Levi's wrists from the cuffs. Vanessa's right breast dangled in front of Levi's mouth as she worked to free her hands. With one hand free, Levi used it to guide the soft flesh into her mouth. She suckled it roughly as Vanessa's fingers worked on the final restraint.

"Oh, yes baby," Vanessa groaned as Levi's teeth grazed across her nipple and her hand plummeted between their bodies. Levi drove two fingers deep inside Vanessa, and as soon as her hand was free she rolled Vanessa onto her back, her fingers thrusting in and out of Vanessa's soaked body.

Vanessa's hand groped between their bodies until her fingers sank into Levi's wetness. Her movements matched the rhythm of Levi's as she drove into her fast and hard. Vanessa buried her hand in Levi's short hair as she thrust her hips upward, driving Levi's fingers deeper inside.

"Almost there, Levi," Vanessa groaned. The dam erupted and she soaked Levi's hand with juice.

"Oh yes, baby girl," she moaned as Levi came with her. She collapsed onto Vanessa as they both struggled for air.

She carefully withdrew her fingers from Levi's quaking core and embraced her lover for a long, contented hug. Her hands stroked down Levi's back. After several minutes she softly whispered, "I love you, Levi."

When no answer came, Vanessa lifted her head, looked into Levi's sleeping face and smiled. She softly sighed and waited for sleep to overtake her, listening to the slow beating of Levi's heart as she watched the shadows of the candles flickering on the ceiling.

†

The following morning Levi awoke with her head resting on Vanessa's chest, rising and falling with each breath she took. She slowly turned her head and looked into Vanessa's face as she slept. A small smile played on her lips as she rested peacefully.

Levi quietly lifted her hand and traced Vanessa's soft lips with a fingertip as she watched her eyes for signs of awakening. Vanessa's tongue snaked out to lick her lips, wetting them as Levi's fingertips brushed back and forth. When Vanessa did not rouse, Levi moved slightly until she reached Vanessa's face. Her tongue licked across her bottom lip, from one side of Vanessa's mouth to the other, and then circled around her top lip.

Vanessa's eyes flew open as Levi took her bottom lip between hers and gently tugged on it, teasing Vanessa awake.

"Good morning, lover," Levi said as she locked eyes with Vanessa.

"It is a good morning indeed, to be awakened by a beautiful woman's lips."

"There are more than lips to wake you," Levi teased. Her hand slid down Vanessa's belly into the valley between her thighs. "So warm and inviting," she purred as her fingers parted damp lips and her thumb stroked across Vanessa's clit.

"Time to wake your body." Levi's mouth hovered above one of Vanessa's breasts. Her tongue flicked across Vanessa's sleeping nipple and it began to grow hard. "Now that's much better," Levi said as she lightly kissed Vanessa's breast.

The fire burning in Vanessa's eyes matched her own. Levi dipped her fingers inside Vanessa's lips, drawing the silky moisture up to Vanessa's clit, circling it slowly as her tongue trapped her nipple against the roof of her mouth.

"You tease me so, my love," Vanessa whispered, burying her hand in Levi's hair, tugging it gently.

Vanessa ached for a firmer touch, but maintained her restraint and allowed Levi to set the tempo, at least for the moment. She was enjoying the sensual caresses of Levi's tongue

281

and fingers too much to allow herself to become impatient. She clenched her teeth to hold back the climax that Levi was so expertly building deep inside her.

Levi saw Vanessa's breath quicken and slowed the pace of her teasing fingers. "What do you want?" Levi asked, her voice husky with desire.

"I want you to fuck me," Vanessa answered as she locked eyes with Levi.

Levi repositioned herself to be face-to-face with Vanessa. Their eyes remained locked on one another. "I want to watch you come," Levi whispered as her fingers slid deep into Vanessa.

Vanessa closed her eyes, fighting to hold back the rising orgasm.

"Open your eyes," Levi commanded.

Vanessa opened her eyes and bit down on her lip as Levi thrust her fingers deep then curled them as she slowly withdrew from her wetness.

"Does it feel good?"

"Oh my god, yes, Levi," Vanessa breathed. "Good doesn't begin to describe how you're making me feel."

"Do you want more?"

"Please Levi," Vanessa pleaded, her eyes begging for relief.

Levi slid a third finger inside Vanessa and her palm rubbed across her throbbing clit.

Vanessa felt the spasms beginning in her stomach and bucked her hips wildly against Levi's hand.

"That's it, Levi," she groaned as her climax exploded from deep inside.

Levi slowed the pace of her fingers then slowly withdrew them, licking the sweetness from her fingers as Vanessa watched her and tried to regain her breath.

Levi lowered her mouth to kiss Vanessa sweetly. "Good morning, my lover," she repeated with a wicked grin.

"You can wake me like that anytime," she said, her eyes still dark with passion as she took Levi in her arms. "What plans do you have for the day?"

"I thought we would shower, get some breakfast, and then maybe catch some rays by the pool," Levi answered. "I would also like to drop by the hospital to visit Simone before I start my shift."

Vanessa looked at the clock on the bedside table. "We better get moving then."

"But you are so warm and snuggly," Levi teased as she cupped a breast with her hand.

"And if you keep that up, we won't be leaving this bed." Vanessa groaned and lifted Levi's chin with her fingertips. "There will be time for more, later tonight."

✝

The deck around the pool was quickly filling with resort guests, and they were lucky to find two chairs together that they could use. They stretched out on the lounges, lying on their backs as the sun began to beat down upon them. Levi reached across and took Vanessa's hand in hers as they dozed in the warm sun. After an hour had passed, Levi prompted Vanessa to turn over onto her stomach.

"I think I'll take a dip in the pool first," she said. "Would you care to join me?"

The cool water welcomed their sun-heated bodies and provided relief from the pounding of the sun on their skin.

"This feels good," Levi said as she dunked her head under the water, careful not to wet her cast.

"Yes it does." Vanessa slicked back her wet hair.

Levi waded through the water until she stood in front of Vanessa and wrapped her arms around her neck. She nuzzled into Vanessa's neck, planting small kisses up to her ear.

"Why do you make me want you so badly?" she whispered, desire evident in her husky voice.

"I have no clue what makes you say that, but I sure have enjoyed being the benefactor of your desire," Vanessa said as Levi's teeth grazed her neck. "You make me feel so desired and special."

"You're very desirable and delicious." Levi's tongue traced the outline of Vanessa's ear.

"Okay you two, the water in the pool is about to start boiling," a voice said from very near the edge of the pool.

Levi looked up and saw NeNe sitting there, smiling at them.

"You two need to get a room if you're going to get so hot," NeNe teased.

"Oh NeNe, you know you would be doing the same thing if Killian were here," Levi said.

Vanessa chuckled. "My Killian?"

"The one and only," Levi replied. "She and our sweet NeNe are the latest of the red-hot lovers."

"I'm very happy for you then, NeNe, and know that Killian is very lucky to have you in her life."

"She's a marvelous woman," NeNe said with a dreamy quality in her voice. She smiled down at Levi. "Must be something about those cruise ship types," she added, with a wink to Levi.

"You're very right about that, NeNe." Levi smiled as she kissed Vanessa's cheek. "They are some amazing women."

Vanessa blushed and turned toward NeNe. "Have you heard from Killian yet today?"

"Not yet, but aren't they due to arrive at home port about lunchtime today?" NeNe asked.

"Yes, they are and she will be filling out paperwork for a couple of hours, so I would expect a call about two our time," Vanessa said. "Please let her know I'm doing well and will see her very soon if I can pull myself away from this beautiful woman."

NeNe grinned at them. "I will. I'm going to head off for an early lunch, so I'll see you two later."

They watched NeNe disappear into the resort. "I guess we should finish our sunbathing and then a shower. Do you want to go to the hospital alone or would you mind some company?" Vanessa asked.

"I'd love for you to accompany me," Levi answered as she lay down on her stomach. "I want to spend every possible moment with you while you're here."

"Very well then, for the next three days consider me another layer of skin," Vanessa teased.

Chapter Forty-four

Levi and Vanessa stopped by the emergency room to have Vanessa's stitches inspected before locating Simone in her private room.

"Everything looks good with your stitches and they should be ready to be removed in another week. Any problems with headaches?" the doctor asked.

"Just a dull throb now and then, but nothing like at the beginning."

"Good. You should be able to fly Monday or Tuesday. Be sure to come see me when you return and I'll take those stitches out for you. Have a great stay and please, will you two stay out of trouble?"

Vanessa grinned at her. "Sure thing, Doc. I think we've both had more than our fair share of excitement lately."

"So, hotshot, you have been cleared to fly," Levi said as they walked toward the elevator.

"I would much prefer to travel by ship," Vanessa answered, "but that doesn't look possible at the moment."

"Is my big brave captain afraid of flying?"

"Not afraid, I just don't prefer that type of travel," Vanessa said with a shy grin.

"Hmm." They stepped inside the elevator and Levi punched the button for the third floor.

"Hmm what," Vanessa asked as she pulled Levi close for a quick kiss.

"I just wouldn't have pegged you as someone who was apprehensive of flying." She took Vanessa's hand and they walked down the hallway until they reached Simone's room.

Vanessa softly tapped on the door.

"Come in," they heard Nat say.

Vanessa and Levi stepped inside the room to find Simone propped up in bed and Nat sitting close beside her.

"Well, it's about time," Simone snarled as Levi and Vanessa walked in holding hands. "I would have thought my lover and my employee would have taken the time to visit before now."

Levi looked at Nat, who sat in shock beside the bed, her jaw hanging open in surprise at her sister's outburst.

"For god's sake, Simone, what are you talking about now?" Vanessa growled at her.

"I'm laid up in the hospital after nearly dying and you are off doing god knows what with my lover," Simone hissed.

"Simone, you need to calm down," Nat said as she stood and hovered over Simone.

"Calm down, you have got to be kidding," Simone shouted.

"Just what type of fucking game are you playing now? Two days ago you didn't even know or care who I was." Tears welled in Levi's eyes. "And, if it hadn't been for Vanessa, your sorry ass wouldn't be in that bed at all. You'd be on some cold morgue slab," Levi reminded her as she rushed toward the bed.

Vanessa reached out and caught hold of Levi's arm before she could rear back and slap Simone. "Easy, tiger," she said.

"It was your stupid arrogance that nearly got you killed by going back and digging up that stupid coin," Levi said, now on a roll. "Of course, the great Simone Taylor had to prove everyone wrong. Look what it has gotten you, Simone. Just look and listen to yourself."

"There was nothing wrong with that coin; I was going to have it set in a necklace for you. But I can see that in my absence you've already begun slumming."

"Slumming!" Levi shouted. "Why, you arrogant bitch! I loved you, Simone, and loved you deeply, until you turned your back on me the first time. I swallowed my pride and fought my better instincts when I agreed to allow you a second chance.

"You're not half the caring and loving woman Vanessa is and you never will be, Simone, until you begin to love someone other than yourself. You can have your money and your games and you know what Simone, fuck you!" Levi stormed from the room.

"You really do take the cake, Simone," Vanessa said. "Levi really did love you and now you have shattered her heart once again. How can you live with yourself?" She turned away and walked from the room not waiting for an answer because there was nothing Simone could say to repair the damage she had done.

Nat was still in shock at Simone's words. "You're one classy piece of work, my sister. You have no idea the torment Levi has been through for you and now you treat her like shit again." Nat shook her head in disgust. "Levi sat for hours beside your bed and waited for you to awaken only to find out you had no memory of her, and now this. I don't know what has come over you, but I sure hope you wise up and figure it out soon."

"There's nothing to figure out, Nat. Levi was no better than all the others. She just wanted to use me for what I could do for her."

"That's where you are so wrong," Nat said. "Levi loved you regardless of your money and the arrogance it brings with it. I had hoped that Levi would be the one to change you, but that obviously isn't going to happen. You've become downright disgusting."

"Get out!" Simone shouted. "Take your high morals and your better-than-me attitude and go, Nat."

"Not a problem." Nat stood and stormed out of Simone's hospital room.

†

Vanessa caught up with Levi just as she reached the elevator. She pushed the call button and looked deep into Levi's eyes. Pain was welling deep in her eyes and Levi clenched her fists trying to quell the rage she was feeling and prevent the flood of tears that threatened to explode from her.

Vanessa folded Levi into her arms and held on to her tightly. When the elevator arrived, she led her inside and they rode down clutching onto one another.

Levi took a deep breath of fresh air as they stepped outside and exhaled loudly. She did not say a word as they drove back to the resort. Vanessa allowed her to remain silent and did not push.

After they parked the van, Levi said, "I need to go for a walk."

Sensing Levi needed some time alone she nodded. "Okay, darling, I'll see you later tonight then." Vanessa watched Levi walk toward the beach.

Vanessa was still standing at the front of the resort when Nat pulled up and parked. "How is she?" she asked.

"I'm not sure," Vanessa said. "When we arrived she said she needed to go for a walk and headed for the beach."

"Will you go update Liz while I follow Levi?"

"Yes, I will, if you think that's wise," Vanessa said.

"You will just have to trust me."

"I do Nat; I know how much Levi means to you and Liz."

"I'll find you later." Nat walked toward the beach.

†

Levi walked briskly down the shore. The skies were growing dark and the wind was howling across the beach as it blew in a storm. Levi's rage had possessed her and she was oblivious to anything other than the hurt she was feeling. How could Simone do this to her again? Why was she so stupid to have allowed her a second chance? she asked herself repeatedly. She found herself walking the path leading to the waterfall. She sat on the rock where she had shared memories with Simone. She tucked her knees up to her and rocked back and forth, fighting back the tears she was desperately struggling to hold back.

Nat followed Levi's tracks in the sand and when they reached the small pathway, she knew where Levi had gone. She walked up behind Levi, encircled her with her strong arms, and turned Levi to face her.

"I'm sorry to admit this, Levi, but you need to let her go," Nat said. "You're much more deserving of someone like Vanessa."

Levi looked up into Nat's face and saw the love and concern in her eyes. "I did love her, Nat, but I just can't take anymore."

"You have already taken more than most people would, Levi, but it's time for you to move on." Nat chuckled softly. "If you haven't noticed, Vanessa adores you and I think would treat you in the manner in which you deserve with love and kindness." She lifted Levi's quivering chin. "Give the two of you a chance. Move past the pain Simone has caused and cherish the love Vanessa is offering."

The tears Levi had been struggling to control poured from her while Nat held her close. Her sobs echoed across the small pool and then fell silent under the roar of the falls. The skies opened and rain fell as tears streaked down Levi's face. Had she looked up, she would have seen tears rolling down Nat's cheeks as well.

When Levi was able to regain control, she and Nat were both soaked to the bone.

Nat could not help but laugh as she looked at Levi. "I'm so sorry, Levi, but you look like a drowned rat in those drenched clothes."

Levi was shocked at first at the apparent poor timing of Nat's humor, but when she looked at Nat and realized they were both sopping wet, their clothing hanging from their bodies and dripping rainwater onto the saturated ground, Levi smiled and then joined Nat in laughter as she hugged her tightly.

"What would I do without you?" she asked Nat.

"To be honest, you would probably be much better off." Nat hung her head.

"That is so not true. You and Liz have been great for me, and if I hadn't come here I would probably never have met Vanessa."

"I know, I just hate that you have to go through the heartache from Simone, before you can enjoy the love you share with Vanessa."

"With your continued support and Vanessa's love I'll be just fine." The alarm on her watch went off at that moment. "Umm, boss, I'm late for work." Levi grinned.

"Liz is covering for us. I'll take your shift tonight if you're not up to working," Nat offered.

"Thanks, Nat, but I need to work. I just need some dry clothes, so I don't scare off all the customers." Levi stood next to Nat. "Thank you for being you, Nat." She hugged her close.

"My pleasure, Levi."

They began to walk back toward the beach. "Looks like we are in for a good storm tonight," Nat said.

"I hope it won't keep the guests from coming out tonight."

"Haven't you heard?" Nat asked.

"Heard what?"

"That *Venus Rising* has the hottest bartender on the island and women will battle the fiercest of storms just to catch a glimpse of her," Nat teased.

"Oh really, do you think you could hook me up with her?"

"I'll see what I can do." Nat placed a protective arm around Levi's shoulders as they returned down the beach.

When Levi entered her room to change into dry clothes, Vanessa was sitting on the bed waiting for her. Levi silently walked over and knelt down in front of Vanessa.

"It's you that I love. I need nothing more," she whispered. Levi smiled sweetly at Vanessa and kissed her softly. "I have a lot of pain yet to deal with, but I also have a lot of love to look forward to with you." She stroked Vanessa's face. "Just be patient with me."

"Oh baby." Vanessa pulled Levi close. "I'll be here to provide whatever you need, I promise."

291

"That's all I can ask." Levi stood and began stripping off her wet clothes. "Liz is filling in for me until I can get dried off. Would you like to spend the night with me at the club?"

"I would love to." Vanessa took a towel and ruffled Levi's still dripping hair.

Levi leaned forward, placing her forehead gently on Vanessa's, careful to avoid her injured area. "Thank you for loving me," she whispered.

Vanessa took Levi's face in her hands. "I'll never treat you badly, I promise, if you will only give me the chance to love you like I know I can."

"I'm all yours."

It was Vanessa's turn to cry. The tears flowed down her cheeks as she held Levi close. "Oh, how I've longed to hear those words from you."

Levi used her thumbs to wipe away the tears and then kissed Vanessa's cheeks, tasting the salt of her tears. "I hope I can make you happy."

"You already do, Levi." Vanessa held her close. "You already do."

Chapter Forty-five

Levi and Vanessa walked down to the club. The weather was indeed not hindering the party atmosphere of the club. The dance floor was packed with women and Karen already looked harried as she rolled to the bar for another drink order.

Liz saw Levi and Vanessa approaching the bar. She could tell that both had been crying and she wondered how Levi was holding up.

"Hi there, ladies," Liz said. "How're things going?"

"Things are fine," Levi said as she stepped around the bar, "it's time to move on and I have a beautiful young lady waiting patiently for my love."

Vanessa sat on a barstool and beamed at Liz.

"I think I have finally chased her long enough for Levi to catch me," she teased.

"Well, she certainly is adorable." Liz winked at Levi. "I can cover the shift tonight, if you would rather take the night off."

"Thanks Liz, but I need to work, and besides I have Vanessa to help make the time pass quickly."

"Fair enough." Liz looked over Vanessa's shoulder and spotted Nat walking through the door.

Vanessa turned to see Nat making her way through the crowded club. "That connection between you two still amazes me."

"I have to admit, I was cheating this time. Nat just called to say she was on her way." Liz chuckled.

"Hello ladies," Nat said as she walked to the bar. "Baby, I don't know about you but I am starved."

"I could use some dinner also," Liz replied.

"Then why don't we go eat some dinner then come back to relieve Levi, so she and Vanessa can have a peaceful dinner for a change," Nat suggested.

"Lead the way, sweetheart." Liz tossed the bar towel to Levi. "We'll see you two later."

"You really have two great employers," Vanessa said.

"They are some truly special women. I feel more like family than I do an employee."

"That's what makes it all so special here," Vanessa said. "Everyone cares."

"Would you like something to drink, sweetie?"

"Hmmm, how about just an old-fashioned cherry Coke?"

Levi poured a Coke from the tap, squirted a shot of grenadine syrup into the glass, and added three long-stemmed cherries.

"Here you are, love." Levi placed the drink in front of Vanessa.

Levi looked up to see NeNe smiling and waving to her from the DJ booth. NeNe gestured for Levi to call her and Levi walked to the telephone and punched in NeNe's number.

"What's up?" she asked.

"How about sending one of those cherry Cokes over my way."

"With extra cherries too?"

"Oh yes, ma'am, the works," NeNe said.

"Will do, consider it on the way."

"Thanks, my friend."

Levi walked back to the bar still chuckling and began making NeNe a cherry Coke. "You have started something here." She smiled at Vanessa.

Karen rolled up to the bar. "I need three dozen Tropical E's, please, Levi."

"Here, let me make that delivery." Vanessa took both drinks and walked to the DJ booth.

NeNe opened the door and welcomed Vanessa inside. "Thanks." She took the drink from her and took a long sip.

"You're most welcome." Vanessa took a seat beside NeNe. "This place is really high tech."

"It looks more intimidating than it really is." NeNe explained the function of the equipment to Vanessa. "Once you set up a routine, the system pretty much runs on its own."

"I don't think the console on the *Sappho One* has this many buttons and switches," Vanessa said with a laugh.

"The big difference here is that if I hit a wrong button, I just play the wrong song, if you hit a wrong button you run ashore," NeNe teased.

"Very funny," Vanessa said but she couldn't help laughing with her.

"So when are you headed back to the States?" NeNe asked.

"The doctor cleared me to fly Monday or Tuesday, I'll probably wait until Tuesday so I can spend more time with Levi."

"Aww, that is so sweet."

"I love that woman so much."

"That is very apparent," NeNe said. "Levi loves you too, I'm sure of it."

A frown crossed Vanessa's face. "Simone was such a fool to treat her so badly."

"Well, that just prompted Levi to do what she felt in her heart and move on with her life," NeNe said. "I know it had to hurt, but I'm sure your love for her will help soothe the pain."

"Thanks, NeNe. I hope you're right and it is enough."

"Have faith that it will be," NeNe said confidently.

†

Liz and Nat sat in the dining room enjoying a quiet meal together. "You know, I was just thinking something," Nat said.

"What would that be, baby?"

"Vanessa will be flying out Monday or Tuesday to meet up with the *Sappho One* to bring her back here, right?"

"Yes, they'll be back in port Thursday," Liz said.

"Well, Levi has been through hell these last few weeks. Why don't we send her off with Vanessa and let them spend some time together away from all the drama here. She can sail back with Vanessa on Thursday," Nat suggested. "Tuesday and Wednesday are her normal days off anyhow, so we would just have a couple shifts to cover."

"I think that's a brilliant idea, my love." Liz leaned over to kiss Nat. "You are such a romantic and come up with some of the sweetest suggestions. I'm a very lucky woman."

"I hate to disagree, but I'm the lucky one to have you by my side every day," Nat said.

"Very well, I won't argue with you about it," Liz teased. "Will you run the idea past Vanessa tonight and see what she thinks?"

"I will indeed, my love," Nat agreed as she took a long drink.

"Where are you with Simone?"

"I'm so completely fed up with her antics right now I could just scream. The doctor said it will be three more days before she is released, so I think I will leave her to stew in her self-induced misery for a few days."

"Maybe a few days spent thinking will do Simone some good."

"I'd like to think you're right, Liz, but I think Simone is hopeless. She certainly was not raised to treat others so poorly."

"I definitely got the pick of that litter," Liz teased Nat.

"That you did, missy, and don't you forget it," Nat said with a smile.

Nat and Liz walked arm in arm back to the club. When they approached the counter, Nat moaned and rubbed her stomach. "That was one delicious dinner."

"I sure hope you left us some," Levi teased.

"I did indeed, but before I send you two off, I feel like dancing. "Vanessa, will you do me the honor of dancing with me?"

Vanessa jumped in surprise when Nat asked her to dance. She had assumed, incorrectly, that Nat would want to dance with Liz. Nat took her hand and led her to the dance floor just as NeNe began a slow song.

"I have an ulterior motive, if you haven't guessed, for getting you alone. Liz and I have an idea and wanted to get your feedback," Nat said, taking Vanessa in her arms.

"You certainly have my attention. What's the idea?" Vanessa asked a little cautiously.

"We think Levi needs a break from all the drama here, and Liz and I want to fly her back with you, if you don't mind, and you can bring her back Thursday when you return."

"I think that's a wonderful idea. I'd love to have Levi onboard for a couple of days, and you're right, she needs a break from the drama."

"When did you have in mind to fly out then?"

"I can go as early as Monday morning, but I had planned to fly on Tuesday to spend more time with Levi."

"I think Liz and I can cover Levi's absence if you would like to go on Monday."

"That would be wonderful."

"Very well, Liz and I will make arrangements for the two of you to fly out Monday morning," Nat said as they swayed to the music.

"Just let me know how much the fares are."

"No way, this is our treat for the two of you." Nat said.

"You don't have to do that."

"I know, but Liz and I insist. Just be sure to bring our best bartender back."

"Oh, I will, Nat, I promise."

"When we finish dancing take Levi for a nice dinner. Liz and I will cover the bar until you return. Tomorrow we'll make the arrangements and bring information on the tickets to you and Levi during tomorrow night's shift, if that's okay."

"That sounds wonderful to me," Vanessa said. "It may take some convincing for Levi to leave the resort you know."

"Just leave that to me. I'm her boss, remember," Nat said with a wink.

The song ended and Nat walked Vanessa back to the bar.

"Off to dinner you two," she said as they returned.

"Thanks Liz and Nat." Levi walked around to meet Vanessa. "We'll be back soon."

"Take your time, I think we still know how to run this place," Liz teased.

†

"What was Nat talking to you about out on the dance floor?"

"She was just asking how you and I were doing."

"Well, it sure looked like the two of you were cooking something up," Levi said.

"Well, she did recommend the porterhouse for dinner," Vanessa said.

Sensing she wasn't going to get the truth from Vanessa, Levi fell silent.

"I'm hungry and I think I'll try that porterhouse steak Nat was talking about, what will you be having, Levi?"

"Steak sounds good, but I'm not hungry enough for a porterhouse so I'll probably stick with a filet. Oh, and a loaded baked potato," she added.

"Definitely a loaded potato," Vanessa agreed. "My taste buds are screaming already."

†

"So, what did Vanessa think of our plan?" Liz asked.

"She thinks we are the two most brilliant people she has ever met," Nat spun Liz around in her arms for a kiss.

Chapter Forty-six

"Thanks for covering for me," Levi said when she returned to the bar. "That was a very nice dinner."

"It was our pleasure," Liz said. "It was like old times having the two of us behind the bar together."

"It looks like business has picked up quite a bit since we left," Vanessa said.

"It has been hopping," Nat said. "Do you want us to hang around a bit longer?"

"I can take it from here," Levi said. "If I get swamped, I'll have the good captain lend me a hand or two."

"Call if it gets too hectic." Liz took Nat's hand and led her from the club.

"I don't know how to bartend, but I do well with instruction," Vanessa teased.

"You do seem to be a quick learner," Levi said with a wink. "It is not too difficult but the orders always seem to come at the same time. So once you survive the rush, you have a few minutes to rest before the next wave of orders hits."

"Kind of like the calm before the next storm."

"Exactly," Levi said as Karen rolled up and blew a stray tangle of hair from her face.

"NeNe has got the ladies wild and thirsty tonight. I just can't serve them fast enough," she said with a giggle.

"It does seem to be an unusually thirsty crowd."

"And a bunch of really nice tippers too," Karen said. "This is probably one of the best night's tips I've had since you joined us, Levi."

"Well, let's keep them hot and thirsty then." Levi poured several dozen more shots.

"I need four Coronas too, please," Karen said.

"I'll get those, Levi, if you'll tell me which direction," Vanessa said.

"They are in the third cooler to the right and after you snap the lids, place a lime wedge in the top of the bottle neck. The limes are right there." She pointed to a rapidly decreasing bowl of wedges.

"Got it." Vanessa filled the order for Levi. "We are running low on lemons and limes, would you like me to slice some more?"

"That would be great. There are bowls of fruit in the refrigerator already washed. If you would slice them for me, I'd be forever in your debt, dear lady."

Levi refreshed the Tropical E cooler while Vanessa sliced the lemons and limes. She could not resist glancing over from time to time to see the look of concentration on Vanessa's face as she carefully sliced through the fruit. She was so adorable, and the big loving heart she had made her even more irresistible to Levi. Her heart raced when Vanessa caught her watching and smiled so sweetly at her.

The rest of the evening passed in a blur of activity, and Levi was relieved to see Susan walking in to take over the bar. The drama of the day's events had caught up to her and she was mentally and physically drained.

Vanessa walked with her up to the owner's suite to drop off the cash deposit to Liz.

"This was a phenomenal night," Levi said. "When we left, orders were still rolling in, so the remainder of the night's cash should be quite large as well."

"That is fantastic, Levi. Would you two like to come in for a drink?" Liz asked.

"Thanks, Liz, but I'm whipped and ready for bed."

"I completely understand," Liz smiled at Levi. "We'll see you two tomorrow then."

†

"I'm completely exhausted," Levi said when they reached her bungalow.

"Why don't we just snuggle until we fall asleep then."

"That sounds heavenly to me. Hold me tight," she said with a grin.

"I fully intend to," Vanessa said as they climbed into bed.

Vanessa lay on her back and Levi snuggled up to her, laying her head on Vanessa's shoulder and draping her leg across Vanessa's leg. Vanessa encircled Levi with a long arm and ran her fingers through Levi's hair. In the stillness of the room, she could feel the soft beating of Levi's heart and the slow deep breaths as exhaustion overtook Levi and she drifted off to sleep.

Vanessa fell asleep with her fingers buried in Levi's hair and did not wake until the sun began to peek through the wooden blinds. She remained as still as possible to prevent disturbing Levi, who slept for another hour before waking. Vanessa made mental plans for how she would spend the time with Levi once they flew from the island. She would ensure that Levi had the most relaxing and revitalizing days possible.

Vanessa was deep in thought when Levi began to stir. She watched the smile grow on Levi's face and her eyes flutter as she coaxed them open. Levi stretched and her naked body pressed into Vanessa's side. When she looked into Levi's face, her eyes were open and smiling at her.

"Good morning, my love," Vanessa said. "How did you sleep?"

"I slept wonderfully thanks to you." Levi leaned up to kiss Vanessa's lips. "You held me all night didn't you?"

"Yes, you were so comfortable there was no need to move."

"Is there anything in particular you want to do today?" Levi asked.

"Just spend it with you. I don't care what we do."

"Well, I'm feeling incredibly lazy. Would you mind if we stayed in bed and snuggled a little longer?"

"Not in the least. I think you're way past due for a day of leisure."

"Thank you for understanding, Vanessa."

"No problem. Do you feel like talking though?"

"Sure, what do you want to talk about?"

"I want to know everything about you, Levi. Who you are, where you are from, everything."

"Let's see." She pondered where to start. "I was born and raised in the mountains of Virginia and was pretty much a tomboy." She smiled remembering back to her childhood. "As a youth, I preferred spending my days wandering the mountainside over sitting inside with Mom, learning to cook, clean house, and sew."

"Somehow I can't see you sitting around knitting or sewing with your mom," Vanessa said.

"That's because it never happened. My mother loved me dearly, but she did not have the patience to teach me household tasks. It wasn't until after her death, in my late teens, that father taught me how to cook. Even then it was only out of necessity."

"What happened to your mother?"

"She died from cancer," Levi said. "It was a very aggressive and fast-growing type, so she didn't have to suffer months or years with a slow death, but her loss was devastating to my father. He was never the same after her death."

"Is your father still alive?"

"No, he was killed during my junior year of college," Levi said. "He was driving home from work one evening and a car ran a stoplight, crashing into his car and killing him instantly."

"You haven't mentioned any siblings. Do you have any other family?"

"I was an only child, as were both my parents, so after their deaths I was all alone. I took the summer off from college and returned home to sell the house and take care of my father's affairs." She sighed softly. "As much as I loved my home, I could not bear to live there without them. So I invested the money and buckled down at school, finishing my bachelor's and now my master's."

"So what lies ahead in your future, Levi?"

"I'm no longer certain. I thought I'd be happy on Wall Street or with some big financial firm, but now I'm not so sure," Levi said. "For now, I'm content working for the resort, knowing that when the time is right, my future will unfold for me."

Levi's hand stroked tenderly down Vanessa's face as she smiled sweetly at her. "One thing I'm certain of is that I have a terrific woman who loves me completely."

"That, my dear, is very true."

"Where do you see us heading?"

"I really haven't thought much into the future. I know I want you in my life, but I don't know where our careers will lead us. I think we can establish a life together if you can tolerate me being gone for a week or more at a time."

"As long as I know I'm the one you are coming back to, I can tolerate anything," Levi said. "I would never expect you to deny your love for the open water and I'm sure I can find a career that is compatible with your lifestyle."

Both women fell silent as they pondered their future together. The silence was broken, by the rumbling of Vanessa's stomach.

"Would you like to order room service?" Levi asked.

"I think that would be a wonderful idea. My stomach will become louder and more persistent if we don't," Vanessa teased.

"I'm feeling like some eggs Benedict," Levi said. "Do you know what you would like?"

"A monster omelet, with hash browns, a pitcher of orange juice, and toast," Vanessa said.

"Well, I guess that is settled." Levi rolled over and picked up the telephone to place their order. "All done," she said and rolled back into Vanessa's arms.

"Do you have any idea just how much I love you?" Vanessa asked.

"Well, you have at least twenty minutes to tell me."

Vanessa was about to speak when the telephone rang and Levi turned over to answer it.

"Hey Levi, this is Liz. I hope I haven't interrupted anything, but Nat and I want to invite you and Vanessa over to the suite for a late lunch."

"Well, we just ordered breakfast, so what time did you have in mind?"

"Okay, so how about two then?"

"Two would be perfect," Levi said. "We'll see you then."

"We have a late lunch date with Nat and Liz at two." Levi rolled back toward Vanessa. "Now, before we were interrupted, you were saying how much you loved me."

"Oh, right." Vanessa chuckled. "I love you with all my heart, Levi."

"Continue please."

"I love you with every fiber of my being, and I love you with every breath I take."

"Now we are getting somewhere." Levi chuckled.

"I love you so deeply I want to be the one to grow old beside you."

"Okay, stop right there. I have no intentions of growing old." Levi took Vanessa's face in her hands. "But if I do, I want it to be with you," she whispered as her soft lips brushed across Vanessa's.

There was a knock on the door and Levi and Vanessa climbed out of the bed and slipped on robes. Levi went to the door expecting the room service staff but was startled to find Del standing at her door.

"Del, what are you doing here? And how did you know where I live?"

"I didn't see you out by the pool so I decided to stop by to check on you to make sure you were okay," she said. "I saw you coming out of this room the other day."

"That was very nice of you, but I'm doing quite well and we are about to eat some breakfast," Levi said as she saw the kitchen server coming down the breezeway.

Del looked past Levi and saw Vanessa walking across the room.

"Sure thing, Levi, I'm glad you are fine." Del walked away.

Levi ushered the server inside and after she had placed their breakfast on the small table, she walked her to the door and slipped a five in the young woman's hand. Levi looked up and down the breezeway and saw no sign of Del, then stepped inside and closed the door.

"That one gives me the creeps."

Ali Spooner

Chapter Forty-seven

Levi and Vanessa ate their breakfast and decided to take a walk on the beach. Instead of taking a left-hand turn when they reached the beach, Levi intentionally took them to the right, away from the waterfall. Even though the place was so beautiful, it held too many painful memories for Levi.

They walked hand in hand as the cool breeze blew through their hair. The storm last night had left the beach swept clean and the air filled with the scent of sea salt. Vanessa breathed deeply of the smell she craved and was filled with the most inner peace she had ever felt in her life. Vanessa's passion for the ocean was embedded deeply in her veins from her childhood, and now she was experiencing a new passion, her love for Levi.

Vanessa lifted their hands to her lips and kissed the top of Levi's hand as their toes crunched in the soft sand. They walked for an hour, their strides perfectly matched until they reached the lighthouse near the mouth of the port. The candy apple-red and white striped tower smiled down on them as they looked up at her shining light room.

"The mighty lighthouses have guided sailors safely into harbors for years, during the worst storms and thickest fog," Vanessa said. "Even though most are now automated and fully mechanized I have to smile at the centuries past that these towers were operated by men and women, waiting patiently for the return of the ones they loved."

Levi placed her arms around Vanessa's shoulders. "You are my lighthouse then. No matter the fury of the storm or the darkest of nights, your love leads me back to you."

"I'll always be here for you, Levi, no matter how tumultuous our lives may become, know that I'll always love you. You will always find safety and love in my arms."

"I love you so, Vanessa." Their lips met and they shared a slow, sensual kiss.

Vanessa glowed after the kiss ended. "I love you too."

They started back toward the resort, following the path made by their footprints in the sand. Vanessa looked out onto the deep green water and smiled when she saw a pair of dolphins swimming parallel to them.

"We have company." She pointed toward the dolphins.

Levi watched the pair swimming in synchrony. "Seems like we are not the only loving couple out here today."

"Not at all," Vanessa said.

The dolphins followed them down the beach, breaching the water several times as they played in the surf and then turned away from the beach.

"They are such beautiful creatures," Levi said.

"Many times during our cruises a school of dolphins will swim alongside the ship, racing the humongous metal fish, putting on quite the show for our guests."

"I bet you have seen many amazing things on your adventures."

"Dolphins, whales, sea turtles, and any other sea creature you can imagine. On a tour of the Galapagos a few years ago we sailed past a small island of sunbathing sea lions." Vanessa smiled remembering back to that day. "It was such an amazing sight to see but the smell was horrendous. I was actually glad to get past that island and onto fresh air," she teased.

Levi laughed and the sound was music to Vanessa's ears. It had been a while since she had heard the sound and it warmed her down to her toes.

"That is such a beautiful sound," Vanessa said.

"What?"

307

"The sound of your laughter."

"You make me very happy, Vanessa."

"I'm very glad of that." Vanessa placed her arm around Levi's shoulder. "I hope to make you happy for a long time."

When they reached the resort steps, Vanessa took Levi in her arms for a final kiss before they left the beach.

"I think we have enough time for a shower before we need to meet Nat and Liz for lunch," Vanessa said.

"Sounds great, and thanks for taking a walk with me."

"The pleasure was all mine," Vanessa answered as they began to climb the stairs.

✝

After they showered and dressed, they walked to Liz and Nat's suite and knocked on the door. Liz opened the door to them and led them into the eating area where Nat was finishing the morning paper.

"Hello ladies," Nat said. "Please come join us."

"I took the liberty of ordering a large chicken Caesar salad." Liz began dishing the salad onto plates. "There is crusty bread too and, Levi, would you be a sweetheart and pour some tea?"

"I'll help you." Vanessa followed Levi into the kitchen.

Levi and Vanessa returned moments later with glasses of iced tea and they sat down to enjoy a light meal with Nat and Liz.

Levi noticed how Liz kept smiling at her during the meal and she finally asked, "Okay Liz, what are you up to?"

"What do you mean, what am I up to?"

"You are wearing a smile like the Cheshire cat, so what's up?"

"You might as well go ahead and tell her love," Nat said.

Liz went into the kitchen and returned carrying a small folder. "Here, these are for you and Vanessa."

Levi opened the folder and took out two confirmations for plane tickets to Miami. "What's this?"

"Nat and I decided that you deserve a short break from the resort and booked flights for y'all on Monday to fly back and meet the *Sappho One* in port. Then you can sail back when the ship returns on Thursday."

Levi smiled at Vanessa. "Did you know about this?"

"Not until last night when Nat shared the idea with me during our dance. I think it's a wonderful gesture."

Levi had tears in her eyes when she turned back to look at Liz. "This is a magnificent idea and I can't thank you two enough."

Nat smiled at her. "You've been through a lot in the last few weeks and we thought some fresh sea air and the company of a lovely lady would do you well."

"I think you're right about that." Levi leaned over and kissed Vanessa. "Wow, now I have to figure out what to pack."

Vanessa took her hand. "Why don't you let me handle that while you work tonight?"

"I have asked Susan to come in a little early tonight too, so you can get a good night's sleep before we take you to the airport," Nat said.

"So all I have to do is work and sleep tonight?" Levi asked. "I could get used to that."

"Well, don't get too used to it," Vanessa teased.

"Speaking of work, I need to get changed and head down to the club," Levi said. "I'll see you all later."

"Don't think you're going without me," Vanessa said.

Levi looked at her friends. "Thanks for lunch and for everything."

"You're quite welcome," Liz said. "Now go on, and get out of here."

†

"Can you believe this?" Levi clutched the folder and took Vanessa's hand as they walked back to her bungalow.

"You mean a lot to Liz and Nat. You're more to them than just a valuable employee."

309

"They treat me like family."

"Yes, they do. They realize just how special you are."

"Will you really pack for me?"

"Yes, darling, I will. It will be a short trip, so you won't need much."

"Thank you, Vanessa." Levi walked into her closet to find on a uniform for work. "Will I see you later at the club?" she asked from deep in the closet.

"Of course you will." Vanessa poked her head inside the closet. "I'll get us packed and clothes ready for tomorrow and then come to see you."

"I'll probably need more limes cut by then."

"I think I can handle that."

"I'm sure you can." Levi walked into the bathroom to brush her teeth and hair.

When Levi stepped from the bathroom, Vanessa had stretched across the bed.

"Oh you look so delicious," Levi said. "Are you planning to take a nap?"

"I might just do that."

"Go ahead, sweetie. I know it won't take you long to pack, so enjoy the afternoon. I just wish I could be lying next to you." Levi leaned down and kissed Vanessa. "Have a great nap and I'll see you later tonight."

Vanessa kicked off her shoes and hugged Levi's pillow close to her stomach, burying her face in the softness, breathing in Levi's scent. She fell asleep wearing a smile as her arms wrapped around Levi in her dreams.

†

Levi walked to the club smiling so hard her face hurt. NeNe was already in the booth selecting music for the night and she looked up Levi entered.

"What has you smiling so?" she shouted from the booth.

Levi told NeNe of the plans Nat and Liz had made for her.

"Wow, what an excellent way to spend a few days off, on a luxury ocean liner in the arms of a really hot babe."

"I plan to enjoy every moment of it too." Levi smiled even wider.

"You deserve nothing less my friend. Just make sure Killian makes it back here quickly."

"I will," Levi said before walking down to the bar to begin stocking.

Like clockwork, the door opened and women started crowding into the club. Karen rolled in a few minutes later and was swamped with orders the moment she arrived.

Levi stayed so busy she didn't have time to watch the clock and was surprised to find that it was nine and Vanessa hadn't arrived yet. She picked up the telephone to call her bungalow, but there was no answer. She tried Liz and Nat's suite and again got no answer. She tried not to worry, but watched the door every time it opened for signs of her lover.

A half hour later, Vanessa, Liz, and Nat walked in together and marched directly up to the bar.

"I was beginning to get worried, when none of you showed up."

"We had a little errand to attend to," Nat said.

"Should I be worried?"

"Not in the least my love," Vanessa said.

"Well, I have to trust you on that, since it doesn't seem like I'm going to get any more information out of you. I thought I was going to have to slice my own limes," Levi teased.

Vanessa sat at the bar. "I would never let that happen."

"Would you care to dance, honey?" Nat asked Liz.

"I would love to, baby."

"So, what have you been up to?" Levi asked once they left for the dance floor.

"I needed to make some purchases before we fly out tomorrow and I didn't have a ride into town," Vanessa said, which was true. "So, I asked Liz for a ride and Nat tagged along with us, simple as that."

311

"Very well, darling." Levi placed a bowl of limes in front of Vanessa.

"I do love you so, Levi Johnson." Vanessa picked up the knife and began slicing the fruit.

Chapter Forty-eight

The night passed quickly. Susan walked in around eleven to relieve Levi. Nat and Liz were still in the club, so Levi turned over the cash bag to them and she and Vanessa left for the bungalow.

They slipped off their clothing and climbed into bed, but they were both too excited about their trip to sleep.

Levi pulled Vanessa on top of her and covered her mouth with a passionate kiss. Vanessa began slowly grinding her hips into Levi's as the fire grew between them. Their hands and mouths teased and caressed each other until they were panting in pleasure.

"That was intense," Levi whispered afterward as they struggled to catch their breath.

Vanessa rolled onto the bed and turned on her side facing Levi. "You always make me feel so loved and needed."

"That's because I love and need you." Levi reached up to stroke Vanessa's face.

"I want to wake up beside you for years to come." Vanessa took Levi's hands and kissed them.

"I think I can live with that." Levi leaned in to brush Vanessa's lips with hers. "Years and years to come."

"Do you think you can sleep now?"

"Only if you wrap your arms around me. I need to feel you next to me."

"Roll over then."

Levi rolled onto her side and Vanessa wrapped her arms around her securely and held her close until she felt Levi relax in sleep. She closed her eyes and dreamed of Levi until the alarm woke them the next morning.

†

Levi ordered breakfast and they showered while they waited. They would eat a light breakfast and then eat a good meal once they landed in Miami. Levi could tell Vanessa was slightly nervous about flying and did not want anything heavy in her stomach. The flight to Miami would only take two hours and Levi planned to keep Vanessa busy talking throughout the flight.

They dressed just as the toasted bagels and juice arrived. Levi spread cream cheese on the bagels as Vanessa finished drying her hair.

Vanessa walked back into the room and sat beside Levi.

Levi handed her half a bagel and bit into one of her own, the cream cheese oozing past her lips as she bit down on it. Vanessa chuckled and leaned forward to lick the extra cream cheese from her lips.

"Yummy," Vanessa winked, "we should have ordered bagels sooner."

They finished breakfast and prepared to leave the room.

"Ready my love?" Vanessa asked as she picked up their bags.

"Ready," Levi opened the door and followed Vanessa outside.

†

They met Liz and Nat downstairs and minutes later had their bags tucked safely away in the back of the van.

"All set, ladies?" Liz asked as she climbed in behind the wheel.

"Very much so," Levi said as she slipped her hand inside Vanessa's, entwining their fingers.

The drive to the airport was short and Nat made Vanessa promise to bring Levi back to them.

"Don't think you can hide the hottest bartender on the island away from us," Nat teased Vanessa.

"I wouldn't dream of it. We'll be back here sometime Thursday afternoon," she promised as they reached the airport.

"Hopefully we can hold the fort down until then," Nat said with a grin.

"I'm sure you'll manage just fine," Levi said as they pulled up to the curb.

"We'll see you two on Thursday." Nat took their bags from the back. "Enjoy yourselves and come back to us safely."

Nat and Liz hugged them both.

"Have fun and stay out of trouble," Liz said to Levi.

"I'll do my best." Levi grinned.

"Have a good flight," Nat said as she watched them walk inside the terminal.

They passed through ticketing and headed directly to the gate. Their flight was on a small jet and Levi hoped the smaller size would make Vanessa breathe a little easier.

"This will be so much fun," Levi said as they took a seat to wait for boarding. "Would you like a drink or anything while we wait?"

"No baby, I'm good, thanks."

A few minutes later, they heard the call to board. Levi stood and offered her hand to Vanessa. "It's time, sweetie." Vanessa followed Levi to the boarding gate.

Levi gave the attendant their tickets they were ushered down the skyway to board the jet. Levi took the window seat, leaving the aisle seat for Vanessa.

They secured their seat belts and sat patiently waiting for the rest of the passengers to board. "How are you feeling?"

"I'm fine, sweetie." Vanessa clutched Levi's hand tightly as the door closed with a thump and minutes later, the small jet began backing away from the gate.

Vanessa rested her head against the back of the seat and closed her eyes as they taxied out to the runway and the pilot accelerated for takeoff. The climb through the clouds was a little bumpy, but once they reached cruising altitude, the ride smoothed out and Vanessa began to relax.

The flight attendant brought soft drinks and snacks as Levi attempted to distract Vanessa with light conversation. It seemed to be working as Vanessa finally let go of Levi's hand as she passed Levi her drink.

"Thanks, sweetie." Levi took the drink from Vanessa.

"You're welcome. When you are on the ship, I want you to take advantage of every amenity," Vanessa said. "We have a terrific heated stone massage and some great facial treatments that will make you feel like a new woman."

"I'll do my best. Will you have to work most of the day during the cruise?" she asked.

"No, I think Killian and the crew have demonstrated they can handle operating the ship without me, so I'll sneak away when I can to relax with you."

"That sounds great. I hope to strike it rich in your casino too," she teased.

"Well, good luck with that," Vanessa said. "I normally make a deposit with no withdrawal."

"I usually have fairly good luck with slots."

The jet hit some turbulence and Vanessa instinctively reached for Levi.

"It's okay," Levi said as the ride smoothed back out. "It's just a little turbulence." She gave Vanessa's hand a gentle squeeze. "We only have a little more than an hour left to the flight. Maybe we should recline our seats and try for a short nap."

"Before we do that, I have something I want to give to you," Vanessa said.

Vanessa sorted through her carryon bag and pulled out a small box.

"This is for you, my love." Vanessa handed Levi the gift-wrapped box.

Levi took the box and tore off the paper. She pulled off the lid and her eyes fell upon a gold lighthouse pendant on a gold rope chain. Her breath caught in her chest.

"Vanessa, this is so beautiful." Levi's fingers caressed the smooth gold of the pendant.

Vanessa took the necklace and placed it around Levi's neck. "Now you'll always have me with you, even when I may seem far away." The pendant rested against Levi's chest.

Vanessa leaned over and kissed Levi. "I love you so much."

"I love you too." Levi's smile grew wide. "Was this the errand you had to run last night?"

"Yes, a friend of Liz's opened up his jewelry store just for us," Vanessa said. "I couldn't leave the island without giving you something special."

"You're special enough for me. But the lighthouse is beautiful."

They reclined their seats and Levi rested her head on Vanessa's shoulder. Vanessa smiled as she watched Levi's fingers stroke the gold pendant and she closed her eyes to rest.

"I will love you forever," Levi heard Vanessa whisper as she softly kissed the top of Levi's head.

This is the end of *Venus Rising*, but watch for these ladies to return soon in *Neptune's Ring*.

About the Author

Ali Spooner

Ali Spooner is a native of Florida, currently living and working in Memphis, TN. As an "Indie" author, Ali has been writing for many years as a hobby, and with the assistance of the Affinity team has taken her love of storytelling to a new level.

Ali's characters range from cowgirls and psychics, to a healthy dose of supernatural beings. She has written stand-alone titles and series. Ali is an avid reader and her other hobbies include photography, outdoor activities and watching college sports.

Other Books from Affinity eBook Press

Anywhere, Everywhere by Renee MacKenzie Gwen Martin's life in the Ten Thousand Islands area changes irrevocably when Piper Jackson comes into her life. Without trust, can the budding relationship between Gwen and Piper survive? Or will the answers to the questions continue to haunt them?

The Devil's Tree by Ali Spooner Torn between her love for the pack and her need to find what's missing in her life Devin Benoit travels to New Orleans. Will the previous happenings at the Devil's Tree help or hinder Devin in the fight of her life, and the life of Tia, the woman who now owns her heart?

The Case of the Beggars' Coppice by Erica Lawson Edda Case is a woman in crisis who discovers that things are not as they seem. Is it truly a message for her from beyond the grave or is something more sinister taking place? Can Edda solve the mystery of *The Beggars' Coppice*?

Locked Inside by Annette Mori How much does the power of love matter to someone who must overcome obstacles far greater than most people face in a lifetime.

Line of Sight by Ali Spooner Sasha and her lover Kara are back. Continue the thrilling adventures of this couple from the Sasha Thibodaux series.

Requiem for Vukovar by Angela Koenig Requiem for Vukovar continues the Refraction series and the exploits of Jeri O'Donnell and her partner, Kelly Corcoran. In an epic siege largely ignored by the wider world, Kelly, who was prepared to give up comforts and certainties when she became part of Jeri's nomadic life, encounters more than physical danger. Her ability to maintain her core integrity is assaulted by the inevitable ugliness of war. For Jeri, the true battle is confronting her attraction to violence as she struggles against losing herself in the exhilaration of combat.

Against All Odds by JM Dragon From award winning and bestselling author JM Dragon, with significant updates by, Erin O'Reilly comes an original tale of romance where everything seems to be stacked against two women whose destinies bring them together. Life however takes a twisted path setting both Steph and Louise in directions they never thought possible. Will love win out against all odds or will love be forever lost?

The Settlement by Ali Spooner The outpouring of love and friendship toward Cadin helps her on her path to healing and learning to trust her heart to love once again. Join bestselling author Ali Spooner on this sensational journey that ends with a heartwarming romance.

Once Upon a Time by Alane Hotchkin Raven only wanted to escape the blows that life had dealt her. She longed to be on the open sea and free. When she came upon a beautiful young girl sitting alone in the middle of a meadow, little did she know that her destiny would be changed forever. Will they become the pawns of the ancient vision or will both paths lead to the same port of destiny? Find out it in this exciting high seas adventure that will capture your imagination.

Asset Management by Annette Mori Follow the twists and turns to the explosive conclusion. Not everything is black and white. There are many shades of gray and sometimes it's difficult to decipher who is good and who is evil. No one is all virtue or all malevolence, but sometimes love helps us rise above.

Do Dreams Come True? by JM Dragon How do two people who really shouldn't get on end up in a relationship? Find out in this deliciously ordinary romance.

Return to Me by Erin O'Reilly Will Salvation bring just that to Ellie, allowing her to find peace and happiness again, or will it have her questioning all that she believes in? A wonderful romance cloaked within an intriguing mystery.

Arc Over Time by Jen Silver This wonderful romantic continuation with the characters from *Starting Over* ties up loose ends. But the question is—does everyone have a happy ending? A must read.

The Presence by Charlene Neal Can Rebecca and Kayleigh overcome ghosts from the past and their own insecurities, or will a presence from the past tear them apart?

A Walk Away by Lacey Schmidt Sometimes chance brings you to the right person to help you resolve some of your baggage, and you learn to like yourself a little more. Kat and Rand are smart enough to recognize this chance in each other, but they also find that there is a catch to every opportunity—walking toward something is always walking away from something else.

Possessing Morgan by Erica Lawson The investigation has barely begun when Andrea becomes the target of a nearly fatal hit-and-run. But was it really aimed at her? Can she and Morgan find the common ground they need to solve the case and stop the attacks, or are the gaps just too wide to bridge?

Twenty-three Miles by Renee MacKenzie This is a story about community, and how it comes together in dangerous and devastating times. When you don't know who to trust, you better have friends who will rally around you. Will Talia and Shay find the answers they need to the mystery of the murders on the parkway, or will justice be elusive? Will they survive their quest for the truth?

Reece's Star by TJ Vertigo Under Faith's guiding, loving hand, will Reece successfully traverse the rocky road of emotion and embrace the positive changes in her life? Or will she panic and be unable to control that Animal part of herself? Will she take that next step to declare herself fully capable of love and devotion? This third installment in the popular series that began with *Private Dancer* continues the passionate and often hilarious romance of Reece and Faith as they both grow in love and in trust.

Confined Spaces by Renee MacKenzie Corporate politics, complicated romance, and long distances conspire to keep Andie and Kara all boxed in. Can love triumph despite the Confined Spaces?

Cowgirl Up by Ali Spooner Ride along with the MC2, for boot scootin', butt kickin', dirt eatin', rodeo adventures, with a love story thrown into the mix.

If I Were a Boy by Erin O'Reilly Will Katie and Helen be able to make a life together work or succumb to doubts and the pressures of family? This story will fill you with the thrill of passion and the tenderness of love.

The Chronicles of Ratha: Book 2 A Lion Among the Lambs by Erica Lawson Can Jordana believe in herself like her Noorthi sisters do? Only then can she fulfill her destiny as The Chosen One. Follow the colorful cast of characters in this action-packed adventure sequel as they traverse the galaxy. Of course, nothing ever goes smoothly when Jordana is involved.

Terminal Event by Ali Spooner Will the killer be caught or continue to evade authorities? Can Tally and Blair's budding romance survive the possibility? Read this intense murder mystery romance and find out.

Love Forever, Live Forever by Annette Mori   Fate intervenes and puts Nicky directly back into the path of her first love, Sara, and the corresponding events send her into a tailspin. Now she must decide—who will be the person she ends up living with and loving forever?

The One by JM Dragon *2015 GCLS Winner for Romance, Intrigue, and Adventure. The One* is a romance with everything, love, intrigue, misunderstandings with a happy conclusion—the only question—who gets the girl?

Reflected Passion by Erica Lawson Through a mirror, Françoise embraces life anew, while for Dale it is a powerful awakening, forcing her to discover not only her sensual nature, but the inner strength she possesses.

Flight by Renee Mackenzie   Some lives will be lost and others changed forever when the sisters' lives intersect. Will they be consumed by the wreckage, or will they be able to pick themselves up and take flight?

Starting Over by Jen Silver   Book 1 of the Starling Hill Trilogy. There's a mystery afoot—whose royal resting place is disturbed at Starling Hill? All is revealed in this classic romance of simmering passions, anguished loss, and the wonder of love.

Starting Over by Jen Silver   Book 1 of the Starling Hill Trilogy. There's a mystery afoot—whose royal resting place is disturbed at Starling Hill? All is revealed in this classic romance of simmering passions, anguished loss, and the wonder of love.

E-Books, Print, Free e-books

Visit our website for more publications available online.

www.affinityebooks.com

Published by Affinity E-Book Press NZ LTD
Canterbury, New Zealand

Registered Company 2517228

www.ingramcontent.com/pod-product-compliance
Lightning Source LLC
Chambersburg PA
CBHW070830280626
47161CB00015B/430